BETWEEN THE SHADOWS AND THE DAWN

JENNA STREETY

ISBN: 9798281818131

Cover Art by ItsMumeii

Cover Design by Jenna Streety

Proofreading by Chesney Infalt

Interior Art by @mgsdesiigns

Formatting by Elle Lavendelle

CONTENT WARNING

This novel contains gory depictions of death, burning, maiming, torture, and more. The content within deals with potentially triggering matters such a suicide, sexual assault, the loss of a child/pregnancy, the death of children, and addiction. There are multiple on-page scenes that build up to full sex scenes in future books.

Please check jennastreety.com for further explanations on tropes and content warnings which may be relevant to you. Read safely.

Check the back of the book for a reference list of characters, locations, and more.

To everyone who fights back against the shadows,
and needs a little bit of hope to meet the dawn.

Playlist

Chapter One - HUNTER (the cacophony) by Paris Paloma
Chapter Two - Kingdom Of Cards by Bad Omens
Chapter Three – Rún by SKÁLD
Chapter Four – Hollow – Lo's Version by Lo Spirit, Dabin, Kai Wachi
Chapter Five – The Fighter by In This Moment
Chapter Six – Artemis by AURORA
Chapter Seven – My Way by PVRIS
Chapter Eight – Warrior by Livingston
Chapter Nine – Burial Plot (Reimagined) by Dayseeker, Seneca
Chapter Ten – I Don't Believe in Anything by DeathbyRomy
Six Years Prior – Into The Light by In This Moment
Chapter Eleven – Intrusive Thoughts by Natalie Jane
Chapter Twelve – Sexual Hallucinations (feat. Brent Smith) by In This Moment
Chapter Thirteen – Antidote by Braeker
Chapter Fourteen – Fall For Me by Sleep Token
Chapter Fifteen – Closer to You by SVRCINA
Chapter Sixteen – Alkaline by Sleep Token
Chapter Seventeen – The Promise by In This Moment
Chapter Eighteen – Take It Or Leave It by James Arthur
Chapter Nineteen – Need Nothing by VERITE
Chapter Twenty - Cosmic Love by Florence + The Machine

The Divide is gone
and only we remain to tell its story.

THE ISLES
KRESSDAER
THE NORT
BRIAR COASTS
WRINIA
AGASTA
SAIKYA
VEMID
RALIA
THE SOUTHERN KINGDOMS
THE DARK LANDS
THE SOUTHER

OSOVAGR
THE DIVIDE
SKAGI
RANNADAL
LYSAFELL
E NORTH
BIRKSON
THE LAND OF
SHATTERED HOUSES
THE SOUTH

PART I

THE DIVINE PROMISE

"It is said in the old texts that the one Promised to us would be heralded by the Gods.

Only it never spoke of which ones . . ."

- Excerpt from Tales of The Hersir

1

THE SHATTERED DIVIDE

SKALD: ADELAIDE AYLARA

The Wild Woods were beautiful.

Every oak and birch branch twisted towards the clear skies, dancing in the warm breeze to the distant melody of crows and trickling streams. On lazy summer days, the sun stretched long and heavy over the mountains and, in the darkest winter nights, the never-ending sky lit up in brilliant colors. Willowherb and dovesfoot blooms blanketed the rolling knolls until the world just seemed to drop off at every unsuspecting cliffside.

Yes, the Wild Woods of The Divide were beautiful.

Until they tried to kill you.

Although Adelaide suspected it wouldn't be her lovely woods that did her in. No, she was certain the humans infesting it would finish her off in the end. There was a reason the perilous mountain range of The Divide existed after all: to separate New Alfheim from the rest of Midgard and all the threats the humans inhabiting their neighboring lands brought to their borders.

Her fate was written on the stone lodged in her gut. That

heavy weight of foreboding and regret filled the emptiness within her after the worst days of her life.

The world had turned six times since then, but the wounds the humans left on her heart festered as if it were a tangible, rotting thing decaying beneath her skin. She tried to find comfort in her purpose. In safeguarding her home from the humans who sought to spoil it, but the sting of the past never ceased.

Her only solace was found in ensuring she wouldn't leave for Valhalla without taking as many humans with her as possible. It was her duty as a Keeper, as an elf whose ancestors lost everything to humankind when their home realm was destroyed. She would sooner die than watch her people's history repeat before her eyes.

Despite her mental preparations for her impending death, its reality being so close at hand still spread a cold pool of dread through her core.

That morning should've been normal. She'd completed a perimeter check of their territory before it was her turn to go hunting. Despite the sabbats claiming it was still summer, winter was fast approaching—too fast in her mother's opinion. The trees changed color before autumn properly began, and there was a bitter chill in the air biting into her cheeks as she crouched atop a tall tree. The day was colder than normal but, otherwise, an average day.

Except there was a human among the frost-tipped foliage of The Divide.

That simply wouldn't do.

Adelaide stalked the man through the woods, throwing stones to entice him into taking paths away from her home instead of towards it. He followed them blindly, tripping over his own feet and every branch on his careless path through the mountains. What he sought, she did not know. But he would not find her family. She would see to that.

Truly, she didn't think of him as a real threat. He bore the penance of age heavily on his shoulders, as if the whole world were resting on his back. He was hunched over with a gray cloak covering his body, and a wide-brimmed hat that did little to hide his wrinkled and hairy chin from her keen eyes.

Still, her heart hammered against her chest with anticipation and fear. She'd witnessed firsthand what humans could do to her people—to the elves who called New Alfheim and the mountainous Divide home. She couldn't wipe the memory of the mutilated and burned remains she witnessed, nor the scent of their charred flesh, from her mind. Years did nothing to smother the burning rage that lit her chest and tightened her lungs, nor the certainty riddling her heart that *this* would be the human who finally killed her.

They stole something precious to me that day; I will not allow it again.

The man paused, his hat tilting back as he took in the tall trees and specks of sky between the branches. She couldn't see his face, so she crept from her perch and lowered herself to the forest floor.

Spending her whole life in the woods had its benefits, including her ability to dance around every twig and pile of crunching leaves. Stealth was needed in her line of work as a Keeper. If she were detected too early, it could mean death for her, her family, and the other clans of Keepers dotting the mountains.

Whatever mistake other elves made to bring the humans to their doors, Adelaide was determined to never make the same error. Even if the old man seemed frail and defenseless, he couldn't remain close to her home. She searched the man for any symbol to denote his faction in the human lands but couldn't find any on his person.

She searched for the entwining ribbons of the Cislenian religion. It was the symbol of The Knights of The Divide, the very same monsters who tore her life apart in their selfish carnage six years prior.

The Knights were the human equivalent to Keepers, their purpose meant to reflect hers, but they'd warped their duty. Instead of keeping the so-called "peace" between their people intact, they often called for bloodshed. She found so many people brutalized by their Brotherhood that she stopped believing in the good of any member of humankind.

Burning, charred flesh. A sword left as a calling card: the ribbon emblem proudly displayed for all to see, for all to know what they've done.

She shuddered at the memory and pushed forward. If her mother and siblings saw her, they'd consider her paranoid, but she already lost too much. And she'd never had so much to lose before. She would not let one man spoil the life with her family she'd fought to protect.

Her pointed ear twitched at the sound of the human moving through the brush, his boots sliding through a muddy patch of earth. With winter coming early, seeming to ignore the existence of autumn altogether, the rain arrived without warning. It drenched the mountains for weeks and barely let up the day prior. It left the hills bursting with greenery and colorful blossoms, but she knew the rush of life would be squashed in winter's cold grip.

She heaved a heavy breath, the scent of the flowers wafting over her, as she steeled her nerves. All she needed was to wait for his next staggered step.

He yelped, slipping across the mud, calling out for help as he fell face-first into the muck. She nearly helped him on instinct alone but held back. She couldn't treat humans as if they were elves, as if they were her people.

They've rarely shown me the same courtesy. Why should I?

Still, it was pathetic watching the poor old man struggle to regain his footing. He was clearly underdressed for the cold, and it would only pain him more after the wet earth penetrated his meager, torn clothing. His hand slipped under his cloak as he turned, his eye catching hers under the wide brim of his hat as he pulled out whatever was beneath his cloak.

A sword perhaps?

Adelaide reached behind her back and pulled an arrow from her quiver, nocking it along her golden bow and aiming it at his heart before he had a chance to reveal what he reached for. Her heart urged her to pull back just a little further and let the arrow fly. His people murdered hers. His people caused Alfheim to fall and cursed elves to live alongside the people of Midgard until Ragnarök claimed the realms.

They don't deserve mercy.

The old man settled himself over the cane he pulled out from under his cloak. The one eye she could see beneath his hat squinted at her, a confused pout turning his lips down over his long, braided beard.

"Young lady, do you perchance know the way out of here?" he asked, his voice timid in a way she didn't expect. He didn't seem afraid of her at all, even with her weapon trained between his eyes. "I've seemed to have lost myself again."

Pity tugged hard at her sore heart as her arm shook with the strain of the bowstring pulled taut in her hands. A storm ravaged her mind, tearing her apart with each tumultuous thought. Half of her wished to see the man dead at her feet for what humankind did to her. The other, more timid part of her wished to let him go. To not cause another family even an ounce of the pain she'd endured.

She wished to kill that part of herself—the weak portion her mother always attempted to train out of her.

The bitter edge of resentment gnawed on her core. Sweat beat across her brow even as the cold stretched its greedy hands through the land, beckoning the setting of the sun and the descent into night. Perhaps if she couldn't stomach watching the man die from her arrow, he'd perish before midnight from the freezing temperatures instead.

Unlike the nights of The North, which stretched out endlessly during the Yule season, she decided she wouldn't be so cold. At least, not that day. Not for that man. Others who were more deserving would receive the full weight of her wrath. She would save it for the Knights.

She would show the old man mercy, but only once.

"Follow the slope of this knoll," Adelaide said as she lowered her bow and pointed at the nearest rise in the landscape. "It will take you straight down the mountain." She cursed herself for the kindness hidden in her tone as she wiped the sweat from her brow, pushing a few damp, white strands of hair from her face in the process. "Just be careful not to fall again."

She could practically hear her mother's scathing comments already.

Damn it, Adelaide, do not fall for their deceptions.

He bowed his head and laced his hands together over his cane, stilling his trembling fingers. "Thank you, my dear. You've helped me a great deal." He took a few steps towards the knoll and her shoulders slumped, relieved to be rid of the man who conjured so much conflict in her heart. But then he stopped, his cloak rustling fallen leaves as he turned his attention back to her. "You've assisted me. It's only fair I do the same."

She swallowed her irritation, returned her arrow to the quiver, and strapped her bow to her back. "It's not necessary. Just return home before it gets dark."

He grew closer and, if it weren't for the stagger in each step, she would've redrawn her bow or disappeared into the woods. She remained still, determined to send the poor man on his way back to his family. She'd already made up her mind to let him go, she wouldn't change it after the fact.

His wrinkled hands gripped hers tight, sending fear down

her spine as the hair on her neck rose. She expected his palms to feel cold and worn by time, but they were warm and smooth even with the signs of age clear across the backs of his hands. Slowly, the fear dissipated as a strange comfort replaced it. She supposed elders always made her feel at peace, their wisdom granting her solace when little else in the realms did.

She just never expected to find comfort from a *human*, elder or not.

"Follow the lights," he said, his focus pinned on the ground between them. "Follow them and find hope in the new dawn. For only *she* can banish the shadows."

Although his words confused her, she knew to remember every detail of what he'd said. The warmth he radiated was magic, something she hadn't felt from a human before. Some of their kind had abilities, but they were few and far between. Many in Midgard were persecuted or hunted for it since magic only entered humans through elf blood in their ancestry.

It was her people who first brought magic to Midgard and, after New Alfheim was forged, it spread like wildfire across the world.

That was why, as a Keeper, Adelaide wasn't just tasked with removing humans from their borders. She was also sworn to prevent any elves from returning to New Alfheim if they chose to depart. Only Keepers were allowed to move between the lands. She'd turned many elves away, along with their half-human children. It was relations between humans and elves that gave humanity magic in the first place—a stolen prize for their destruction of Alfheim.

As she slipped her hands from his, she knew why she'd allowed the man to live. He wasn't any feeble old man. He was a seiðmaður, a seer and spellcaster blessed by Odin with great sight. He was of her blood, as any witch was. She was certain of it.

"Thank you." She bowed her head and backed away, giving him room to leave. "I will remember your words."

His lips twitched into a grin beneath his beard. "See to it that you do. Shadows are brewing all around us, and smoke litters the breeze." He sniffed at the air, as though the scent already lingered there. "Hurry to your kin now, child. I will endeavor to do the same."

Without another word, he hobbled down the hill and disappeared on the horizon as she contemplated the weight of what he said. The words themselves were simple, but every letter was drenched in whatever deep-seated knowledge he'd obtained from the Gods.

Adelaide was not one to ignore the heavens, so she turned back home. Surely, her mother would know what to make of his vision. She was wise beyond her time, accounting for the fact that her life stretched far beyond average. She never admitted to her real age and her youthful face wouldn't give it away, but all her siblings knew their mother wasn't what she seemed.

But what she was, none of them were ever quite sure of.

Her sister, Nissa, was certain Mother used her gift for shapeshifting to turn into a more youthful version of herself every morning. As kids, she convinced Adelaide to sneak into her room before dawn broke and see her true face, but she appeared the same even in sleep. Their other siblings were certain she was a powerful witch who touched time but time couldn't touch her back. Whatever she was, she would have answers for what the seer spoke of.

Hunting could wait. Something about the seer's words felt important. As if the future of shadows he foretold was just around the corner, waiting with bated breath for the sun to fall and consume all the world.

Time slipped away from her that day, so she quickened her pace as the sky bled into night above her. Being caught unawares in the dark of the mountains was always a mistake. The Wild Woods were named that way for a reason after all. Untamed creatures and wicked spirits roamed the cliffs after the sun descended and, during the darkest days of winter when the sun never rose, they seemed to claim the whole realm.

A shadow darted past her, a rabbit speeding through the woods. Like her, she supposed they were trying to return home before the sun fell. As a deer followed the smaller creature at a frantic pace, unease burrowed into her core.

Something's wrong.

She ran, her heart hammering against her ribs as she rushed deeper into the thick of the woods and the growing night. Animals continued to run past her, fleeing in the opposite direction.

They're running away from home.

There was no logical reason for every living being of The Wild Woods, from the meekest bunny to the largest bear, to run away from the same source. Nothing natural could cause that. There was no normal force in The Divide which could cause creatures of such opposing ways of life to agree on anything, let alone that running from their mutual home was necessary to survive.

Dread bared down on her shoulders as she grew closer to the cabin she called home all her life, the sickly taste of unknown magic heavy on her tongue.

The ground shook beneath her feet, and a deafening roar thundered around her. She was thrown backwards and the air left her lungs as she collapsed, a cloud of debris rupturing from the tree line and bathing her in soot.

The tremors subsided enough for her to regain her footing. Smoke and flames rose towards the twilight skies in the distance, casting a waxen orange glow across the mountainside. Her stunned fear turned to horror as she realized her home lay somewhere near the epicenter of the explosion. She ran, her heart hammering against her ribs as she dodged fallen trees and small landslides where cliffs once lay.

The closer she drew, the more her body shook with fear. Destruction lay in every direction. Not even the familiar paths her family carved through the mountains were untouched by the ash and cracking earth beneath her feet. She could feel the heat of the flames before she ever saw them. And, somehow, deep in her soul, she knew one thing to be abundantly true.

The seer's prophecy is already coming true.

She broke through the final thicket separating her from the homestead. Since she was old enough to hold a bow and defend herself alone in the woods, she'd always crested that final hill and parted those buckthorn bushes with excitement to be back with her kin. To welcome the warm embrace of the fire and her sisters' solid hugs. She'd pick lingonberries in the garden and watch ravens dance for the smallest remnant of purple-red berry stuck to her fingers. But that day, she climbed the hill and parted the bushes with only terror leeching off her heart.

A crater lay where her home once was.

The haze of billowing black smoke twirled into the sky, blurring her vision as she stood on the precipice of chaos. Tears filled her gaze, blocking out the scene before her as something deep within her broke into a million shards. She only had a moment of sorrow before panic kicked her into action.

She slid down the devastated hill and collapsed at the bottom, nearly rolling straight into the chasm torn into the mountain. Flames licked at her feet as she scrambled from the depths which threatened to swallow her whole. Her home was somewhere below, burning in the darkness as the bitter tang of magic choked her as much as the smoke.

Mother would sense this coming. She would've protected our clan. She had to.

But those thoughts provided little reassurance as she

teetered on the edge of a certain plummet into death. The earth slipped between her fingers as she crawled across the ledge, looking for any remaining evidence of her beloved cabin and her missing family.

There, mangled in the muck between her fingers, was a sliver of metal. She clutched it tight and pulled it into the light of the raging fires. A familiar raven pendant materialized between the debris she wiped from its surface. It was intricately carved, with delicate feathers and a rune for protection etched on the back. It was out of place amid such destruction, a memento of fond memories replaced by sheer despair.

Its wing was chipped and the necklace itself was mangled nearly beyond recognition. There was no way in all the realms Adelaide wouldn't recognize that necklace. She helped the smallest of their clan put it on every morning before Mother called out to say breakfast was ready.

Her body was soaked through with mud and her legs trembled as she hoisted herself over the nearest ledge so she could scurry away from the broken piece of the mountain that stole her home. She stared out at the devastation before her and, from her vantage point, could see the mountains dotted with fires burning bright in the distance. It cast an ominous glow over what seemed to be the whole world.

At least, it was once *her* whole world.

Smoke and ash swirled in the air, soot matting around her lips and filling her nostrils as she clutched the silver raven pendant tight. The chasm gaped open, swallowing more of the earth around it.

Everything she'd once loved stood right there, waiting for her to return.

Heavy tears stung her eyes and, when mixed with the ash, caused trails of black to rain across her cheeks. Surges of grief and rage coursed through her. Had she not been through enough? Hadn't her family deserved peace? Why did everything she'd ever cared for been taken from her?

A sob tore through her chest and echoed in the dark forest around her. She no longer feared the spirits haunting the land. She would let them claim her if they wished. There was no light from the absent moon and only pain came from getting closer to the flames, so there was no light to help guide her through the darkness.

She was certain she wouldn't live to see the dawn, and part of her was glad for it.

But then a whisper of light unfurled in the sky. A streak of brilliant emerald curved around the constellations she'd memorized as a child. She looked up, begging the All-Father, Odin, for another glimpse of beauty when all around her was hideous destruction. Rouge blossomed above, twirling through the constellation of the two missing brothers. Further west, more colored light twined itself with the stars of the three sisters—stars their mother swore were for them.

"Follow the lights," the seer said. *"Follow them and find hope in the new dawn."*

All at once, Adelaide knew her family lived. She couldn't say how or why, but a certainty rooted deep in her core made her press on through the night. She donned the mangled necklace, hid the raven under her tunic, and entered the shadows of the night. With the dawn, she would find her family and, together, they'd discover who destroyed their home.

And Adelaide would ensure they begged for death before she ever granted it to them.

THE SONG OF SPELLS

"Those songs I know, which nor sons of men, nor queen in a King's court knows . . .

An eleventh I know: if haply I lead my old comrades out to war, I sing 'neath the shields, and they fare forth mightily safe into battle, safe out of battle, and safe return from the strife.

A fourteenth I know: if I needs must number the Powers to the people of men, I know all the nature of gods and of elves which none can know untaught.

A fifteenth I know, which Folk-stirrer sang, the dwarf, at the gates of Dawn; he sang strength to the gods, and skill to the elves, and wisdom to Odin who utters."

- Stanzas 145, 155, 158, and 159 of *Havamal*

2

THE DELIVERED OATH

SKALD: KARSTEN STROM

The Gods tested him before, but never like this.

What was once a blissful summer's day—one of few Karsten Strom was ever lucky enough to have—rotted into a night of terror. The fresh scent of late-blooming eucalyptus was replaced by the tang of burnt flesh and the copper taste of blood on his tongue. With every order to the brave warriors under his command, he bit his cheek and furthered the flow of crimson into his mouth. That injury was minor compared to the wounds scattered across his body.

Still, he bit a little harder whenever his mind dared to sway from the task at hand.

Focus, you fool. Otherwise, we'll all be dead.

The itch still clawed at his throat, an ever-present reminder of his weakness when it came to an addiction which could grant him reprieve from the horrors around him.

Just one sip and I can focus. It will help me fix this.

He bit harder. He'd take the taste of his own blood mixing with the ash of the burning mountains over the sweet taste of the elixir he'd once craved. It was a year since he'd succumbed to such vile delights. He couldn't falter—not with so much at stake.

The Divide had fallen and, with it, his world turned into chaos. What remained of the mountains was set ablaze, and the sky was thick with growing plumes of black smoke. Debris was thrown far and high from the epicenter of the explosion, raining flames from the skies. It burned every farmhouse and village littering the path from his home in Rannadal to the gaping mouth carved into the mountains. With the destruction so close to their home, every warrior in town picked up a weapon and rode alongside him into the heart of sheer mayhem.

Once they crested the final hill and received a perfect view of the tear in The Divide, he closed his eyes in prayer at the horrors lying before them.

Olena, Goddess of Order and Light, hear my plea to keep us safe and grant me the strength to fix this.

But when he opened his eyes, he was certain for the first time in his life that his prayers would be unanswered. For not only was the sky blackened and the earth marred with the stench of magic, but spirits were leaking from the cavern where the mountains once stood.

The Divide wasn't just a natural force separating elves and humans; it encapsulated some of the world's greatest evils. When it was formed, it was said Olena herself trapped the God of Chaos' spirits of calamity within. They were his agents of destruction and, in a single night, they were bursting free after ages of captivity.

Living to see the dawn would take a miracle.

That would not hinder them from trying to protect their lands from the spirits wishing to do it harm. No matter the creed or faith of those under his command, they fought with the same vigor as soon as Karsten ordered them to strike at the spirits pouring from the crevice torn from the earth. They would not wait to be saved by the divine intervention of any God, and they would not fall to their knees in prayer or anguish either. Rannadal and its people were largely forged in the blood of wars and the raids of lands double their size.

They would not kneel to any King or Jarl, let alone to the damned.

Blood poured down the side of Karsten's face as he heaved his sword out of a spirit that, like many around them, was foolish enough to take physical form. The others, which remained in their ghostly, untouchable but weaker depositions, fled further into the mainland of The North. They flew above them, dark shadows they felt more than they saw, and were certain to infect everything they touched.

'They'll run rampant all over the world, corrupting every corner of it, and there's nothing I can do. Nothing any of us can do. I cannot stab a spirit any more than I can stab a cloud unless it's in the process of haunting someone, tethering itself to the mortal plane to feed just in time to be cut down. My effort here will do nothing. We will die for nothing.'

Panic welled up fierce and bright in his chest, forcing his bruised lungs into overdrive as he heaved in ceaseless waves of ash. The nearing flames were hot on his skin, searing him inside and out as the world blurred. Gone were the screams of his men and the visions of their bodies dropping heavy across the blood-soaked ground. Everything was replaced by a harsh buzz and a white film which turned the world around him to glass—a precious thing he knew would shatter.

"Karsten, duck!"

A shriek echoed in his ears as he dropped to the ground. The sharp tang of magic surrounding him ceased as someone pulled him to his feet. The face of his savior came into view, silhouetted by the burning summits and pines smeared with crimson.

"Damn fear spirit had its claws in you," Zamir shouted over

the roar of the flames and the clash of swords against the oozing, half-formed flesh of the spirits manifesting around them. "Shake off the visions and thoughts. There's work to be done."

He gripped his friend's arm tight, more thankful than he'd ever been that Zamir was not only his closest companion, but also the only witch he trusted. "Thank you."

Zamir shrugged off the thanks and beckoned him further into the throes of battle. "Thank me when we leave these mountains alive."

Even though the spirit which conjured such fright in him was dead, Karsten still questioned whether they'd ever make it out alive. In every direction, their odds worsened. Spirits could manifest in physical form, but then they could be killed by average weapons like a sword or axe. Those lingering spirits that remained in their spectral forms were creatures far more difficult to defeat.

Battling spirits such as those was a fight in the mind, not on the battlefield.

They could make a person see, feel, and think about things they normally wouldn't dream of. They pushed good men to do terrible deeds and drove others mad. Only magic or a strong mind could dispel them, but either option took a strength that weighed heavy on the shoulders of any who dared attempt the task. Karsten could already see the signs of fatigue wearing Zamir down. His shoulders were slumped over his bronze staff and there was a tremble to each of his steps. Both men knew Zamir was all they had until their scouts returned with another witch or magically inclined healer.

If he falls, we all will.

On his left, a warrior cried out as she stepped, purposefully, off a cliff. Her body cracked on the rocks below, and a spirit of Suicide laughed as it hunted for its next victim. On his right, a guard he'd known since he was a child, who always snuck him an extra dessert on his name's day, was sobbing like a child as a spirit of Sorrow latched onto his heart with astral claws to suck every shred of love from its depths.

No, they would not make it out of The Divide alive.

Somehow, that made him fight harder.

They pushed through the night, working tirelessly to hold the tides of darkness back. Their makeshift army held the line as nearby villages sent their own to aid their efforts. Over the highest trees perched atop the broken mountains, light finally began to break the night apart.

The spirits will be weaker in the sunlight. If we can survive a little longer, we might live after all.

It was only a moment later that his hopes were dashed as a streak of green lit up the sky. It was not the sunrise breaking the sky in two; it was the aurora. While he would usually marvel at the beautiful sight associated with his Goddess, he found no peace in it. The presence of the aurora meant the dawn was still too far away to be of any help.

One of his warriors ran to his side, her face caked in blood and sweat to mirror his own haphazard state, and gasped as she pointed at the sky. "Commander, it's a sign of Olena."

Karsten tried to seek comfort in the symbol of his Goddess so present at their side, but it was hard to find any ounce of hope with the sounds of death growing all around him. "Don't get distracted now. We must stay vigilant," he ordered, his voice straining and cracking beneath the smoke strangling his throat.

"She's right, you know," Zamir said as a small reprieve in the waves of spirits allowed them to rest for just a moment. "For your Goddess, it's a sign of her love. For mine, it's the gateway to The Old Gods—the Bifrost." He smirked as he readied his staff for the next group of encroaching spirits which dared to make themselves into mortal form. The sky above erupted in brilliant color as the aurora grew, spreading its light across the battlefield. "With both pantheons aiding us, I see no reason for us to fail."

Hope could be a powerful force, one to challenge the fate of Gods and conquer any spirit. Karsten watched as it renewed the strength in his men's attacks and the power radiating from Zamir's spells. Determination returned with a fierce conviction in their hearts, forcing them forward when even the bravest of them considered fleeing for the valleys. A renewed energy permeated the air that had died when they bore witness to the chaos claiming the mountains.

They would hold back the spirits, even if it killed them. Even if most would not live to see their efforts bear fruit. They would hold the line and the light for those who lived beyond that night and all the lives it took.

But Karsten wondered if that new sense of hope was an intervention of the divine right before their eyes. The aurora was a subtle sign, yes, but strange enough it made many believe it must be godly in origin. It was too early in the year for such magic as the aurora. It shouldn't have been glowing above them in the summer, and yet it was shining regardless.

"If the aurora was sent by the heavens," Karsten began as he switched from his sword to the axe strapped to his side. "Then let's give the Gods a show."

He reentered the fray, his weapon cutting through every spirit who dared to feed on his people. They burned with rage and bit into his skin with sharp teeth as they tempted him, twisting at the edges of his mind to seed fear, doubt, and darkness into his heart.

Sweat dripped from his brow into his eyes, mixing with ash and blood until his vision was blurred black and red. He paused for just a moment to wipe it away on his cloak, the burning in his irises only ceasing when the muck was cleaned from the corners of his gaze.

He looked back up, expecting a spirit to be too close for

comfort, only to find the entire clearing they fought within frozen in awe. The light of the aurora lowered and, instead of flowing freely through the sky, it whisked itself between trees and cliffsides to cut a path straight through their ranks. It lit the woods in brilliant shades of mint and wine so beautiful even the spirits halted their attacks to watch in wonder at the display. The sick, bitter taste of magic and blood on his tongue lessened. In its place, the soothing flavor of lavender and snow invaded his senses, filling him with a peace he'd never known and shouldn't have felt in the heat of battle.

A shadow stepped out of the cavern tearing open The Divide.

The aurora wrapped around them, lighting them in shades of scarlet and emerald. From such a distance, all Karsten could make out was a shocking head of white hair, a feminine frame, and the unmistakable glow of their eyes. He should've apprehended them, seen if they were responsible for the devastation, but he couldn't move. All he could do was stare and feel a tranquility he hadn't experienced since he was a child—but perhaps not even then.

The woman raised her hands to the sky, teasing the edges of the aurora, before she spread her arms almost like she was pulling the light close for an embrace. Only, her demeanor shifted the moment that power was within her grasp. Gone was the feeling of safety and, in its place, was a sharp tug of apprehension as her fingers curled into rabid claws.

The spirits jerked in unison, wrenched back by an invisible thread connecting them to the mysterious figure and the lights she commanded. They screamed and cried out, fighting with every ounce of energy they had to grasp onto their freedom. As soon as they passed through the lights, they morphed. Their violence was replaced by disquiet as they willingly flowed back into the cavern they escaped from.

Hundreds of spirits flowed from states of aggression into

passiveness as they whisked past the woman's still form. It was only when the last of the spirits was returned that the woman lowered her arms and every light disappeared, casting them back into the shadows.

Except for the light in one of her eyes.

Karsten ran, finally able to move even as surprise and relief made him want to collapse. When he was within reach of the woman, he slowed until he could see the weak tremble in her limbs and the blood streaking from a wound marring her glowing left eye.

"You're hurt," he said, unsure where the tenderness in his tone came from. He should have questioned her motives instead of seeking out her wounds. Yet, he somehow knew in his core that she'd saved them, not damned them.

At his question, the glow in her eye flickered. Behind it, he could just make out her piercing but exhausted eyes, the color of the forest around them when the trees weren't covered in cinders.

Once the light fully died, her eyelids fluttered closed and she collapsed. He caught her as she fell, his weapon clattering to the ground beside them.

"Healer!" he called, praying his voice carried beyond the charred fissure carved into the mountains.

He hated that he sounded so desperate when he was standing before his warriors, but he couldn't stop the miserable edge to his voice when he felt how fragile she was in his arms. She'd stood before them, radiating with the light of the heavens, only to fall from grace between one blink and the next. No matter how strange the woman's sudden appearance was, she saved them.

He would not let her die for them.

As he waited for the healer to reach them from the other side of the battlefield, a crowd formed to look at the maiden in his arms as he knelt to hold her better. He swept the blood from her face to reveal the wound snaking across her eye and, in doing so, moved the white, tangled locks from her face.

Only, his movement revealed her pointed ears.

"She's an elf," someone whispered.

"Her people won't want her here," another said.

"We should just leave her. Better that way."

"And let the elves think we did something to her? Absolutely not."

"But what if she did something to cause this? It must be addressed."

"She was sent by The Old Gods—did you not see the Bifrost?"

"It could've been a sign of Olena just as well."

"Let her die either way."

Zamir ran through the growing crowd, pushing past any who dared get in his way, before he dropped to his knees beside them to look over the injured woman in his grasp. In his frantic effort to save her, he only stopped one time to lean towards Karsten and whisper for only his ears, "We can't leave her alone. I don't like how they're looking at her."

He gave his friend a curt nod and only dared to release some of his grip on her when Zamir maneuvered her away to better inspect what was sure to be the woman's vast amount of injuries. Her clothes were burned, and she was heaving desperately for each breath from her strangled lungs. She was caked in mud, sweat, and blood. Half her face was covered in crimson, and the other was scrunched up in pain even as she slept.

Still, she's the most beautiful woman I've ever seen.

He tore his gaze away.

She's an unconscious woman who just saved your worthless life. Don't act like a fool.

Zamir stayed with her as Karsten rounded up what little remained of their forces to gather the injured and build a pyre for the dead. It was only when dawn broke over the mountains that they were ready to return to Rannadal. The mysterious woman survived the night and was towed on a cart behind his horse, separate from the others just in case anyone had poor ideas.

Olena granted us a miracle after all, he thought as he checked on her halfway through their ride back into town. *I just never expected to see divinity in the flesh.*

THE PROMISED PROCLAMATION OF JARL THURSTAN II:

To the dearest people of The North and all those whose faith lies in our esteemed Goddess Olena, the benefactor of peace, I write this proclamation with both joy and anguish in my heart. The mountains of The Divide have been torn asunder, the spirits of Chaos trapped within now free to taint our world in darkness. In this time, be wary of possessions and question any thought which leads you astray from your convictions. All forces within our great city of Rannadal will do everything we can to secure the valley's borders and find those responsible for the death and mayhem which has befallen our neighbors—both elf and human.

Despite this, I bring joyful news to our growing ranks within The Covenant. On the very night our mountains shook, we have been granted with the Promised of Olena. Down from the mountains she came, a mysterious woman who controlled the aurora and spirits like the prophecy foretold. She is housed by and under the esteemed protection of The Covenant ever after.

Blessed be The Divine Promise,
Jarl Lefa Thurstan, Daughter of Thurstan the Cruel, Visionary of The Covenant

3

OF MISSING GODS AND UNHOLY SPIRITS

SKALD: ADELAIDE AYLARA

Everything fucking hurts.

A deep ache bloomed around Adelaide's left eye and a sharp dagger of pain lanced up her back, across her ribs. She could tell she suffered from a few bruised or broken ribs along with whatever other ailments claimed her prone body. She couldn't move, so she remained trapped, frozen in place, with an eye that refused to pry itself open.

She recalled the lights and the hope they'd brought her, but everything beyond that was fuzzy. It was as if a fog was placed over her memory. By the soft fabric wrapped around her shoulders, she assumed she wasn't still lost in the madness of The Wild Woods. Where else she could be, she did not know.

Falling.

Adelaide couldn't piece together much more than that while still fighting for control of her body. The memory of the steep cliff side and the jagged rocks below flashed through her mind. She was blindly following the lights, believing the Old Gods and the All-Father would guide her. She hadn't noticed the ledge in her haste, and she hit her entire body on the way down before everything turned black.

No wonder I'm a Gods-be-damned mess.

Finally, her unmarred eye peeled open and she winced at the light of the fire in the nearby hearth. The world was too bright and saturated—a harsh parallel to the darkness of sleep she'd once been cocooned in. How long was she teetering between Valhalla and the land of the living?

Relief greeted her as she focused on the wooden ceiling of the cabin above. Whoever saved her wouldn't have gone through such efforts to keep her alive if they only planned to kill her when she awoke. It was probably other Keepers who found her in their own efforts to protect their homes from whatever maleficent magic endangered it in the first place. Yes, that was the only explanation. No one else would've been near enough to pull her from the remnants of ash she could still taste on her tongue.

Unless my kin found me.

The thought sent her lurching forward, gasping in pain as she clutched her bandaged ribs in one hand and the gauze covering her left eye in the other. The agony grew, encapsulating her chest and pressing down on her core as her heart beat a little faster every moment her heavy breath echoed back to her.

If her family or a Keeper saved her, they wouldn't have left her alone.

So, who did?

The door creaked open, and a man stepped across the threshold. He was tall and lean with bronze skin that hadn't faded even when The North got so little sun. A staff was strapped to his back and a tome clutched in his willowy hands—a witch if she'd ever seen one. His shaggy black hair did nothing to hide the flat tops of his ears.

Human.

His hazel eyes widened as he regarded her with an anxious glance. "I'm surprised you're awake. You had quite the adventure before you fell unconscious," he said, his voice holding a low timber she found calming even as her back stiffened with each step he took further into the room. "I'm Zamir. Perhaps you would like to tell me your name?"

She remained silent, not daring to move as he ventured closer and sat on the nearest chair between her and the hearth. He left the path to the door open, as if proving she wasn't trapped. Still, she found her fear roaring to new heights with every word Zamir allowed to pass from his lips.

His kind kills mine. His people destroyed Alfheim. Humans only took and took until there was nothing left to take. All-Father, don't let him take me too.

"You may not believe it, but you're safe here. I won't let any harm fall upon you. You have my word." He tilted his head, seeming curious at her silence. "You're in a spare cabin in the village of Rannadal. Do you know where and *what* that is?"

She scowled on instinct, her panic piquing. Rannadal was the stronghold of the Knights of The Divide. The very Order which destroyed her life when she was still a foolish youth. They wouldn't let her leave town alive; she was certain of it. They'd probably pin some Knight's death on her shoulders and use it as the reasoning for her undoing.

Not that she hadn't killed plenty of their kind as a Keeper, but it was her duty. She was meant to protect her people from their wretched ways with everything she had.

Perhaps they would even lay the blame for the destruction of The Divide on her. If any of them truly believed she'd destroy her home, they would be idiots. Humans had little in the way of coherent thought anyways. They'd accuse her because they always yearned for any excuse to kill an elf. Her life would matter little in their quest for revenge.

The Knights would kill her, and her family would never know what tragic fate befell her.

Zamir grinned at the downturn of her dry, cracked lips. "I

figured as much, but I'm not telling you where you are to frighten you further. I'm letting you know how far away you are from home, should you seek it out. Although, I suggest that be after you've properly healed."

Adelaide let out a breath and forced her stiff body to recline back on the bed. The human had a point. Her mind already conjured an escape route through the woods and back to the tear in the mountains where she'd last seen her family. Once she gathered her strength, she'd make the trek back through the forests.

She just needed to survive until then.

"You know, your powers are quite remarkable," he mused as he pushed his chair just a little closer. "How did you obtain them? Birth, curse, training, or something else?"

She snorted. By the Old Gods, the man must've been daft. "I don't have magic," she said, her voice cracking with each syllable.

"So, you *do* talk," he mused as he poured a glass of water from a nearby pitcher and passed it to her.

She was careful to sniff the liquid for poison before she took the offered drink to calm both her nerves and her smoke-damaged throat.

"But I'm afraid you are incorrect in that regard," he continued. "You put on quite the show at the crevice torn into the mountains."

A choke ripped through her, burning her lungs as the water went down the wrong way. "*What*?" she gasped, still coughing the water out of her chest.

He chuckled. "Figured you didn't remember. You took a nasty blow before our forces found you," he said, tapping his own eye where hers was wrapped in a bandage. "You came out of The Wild Woods, cloaked in the aurora like a goddess of old. All you did was stick your arms out and all the freed spirits of The Divide were yanked straight back into the mountains.

They're still slipping free, but the casualties and danger decreased greatly since your little stunt."

The human had no reason to lie. Adelaide knew that. Still, she wished she could shove his falsities away and bolt straight for the door. All elves were supposedly born with magic, but some were more gifted than others. Many specialized in certain crafts. Her siblings could heal, manipulate water, and conjure shadows. Their mother could shift her shape on command to become any animal or person. Adelaide never even managed to heal a papercut. Her mother was certain she didn't have an ounce of magic in her blood.

It was quite a disappointment for Mother.

But the powers he described were unknown to her, and she'd read every book in her mother's library of magical texts. Books which were now burned, rotting at the bottom of a spirit-filled cavern.

The ability to control the spirits was beyond what mere mortals were allowed to do. It was a thing for the Gods to handle and mortals to leave up to the heavens to contend with. Zamir claiming she held any sway over their kind seemed like pure insanity, but she didn't detect any lies hidden in his tone. At the very least, he believed he was telling the truth.

Until she was healed, that was all the information she could rely on as she handed the empty glass back to him.

"You didn't answer my question," he noted, and she turned her head to him even as her eyes grew heavy. "Birth, curse, training, or something more?"

The pain must've been getting to her head because she smirked at him, although it was a pitiful excuse for a smile with her face half covered in bruises and the other half wrapped in bandages. "What do you think?"

He huffed a short laugh and reached over to stoke the fire, sending more warmth her way and dragging her mind further into the realms of sleep. Her eyes were closed, and she figured he must've thought she was asleep since he sighed, his seat groaning as he grew more comfortable.

Whether he stayed to protect the villagers of Rannadal from her or protect her from the Knights, she couldn't tell.

"You're certainly something more," he murmured as she drifted off to sleep.

THE SUN WAS high in the sky by the time her eye cracked back open. The light from the hearth was replaced by the warmth of the sun kissing her cheeks, rousing her from slumber and casting her back into her new, stark reality.

She was in the stronghold of the Knights, the faction of humans that ruined her life. Her body ached fiercely, preventing her from a quick escape. Even if the exact Knights who tormented her six years prior weren't posted in Rannadal, since the Order was comprised of thousands across The North, she couldn't remain in the base of their brothers-in-arms.

Worse yet, her family was still missing in some unknown crevice of The Divide, which was at least a half day's travel on horseback and a full day's trek on foot from Rannadal. There was no way in all the realms she would leave her family waiting for her.

Injured or not, she had to escape.

A long, deep groan peeled from her lips as she forced her body into a sitting position. A sharp pain spiked down her spine, and her head pounded with each rush of blood in her skull. Her heartbeat rose, panic crashing through her. She had to get away before Zamir returned, but she felt like Hel crawled inside her body and rotted half of it, transforming her into half-death just like the Goddess herself.

But for her family, she would find a way.

Above the hearth, dried sprigs from the spring hung upside down. The evidence of their drying process littered the mantle, warping the wood. She recognized mugwort and waybroad, two herbs her mother used for healing. Across the room were dusty bottles typically used for tinctures. Whoever abandoned the cabin was most certainly an apothecary or herbalist. By the looks of things, they departed in a rush.

Maybe they left something behind.

She hoisted herself to the end of the bed, clenching her jaw the whole way to clamp down on the sounds of pain wishing to slip free. Her trembling legs were limp as she dragged them with her hands to the ground, steadying them before she dared to put weight on them.

She fell.

A yelp tore through her as her ribs met the solid oak floor, her body sending a cloud of dust into the air as she rolled onto her back. The rafters above swirled, the hanging herbs latched to the ceiling turning the one-eyed vision around her from shades of wooden brown to faded greens.

After all that work, I'm lying down again. Fucking great.

She ripped the bandage from her face in anger, biting her tongue when she really wished to cry out in frustration and sorrow. Her kin were gone, and she was far too weak to reach them. The eye she'd uncovered was heavy before it filled with tears she wiped away with a harsh hand.

She touched her face again, curious at a ridge she'd felt as she brushed away her tears. Her finger started above her left eye, following a serpentine path across her forehead, over her eyebrow which was split in half, skipped directly over her eye, and continued beneath until mid-way to her cheek.

It was already a scar. No doubt healed by Zamir's magic. It would be a permanent fixture on her face for the rest of her days, however short the Knights decided that would be. She'd forever have a branding of failure in her duty and to her family marring her complexion.

As if she could ever forget.

A broken sound erupted from her throat, as if it came straight from her burdened and shattered heart. She fought with her tunic's burned edges, seeking out the warped raven pendant against her chest. She clutched it with trembling fingers as a few more tears she refused to acknowledge slipped free.

Despair threatened to claim her, but she resisted as she trucked the pendant away and clawed her way across the creaking floorboards to the cabinet at the corner of the room. Using the table and wall as leverage, she hoisted herself into the chair Zamir sat in the night before. She was level with the doors of the cabinet which, to her relief, were unlocked. Inside, numerous vials of shimmering liquid stared back. They were covered in dust and no doubt passed the recommended application date, but they would do in a pinch.

And Adelaide was definitely in a pinch.

In a lazy script, she struggled to read the words '*healing tonic*' in Common and chugged the liquid without a second thought. It ran thick down her throat and left a sour tang behind, but the effects were nearly instant. The sore ache in her bones lifted and her mind seemed to right itself so she could focus beyond the pain. Her aching, cracked ribs knit themselves back together and the pressure behind her eyes faded. She still staggered, her legs weak like a babe just learning to stumble through the world, but she'd have to live with it. The tonic did all it could for her, but the effects wouldn't last forever. She'd need to be out of town before the magic faded or she'd end up bedridden and stuck in Rannadal forever.

A new pair of clothes and fresh boots lying on a table caught her eye. She dressed in a hurry, eager to get rid of her soot-soaked clothing. Briefly, she searched for her bow, arrows, and daggers but found none of them within the cabin. She expected the humans would take them, and she mourned for their loss as she pulled the new boots on. Her family, the Aylara Clan, were all given golden weapons passed down by their ancestors. Her bow was priceless, but the risk of getting caught while trying to retrieve it from wherever the humans took it wasn't worth it.

Her skin buzzed at the telltale signs of magic in the brew, which slithered through her veins. She used the rush from the tonic to hurry across the cabin. The window above her bed led straight out into a patch of trees. The sun may have been shining bright, but she could use their shadow for cover until she found a weakness in Rannadal's defenses to escape.

Anything is better than waiting in silence and pain for my death.

Her hands shook as she pried the window open and slid outside, the new boots crunching in early-fallen leaves dusting the ground. Luckily, with the bustle of the town, no one heard her escape or noticed her disappear into the shadows. As she hurried through the thicket of trees, she knew she couldn't stay there for long. There were too many humans and the vaguest outlines of the shining silver armor of the Knights. They would eventually catch sight of her in the tree line and if she wasn't already a goner before, her discovery would seal her fate.

Walls encapsulated the entire town, and she couldn't reach their peaks on her own. Her first idea was to scurry up a tree and hop the gates, but the trees around her weren't as tall as the giants in the forest she called home. They wouldn't support her weight, nor reach the heights required to flee the fortress.

There must be another way.

She followed the line of trees, slipping in and out of the shadows, until a familiar shape caught her eye on the horizon. A temple to the Old Gods stood proudly nearby, a path twisting towards it from the center of town. She would find solace among followers of her Gods. The All-Father would protect her, as he always had.

As the heavy door shut, darkness enveloped her for just a moment before her elven eyes adjusted to the dim candlelight bathing the temple in warmth. Pillars stretched above before curving to create beautiful arches around the main floor. A second floor wrapped above her, open in the center to reveal a few specks of sunlight filtering through the thatched windows.

It was the closest thing to home she'd seen since she ventured out to hunt. It was the only time she felt as though the Gods were with her since she allowed that old human in the woods to live. But the longer she stood in the threshold of the temple, the further her heart sank.

She didn't dare make a sound as she tiptoed through the first row of melted candles dripping onto the floor. Where she would expect to see offerings to Odin, Freya, or Thor, there were instead long benches lying barren of both worshipers and idols. Rather than smelling lavender incense and spilled mead, she tasted the thick scent of roses and wine.

It wasn't until she came upon the back of the room that she realized she hadn't sought sanctuary in the temple of her Gods but in a chapel of the human's divine, and her dismay didn't end there. No, she discovered the people of Rannadal hadn't merely built their own religious space.

They'd stolen it from her people.

What have the humans done?

In every etching and in every marvel of woodworking genius, she could see the hand of either an elf who long ago left New Alfheim or the touch of a human believer of the Old Gods. The building was given so much love and grace by those who built it, only for it to fall into the grasp of followers of a far newer religion than her own.

Adelaide heard whispers about the Cislenian religion from

other Keepers, but she'd never seen the evidence of their deeds until that very moment. A "conversion to the new world" is what they'd called it. Some were converted by choice, but many were not.

As she stood in the heart of a place once meant and made for her people and those who believed in their ways, she mourned for what once was—for those who were misplaced. She knew of the methods some Cislenian used to tame the so-called pagan *'filth'*. They were no better than the Knights. It would make sense for their stronghold to cater to such destruction.

Her knees buckled, so she lowered herself into a pew and stared hard at her findings, wondering what horrors preceded the changing of the temple into a chapel. Gone were the typical statues of Odin, carved from delicate hands and steady hearts. In its place, a golden relic stood proud, surrounded by offerings of meager silvers.

As if gold needs its own accessories.

The sculpture depicted a woman basking in her higher purpose, her hair billowing behind her and her hands clutching a thick tome Adelaide didn't know the title of. Around her, weaved like a ribbon in and out of the woman, was a cloaked man forged from obsidian. He held another book, and his eyes sucked Adelaide in and wouldn't let go.

Humans have such strange ways.

She would never understand them or their need for greed and conquering everything they saw. It was those traits that destroyed Alfheim. It was those dark, natural qualities that formed the Knights, the Cislenian faith, and killed those she cared for.

"They simply cannot help themselves," her mother always said. *"We must only hope we live to see them kill each other off before they endanger the entire world."*

"And if they don't?" she asked her mother.

"Then we will have no choice but to stop them."

How was she to stop anything horrible from happening to the world when she couldn't even protect her own family?

Her breath deepened as she sunk further into herself. What if she couldn't find them? What if she traversed the rest of her days with desperate vengeance but never got them back? She'd never been so determined to accomplish something in all her days, but what if it wasn't enough? Worse yet, what if she found her family's corpses instead of their welcoming arms?

A heavy weight settled on her chest as her heart quickened. The temple-turned-chapel around her faded as her vision blurred with tears. She'd never been far from her kin and, the one time she had, she'd been searching desperately for a friend who was already dead—their life stolen by the Brotherhood. Would she find her family the same way? Their bodies broken by the very people who'd taken her from The Wild Woods?

Dread dug into her heart and bit down, forcing her to gasp as she doubled over, clutching her chest as if her heart threatened to leap free at any moment. Her scarred eye ached, the pulsing beat of her blood around the wound making her head swim. The world around her danced in darkness as she tried to push the worried thoughts away.

I'll find them. I'll find them.

'And if you don't?' a whispered voice replied. *'What if you find them broken and bloody at the bottom of that ravine—their skin scorched by flames and their lovely gazes pinned right back at you? Did they wait for you, thinking you would save them, and you never came?'*

"No, they could save themselves," she told the voice aloud between her desperate gulps of air. Her chest was squeezed so tight it burned each time she breathed and it hurt worse to speak. She clutched at her heart with one hand and laid the other over her stinging eye. "They *did* save themselves," she corrected.

'You already know they didn't. That's why you left. You weren't searching for them; you abandoned their final resting place. You didn't want to risk seeing their bodies, crushed at the bottom of a ditch. Adelaide, you didn't want to see them like you saw the others.'

"That's not true," she cried, her head in her hands as the steady stream of tears running down her face grew to a flood. "I would never abandon them."

'But you already did.'

Somewhere on the chapel floor, pieces of her heart shattered around her. She'd never be able to put the shards back together, not if her family was truly gone. She trembled with each soul-wracking sob as the world around her shifted to darkness with every wheezing breath. She dared to open her damaged eye and, at the corner of her gaze, caught sight of a watery shape that didn't belong to her tears.

Adelaide rubbed that eye clean and tried to focus on the ghostly outline hovering to her left. It shimmered in shades of turquoise and midnight blue, curving around her and yet just out of reach. She'd seen such creatures before in both their astral and physical forms, but they'd never worked their way into her blood so thoroughly.

"Sorrow," she said, forcing the spirit to twist in her direction. "Why do you torment me?"

The voice from before replied, *'It is my nature, Adelaide.'*

"It doesn't have to be," she told it.

The spirit of Sorrow paused, as if to consider her words, but each second it hesitated caused the pain in her eye to worsen. She tried not to blink, nor look away from the vision of the spirit, but eventually the pain surpassed her determination. She closed her eyes as they filled with tears of pain instead of sadness.

That was all the spirit needed.

It began barraging her again with every word she never wanted to hear.

'They died because of your failure. You will never see your family again. Everything you've done was for nothing. Now, you will die here like so many elves before you at the hands of the Knights. They would be ashamed of you. Your mother is watching from Valhalla, disappointed in what you've become. The real tragedy is that she knows she'll never see you again, for you will never die an honorable death in battle. You're too much of a coward for that honor. Your siblings will never forgive you for cutting their lives short. To think, you will never see Sophie grow up.'

All at once, the growing darkness around her fractured. Awareness snapped back to her as if a cold bucket of water were dumped over her head, shocking her veins. She wiped her heavy eyelids on her sleeves and turned to the place where the spirit once was. It lay on the ground, frozen in a state where it was half-physical and half-otherworldly wisps of greenish blue light. An axe pierced its core and, slowly, the spirit cracked.

She stared with wide eyes that continued to spill stubborn tears until the last visages of the being faded. In its place, the deceased spirit's essence flickered, transforming into sparks dancing through the air like blossoms on the spring wind. Its remnants would return to The Divide, becoming one with the realms again. With the mountains broken apart, she wondered if it would simply escape once again. If it would haunt some other poor soul who'd gone through too much.

Boots echoed across the chapel as someone walked past her. A man came into view, his gaze focused solely on the axe embedded in the wooden floor. He yanked it free and turned to her. When she saw his flat ears and the heavy weapon in his hands, the reality of where she was snapped back to her. She scurried backwards until she hit an ornate planter. Her nails tore through the wet earth, her fists full of dirt. If he advanced, she'd toss it in his face to obscure his vision and dart out of his grasp. She'd done so on many occasions when humans found her gardening and wanted a taste of more than the fruit she grew.

Humans are always out for elf blood.

The man's scowl and tense grip on the axe loosened. He secured it to his side and crouched before her, his expression unreadable except for the concern in his down-turned brows.

"Are you hurt?" he asked, his voice far quieter and softer than she had expected. He spoke like he feared any loud noise would startle her, as if she were a timid animal in need of coaching to leave the safe confines of a cave or bush.

And that's when the hunter entraps you.

She searched for any twining symbols of the Knights adorning his person and was surprised to find it lacking. Still, he bore the intense presence of the Brotherhood with a watchful gaze and sturdy build she'd come to expect from a Knight. It caught her off guard, seeing someone so attuned to their order treat her gently, but maybe that was how every warrior in Rannadal appeared.

"Are you a Knight?" she demanded, ignoring his previous question.

He paused to study her, his brows furrowing before he answered, "No."

Relief washed through her. Perhaps all the people in Rannadal simply trained like a Knight in battle? He had no weapon or insignia from their Order. There was a greatsword on his back and an axe strapped to his side, not a sword and shield like a Knight would have.

If she wanted to survive, she couldn't appear as a threat or kill any of the humans within Rannadal's borders—even if she wished to see every Knight dead at her feet. It was against the treaties signed by the Keepers and the Order decades prior. Her duty came first, even before her own life. She wouldn't break their agreements just to ensure her own escape back to the safety of her mountains. Especially not when diplomacy was still an option.

Being friendly to any warrior within Rannadal, Knight or not, still sickens me.

They were all still complicit in their connections to the Brotherhood. It was an unforgivable sin in her eyes, but she was not the All-Father. She could not see through their hearts and into the heavens. The only thing Adelaide could do was find a way to make it back home alive, even if that meant setting her morals aside. So long as she didn't break any treaties in the process, she'd force herself to accept the aid from a Rannadal warrior.

Besides, this human just saved me from a spirit. At least at this moment, he doesn't seem like a threat.

Her hunched shoulders fell, and she loosened her grip on the earth bunched in her palm.

I once believed it was impossible to find a kind human, and yet I've supposedly discovered two in one day: Zamir and this man. One must be lying. I would never be so lucky.

At her silence, he sighed and rubbed the back of his neck. "Sorrows are never fun to deal with, and I will not force you to share your pain. However, I can at least escort you back to your cabin and call for aid, should you wish it. There are many in town who are willing to listen to the pain in one's heart."

He pulled off his gloves, as if to show her he had nothing to hide. She stared at his offered hand, each crevice on his skin running like rivers towards his future. Her mother could read life paths on people's palms, but she constantly refused to do Adelaide's. She always wondered why and, as she recalled what little she was taught of the art, she read the man's past instead of his future with every scar and line carved into his skin.

Whoever he was, he'd once been in incredible pain. Perhaps, he still was.

Her gaze slid up his arms covered in leather vambraces, which were crafted with patterns she'd never seen before. His matching chest plate differed only in the symbol on his chest. It reminded her of the statue in the center of the room: two souls colliding in an eternal dance. Beneath the armor was a white linen tunic, trousers, and worn boots that had seen better days. Atop it all, he wore a bear fur cloak that wrapped around him like a shadow.

Gods, she longed to be wrapped in that cloak and take a long, much deserved nap. She could already feel the effects of the healing potion wearing off since she'd overexerted herself.

But she couldn't rest yet, not until she was back with her kin, so she schooled her wants and focused on practicality.

"Why did you save me?" she asked, locking her jaw. The healing tonic waned, draining the strength from her body with each passing moment.

He stared at her, his gaze piercing and warm all at the same time. Like a molten dagger digging into her ribs, staving off frostbite even as it pierced her heart. "It was the right thing to do," he said, his head tilting to the side as his curiosity remained fixed on her.

Why would a human show her such kindness? She was an elf obviously out of her depth and inside the village that the Knights called home. Although the man before her bore no symbol of the Brotherhood and he claimed not to be a Knight, she knew Rannadal's loyalty to them ran deep. That knowledge should have sent her running.

But then she truly looked at the man behind the armor.

His mouth was turned into a sad but welcoming smile, the edge framed by a scar running across his lips. Thick stubble shadowed his strong jawline and, as she followed it, his hair lightened as she reached the strands atop his head. Wisps of curls sprung out of an otherwise polished style. With the fine cloak adorning his broad shoulders and a crown of golden locks, he could've been mistaken for Rannadal's chief.

What do the humans call their leaders again? Jarls?

But no, the scars on his face and hands told her a different story. He'd seen the horrors of battle and, if she were to hazard a guess, he was one of the famed Viking explorers she'd heard about as a child. They traveled the vastness of Midgard, trading and fighting in the name of The Old Gods. She'd met an elf who left for that life once. She trained Adelaide in the ways of a shieldmaiden, and she fancied joining her in the open seas.

In the end, her family needed her and she stayed.

If that were true, what was a Viking doing in a landlocked village, far from the sea?

She shook off the rampant thoughts and peered back at his hand. He hadn't yanked it away in disgust, but she could see his patience wearing thin as he balanced on his creaking, old boots with his entire weight.

Taking pity on him, she sighed and began to tell him to just leave her and she'd be out of his hair for good, but then their eyes met. Her deep green on his piercing amber. There was something there, hidden in the honey color of his eyes that made her pause.

Sincerity.

As far as she could tell, he genuinely wanted to help her. Zamir assisted her as well, but it didn't feel the same. He spoke to her in the same way Adelaide would handle a wounded fawn, always questioning if it would lash out at the smallest transgression.

With every other human she'd encountered, there was always an ulterior motive. There was always something they wanted: a trade they wished to barter, a secret they wanted to pull from her lips, her blood mixed into the snowy earth, her body beneath theirs. Always something they wanted, but they wouldn't simply come out and speak.

But not him. He did not offer his hand like she was a scared animal and he feared her bite. He had not saved her from her sorrow merely to demand repayment for his kindness in the form of crimson or gold. He just wished to help for the sake of being *kind.*

She took his hand.

HEALER'S NOTES ON UNKNOWN ELF PATIENT

"The patient has slept for nearly four days, tossing and turning when she isn't screaming in her sleep. She calls out to Gods I do not know, and for a family who certainly perished in the onslaught of spirits leaking from the mountains.

There aren't any tears left to shed on the tragedy, on both our accounts. Her cries have turned to whimpers and my own anguish at the constant flow of death into my clinic has numbed. There is only so much one man can see before the darkness creeps in. I long for the days when my most interesting patients were those who spilled love tonics on the wrong man or couples I never expected to be with child. Now, I must deal with a patient the Jarl has claimed as divine providence across the lands. But I am getting away from the point.

The unknown patient's injuries are as follows:

A concussion, most likely caused by a bash to the face which granted her a scar.

Two broken ribs, another fractured, and all the bruises to match.

A broken heart, but I have no droughts to aid in such an injury."

- Healer Bo Sigvidsson

4

STRANGERS IN THE TEMPLE

SKALD: KARSTEN STROM

Karsten helped the elven woman to her feet and grimaced when his palm came back covered in sweat and earth.

"Apologies," she said, turning her gaze to the floor in a weak attempt to hide the blush burning across her cheeks. She wiped her hand on her trousers, and he copied her movements to rid himself of the dirt.

"That's alright. I know a good distraction technique when I see one. I should've asked you to drop the dirt before helping you up," he said, a sparkle of mirth escaping even as he tried in vain to school his features.

She snorted. "Do you really think I would've dropped it if you'd asked?"

Finally, a full smile was pulled from his lips, and it was his turn to blush. "I suppose not."

They lapsed into silence, their breaths the only sound to echo through the rafters above their heads. Her gaze was transfixed on the statue of Olena and Cismir he'd originally entered the chapel to pray near. She looked at its marble and obsidian form as though she'd never heard of the largest religion in The North.

Her lips screwed into a scowl, and her eyes narrowed at the golden veins on the relic's carved skin. "Where are the idols to my Gods?" she asked, and he immediately felt like a fool.

No doubt she'd sought sanctuary just like he had on those holy grounds. Unlike her Gods, his were still present in the central chamber. His shoulders fell as he beckoned her to a stairwell at the back of the building, but she remained fixed in the same spot he found her weeping. The tears were long gone and, in their place, a fierce stubbornness remained.

"I usually don't follow strange human men into the darkened bowels of a stolen temple," she remarked, her dry tone full of sarcasm that did little to hide her genuine frustration and fear.

He arched a brow and took a step down. "And I usually don't save strange elven women from sorrow spirits, but the world certainly isn't usual anymore, is it?"

She huffed but followed him down the stairs. Below the chapel, they entered a room at the end of a stone corridor. Inside, the walls were covered in the tapestries once adorning the entire temple. Tables were covered in idols to The Old Gods, carved from wood and stone. In the center, a statue crafted to resemble Odin welcomed them inside.

Her silence lay heavy over the room as she placed a pale hand across the long beard stretching down the middle of the statue. Dust flew into the air with each wipe of her hand until, finally, it was clean enough to reveal the runes on his sleeves and the blindness in one of his eyes.

Karsten had only seen Rannadal's temple in all its pagan glory once, long ago as a child, but he could hardly forget it. He'd been in such awe at every turn and, while the church's conversion to the Cislenian faith brought its own beauty, he had almost forgotten what it replaced.

What it stole.

She pressed her forehead against the statue and breathed deeply between her hushed words. "All-Father, grant me the wisdom to find them," she murmured, her voice so soft he nearly couldn't make out the words. "Freya, give me the strength to endure without them. Thor, strike down any who would keep us apart. Frigg, care for them in my absence. Gods, stay with me—always."

In the following silence, he awkwardly shifted his stance and resisted the urge to leave the room entirely. He had to ensure she returned to her cabin before anyone discovered what was most likely her attempted escape, but watching her plea to the Gods he once knew for safety felt like a violation. They had no idea what she went through or who she lost. It was a miracle beyond measure she hadn't ended his life or Zamir's on mere principle. Humans and elves weren't known for their cordial relations, let alone those who called the mountains home.

That wasn't even considering the fact that he was once a Knight of The Divide, the very wards Keepers like her despised. Their factions were at war for generations, and it was only by Olena's grace that the nameless woman took his word when he claimed he wasn't a Knight.

When I lied.

He shook the thought off. It wasn't exactly a falsity, but it also wasn't the truth. Karsten was no longer one with the Brotherhood, but he'd been among their ranks for most of his life. If he was certain she wouldn't kill him outright, he would've clarified the situation then and there to avoid any further blunders on his part.

Yes, tell the elf you're alone with that you lied and were one of the Knights who stalked her home. That will end well.

He bit his cheek until it bled, his tongue dancing on the old scars lining his mouth from repeating the same action time and time again. By the Gods, both old and new, couldn't he stop overthinking and obsessing over every tiny detail of his life and each of his many regrets? If he could, at least he would sleep better at night for the few winks he was granted between the ceaseless reports of death pouring in from their warriors who still defended their borders from the spirits who continued bleeding into their realm.

This woman slowed their approach before. Perhaps she can stop it altogether.

That was the hope of their Jarl, anyway. If she could seal the tear in The Divide and prevent anymore spirits from escaping, they would finally have enough manpower to track down the spirits who already fled and find whoever was responsible for the destruction in the first place.

Unless she's the one responsible.

It was a paranoid thought, one which lingered in the minds of everyone in Rannadal who doubted the Jarl's claims of the elven woman's divinity. Karsten wished he knew what to think one way or the other—was she their Promised savior or a fluke meant to damn them all?

His mind, which was full of compulsions and doubts ceaselessly looping in the quiet between his thoughts, seemed to be convinced it was the latter. His heart, however, told a different story entirely.

Karsten witnessed the pull of her magic over the mountains and her command of the aurora. He'd felt the peace and wrath in her abilities which even caused the spirits to take notice of her power. Yet, he saw her weeping at the loss of people she cared for who were no doubt stolen by the very destruction that killed many of his men.

He'd held her in his arms, her weak limbs cold to the touch as their healers tried to save her life. The reports of their progress lined his desk, notes on her screaming as her ribs were rapidly mended by a potion speeding her heart to dangerous levels.

His gaze fell on her, and he watched as she remained focused on the idol of Odin before her. Her emerald eyes were still closed, her lips trembling with words only meant for the Gods themselves. He hated to tear her from prayer, or whatever followers of The Old Gods did, but he needed her to willingly return to her cabin before anyone saw her.

That means she'll need to trust me.

He tested his next words on his tongue before he spoke, making sure he wouldn't stumble over them and make a fool of himself, as he often did. When he was certain his lips would cooperate, he cleared his throat. The sound broke the spell the statue seemed to ensnare her in. "They moved the statues here when Rannadal converted," he explained. "Some still celebrate the old ways, so the local völva ensured there would still be a place for her people to worship."

"We don't need relics or temples to worship the Gods. They are all around us," she said before peering up at the ornately carved rafters above her head. "Although, it is nice to have a place to go. Something that feels like home but isn't."

It truly crashed into him then, what exactly she must've lost.

Many of his warriors lost their lives when the spirits spilled into the edges of Rannadal, and even more people were displaced by the encroaching hordes of the damned, but at least those who lived still had a home in the first place. The elven woman before him had lost everything. His certainty of that only grew with each of her desperate pleas to the Gods.

Does she call for the safety of her people or for her family?

Either way, she'd lost too much, and that small temple nestled in the depths of a stolen chapel was the closest thing she had to a home. A home which no longer stood in the wake of such destruction

"I know this must be hard for you," he said, not realizing the words fell from his lips until her attention snapped to him, her green eyes piercing straight through him. "You should return to your cabin and continue to rest before the others want to speak with you. I'm sure they have an endless sea of questions you're not feeling up for."

She doesn't have the energy for an interrogation, Karsten noted as she swayed on her feet like a willow tree blowing in the slightest breeze. *She's nearly dead on her feet.*

Despite that, she squared her shoulders and hardened her gaze.

"What would you know of *hardship*?" she asked, spitting the words at his feet as though she wished they could curse him. "Although, I'm sure you understand plenty about *rest*. Rannadal sleeps easy at night knowing they've created monsters who cut down my people for the slightest offense. For no reason at all. Do you truly believe an elf such as I could rest while imprisoned in this—"

She stopped, her harsh tongue froze as her eyes rolled back and her body went limp. She crumbled, and he was barely able to catch her as she slumped to the ground. Under his fingers, which were wrapped around her wrist, her pulse beat hard and fast. She was still alive, but the rapid increase of her blood flowing beneath his touch frightened him beyond measure. His hand came back damp as he touched her sweaty forehead, and he shivered at the coldness of her skin.

"Don't—" she pleaded, her voice hoarse and tone panicked. "Don't let it be true."

Her hands flailed in her fitful sleep as Karsten questioned what in all the realms he should do with the incapacitated and deeply troubled woman in his arms. A healer was ideal, but then someone would discover that she tried to escape. Their Jarl wouldn't take kindly to that.

And yet, after seeing the full strength of her abilities, he wasn't keen on ending up on the other side of her magic. They needed it to aid their plight to stop the spirits, not end up on the receiving end of her wrathful enchantments.

His only option was to sneak her back to her cabin and call the healer from there. It would be a troublesome task heaving a sleeping woman through the thick tree line to conceal her until they were safely hidden inside her cabin, but it was his only option.

"F-fuck," he muttered as he imagined the scenario ending horribly in a million different ways. If caught, someone would assume he was kidnapping her or had plans to murder her. Still, he needed to try. She just needed to stay strong until he returned her.

Her fit worsened as he laid her fully on the ground, her eyes moving frantically behind her heavy lids.

"Knights, I beg of you. Not again."

His stomach lurched at the pain in her voice. Gone was the vicious gaze and the brash words of the woman who stood before him, defiant even in the face of her own exhaustion. Only the pain she endured that made her so fierce remained as she slept. He knew what that was like. He often spent his nights tossing and turning just like she was.

The past does that to a person.

Karsten met plenty of people haunted by their past, and they never tugged at his heart with such wild abandonment. Perhaps it was because he felt indebted to her for saving his warriors at The Divide and understood Rannadal was the last place a Keeper wanted to end up.

Or maybe her sorrow carved into his chest with a dull blade because he could still taste the lie on his tongue. He could shake the Brotherhood's armor from his shoulders, but he couldn't rid himself of their training completely after it was thoroughly beaten into him. The very hands that caught her falling were the same blood-soaked palms he couldn't cleanse.

No matter how hard he tried, he would always be what the divine feared most.

AN UNSENT LETTER SHOVED IN THE BOTTOM OF A DRAWER

Dear Caroline,

I apologize for not answering your letters sooner. ~~I don't know what to say to make up for everything.~~ You send far too many, but you needn't worry about me. I may have left the Brotherhood, but it was not a great loss. ~~I finally quit it.~~ There is a bigger purpose to The Covenant than the Knights could ever accomplish. I hope to one day show our family exactly what we've been building. ~~It won't be enough for father. It never is.~~

Your name's day just passed, how was it? ~~I miss you.~~ I'm sorry for not sending a gift. ~~I'm a terrible brother.~~ Has mother been well? ~~She's never well if he's home.~~ As for your questions in letter number four that I missed responding to: yes, Zamir and Zareen are well. I'm uncertain when I'll visit next. ~~He doesn't even want me there.~~ My role keeps me busy but yes, I'm sleeping. ~~No, I'm not.~~ I'll try to write more often. ~~Another lie.~~ Our forces require my utmost attention, so it leaves little room for correspondence that isn't related to my work. ~~You always pull the truth out of me. It's why we can't talk. You'll know too much.~~

I love you all. ~~That's not a lie.~~

- Karsten

5

NIGHTMARES FOR A TIMID HEART

SKALD: ADELAIDE AYLARA

A wicked thing slipped through the cracks in her mind, tugging at loose memories and mangling them into something new, dark, and horrid.

Something for its namesake—*a nightmare.*

Her burning home was alight again, as if Adelaide were there to witness it smolder when she'd truly only found it after it was destroyed at the bottom of a ravine. The vision was so like the one she'd seen six years prior, when another clan's cabin was smoldering in The Wild Woods, that it stole the breath from her lungs. Inside the roaring flames and melting memories, small arms stuck out from the timber and clawed desperately for fresh air.

No, she quickly realized. *They're reaching for me.*

But she was too far, and every step she took closer only seemed to push her farther away. She ran but all she gained was an ache in her chest and ash coating her tongue. The screams of her family echoed into a symphony of chaos around her. All she could do was cry, but no sound came out no matter how hard she tried.

On the horizon, the shapes of Knights overtook the once peaceful mountainside.

Not again.

LINGERING remnants of Adelaide's dream clung to her mind like cobwebs as she drifted in and out of sleep. The scent of charred flesh mixed with the growing voices echoing around her. Even as the last remnants of her horrid nightmare crashed through her, soaking her to the bone in sweat, she'd never felt so comfortable.

That's not possible.

In an instant, she knew she was being bathed in magic. There was nothing in all the realms except for magic that could calm her frantic mind after a nightmare like that.

As she cracked her good eye open, she saw the proof of it shimmering above her. Green swaths of magic shone in the air, the light dancing around her and across the cabin. How she'd returned to her spot in bed as though she'd never left, she wasn't certain.

Then, she heard his voice. The man from the temple was arguing with Zamir across the room. As her mind came back to the lands of Midgard, so did their voices, which grew more and more irate by the minute.

"She tried to escape," Zamir said, his voice pitched low with brimming irritation. "We need to tell the others."

The other man folded his arms over his broad chest and glared down at him. "She's clearly unwell. Telling anyone she left won't garner her sympathy. I'd rather *ask* for her assistance than have Zareen demand it from her, wouldn't you?"

With a sigh, Zamir turned away and tugged viciously at his

hair. “She won’t take kindly to the news, but that doesn’t make this right.”

“Her being killed after she saved us wouldn’t be right either,” the other man said as he laid a heavy hand on Zamir’s shoulder. “I know lying to your sister isn’t your usual code of conduct, but for this woman’s safety, we must pretend as if she were here the entire day.”

The humans are . . . arguing over my safety?

She would’ve been certain the conversation was just a dream if she hadn’t already come from her own personal land of nightmares just moments before. So, no, the people before her were real and they truly did seem to care for her safety. Even if it was simply to ask for her help, she’d never experienced such a thing from humans before. She wasn’t sure if it was the sheer shock of that revelation or if it was her scrambled brain still swimming in pain, but their conversation struck a chord in her.

“My name is Adelaide,” she said, her voice hoarse and barely above a whisper. Still, the two men heard her and turned in surprise. “I am Adelaide Aylara, Keeper of The Divide, and you both are incredibly loud.”

The unnamed man blanched while Zamir threw his hands into the air, breaking the shimmering spell around her. “She lives and finally has a name!” He jabbed the other man in the ribs with his elbow. “Told you my magic would work better than any traditional healer.”

The blond human’s scowl grew, the downturn of his lips tugging on the scar that ran across it. “I think her face marred by pain would say otherwise.”

She realized she was indeed grimacing as the once dull ache grew into a stabbing pain across her side in the absence of Zamir’s healing magic. Adelaide schooled her features to the best of her ability, as her mother always taught her. “While I appreciate the application of magic for healing purposes, I would also kill for a healing draught."

Zamir clapped his hands and rubbed them together as if for warmth, no doubt hiding his embarrassment at his lackluster healing magic behind a façade of bravado. "Let me get right on that for you, my lady." He hurried to the corner of the room where she previously found a healing elixir and busied himself with the ingredients.

"How are you feeling?" the other man asked and, when she turned to him, he was closer than she expected. He'd made tentative steps, no doubt in an effort not to scare her off.

She did, ever so slightly, feel a little like prey under his watchful amber gaze. Like she was a shorebird caught in a cage. Whether he was the hunter who set the trap or the one who planned to set her free, she had yet to tell.

"Like I fell off a cliff," she answered honestly, forcing herself to sit up. Sitting up would keep her aware and awake, just in case he was the hunter she feared.

He hesitated, fiddling with his hands as he glanced at the end of the bed before he dared sit on the edge furthest from her. The cot sank beneath his weight and, at the shy glance he sent her, she couldn't muster the effort to fear him. Exhaustion snaked through her, tainting her ability to distrust him. She wanted to scream for every human in the room to leave her alone so she could heal in solitude and escape as soon as she was able, but she could hardly keep her eyes open.

A huff left his lips as he fought back a grin. "That's funny since you practically did."

Adelaide arched a brow, not following his train of thought and silently questioning what in all the realms he was talking about. She knew she'd fallen somewhere in the mountains, but she'd been alone then.

Any remnants of mirth fell from his expression. "You don't remember?"

She shook her head. "Zamir said I helped save some people from the spirits, but I don't recall any of that. Last thing I remember, I was stumbling through the woods looking for—" She bit down on the words as she recoiled into herself.

Adelaide might not have remembered saving anyone, but she remembered letting her family down and losing them in the darkness perfectly.

"Well," he said as Zamir returned with fresh bandages and an elixir that smelled far stronger than any she'd taken before. "You ended up stumbling down a cliff side and right into the throngs of battle. That's where I found you."

He found me?

Zamir scoffed. "What he means is that he saved your life—*twice.*" He sat the gauze and bandages on the bed beside her before leaning over to inspect her eye. Usually, any human getting so close would make her shrink away, but the mixture of pain and the healing spell he'd woven made her weak. Being at their mercy set her on edge, but even those nerves were dulled by pain and magic. "You were practically glowing under the light of the aurora, basking in the light of the Bifrost as you floated down the gods-be-damned mountain."

She shared a perplexed look with the other man who mouthed, *'He's dramatic.'*

Zamir covered her scarred eye in a healing solution and wrapped it with gauze, shutting light out from that side completely. Normally, she'd object to the mere idea of anything hindering her line of sight. But her eye ached fiercely with the rest of her body, so she allowed it.

Yes, I'm allowing all of this. I'm choosing it. That feels better than saying I can't do anything to fight against whatever these humans decide to do with me.

"We watched in awe as, with just a wave of your hands, you beckoned every spirit back into the mountain," Zamir continued as he placed the elixir in her hands. "Then, you were simply frozen. Standing there like you didn't have a care in all the realms even as you were surrounded by a blood-drenched battlefield. He" — he jerked his thumb at the other man — "approached just as you started to collapse. Caught you and called for a healer immediately. Even as spirits began to leak into the world again, he held onto you in one hand and swung his sword in the other until we could all escape, save for a rotating contingency of warriors to ensure these spirits don't infest the entire realm anyways," he said before dropping the ingredients he used for the elixir back in a box in the corner of the room. "Healing magic isn't my forte but even I could see it was anyone's guess if you'd make it."

The other man's cheeks were tinted pink as he cringed at the praise Zamir loaded onto his shoulders. "I assure you: it wasn't notable. I'm sure Lady Aylara could better spend her time resting from her injuries than listening to your tall tales."

"I didn't control the spirits then?" she asked, relief heavy in her tone.

"No, you most certainly did," he said, his amber eyes darting back to her as he bit his lip. "You were quite notable in fact. I, far less so."

"You're too humble for your own good," Zamir chastised with a roll his eyes. "It'll leave you miserable. Better to stroke your own ego sometimes than to remain un-stroked."

The stranger sputtered at Zamir's obscenity and she snorted, although both sounds were drowned out by the other man's barking laugh as he ambled to the door.

"Now, dearest Lady Adelaide," he began as he opened the door, "make sure to drink the elixir and get some much-needed sleep. I will fend off the leeches who wish to bathe in your gods-touched glow for as long as I can." He laid a fist over his chest, as if he were making a vow. "It is a tremendous task before me, but I shall endeavor." The door slammed shut behind him, leaving Adelaide and the mysterious man alone.

His eyes fell to the elixir in her weak grip, his lip curling. "Don't drink that."

She sat the bottle aside. "The second he said healing magic wasn't his expertise, I had a feeling I wouldn't be taking it."

He scratched at his stubble-covered jawline. "Zamir means well, but I'm afraid tonics and potions weren't part of his training."

She shrugged as she leaned back against the bed, her body heavy and eyes sore. "I appreciate the sentiment." Just then, their previous conversation with Zamir floated back to the forefront of her mind. "But he didn't exactly explain how you saved my life *twice*?"

"Aside from dispelling the Sorrow spirit?" he asked, and she paled at the reminder. "When you fell unconscious at the chapel. It was obvious you were attempting to flee and there are some here, like Zamir's sister, who wouldn't take kindly to discovering that. With his help, I discreetly brought you back here so they wouldn't find out."

Part of her thrummed with gratefulness, but the other, larger part of her was on the edge of defeat. She was a prisoner after all, no matter how kind the two humans she met appeared to be. With the title of prisoner hanging around her neck, it would be far more difficult to find her family. Still, she would find them. She knew it in her heart. It was only a matter of time.

And a matter of how many humans I'll have to cut down to do so.

"I truly thank you for saving my life," she said, surprised by her own sincerity as the words slipped free unbidden. "Not many humans would—" she stopped, hating the words she couldn't force herself to say.

Not many humans would risk their life for an elf.

His brows pinched and he focused on his calloused hands

instead of her, the unmistakable darkness creeping over his gaze. "I know."

She pursed her lips as she drank him in. In the light of a stolen temple, surrounded by gilded statues and with a weapon in his grasp, he'd seemed like every other human she'd ever met. Far too brash and bloodthirsty for her liking.

In the soft firelight filtering in from the hearth, the edges of his hard exterior were softened to reveal a gentle nature. His metal chest piece and vambraces were missing so only his linen tunic stood between him and his enemies. Warriors wouldn't remove such crucial pieces around just anyone. Which meant he didn't think of her as a threat or an enemy.

She wasn't sure if that brought her comfort or offended her.

She decided to take it as a good sign as she tilted her head, peering at him from every angle as if looking at him sideways would give her a better view of his character. "I just realized I don't know your name."

He shook off whatever spell encapsulated him and gave her a small smile that briefly pulled on a jagged scar running across the side of his lips. "My name is Karsten."

She smiled back and said words she never expected to utter to a human, "Well, Karsten of Rannadal, thank you for saving my life—*twice*."

"It was my pleasure," he mumbled in a deep timbre as his honey eyes drank her in. The warmth of the hearth and the unbreaking, soft gaze he bestowed on her drew her in like a sailor to a siren song. With that scarred lip and the loose curls springing from his styled hair, she was more than willing to drown.

Gods, I must be exhausted if those thoughts are flowing through my mind about a human.

Still, she decided, *if I must kill my way out of Rannadal, I might just let Karsten live.*

It was in the darkest hours of the night that she stirred, aware of her surroundings even as her eyelids remained stubbornly closed once again. Her dreams were empty save for the vaguest outline of the moon shimmering over her head, always watching, but that was preferable to the nightmares she fought off the last time she dared to sleep.

Voices drifted towards her, hushed and anxious in the shadows. She kept her breathing steady and deep as she listened in, her keen elven ears picking up on their words easier than a human could. They probably believed they were being quiet, but it was their voices that raised her from slumber in the first place.

If they believe I'm still asleep, perhaps they'll let their true intentions slip. They must not be as kind as they appear. There's always an ulterior motive with their people, and I will find it.

"How long do we have before they interrogate her?" Karsten asked, his gruff words the first to filter through the fog of sleep.

"That depends on Zareen," Zamir explained as he shifted in his seat. "She'll be the one doing the questioning. I can stall for as long as possible, but eventually she'll demand access to her, whether she's still injured or not."

"I doubt your sister will take kindly to her investigation being obstructed."

The dark-haired human laughed. "Have you ever known her to *take kindly* to anything?" he asked before pausing, and she could imagine him giving a dramatic roll of his eyes in the brief silence. "Still, she's not unreasonable. Once she realizes Lady Adelaide had nothing to do with the destruction in The Divide, her anger can be redirected to the true culprits."

Karsten gave a harsh sigh and the floorboards creaked under his shifting weight. "You're clearly still troubled," Zamir noted. "Out with it."

"I still don't like this," Karsten rushed to say, and Adelaide could hear the telltale signs of his pacing across the old wood floor. "Lady Aylara already saved our lives. We've repaid that debt by keeping her alive. To ask for more from her feels wrong, but the Jarl demands it anyways."

There it is, she thought, the bitter edge of resentment coiling in her core. *Their reason for saving an elf at all. Humans never act because it's the right thing to do, it's always for something more they can gain. They're never satisfied with what they have.*

"What other choice do we have?" Zamir asked. "We cannot defy our Jarl, and we also can't abandon those suffering from the spirits. For that matter, what choice does Adelaide have? She's a Keeper and duty-bound to protect her borders. Our goals are the same. It would be foolish on all our ends to part ways now."

Gods-damn-it, he's right. If what they say is true and I hold any sway over the spirits, they can't let me go. There is no peaceful way I will get to leave this village.

"It should still be her choice," Karsten replied, his voice soft and delicate on the warm night air. "I will not hold saving her life against her by calling a Blood Debt, even if Jarl Lefa wished me to. If she agrees to aid us, it should be of her own free will and not by whatever trickery Lefa no doubt has up her sleeve."

Adelaide's mind raced and her heart beat with raging fists against her ribs. Blood Debts were powerful social bonds and magical incantations that bound life forces together for a pact. Those contracts were formed between a person and whoever's life they saved, forcing the one saved to serve their savior for however long the agreement lasted.

Sometimes, they stretched for lifetimes.

"Yes, you've made that clear already," Zamir drawled. "And I already made it clear that I agree with you." He stood, the chair squealing across the floorboards. "However, that doesn't mean an agreement can't be reached that's beneficial for us all. We need her magic, but Lady Adelaide must have requests for us as well. If she can strike a pact with Lefa, no blood required, we can work together peacefully." He stopped then to mumble beneath his breath, "As long as Zareen doesn't mess it up."

Adelaide swallowed, her skin itching with the revelations she overheard. Yes, perhaps she could make a deal ensuring her safety, but what of her kin? She was bound by her duty as a Keeper to protect their lands from any threat. She couldn't leave that in human hands, but then who would search for her family? Just as she had responsibilities as a Keeper, she had an obligation to the Aylara Clan as well. Her family needed her.

She felt Karsten shift closer to her bed and she was quick to school her breathing so they still believed she was asleep. His shadow hovered over her, blocking the warmth of the hearth. "She asked me why I saved her," he murmured, and even her pointed ears struggled to make out the words. "I told her I did it because it was the right thing to do." She heard him shift, turning back to Zamir. "But this doesn't feel right at all."

Mentally, she agreed. Even if she could somehow learn to conjure the magic they claimed she had, she knew the toll such powerful forces could take. There was no amount of gold that would justify the pain such power could cause. If she refused, their leader would force her hand by whatever means necessary. Adelaide couldn't even blame them. In their place, if it were to protect her home and kin, she would've done the same.

Despite that, Karsten still hesitated to follow those orders. He battled with the mere idea of forcing her into anything. Both humans thought she was asleep, so their conversation wasn't for her ears. The tangled emotions of his own duty and morals rivaling each other was laid bare for all in the cabin to see.

It endeared him to her, just a tiny bit.

ZAMIR'S HAND was ice cold as he unwrapped the bandage from her eye, careful not to touch the scar beneath even though it held no feeling. The pain in it and the rest of her body lessened greatly in the two days she rested after first waking. Her only visitor was Zamir. It was her understanding that he was exaggerating her injuries, allowing her to gather her strength.

What she needed her strength for, he wouldn't say.

She daydreamed it was to help her escape from the village and back to the mountains, but she wasn't that foolish. He just wanted to ensure she'd survive whatever horrid interrogation techniques awaited her on the other side of the door.

He sighed as the last evidence of the bandage was removed. "I'm afraid you're as healed as I can make you. Which means Zareen will hurl her questions and accusations at your feet." He offered her a tattered cloak hanging on the back of the creaking chair he usually occupied. "Think you're ready for it?"

She secured the fabric around her shoulders. "I've fought rabid bears and demented Knights for two decades, Zamir. I think I can handle your sister."

"You say that now," he chuckled. "But wait until you meet her." He was about to open the door, but stopped to lean against it, blocking her exit. "I should also warn you: the townsfolk are torn over your arrival. Some see you as a symbol of the Gods, no matter which religion they belong to, and some see you as the reason for The Divide's destruction."

"I would never—"

He held up a hand, silencing her. "I believe you, but the

others haven't spent two days cooped up in a small cabin chatting about magic and autumn recipes with you like I have."

Regrettably, she did acknowledge that he had a point. When she wasn't asleep, she spent long hours conversing with the man. She was even surprised to find that she *actually* enjoyed his company. He had a flare for the dramatics, but he was genuine enough to make her laugh. In a situation such as hers, that's all the company she could hope for. Anything to make her forget the people she was missing.

Even if that means sharing pleasantries with a human.

If she was stuck in a foreign village surrounded by humans and Knights who normally wished her dead, she'd accept any small kindness she could receive. It was far better than the alternative: being bound in chains and left to rot. Until she was fully healed, she wouldn't be able to fight back against anyone who wished to see her imprisoned or dead.

All she had to do was get through one session of questioning, use the trip outside to get a better lay of the land, and she'd make her next attempt to escape a successful venture.

I'll be long gone then, and this will all be a strange footnote.

The weights in her boot and waistband were also a small comfort whenever Zamir got too close, testing her willingness to speak with him at all. She'd pilfered two dinner knives from the trays of food he brought her, hiding them in her clothes even as she slept. They were pitiful excuses for weapons, but they were the only sharp objects she managed to get her hands on. With her bow, arrows, and daggers still missing, they were the only armaments at her disposal.

It doesn't matter if they're from a kitchen. They'll still make someone bleed.

Adelaide shook off such dark thoughts even as they tried to coil back around her heart, shouting in her mother's voice that humans were dangerous and couldn't be trusted. She had learned that lesson long ago. That was the very reason for the stolen knives. That didn't mean she'd completely ignore diplomacy and the art of talking her way out of harm's way.

I will swallow my distaste for humanity as long as I can. I will not pose as a threat. I will bite my tongue, lest they cut it off.

"No matter what happens," she began, swallowing her nerves as she carefully fixed a smile to her face, "you'll try cinnamon in your hot chocolate this winter, right?"

He cracked a smile and pushed the door open, letting the sun's light shine through. "You've made it sound so sweet; how could I resist?"

She stepped through the threshold with Zamir on her heels. She'd only seen Rannadal through the fogged windows of her cabin or from a distance in the tree line, so she drank in every new feature of the town. There was a stone road twining through the village, connecting the merchants who eagerly sold their wares to anyone foolish enough to be caught bartering with them. Homes squeezed themselves between shops, and a deep ache wrapped around her chest at the sight of every family who passed by.

It smelled of dewy moss and flowers she couldn't name. It was only when she passed a thicket of close-knit purple and white bulbs that she knew they were the culprit of the sweet scents she gravitated towards. Her awe dissipated as she realized what lay before her.

They were linnaea flowers, the very plant her mother was named after.

The first question Adelaide asked, when she finally wasn't so disorientated from the tonics and healing spells, was if any other elves were seen around the area Karsten found her. She wasn't sure what kind of response she was expecting—confirmation that her kin were found dead at the bottom of the ravine where their home once stood, or that they were witnessed fleeing the battlefield to avoid human swords and the sharp tongues of the spirits?

Were they buried beneath the rubble, or were they seen leaving me behind?

Zamir's response that no other elves were seen and no bodies were recovered yet didn't deter her anguish or solidify her hope. She drifted between realms—one where her family lived and one where they'd left for Valhalla without her at their side.

She sighed, her shoulders dropping as the reality of where she was rushed back to her. That brief, memorized moment when she was caught up in the intrigue of a new place vanished into the brisk air. She was still in Rannadal, surrounded by people who either hated her for being an elf or despised her because they believed she destroyed her home.

That's when she began to sense the stares. Eyes were glued to her every move, and each breath she took was followed by a dozen whispered words. She was foolish for having forgotten after only two days that not all humans were as polite as Zamir and Karsten.

"Isn't that the elf?" someone whispered.

"The one who stopped the spirits?" another asked.

"What other one would it be?" a woman snarled.

"Surely they're not letting her walk around unchained," someone gasped.

"How unkempt she seems," the first person said, their voice far louder than before.

"Just wait until they get their hands on her. She won't last long," a man laughed.

Zamir's hand on her shoulder pulled her attention away from the voices of the townsfolk she picked up at every turn. He settled her with a sympathetic smile and quickened his stride, forcing her to keep up.

"Ignore the rabble, Lady Adelaide. They speak with malice, but few have any real intent," he said, probably trying to ease her nerves even though his were plainly shown by the anxious quality of his voice.

"It only takes one stupid enough to make the others bold," she muttered back, hoping no eager flat ears could hear her.

"True, but you don't seem like a person easily gotten rid of," he said with a small laugh.

"You'd be correct in that assumption."

He smirked as they rounded the final corner, which opened to a large square overseen by an impressive longhouse. Her tense nerves fully returned as she stared at the imposing structure they were heading towards.

"I wish Karsten was joining us. He's a force to be reckoned with, so I doubt anyone would attempt to harm you in his presence, but he was pulled away," he said with a sigh as they ascended the steps to the longhouse. "But fear not, I won't let anyone hurt you."

Regrettably, she agreed that having the other human alongside them would be useful as a shield if nothing else. They both saved her life in their own ways, proving they at least wished for her not to die. It would be a lot of wasted time on their part if she were murdered the moment she stepped out into the village. In some small way, she supposed that meant she could trust them, even as she recoiled at the mere idea on principle.

Every instinct in her core told her to run, to gather every ounce of energy in her still-fragile bones and make for the mountains. Her kin would protect her better than a human ever could. Yet, she couldn't shake the feeling that she could rely on Zamir to keep her safe. He wouldn't let any of Rannadal's inhabitants harm her if he could help it. That was clear from all the effort he put into healing her and his watchful gaze piercing through any who dared to step too close. Still, she doubted he would be enough to deter anyone who truly wanted her dead.

The heavy doors opened, and Zamir held them ajar long

enough for her to slip inside. They closed with a heavy echo that bounced off the towering wooden walls around her. In the center of the room, a large firepit blew smoke up towards the hole in the ceiling. The aroma of the night's community feast of ox stew, flatbread, and some of the last fresh fruits of the year coated her senses with every breath. Zamir brought her food throughout their time together, but it was always after the usual mealtimes and, as such, was cold to the touch. It was half a week since she'd had a warm, home cooked meal.

I must get through this. I just need to prove my innocence, and then I can find them. Gods, if you help me, I'll never complain when it's my turn to make dinner ever again. I swear it.

She blinked her unwanted tears away, acting as if they were caused by the smoke and not from her sorrow as she followed Zamir deeper into the longhouse. The rafters above were covered in drying herbs and summer flowers, and each wall was draped in fine tapestries. A woman worked on a loom in the corner, crafting another magnificent piece for the grand hall they strode through. Every pillar was carved in symbols she almost knew but couldn't place. It was clear they were runes, but their shapes were crafted as if from someone's poor memory, leaving everything askew and filling her with unease.

Just another case of humans' theft of things they don't understand, she thought, her tongue heavy with bitterness that only grew the further she got into the grand hall. *Such a beautiful place, but it lacks substance.*

Heavy footfall echoed on the other side of the room, causing the hairs on her neck to stand straight. A woman approached and, from fierce presence alone, she knew the figure before her was Zareen. Her dark hair was chopped around her flat ears and made spiky from the winds beckoning her inside. The glare she settled Adelaide with made her stomach curl into knots.

Zareen was made of stone; Adelaide was sure of it. From her

chiseled jaw that set her lips into a firm scowl, to the deep-set of her piercing hazel eyes, there was no way in all of Midgard that her body was merely flesh and blood. She seemed too hard for something as soft and breakable as skin. It was a wonder Zamir and she were siblings at all, when the man seemed to be all soft edges and smiles.

As each of her determined, unfaltering steps dragged Zareen closer, she began to see the similarities between them. They had the same warm, russet skin that hadn't faded by life in The North, where the clouds often hung heavy and the snow would lay its burden across the world for days on end. Although, Zamir was a touch paler than his sister, which was no doubt a byproduct of his life reading tomes of magical texts. More obviously, they shared the same piercing gaze glinting like flames in the night.

"They've been calling you a vision of divine intervention, but I have my own names for you," Zareen said, her gruff tone echoing across the hall as she came to a stop right before Adelaide. She was so close their noses almost touched, her sharp exhale painting the other woman's face.

The last time a human looked at me with such malice, I nearly died.

"And what is that?" Adelaide questioned as she fought to keep her tone controlled and free of the anxiety running rampant beneath the skin.

"Destroyer of The Divide, Pretender of our Prophet, unholy elven witch," she said, her voice rising with each twisted name.

Adelaide thought anyone calling her a sign of the divine was foolish, but to claim she destroyed her home was lunacy. She bit her cheek until she drew blood, forcing the harsher words she wished to spit at the woman back. Zamir's kindness to her would run short if she tore his sister apart, both verbally and physically, but she wouldn't remain silent either.

"I assure you, the destruction of The Divide had nothing to

do with me," she explained before taking another settling breath to calm the rapid pace of her heart. "I was there by chance, nothing more."

Zareen's harsh laugh came straight from a heart full of hate. "You possess never-before-seen magic so powerful it can control the spirits and were found at the epicenter of that destruction which allowed those spirits to escape in the first place," she challenged as she began circling her. "And you want us to believe it was by mere chance?"

At that moment, Adelaide felt like an injured animal waiting to be slaughtered by a hovering ravager. "The only other explanation is that I destroyed my own home," she snapped.

"It makes sense if it wasn't much of a home to begin with."

She bristled at that. Her home—*her family*—was everything to her. After the Knights destroyed so much of her life, they were all she had left. She would not forsake them for any riches, gold, or magic.

"For what purpose? To further the hatred humans and elves have for one another? To control spirits when I have never held an ounce of magic before? To murder a few humans who've never raised their swords against me? To strike a blow at the Knights in this town, knowing they are only a day's ride away from my home?"

On those last words, she choked on her building tears and lowered her gaze to the floor.

They're okay. They're not hurt. They're not dead. They're missing. That's all.

Zareen stopped behind her and Adelaide could feel her hot, angry breath on her shoulder where it rustled the fine hairs on her neck. She was tense, that much the elf could tell, but her anger wavered like a receding tide.

"Where is your family now?" Zareen asked.

She needed to clear her throat to get the words out. "I don't know."

The other woman slipped around her so they were face-to-face again, her expression somber and guarded. "You are not the only one who lost their loved ones in the destruction. Many perished in the aftermath."

She shook her head, her fists curling at her sides until her knuckles turned white. "They aren't dead. I couldn't find them with all the smoke and fire."

"I can tell you believe that," she said, her shoulders finally deflating from their once high, proud position by her flat ears. "However, we haven't found any survivors since you stopped the spirits."

"It is still early in our search, Zareen. We may yet discover survivors," a melodic voice said from the back of the hall, forcing both women to turn towards the sound. The door to the furthest, private section of the hall opened for a woman with a head of untamed copper hair, behind the heavy steel crown and black hood that sat atop her head.

Zamir leaned close to her and whispered, "That's my sign to leave." Before she could protest, he was already halfway to the door.

His sister clasped a fist over her heart and gave a curt bow of her head. "My lady, I have yet to complete my interrogation."

The other woman waved a dismissive hand and stopped before them. "We both know your ability to sniff out lies is world-renowned. If she were lying, you'd have sensed it by now." Finally, she turned to Adelaide and their gazes met. "Hello, Keeper Adelaide Aylara of The Divide. I am Lefa Thurstan, Jarl of Rannadal." There was a small twitch of a grin on her lips. "You have drawn a lot of attention to yourself."

"Believe me, that wasn't my intention," Adelaide said under her breath, although she knew the other woman could still hear her. She just hoped her quiet tone would mask her growing frustration.

I need to get out of here. I need to find my family.

A huff that was nearly a laugh slipped past Lefa's lips before she caught herself. "I figured as much. The others just wanted to be sure. Now that we're in agreement regarding your innocence, we should really move along." She beckoned them towards the long table at the center of the room, where her throne sat proudly at the end. "There is much to do."

Adelaide stopped, her gut twisting into knots. "I simply wanted to clear my name so I could return home since I've healed. There is nothing more I can do for you."

Lefa's robes elegantly swayed behind her as she sat in her throne of thick bear furs and intertwined birch branches. She seemed posed, but at the same time fully natural in the way she lounged upon a chair far too large for her lithe body. "On the contrary, Adelaide, there is much for us to accomplish together."

Zareen pulled out a chair beside Lefa and jabbed a finger at it. "Sit."

With a tone like that and her eyes of steel, she was compelled to follow their instructions. She wasn't truly being asked to listen to their demands, even if they pretended that was the case. They needed her and, while she'd been busy playing the role of polite guest, they were also pretending as if she wasn't their prisoner.

All that kindness and honey-coated words ensured I stopped trying to escape, and my willingness to play along has kept me alive so far. I just need them to turn their backs. To trust me long enough that they'll make a mistake and I can run away for good.

She took the offered seat and sat opposite Zareen, with Lefa stationed between them.

"We're only waiting for one more," the Jarl said, scanning

the entrances for any figures that had yet to approach. "We are normally a council of four, but Commander Strom was called away to continue beating back the spirits, and Ylwa is *always* late."

Her curiosity piqued and she sat a little straighter in her chair. "I'd heard the spirits dissipated due to something I did. Have they returned?"

Zareen clasped her scarred hands on the table. "This world will never be without spirits; they merely lie dormant in vessels like The Divide. With it torn permanently open, there is no barrier holding them back besides our swords. Even then, we can only harm the spirits that choose to make themselves into physical manifestations. The others, only magic can interfere."

"Your magic, more specifically," a new woman said as she swiftly entered the room, the sun trailing her every step and glittering off her umber skin since the door was left cracked open behind her. "Controlling spirits has been highly frowned upon across the world due to the darkness with which the spirits are commonly summoned, but your magic was like the light itself. Many are seeing it as a symbol of the divine." She stopped beside Adelaide and raised one thick brow at her. "I'm told you put on quite the show."

She couldn't help the blush rising to her cheeks at the woman's praise and enthusiasm. "I don't even remember it happening."

The woman sat beside her and scoffed. "That matters little. The people saw what they saw, and they will interpret it however they wish." Her dark brown eyes twinkled as they met hers. "I know I sure will."

Zareen sighed, heavy and long, as her shoulders deflated under her armor. "This is Ylwa Laxness, Matriarch of Rannadal's Chapel. She would be the incredibly late individual we were waiting for."

Ylwa's lips screwed into a deep frown as she turned to Zareen. "The people require faith, not merely brute force, dearest Zareen. I cannot help if my time and duties are split between the council's needs and theirs."

Lefa rolled her eyes. "I wouldn't consider my cook a person requiring faith."

A wicked smile graced her lips as she fixed the nape of her ornamented gown. "He still has needs, does he not?"

Adelaide loudly cleared her throat, silencing the bantering woman around her until each gaze settled on her. Her blood thrummed in her pointed ears, and she swallowed the irritation welling up within her as best she could. The women around her were giggling with mischief in their eyes while she was questioning her own escape. The entire interaction sent her on edge, even if it was a little humorous.

"Am I a prisoner here?" she asked.

Ylwa's gaze turned to one of concern as she shook her head. "No, we do not wish to keep you as one."

"But we will, if necessary," Zareen clarified, causing Adelaide's heart to pound harder in her chest. A terrified thrill coursed through her, and she dug her boots against the floor. She shifted and braced herself against the table, ready to bolt for the door if she needed to.

If she truly needed to flee Rannadal to reach her family, she would. Still, something told her Zareen would outrun and tackle her if she dared to even try.

Ylwa placed a gentle hand against one of hers. Adelaide's grip on the corner of the table tightened, her nails biting into the surface and scuffing the veneer. "We would rather not go to such measures and allow you to stay here of your own free will, but we do require your assistance," she explained.

"The entire world does," Lefa added.

"It's not truly free will if it's the only option you'll allow me to make that ensures my safety," she snapped, Karsten's murmured words in the dead of night roaring in the back of her mind. She despised that they brought her comfort or that humans could be right about anything at all, and that anger fueled her biting words. “Besides, what could you even need me for? To perform some so-called miracle I don’t even recall doing. To help a bunch of humans who’ve never thought twice about hurting my kind. To assist in your deranged efforts to continue erasing my beliefs from existence.” She yanked her hand from Ylwa’s and leaned away from her. “You try to comfort me as if we were equals, but I don’t see your temples desecrated with the symbols of a faith belonging to another person who has done nothing but hurt you.”

The sister had the decency to look ashamed, but Adelaide doubted it would last long. Humans would never accept elves. The only people who understood her were her kin, and she was wasting precious time better spent searching for them. She couldn’t waste her days playing nice with the same beings who murdered her kind for sport.

At the same time, the entire realm was bigger than just her. She was a Keeper after all. It was her duty to protect the world, both elves and humans, from the spirits within the mountain.

Mother would know what to do. My siblings would all be far better at this than I. When I find them, maybe they can help.

Lefa motioned towards the open doors, where the lively town echoed towards them. Birds called to one another in the trees, children laughed as they burrowed into the falling leaves of a too-early start to autumn, and merchants beckoned customers closer.

“The world outside this hall is teeming with life, but we each saw the devastation that can rain down upon that life in a single moment,” Jarl Lefa said, her gaze going dark with memories better left forgotten. “You have lost your home. We’ve lost many warriors. The rest of Midgard will lose even more if the spirits continue to be a festering blight on this world.”

Ylwa straightened herself and all discomfort from before seemed to wash itself from her shoulders. "We will never be fully rid of those creatures, but we cannot allow them to run free either. The Divide must be closed, and the spirits need to be returned to their rightful place. There will not be a world worth living in unless we can complete that task."

"And once that is done," Zareen continued, "we can focus our efforts on finding whoever is responsible for this destruction, how they accomplished such a feat, and hold them accountable to the highest degree."

If she dared, she could seek to heal The Divide on her own after she found her family. How would she accomplish that when her body still ached and the humans planned to entrap her if she dared to leave? If she escaped and found her family, the only thing she'd accomplish would be bringing Knights to their doorstep.

She could not allow that to happen. That was the one thing she'd promised her family after she watched another clan burn at the Brotherhood's hand. She would never bring the Knights to their home.

Perhaps it's safer to stay away.

There was a possibility, however slim, that she could use the human's resources to find her kin. She could complete her duty as a Keeper while others searched the mountains in her steed. Rannadal always stationed scouts at the border to watch her kind, and they could reach where she could not.

As long as they don't send any Knights.

"If I am to help," Adelaide began, her blood rushing loudly in her ears. *Am I truly doing this? Are they really going to convince me to help their kind? I feel like such a fool but what am I to do if I resist? Be held captive while the world burns around my family?* "My assistance ends when The Divide is sealed and not a moment longer. That is my duty as a Keeper, and that's where my duty ends. I will also have conditions."

Zamir's words rang in her ears. He claimed she could strike a pact for anything she desired, and she was more than prepared to make them pay the highest price for her assent.

Lefa lowered her head. "I understand."

"Then we are in agreement?" Ylwa asked, excitement filling her soft voice. She was on the edge of her seat, ready to bounce into action at a moment's notice. "Adelaide shall be our guest and assist in this quest. In return, you shall receive our protection, the dwelling you're already accustomed to, and any other provisions you shall require." Adelaide opened her mouth to interject, but the other woman was quick to correct herself. "And of course we will continue discussing your conditions."

"There's one more issue," Zareen said, forcing Ylwa to resign herself to further discussion.

Adelaide thought every woman in the hall was built for action, but in far different ways. Ylwa was a bundle of excited nerves flaring to life at the idea of planning every actionable step ahead of them on the quest they forced upon her. Zareen was a woman of action in combat. She could tell by the scars littering what little skin she allowed to show. She was a Viking to her core in every way. Lefa may have been soft spoken with a gentle, noble quality to her, but she held secrets in her blue gaze telling everyone in the room she was not to be tested.

But Adelaide? Well, she wasn't sure about herself. She simply knew whatever steps she needed to take to reunite with her family, she wouldn't hesitate.

Even if it means working with humans.

"Commander Strom," Ylwa said, shaking Adelaide from her musings. "Despite our differences, we have had a mostly civil discussion thus far. However, I'm afraid that thread of trust will break if we do not disclose the nature of Strom's position within our organization. He is the leader of all factions in our growing army. As such, you will need to work with him to get close enough to the spirits to command their return to the mountains."

"I understand," Adelaide murmured even as the hairs on her arms stood straight. Whoever their commander was, they would need to trust each other in combat—to turn her back on him in a battle and trust he wouldn't strike her through.

Not likely.

Ylwa shifted in her seat and bit her lip. "Well, you see, I don't think you do understand. Commander Strom has an incredibly diverse background—"

"He is a Knight of The Divide," Zareen said, cutting Ylwa off. The two women glared at each other. One annoyed with the other for taking too long to get to the point, the Sister annoyed with the shieldmaiden for not being tactful in her approach.

Adelaide cared little for either party's petty squabbling. She rose from her seat and marched to the door.

That was to be one of my only conditions. The only two conditions I would ask of them: to find my family and not force me to be near any of the Brotherhood. I haven't even had a chance to demand those very things, and I am already being asked to abandon my principles.

They're going to demand I remain diplomatic in the face of the Brotherhood who took the lives of so many I cared for. I won't even listen to it. Their scouts would be beneficial in finding my kin but I cannot trust them if they're aligned with the Knights. Besides, I know my home. I can find them far swifter than any human could. Then I can deal with the spirits alongside my kin, as it was always supposed to be.

"Where are you going?" Lefa called, rising from her chair.

"I'm leaving," she yelled back. "There is no way in all the Nine Realms I'm conversing *pleasantly* with or fighting alongside a *Knight*! I will work with humans, even those associated with the Brotherhood, but I will *never* conspire with a Knight. Try to hold me prisoner and see what happens."

As a Keeper, I am honor-bound to many things. Protecting the mountains and my family. Ensuring no human or banished elves breech New Alfheim's borders. Prevent the Knights from invading my home or hurting my people—and I already failed at that once.

Never again.

Zareen grabbed her arm, yanking her backwards and nearly pulling her off her feet. There was a short scuffle, Adelaide's claws digging into the heavy padded shoulders of the other woman as she tried to pry herself free, but the warrior quickly pinned her arms at her back.

Lefa stopped a short distance from them, her hands clasped formally in front of her. "Zareen is not entirely correct in her assessment, Keeper Aylara," she said, causing Adelaide's racing heart to slow just slightly. "But neither are you."

"I would sooner perish in the bottom of one of your cells than follow a Knight into battle," Adelaide shrieked, her words morphed by the sharp pain of Zareen yanking her arm back. "That was to be one of my only conditions, and you cannot even manage something so simple. How can I trust you to accomplish anything else?"

The Jarl put up a fist, a short motion which commanded Zareen to release her arm. She was free for just a moment, her blood in her ears and her arms shaking from the general weakness of her ailing body and the fierce knot Zareen had her arm in, but she made quick use of that moment. Her fingers grasped the hilt of the kitchen knife in her waistband, and she pulled it free with quick ease.

It was pathetic in a fight. Everyone in the longhouse knew that much as they stared at her useless weapon with a mild amusement that sent Adelaide's blood boiling.

She slashed the knife backwards and spun, catching on the harness to Zareen's dagger strapped to her waist. Their small grins vanished as the weapon slipped free, and Adelaide quickly abandoned the knife in favor of the jewel-tipped dagger she placed between her and the humans.

Zareen lurched forward, nearly knocking the blade from her hand completely, and was only halted by Lefa's firm hand on her chest holding her back. They watched in silence as she put a short distance between them as she backed up towards the doors.

"I would've been fine remaining within Rannadal. I could've made peace with the idea since I've been safe here these last few days. It's not like I have anywhere else to go," she said, pausing to swallow the lump of sorrow wedged in her throat. "But I cannot fight beside those who've murdered my people since we first stepped foot in Midgard. You cannot expect me to foster peace with those who wish to kill me."

Ylwa raised a placating hand, but all it did was force Adelaide's temper to rise until her ears burned red with rage. "He is no longer a Knight of The Divide, Lady Aylara. He is a former Knight, this is true, but he left the Brotherhood long ago."

"However," Lefa continued. "You will need to work with current Knights regardless. That is the bulk of Rannadal's forces since our Vikings are currently establishing a settlement several lands away. Strom is simply the one you will work closer with and thus is the one you need to know about."

"You're all insane." She knew she was shaking, and yet she couldn't stop the trembling in her limbs nor identify if the movement was from fear or her contained anger. "You truly expect me to leave my life behind to aid you, for a roof over my head and food in my belly, when my life is constantly endangered by both spirits and Knights? There is no fair trade in this."

Lefa seemed as though she was going to interject, but the main door to the hall was pushed further open, cutting off her words. The other women waited patiently for whomever was lingering to fully emerge from the blinding light of the sun outside, but Adelaide couldn't stay. She needed to sow doubt in their minds, discourage them from following just long enough for her to flee. She would be gone before they realized that they were supposed to hold her and enslave her to their cause.

"I would not need a roof over my head or provisions if my own weren't destroyed by some mad force your kind is no doubt behind," she continued, rambling on as though they were still listening to her. She was sure they weren't. They were too busy scheming some horrid plan to hold her against her will. "I had a perfectly lovely garden with a plethora of food ready to harvest and game to hunt in the woods. I had everything I needed until it was burned to the ground. Why would I risk the only things I have left—*my life and my honor*—for yours?"

"What more would you ask of us?" a far too familiar, deep voice asked from behind her.

Despite her better judgment, her shoulders fell. Karsten entered the hall and, as his golden gaze adjusted to the dim light and settled on her, she somehow knew he would listen. Even if Lefa, Zareen, and Ylwa did not, he would. She'd heard him whispering with Zamir late in the night about how unfair it was to demand so much from her. He lamented how Jarl Lefa's plans weren't the right thing to do. He'd saved her life for no Blood Debt or honor, but simply to do something good. If anyone listened to her, it would be him.

And if he didn't, she could make him.

They were already standing close, so it only took one step for her to be chest to chest with him, the blade against his throat as she craned her neck up to force his burning gaze onto hers. He stood frozen, staring down at her as the blade drew a thin line of crimson beneath his chin from where her shaking limbs struggled to hold the weapon straight.

There is only one thing in the whole of Midgard that I want.

"*Find my family*," she commanded, hating how her words sounded like a desperate plea. She cleared her throat and tried again, her focus drifting to her rapidly weakening grip on the dagger. "Find my family."

Ylwa awkwardly shifted her stance and fiddled with her hands. "I didn't know you had any family in the mountain with you."

Zareen's expression pinched. "As I said before, there are no survivors in The Divide."

Adelaide shook her head. "I was there when it exploded. I know what I saw and it wasn't my family dying. There were no bodies nor blood." With her free hand, she grasped her chest and spoke as if she were calling to the Gods for confirmation of her words. The raven pendant bit into her chest where it was still safely tucked under her tunic. "They are alive. I know it."

Zareen moved, the sound of the sword on her back unsheathing in warning, but Karsten held up a hand to stop her. He never looked away from the woman holding the dagger. "What more do you require from us?" he asked, his throat bobbing against the blade and further cutting his skin on the sharp edge.

"I don't want to work with any Knights," she explained, her voice coming out far quieter than she liked. Her strength was failing her, and her ribs ached from the quick movements she made to get the dagger in the first place. "They cannot look for my kin, and I can't trust that they won't turn on me in battle."

"I can't promise that, Lady Aylara," he said before he took a sharp inhale when she added a bit more pressure on the weapon. "Rannadal has been a base for the Brotherhood for generations. They are too intertwined with our army. However, none will be sent to look for your family, and we can limit contact between you and them as much as possible."

"And what about my kin?" she demanded, hardening her gaze on his. "If I am to do anything, I *need* them."

"We will search for your family and bring news of their whereabouts, or fates, if you agree to help us of your own accord," he said, sincerity bleeding from his voice and calming her nerves. "If they still live, they will be found and no harm shall fall upon them. I swear it on Olena's very heart."

She shook her head. "I care not for promises made on a false Goddess' heart. Swear it on yours." He paled, his gaze snapping to the others behind her before he stared back at her. "Swear on your heart and on your life that you will do everything in your power to find and protect my family. I will make the same oath to assist your asinine plans to hold the spirits at bay." His lips parted in answer, but her next words forced them shut again. "*Please,* bring them back to me," she whispered, the pain in her tone so obvious it made her skin crawl. "It's the right thing to do."

Something shone in his gaze and, a moment later, he gave one curt nod as she lowered her weapon. Despite the brewing protests from the others, he agreed, "I swear it on everything I am."

And what exactly are you?

After Lefa's next words, she wished she'd asked that question as soon as she met Karsten. "I would introduce you," she began. "However, it seems you and Commander Strom have already met."

Everything inside Adelaide, from her heart to her lungs to her gut, froze and shattered somewhere between her feet. It left her cold and stuck, standing with her eyes locked tightly on Karsten as he took a step back—putting distance between them.

He's a liar, and I'm a fool for believing him.

His brow rose at whatever marred her expression before he turned to Lefa with a face full of guilt, rubbing at the back of his neck. "We may have bumped into each other," he explained, a small and nervous edge to his tone.

Zareen peered between them with pinched brows. "So, you two should have no problem working together then?"

He shrugged. "I don't see why not."

Adelaide smoothed her white hair behind her pointed ears, making the shape of them more pronounced, as she turned on her heel and once again made a beeline for the door. Each step was faster than the last until she skidded to a stop right at the threshold, knowing if she truly fled, she wouldn't have any help in finding her kin.

And she already told them about her family: something they could use against her. If she left, she'd only put them in danger. If she found them, the Knights would be following shortly behind her. If these people found them first, they could use them to force her to comply with any of their demands.

When I find them, not if.

Commander Karsten Strom, the damned Knight who lied about who he really was the moment they met, already swore an oath on his life to find her kin and protect them. She had the proof in his blood on the dagger still clutched in her hand. Long before he saved her in that stolen temple, she saved his life in the so-called miracle they claimed she performed.

That meant, in a way, they already forged an informal Blood Debt tying their fates together. If she didn't uphold her end of the bargain and aid their mission, there was nothing stopping him from finding her family anyways and ensuring they met swift ends. The pact they just forged may have been the only thing stopping him from harming her family.

The only thing I can do to save them now is to stay.

If she fulfilled her end of the bargain and he didn't, it allowed for a loophole in their oaths. If she found her family before he did, his failure would ensure he could never harm them for the rest of his days and he would be forced to protect them—even against his own kind. With the sealing of The Divide, her end of the bargain would be closed and she would have no obligation to those humans, but he would forever be bound to his promise to protect her family.

She smothered the timid grin threatening to stretch across her lips as the blood dripped from the weapon onto the stone floor. The tip of the blade bit into her thumb, bubbling her own crimson essence to the surface so it mixed with his. It gave a small shine, sparkling in the sunlight filtering out of the crack in the door as the magic took hold.

I just might be able to make this work after all.

"Where are you going?" Lefa asked, her tone less panicked than before.

Everyone in that room knew Adelaide couldn't truly leave, even if her feet resumed taking her to the exit anyways. That didn't mean she wasn't going to make them regret ever bargaining with her.

I agreed to aid their efforts. No part of our agreement said I couldn't be a menace while doing so.

She peered at them from over her shoulder. Lefa's fingers were steepled before her and her brow was raised in question. Ylwa was chewing on her nails. Zareen folded her arms and widened her stance, preparing to chase her down if necessary. As for The Knight, he looked utterly lost as to why she was upset in the first place.

Fools, the whole lot of them.

"If I'm being forced to deal with your insanity, then I'm going to need a heavy drink of mead first," she explained.

Zareen snorted at that and they all seemed to relax at the sound. Adelaide turned back towards the doors but froze once more when Lefa spoke.

"One last question, Keeper Aylara," she said, forcing Adelaide to peer at her from over her shoulder. A heavy look of contemplation pinched the Jarl's red brows and lowered her pink lips into a deep frown. "You said you would leave once the spirits are enclosed in the mountains. I'm surprised. Why wouldn't you want justice against the one who destroyed your home?"

She clutched the bloody dagger tighter, her knuckles turning white and her fist shaking with the building rage she fought to control.

"Because I will not pursue justice like the rest of you," she said. "I will seek revenge."

AN ANONYMOUS LETTER SCRIBED FIVE YEARS AGO

"Rannadal was founded by exalted members of the Brotherhood, and yet our current Jarl wishes to stand with those who desire their Order completely disbanded. What will we do without the protection of their holy army? Who will guide us away from disorder and chaos? Certainly not Lefa and her brash tongue encouraging so many of our Knights to flee, least they face the wrath of her lackies.

Karsten Strom is nothing but a lap dog of the Jarl: a pacifist who couldn't stomach what was required to secure our borders. He returns with vengeance in his steps and declares he can cull any Knight from the ranks who does not cater to his whims. We believed Lefa wouldn't stand it—her father The Cruel wouldn't. Yet here she is, bending the knee to a farmer's son and his selfish crusade against his own kind.

We have turned our backs on who we once were, and we deserve every horrible fate that befalls this town because of our cowardice."

- A Concerned Citizen

6

TO ANGER A BEAUTIFUL WOMAN IS A DEADLY SIN

SKALD: KARSTEN STROM

There were many times in Karsten's life when a woman looked at him with pure and utter malice.

Usually, he could piece together why he'd received such a look. Half the time, he even agreed that he deserved it. He spilled stew on the bear rug in the great hall and earned a rather murderous glare from the Jarl. He broke an ancient rune that was held dear by the local völva. He even ruined one of Ylwa's most prized Cislenian tomes.

But it wasn't until that late summer day that he hadn't the faintest idea as to why he was graced with such a dour look by someone who, only a few days prior, was smiling at him. It was a timid, uneasy sort of smile, but *still.*

Zamir stepped through the front doors, nearly bumping shoulders with Adelaide on her way out. He grasped his chest and sent them a shocked expression. "I leave her alone with you lot for a few minutes and she's tangled into knots!" He stopped beside his sister and scowled at her. "What did you do?"

Karsten cleared his throat and tore his gaze away from the space the elf once occupied. "Actually, I think I did something."

At the other man's intensifying look, he shrugged. "I haven't the faintest idea what."

Lefa began returning to her bedroom at the back of the hall as she snickered, "Why don't you ask her yourself, Commander?"

"I'm sure she'd answer your question most thoroughly," Ylwa continued as she followed their Jarl. He was sure they were going to further gossip at his expense once they were in private, but he didn't truly mind. It irritated him some days, when his body ached and his mind wavered, but mostly he was just happy to see the Matriarch and Jarl in such higher spirits.

Making their Commander into a private joke seemed to be the only way to make the two women forget, just for a moment, that there was a horde of spirits on Rannadal's borders.

"And with plenty of expletives," Zareen said with a roll of her eyes. She headed for the doors but stopped when Karsten laid a heavy hand on her shoulder. He wasn't sure what expression he wore, whether it was confusion or embarrassment, but it must have been pathetic enough for her to take pity on him. "We told her, Karsten," she sighed. "About who you are or, more accurately, what you once were."

Understanding dawned on him as the heavy doors at the back of the hall closed, leaving him alone with the siblings and a head full of swirling thoughts. She must've thought he was a liar. He told her he wasn't a Knight but that wasn't the full truth. He'd left the Brotherhood long ago but there was no way to explain that while Adelaide was half-dead on her feet. He needed her trust that day to ensure she was returned safely to her cabin and didn't have the chance to explain himself.

Even if all I want to do is lie to both of us and pretend that I was never a Knight in the first place. Of course, the others would be more truthful than I could be.

"I asked you not to say anything," he said as he pinched the bridge of his nose. His wool-gloved wrist rubbed uncomfortably against the scar that ran across his lip, bringing a swath of memories back with that slight pain.

Those dark chambers, surrounded by swirling crimson red mist. The tang of honey on his tongue and the ache of his back as he lay on the cold stone floor. The sharp blade, tearing him apart. There had to be another way. This was not their calling. This was not what they were meant to be.

His protests mattered little in the end. He'd watched the Brotherhood do unspeakable deeds to all they encountered, even their own brothers-in-arms. It was why he left that life behind. Yet his connection with them still haunted him—a shadow forever lurking over his shoulder that never looked right.

If Lady Aylara knew the truth, their work to seal The Divide would be hindered by mistrust. The gap between elves and humans was something they could all cross together if she wished it. But the gap between Keeper and Knight? That was something he'd never seen mended before. That was not the foundation armies were built on. If they were to survive the growing spirits leaking from the darkest depths of the mountains, trust was exactly what they'd need.

His unease grew as he pictured working so closely with Adelaide. He doubted the others shared the full nature of their work with her. How she'd need to train, tirelessly, to strengthen her powers and keep herself alive long enough for them to succeed. She was the only one who held sway over the spirits and, if she fell in combat, they would all burn at the hands of the damned.

Their numbers were already faltering, the death toll since The Divide fell only growing as the injured succumbed. What remained of their forces at their borders couldn't hold on without reinforcements. *Something* needed to stop the flow of spirits or they would be the first village to fall. With their Vikings still in a distant land enforcing their newest settlement, there was no one else who could aid them if Lady Aylara's magic didn't work to stop the spirits completely.

Then there would be no one left alive to search for her family.

"You know how the saying goes. To anger a beautiful woman is a deadly sin—so what do you think would've happened if she discovered we all lied to cover for you? Do you truly believe it would have been better?" Zareen asked, pulling him from his jumbled thoughts.

"*No.*" The word left him immediately. There was no hesitation. They'd done the right thing, even when he hadn't wanted them to. He could live with her distrust, as much as he didn't want to, so long as their mission succeeded.

At least, that was what he told himself.

"Listen," Zamir said as he patted Karsten on the back. Somehow, even that small comfort felt sarcastic coming from him. "I know you come from a background where trust and Brotherhood are core to your beliefs, but things don't always work that way."

Zareen nodded. "As long as we succeed, it matters little if she trusts us. If she does her duty, I don't see the issue."

"That's exactly the problem," Karsten said as he pulled away from them, following in Adelaide's footsteps outside. "If she doesn't trust us, how can we expect to trust her? To believe that she'll fulfill her end of the bargain?"

Yes, he thought. *That's what I should focus on. Making sure she does as she says and that I keep my promise to her as well. Then, everything will return to how it should be.*

He took a deep breath as he pushed the doors open, re-entering the sunlit world outside.

Zamir claimed Adelaide needed another day of rest before training, but the entire leadership council knew better when he left her cabin smelling heavily of mead.

She got absolutely sloshed at Rannadal's tavern, the Gilded Raven, and needed to nurse the effects of her hangover before she could even stand straight. He wished he could reprimand Zamir for indulging, but he was glad someone was there to protect her in the tavern.

Besides, I honestly don't blame her.

Between her home being destroyed, her family lost in the aftermath, and the knowledge that an army of spirits was lingering on the horizon, he was surprised she was functioning at all. Even with his own family miles away in the village he grew up in, safe from the effects of the spirits for the time, anxiety gnawed at his bones and one of his usual migraines beat against his temple with a growing urgency.

He couldn't imagine how she felt with her loved ones lost in the chaos. She was strong, but it obviously weighed on her. So, he let her incident with the tavern go. If she needed one night of heavy drink to steady her nerves, that was a small price to pay for all the good they hoped she'd do.

Still, there were those in the village who doubted Adelaide's innocence and her ability to help with the spirits. They were a growing danger to her, so he made sure to station some of his best guards at her cabin doors to keep watch while she slept and follow as she moved around town. She wasn't a prisoner and the guards were meant for her own protection, but that didn't stop her from slipping away from their line of sight like a jailbird trying to fly the coop.

"Rein her in, Commander," Lefa ordered that morning. *"You may find her indulgence amusing and excusable, but her appearance to the people matters. She at least needs to look the part of a holy woman instead of getting drunk at the tavern."*

He'd scoffed. *"Why does her appearance matter? She saved our lives with the aurora itself. That should be proof enough for any true believer."*

Doubt tugged at the back of his brain. Did he believe she was divinely touched? If he didn't, was he not a true believer? The words came to him so naturally, he hadn't questioned what they meant for him until they were already free.

"What will our Vikings think when they return?" the Jarl had asked, her grim tone and the mention of their missing warriors sending a cold sweat down his back. *"They have kept firm grasps on their pagan beliefs even in the face of the massive Cislenian conversion efforts and they weren't here to see her powers. Even if a few heathens in Rannadal saw her control what they believe to be the Bi-frost, we don't know if they will believe the stories."*

"Their doubt could be our downfall," Ylwa had said in agreement as she scribbled something on a piece of parchment. *"Before the Vikings return, Adelaide must appear to all as our Promised, not just in her power but in all she does. We cannot leave any room for doubt in any of our warriors or the clergy."* She had signed the bottom of the paper with a flourish and rolled the scroll up. *"I will send word to Lysafell and ask for an audience with the Grand Clerk. It will legitimize our cause, but we need Adelaide to convince everyone of her divinity before they ask for our attendance in the holy city."*

Lefa had leaned back in her throne, tilting her head and closing her eyes as though she was suffering from her own headache that morning. *"Our claim that she is the Promised of Olena is the only thing that can keep her safe—from our own townspeople, our warriors, and the clergy itself. Otherwise, they will lay the blame for The Divide's destruction on her shoulders. A convenient scapegoat whose death would only ensure we all perished."* She had peeked her pale blue eyes out at him, her words sinking into his bloodstream. *"And if our Vikings doubt she was sent by The Old Gods, none of us will be able to stop their demands for her head."*

The memories of their meeting during the first rays of

sunlight that morning still chilled him. They were right. The most devoted heathen in their guild of Vikings, Njarl Magunusson, was also their strongest Berserker. If he set out to kill Adelaide because he believed she was an imposter, even the Commander couldn't stop him. They'd dared to fight in the training field only a handful of times, and he was the only warrior in Rannadal that Karsten couldn't beat.

For her safety, there can be no room to doubt the Gods—both new and old—sent her.

Others who witnessed her powers firsthand were dedicated to their cause, and Adelaide by extension. Most of the townsfolk remained unsure of what to believe. Hesitant hope hung in the air like the buzz before a lightning strike. Karsten knew that it only took a few simple words for that feeling to dissolve from hope into fear.

"I thought you of all people would have a clearer view of this deceiver, Commander," a woman said as she slithered up to his side, sending every hair on his arms straight up. "I'm surprised you didn't behead her from the start."

He schooled his features before turning to the woman beside him. Sister Jill Gorm clasped her old, wrinkled hands in front of her and sighed as though the entire world rested on her shoulders. He'd seen firsthand what her words could conjure in even the most levelheaded men. Once, she'd spun hope around his heart and fueled him with the faith of Olena.

Now, she only brings me dread.

"I saw her abilities up close, Sister," he said with a tiny, futile sliver of hope that he could change her mind about Lady Aylara. Once, she'd been his confidant in the chapel. She raised him when he left his real family behind for the bond found with the Knights. At that time, she hadn't made him shiver at the mere sight of her, but those days were long gone. "I assure you, she can and will help us."

"Her help hinges on her family's recovery, does it not?" she asked, forcing him to mentally curse Ylwa's name to the Gods. He loved her like a little sister, but her big mouth would get her killed one day. "What do you suppose happens if one of your men discovers them brutalized or rotting somewhere in the mountains? Do you truly believe she would not blame our kind? That she would continue to aid our efforts?"

He and the rest of the leadership wondered the very same thing. It wasn't until she said it with such contempt that he truly feared that outcome becoming reality. Lefa insisted that, should they find her family dead, they wouldn't tell her until she completed her end of the bargain. They would simply keep up the act of searching for people they already found.

The mere idea makes me sick. I cannot allow it.

Jarl Lefa may have had the final say, but he'd never been one to follow the rules completely. Should that unfortunate reality come to pass, he'd mentally already decided to find some way to tell her. Even if she hadn't saved their lives, she deserved to know.

If humans were responsible for the destruction of The Divide—*her home*—she deserved to know that too. He would not blame her if she refused to assist after that, even if it broke their deal in the process. He wouldn't force her to stay. He'd find a way to get her out safely and ensure she could start over somewhere new, no matter what side of The Divide that was on.

It's the bare minimum I can do to try and make up for all I've done.

"I truly don't know, Sister," he said as his attention slipped to a familiar head of white hair that weaved through the bustling village beyond the doors of the chapel. She looked better. A little more focused and not so distraught. She walked with a purpose and all he could wish for was that her purpose aligned with theirs. "I can only pray that she will try, just as we all must, to right the wrongs that have been done."

He turned back to Sister Gorm and squinted against the sun to see her lithe shadow in the dim light of the chapel. He'd only come that morning to pray, but of course she'd stalked him down to voice every one of his fears aloud. So long as she kept that dread to herself, he would let it pass.

Unfortunately, I've never known Jill Gorm to be a quiet woman.

No, she constantly and insistently whispered in the ears of the people of Rannadal. Spilling secrets, spreading lies, and inciting violence for any slight or perceived offense. Once, she whispered in his ears and he bothered to listen. He was no longer that foolish young man who adhered to the words of any elder who outstretched a kind hand to him.

Adelaide wasn't wrong. We stole her people's temple and claimed it was our own, and we have done it before, time and time again.

Jill was one of the oldest and the first to take part in such an act. She ventured across the world, something she was quite proud of. She told stories of her so-called adventures to the children around town where she reaped other temples to assist in converting the population into the Cislenian faith. The temple in Rannadal was one of many.

It sickened him to think that, only a few years prior, he wouldn't have blinked twice at the idea. He had truly thought it was normal. That was just the way things worked.

Now I know better.

And he knew that the wicked whispers of the woman before him would turn the entire town against Adelaide. The only people who wouldn't listen to her would be those who replaced Jill with Ylwa as the head of the chapel, removing some of her power. Still, the rest would listen to her every word with bated breath.

He squared his shoulders and, with his eyes finally adjusted to the weak light, stared into her narrow grey-blue eyes that had seen atrocities and, if the wrinkles around her mouth and eyes were any indication, *laughed* at them. Her wispy red hair was mostly hidden by the ornate hood she never removed, and the tinge of her skin was yellowed from a sickness that rolled through her every few seasons.

"I never expected such soft sentiments from a man who was once a trained killer twice over," she huffed as she straightened the teal and white robes she wore. "You may trust who you wish, but do not expect the people of Rannadal to."

"If you try to poison these people against her when she has done nothing wrong, I will ensure your punishment is as painful as I can make it," he snapped, jabbing his finger at her face even though it quivered with his barely contained rage. "Give her a chance and, if we're wrong, you may say or do all that you wish. But don't subject a potentially innocent woman who just lost her family to your insistent antics."

She pursed her thin, dry lips until the edges around her mouth seemed to crack. He'd never spoken to her, or any clergy, in such a manner before.

He had to admit, it was *thrilling.*

"The elf gets a single chance," she said, her faded gaze flickering over his shoulder and out into the bustle of Rannadal. "The Jarl asked you to rein her in, did she not? I assume you know what that means." He remained silent, unable and unwilling to bend to her patronizing tone. "Consider yourself her personal guard, Commander, because she will need the protection once our people realize she's a fraud: a pretty and exotic face whose claims to divinity are built on a fragile lie crafted from Lefa's sharp tongue." Her lips quirked into a small, devilish grin as she turned away. "Regardless, it seems like I may not have to wait long for her to make a mistake."

If he was scowling before, he had no idea what his face must have looked like as he spun around to check on where he'd last seen Adelaide. She was on her way to the great hall, he was sure, but as he backtracked her steps, he discovered that she'd veered off course.

She was closing the door to the tavern behind her.

"Olena's sacred heart," he cursed as he bolted down the small hill the temple was perched atop, the sound of Jill's crackling laughter echoing behind him.

"One chance, oh mighty Commander!"

He was sweating by the time he slammed the tavern doors open, much to the surprise of the people inside. Several of his men, who were no doubt absent from their duties, gave him timid glances and apologetic waves as they slunk out the door behind him.

He would deal with them later.

Lady Aylara was curled into a corner, a heavy pint in her hands and a scowl marring what would otherwise be the pretty face that Jill described. Despite his prior certainty that the sister could no longer influence his thoughts, he found himself dissecting and repeating every whispered word in his head until they made him nauseous. Doubt in the elf's ties to the divine would get her killed, but even he felt that uncertainty gnawing at him as he stared at the already drunk form hiding in the darkest corner of the tavern.

I witnessed her magic. It saved my life that night. Yet I cannot shake the feeling that she is merely a woman in pain with far too many lives in her hands. I was so certain of my Goddess sending Lady Aylara to us in our greatest hour of need, but now I hesitate in the presence of that which is holy forged in mortal blood.

The Cislenian religious text, The Codex, described The Promised of Olena the very same way. The old scrolls and standing stones swore their savior would descend from Olena's very hand, held within the aurora, but that she would be mortal in every way. She would be cut and bleed, she would die, and she would rage at heavens that forgot their children.

I suppose she would get intoxicated too.

Karsten shook that thought away as he neared, his shadow cast by the open tavern door looming over her. He hated to admit it, but Jill was right. She wouldn't be safe with doubt like his spreading throughout town, and her public displays of drunkenness wouldn't help matters. It left her vulnerable, and her constant ability to slip away from her guards prevented them from protecting her from those with ill intent.

Yes, I suppose I will need to be her personal guard after all.

"I wouldn't recommend training on a stomach full of mead," he said, silently hoping that would be the only words they'd need to exchange before she agreed and left the pint behind. But Karsten Strom was never a lucky man, so he doubted she would come along with him willingly.

His suspicions were confirmed when she turned that wicked scowl on him, her eyes alight with a dark malice he understood far too well. He'd witnessed it when he was a Knight whenever elves saw him. Those days were long since passed, and he no longer felt himself accustomed to the rage behind such brilliantly green eyes.

"I wouldn't recommend getting between a lady and her drink, and yet here you are," she said, slamming her tankard so hard the foam splashed over the side and dribbled onto her pale hand. "Tell me, has this elf done something to warrant such scrutiny or shall I simply be shackled for the most minor wrongdoing?"

He was quick to school his features, not having noticed the rigid turn of his upper lip until then. "I assure you, I'm not here to be your warden." He fought the urge to wrinkle his nose. "You merely smell *rank*."

She stiffened but had the decency to blush as she returned to sipping on her drink. "You try being cooped up in a cabin for a week after falling down the face of a mountain. See how your hygiene is after that," she grumbled into her drink, as if sharing a secret with the mead.

He stared at her, not quite meaning to, but not able to stop himself either. Even with her being "cooped up" as she'd said, he hadn't thought twice about her beauty behind her messy appearance after she was dragged into Rannadal. Zamir mentioned that he'd had Lefa's handmaiden assist Adelaide with a sponge bath when she still couldn't sit up straight without doubling over in pain. He wasn't sure if that routine remained or if she'd been given access to the baths. Since he knew better, he would rectify the situation.

He held out a hand to her and, for a moment, he thought she would bite his fingers clean off. Instead, she glared at his outstretched, gloved fingers like they were five venomous snakes.

"I can show you where the bathhouse is and anything else you require. Will you be civil enough with me for that much?" he questioned with an arched brow.

She thought it over for a long moment and, at his grunt of disbelief, she finally gave in. "For a bath, I will put my morals aside and pretend you're just a regular, kind gentleman instead of a murderer and liar," she said, although it almost seemed like the words were meant to stay inside her head rather than slip past her lips, if her growing blush was any indication. She muttered under her breath, "Odin, forgive me."

He rolled his eyes and pulled her to her feet, her lithe form far heavier than he anticipated thanks to the drink. She was quick to grab her jug and drank deeply as he tugged her out the back door of the tavern. Outside the rear doors, there wasn't as much noise or foot traffic, so he released her, hoping she could follow along even in her intoxicated state.

She was barely in the tavern before I got there. How much could she have drunk?

"What if I was just a regular, kind gentleman?" he questioned as they walked. He peeked at her over his shoulder as he led her down the tree lined path. "What if I wasn't this murderer and liar that you imagine me to be?"

She hummed in thought as she tilted her head to the sky, where a flock of birds were flying south. With the light of the midday sun basking her face and her expression softened by the cool breeze, he could see just how much she'd gone through. Her skin hung on her bones in some places where, when he'd first found her, there had been a tender roundness to her. Dark bags hung heavy under her eyes, and her white hair looked grey in the parts that weren't matted to her head. How no one noticed that she looked so haggard, he wasn't sure. He also wasn't certain as to why she hadn't asked anyone for directions or assistance before.

Or why she trusts my help at all.

He blamed it on her being thoroughly inebriated from the moment she could mill about the town on her own.

"That would be too complicated," she finally said, her eyes still glued to the birds. He noticed they were a family: a flock of partners with a few trailing babes who were still novices in flight. "Then I'd have to admit a good person can wear a Knight's armor."

"Is that such a horrible thought?" he asked. "That good people exist in every shape and under every creed?" He was sure the thought was comforting. That, no matter where one went, something good could always be found.

She turned away from the sky and settled him with emerald eyes full of sorrow: the kind that made meeting her gaze impossibly painful. "No," she said, her voice timid. "Because that means good people can still commit atrocities." She shook her head and strode a little faster down the path. "Believing some people are just evil is much easier than the alternative."

"I don't think any realm is that simple or easy, Keeper Aylara."

She stopped as the entrance to the bathhouse appeared around the next turn and spoke without looking at him. "Perhaps not, Knight Strom," she said before finally looking at him again. It had only been a few moments since the last time their eyes locked, but she'd resolutely locked her hard gaze back into place and narrowed it on him. "But until my family is safely returned to me, that's the only reality I can see."

"We'll find them," he said, his voice full of more conviction than he felt. She began to walk away, the swaying of her stance gone and her sober, aggressive attitude back in place like a solid curtain. "I do have a question," he said, forcing her to pause. "Why didn't you ask for directions earlier? They could have been easily provided."

Her shoulders nearly touched her pointed ears with the way she hunched forward. "Bathing leaves you quite vulnerable," she explained as her gaze darted back to the bathhouse doors. "I didn't trust anyone to know when I would be in such a state."

"But you trusted me?" he questioned, his jaw slack.

She doesn't act like she trusts me.

"My drunken, desperate mind did," she grumbled as she continued up the small slope to the bathhouse. "Don't get confused."

"One more thing," he said, stopping her trek up to the bathhouse once more. It earned him an annoyed groan as she shot a sharp glare down at him. "I'm sorry for lying to you. While it's true I'm no longer a Knight, it was wrong of me to pretend that was never the case."

She didn't respond, but her shoulders dropped, and he saw just the briefest flash of something vulnerable cross her expression before she turned away and continued her march. He watched her leave, a tightness in his throat that wouldn't stop growing with every step. He wanted to call out to her, to convince her he wasn't the man she thought him to be. No words felt adequate for the fierce burn that ravaged his chest with every look she gave him.

For a brief time, those looks were alight with small glimmers of something he couldn't name. They'd turned to looks of rage and a sorrow so deep he feared they'd both drown in it so quickly that it shook him to the bone. He wondered if she would ever dare to change her mind about him.

I doubt it. I deserve her anger.

It annoyed him to no uncertain ends that he could be so twisted up on the inside by a woman he hardly knew, but his feelings ran so much deeper than merely a desire to be liked. No, he didn't care all that much if Keeper Aylara tolerated his presence or not. She wasn't really the one he was trying to convince that he'd changed.

He was really trying to prove it to himself. That was all he'd done from the moment he left the Brotherhood all those years ago: try and fail to believe that he could be more than his worst moments. However, there were no words, no matter how eloquent, that would change his own mind about himself.

Adelaide is right. A good person doesn't commit atrocities.

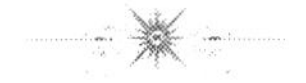

ONCE ADELAIDE WAS sober and freshly bathed, she seemed like a different person.

She still wasn't the nervous but pleasant woman Zamir claimed her to be, but she wasn't a complete mess either. There was a hardness to her that Karsten found compelling—when it *wasn't* directed towards him, anyway. She kept her shoulders squared, as if ready for an attack from any angle. Her hands were calloused from years tending to the mountains, but there was a softness hidden there too. One she couldn't rid herself of entirely.

When he was stationed as her guard, which was becoming a regular occurrence with each of her attempted escapes from the warriors he originally organized to keep an eye on her, Karsten often found her bewitched by the smallest creature racing across the training yard. She bathed in the first rays of sunlight every morning and the first flickers of moonlight in the evening before bed. He slept so little anyway that it was easy to catch her attempting to slip away from her guards no matter the time. No one was certain if she was truly trying to escape Rannadal or if she merely hated having guards in the first place, but she was always quick to act as though she wasn't doing anything wrong the moment she was caught.

There were no words shared in those awkward moments when he found her trying to slip out of the gates with a hood pulled tight over her face. She merely gave a sheepish look, a blush burning across her cheeks even as her eyes sharpened to daggers the moment she thought he wasn't paying attention. In those brief seconds she blushed and met his gaze with her shy smile, he could almost forget how much she hated him.

Then she'd pin him with that green glare and reality returned to them both like a leap into a frozen lake.

Zareen put her on a strict training regimen to help her regain her strength, but it was clear she believed it was a punishment for her escape attempts. With how harshly Zareen treated her, he couldn't blame her for that misconception, but she was simply like that with everyone.

Even the strongest Knights and Vikings tended to cower in her presence, which he was grateful for when they ordered every Knight still in Rannadal to move their training camp. Their complaints were loud and numerous, always piercing a migraine into his skull, but he'd made a promise he planned to stick to. That meant Lady Aylara would have minimal interactions with any Knights. It was only through Zareen's fierce glare and biting words that the few members of the Brotherhood who dared to raise complaints were finally silenced.

She was only training, but there was still an obvious shift in her demeanor whenever she caught sight of a Knight out of the corner of her eye. She would curl into herself, making herself small as her steps quickened and her breathing accelerated. There was no way she could train like that, so they all considered it the right call to keep the Knights out of her sight until they were undressed from their armor. She could still tell sometimes which members of their forces were in the Brotherhood, even without the emblem on their clothes, but she didn't seem as panicked.

I should just be thankful she doesn't react like that around me. The instant rage is still preferable to the heart-aching fear.

It was only a week into her new schedule, with Karsten always close behind her as he trained his warriors not far from her, and there was already progress in the sheer strength of her body and the brightness returning to her eyes. It gave her a sense of liveliness that was once absent, the energy returning to her eyes and sharp tongue with equal measure.

"Have you discovered any evidence of my kin yet, Knight Strom?" she asked, pulling him from his thoughts.

If he were a less trained man, he would've laughed at the question. She already knew his men hadn't found anything. Just the night prior, Zareen caught her rifling through Karsten's reports on the subject when she slunk out of her cabin *again*. On the rare occasion that Karsten got any sleep, the guards he stationed at her door claimed it was a nightly occurrence. She'd sneak out through the window, mull over the reports she wasn't meant to see in the rookery, and attempt to make it over the town wall to escape. Her injuries always caught up with her, and she was forced to return bruised and battered to her cabin.

As the days dragged on and her healing progressed, he began to truly doubt if she needed the protection his warriors provided at all. Even if the entire town doubted in Lefa's claims that the elf was their Promised, she was a force to be reckoned with—injuries or not.

He shook his musing away and grounded himself on the training field, his boots digging up the earth around his heels.

Such a daydreamer, his mother once told him. *Keep yourself out of the clouds.*

After leaving the Brotherhood, that habit worsened. He was reliant on them for everything that he once thought he needed. Without their training, regimen, and *other* methods, he often found himself adrift. So, he bit his cheek until blood pooled across his tongue and drank it down to keep himself in Midgard and not some other realm that only existed in his mind.

It smells of oakmoss, and there's a distant ting of blunted training blades connecting.

He refocused his gaze on what lay before him. The training yard outside the gates of Rannadal stretched out until they met the vast fields where their grains and vegetables came from. Even if Adelaide made it over the wall, it would be a long trek before she could break into the mountainous tree line and properly disappear. On the other side of the village, farther from the mountains, were the herds of livestock he could still smell and hear when the wind carried them right.

It's been so long since that simple farmer's life was my own.

"Are you ignoring me?" she asked, her angry tone ripping him from his thoughts.

Despite the furrowed brows covering her gaze in shadows and the scowl on her upturned lips, he found her grounding in a way the world around him wasn't. She was sweaty, her clothes plastered to her skin and her white hair a wild crown wrapped around her head. A training sword was gripped tight in her trembling hand.

"No, I simply notice you're only asking that question the first moment you've been given a weapon," he mused as her vexed expression faltered and her grip loosened on the sword. "Will my answer alter my fate?"

She rolled her eyes and swung the sword away from him. "I don't even know how to use this thing," she said, the hilt nearly slipping straight out of her hands. "But you still haven't answered my question."

Most Keepers are masters in combat or magic. She claimed she didn't possess magic before The Divide was destroyed. She must know combat but not a sword. What did she specialize in?

"It's only been a week, Keeper," he said as he placed his hands atop the pommel of the axe strapped to his side. "My men haven't reported back with any of their findings yet, but you will be the first to know once they do."

Her entire stance seemed to deflate as she stepped away, rounding the practice dummy that she barely managed to dent. Some of the straw was slipping out of the shallow cuts around its torso, but otherwise it remained unharmed.

If it were a real enemy trying to strike her down, she'd be dead.

In a way, the dummy reminded him of her. Although, if he were to say that out loud, he knew she'd take that in all the wrong ways. When he had carried her back from The Divide, she had been frail and broken. There had been numerous cuts across her body that bled profusely at the smallest movement. They had worried she wouldn't live, and some in the town had even prayed for her death.

He was determined not to allow such fate to befall her again. Not under his watch. Her powers were their only hope against the growing hordes of spirits. Whatever she did that fateful night to calm the spirits was waning, their numbers growing each day. If they couldn't whip her into fighting shape quick enough, he knew his men would eventually falter. He'd already split some of his warriors off to search for her family. If they lost any more before their Viking forces returned from their latest raid, Rannadal would fall. After that, it would only be a matter of time before other villages and kingdoms followed. That doubt in her magical ties to his Goddess welled in his chest again, sharp and poisonous, as it dug fiercely into his heart.

Olena, if she is for you, I will do everything in my power to protect this answered prayer made flesh, but I need a sign. Tell me I am on the right path and I will never doubt your Promised ever again. I swear it.

"Your grip on the hilt is wrong," he said, following her to the dummy that she continued to glare at. "You're holding on so tight you're not allowing movement. I know your arms must feel weak after being unwell, but give your wrist and fingers more space. It will allow you to switch from defensive positions to offensive ones easier as well."

She grumbled something in the elven tongue he didn't understand, but she still loosened her grip and followed his instruction. He grabbed another blunted blade and walked her through the motions, allowing her to mirror him in every swipe and footstep as the day bled on. The bright glow of the sun receded, welcoming the coolness of the moon as they moved in sync. The training yard was long since emptied until only the rotating guards on the ramparts remained.

Down the hill Rannadal was perched on, flickering lights lit up the fields. Small homes were scattered around the outskirts of farmland, each resident tending to another crop or animal that allowed the town to thrive in both food and trade.

That year, autumn was approaching faster than normal, and many wondered if they'd survive the cold months ahead if the crops were frozen before they were picked. As the leader of their fighting forces, he wasn't typically concerned with such things, but Ylwa and Lefa whispered about it nonstop. It caused that worry to creep into his head as well.

While training, all that fell away. Maybe it was that moving his body through such fluid motions always calmed his racing thoughts. Maybe it was the coolness of the night sweeping over his sun-kissed cheeks and chilling the pools of sweat on his neck.

Or maybe it was the steady presence beside him. The silent woman who stopped all pretenses of glaring at him as they practiced. Instead, her face smoothed as her focus grew. By the time the last dinner bells chimed, she still wasn't the strongest swordsperson he ever trained, but the dummy was hacked to impressive pieces at their feet.

If it were her enemy, it would be a cold corpse.

She turned the practice blade on him, her hair appearing darker due to sweat and the growing night. Only the lights in the distance and the lanterns at the gates lit their features.

"I think I've practiced on a still object enough," she said, her lips curling back over her teeth in an almost-smile that was closer to a grimace. There was a bitter edge to her voice that bit on the edge of competition and condescension. As if, in a single day, the pupil believed she could outmatch the teacher. "I want to see what you can really do."

It's far more likely she just wants the smallest chance to hurt me.

He smacked his sword against hers without replying, his strength immediately forcing her to stumble back and cry out as her sword flung out of her hand. He grinned as her almost-smile turned into a full scowl.

"Let's try a fair fight next time. Didn't you hear? The bells chimed. The hall will close soon, and I'm sure we're both famished."

She grabbed her fallen sword and grounded her heels into the earth. "I'll go as soon as you show me what you just did."

She held out her sword in the same fashion and narrowed her gaze on him.

Of course she'd want to know. I left her without a weapon. I made her vulnerable.

"Very well," he said as he holstered his sword on his back. He stepped around the practice sword to scrutinize her stance and hold of the weapon. She was doing everything he taught her, but he would always have one advantage over her. It was the same advantage he had on most of his opponents.

He wasn't a small man by any stretch of the imagination. He'd trained for so long around other Knights and, for a short time, the Vikings of Rannadal, that he sometimes forgot how large and imposing he must come across to others. There were certainly men and women who towered above him, but they were usually Berserkers, like Njarl, who kept to themselves.

A shiver ran down his back at the image of the Berserker's towering form bearing down on the woman before him. If that giant truly wished for Lady Aylara's demise, she would need to learn how to defend herself from even the largest opponent.

"The tactic I used is most effective when you're larger than your opponent. For you, that won't happen often, but should you find yourself against a smaller adversary, you can buy yourself time to escape by surprising them. I'll show you a trick to it." He positioned himself behind her and grabbed her hands over the sword. In her weakened state, she needed two hands on a single-handed sword.

"Once you've regained your strength, you should be able to hold onto both a sword and a shield with ease," he'd explained earlier in their training session.

She'd looked like she wanted to throw up at the mere idea. *"Those are weapons of the Brotherhood. I will never wield them."*

"Move fast and strong at the same time," he continued as he shook off the memory. "Don't let them prepare themselves and don't hold back. Put all your power into one swing and let them have it. If you falter, you'll spend your energy before they're cut down and you'll need time to recover. If that happens, they can rebound and come back for you. That's how you die."

He could feel her breathing quicken from his place behind her. Her back was pressed to his chest so that every time she took a rapid breath in, he felt it in his ribs. In his grip around her hands, with his thumbs to her inner wrist, he felt the rush of her pulse even through his thick leather gloves. In the back of his mind, he figured he must've been scaring her with the very real possibility of her death or upsetting her with his proximity. If she was truly afraid, she hardly showed it outside of her breathing and rushing blood.

"Let me try," she said, her voice softer than he expected.

Her warmth left him the moment he stepped away. He returned to the same spot as before and pulled out his sword, bracing himself for a fierce swing that didn't come. Instead, she merely stared at him over the top of the blade, her gaze reflecting on the blunted steel. It forced a pair of piercing green eyes on him. He stared right back, wondering what in all the realms was going on in her head.

She smiled and widened her stance so her leg slid backwards in the dirt. His attention remained fixed on the upwards tick of her lips that was so like the smile she gave him before, in her cabin when she didn't loathe his very existence, that he didn't notice her true intentions.

Her boot dug into the earth and pulled back out, raining dirt across them and straight into his eyes and mouth. He sputtered in surprise, losing his stance, and that's when she struck. Karsten could tell she put every ounce of herself into the swing. She even managed to slightly loosen his grip on the sword. He stumbled a few steps back, but his weapon met hers even as he kept his eyes pinned closed.

"How?" she gasped in surprise.

He yanked his axe free with his other hand and used the

hooked, blunted side to sweep at her knee. A rush of air greeted him as she collapsed, some sort of elfish profanity spilling past her lips as she groaned from her spot on the ground below him.

"I'm afraid I can't teach you everything in one day, Keeper," he said as he holstered his axe and rubbed his cloak against his burning eyes. "Although, you have some tricks of your own already."

Once his vision cleared, he found her lying in the same place. Her hair was dotted with grass, and smudges of dirt lined her face before running across her torso in dirty streaks. He would've laughed at the sight if he thought she'd let him live afterwards, but he decided his life was worth keeping that day.

"Come," he said, offering his hand. "Before dinner spoils."

She rolled her eyes and pushed herself to her feet. Her hands came back caked in mud and she scowled at each flexing finger as if they were foreign to her. "Go ahead. I can't fathom eating like this."

"I'll save you a bite then," he said as he returned her training sword to its rightful place in a large, emptied keg at the end of the yard. He placed his own sword in the sheath on his back and headed for the town gates. "The hall cooks don't take kindly to people poking around their space once they've closed for the night." When he realized she wasn't following him, he stopped and turned around only to find her standing perfectly still in the same spot. "Keeper Aylara?" he asked, the concern in his voice obvious enough to shake her from her thoughts.

"Why are you being kind to me?" There was a deeply rooted accusation in her tone. "You've spent the entire day training me. You're saving me food. Walking me to the bathhouse. Why bother?"

He shrugged. "We need your abilities."

"Bullshit," she spat as she picked her heels out of the mud and rushed towards him. "None of that is required for my assistance. Only finding my family. That was the deal. So, what is it then? What compels you to do such things?"

He sighed, his breath forming a small cloud around his lips that he was quick to frown at. *Winter is coming too early.* He shook the thought off and instead focused on the storm of emotions her words brought forward and the tempest she held in her eyes. He could tell she was grateful, even if she would never admit it, but he was uncertain of whatever other truths remained hidden behind those fierce green eyes.

Why am I doing this? he questioned in the silence that lingered between them. *Perhaps I feel it's penance for the wrongs I've done. That I must treat everyone who distrusts me as if they had no reason to. If they can trust me despite my wrongdoings, maybe I can finally trust myself.*

But there was no way to tell Lady Aylara about any of that. No way to pour his heart into the hands of a woman who would sooner crush it than treat it like the tender, war-torn thing it was. As he looked at her, he thought there could be a different reason for his kindness towards her.

In the nightfall, when the world was painted in swaths of dark azure that tinted the world in its icy hue, she stood as the only warmth in a cold sea. The distant candlelight melded with the bright stars beyond: a beautiful backdrop that still paled in comparison to the alluring sight before him. Even streaked in mud, covered in grass, and menacingly scowling at him, there was still *something* about her that compelled him to remain in her orbit.

She reminds me of someone, but I can't remember who.

That's when he saw it. The streaks of dirt that wrapped around her lithe form seemed to dance across her chest and wrap possessively around her hips. With her white hair framed by the dark night and the earth smeared like paint strokes around her body, she looked exactly like the statue of Olena in the chapel: a marble sculpture interweaved with obsidian.

Marble for Olena. Obsidian for the God of Chaos, Cismir. Had I not found her weeping while being attacked by an agent of the Dark God in the shadows of that very idol?

Karsten's shoulders fell in both defeat and relief. He'd prayed for a sign, and there she stood like a myth come to life that caused hope to flutter in his chest. And yet, his newfound certainty in her holy nature didn't stop the rapid descent of his heart into his stomach.

Because if something divine hates my presence, what does that say about me?

He blinked the darkness on the edge of his gaze away, forcing his eyes to refocus on the angry woman before him. In the silence stretching between them, her rage dissipated. In its place, a quiet suffering rose unbidden from the depths of her heart.

The Codex claims The Promised of Olena would be mortal in every way. It spoke of how she could bleed, but it never told them that she would cry.

"I know you're in a lot of pain, Lady Aylara," he said, turning back towards the gates so he could pretend like he didn't see the tears in the corner of her eyes. "It makes you lash out when you don't truly mean to. I understand that." He started walking and was relieved to hear her follow. "I was like that once. So consumed by my hatred that I allowed it to blind me. I only wished someone had shown me kindness even when I only wanted to show my anger. It would've made me stop and think. Perhaps then, things would've turned out differently for me."

He paused once they passed the threshold, and she moved to stand beside him, confusion written in the downturn of her brows as the gates closed with a resounding, hollow echo.

"You're being kind to me because you wish someone was kind to you?" she asked, disbelief heavy in her voice. He lied to her already and she caught him in the act, so *of course* she'd assume every word from his lips was a lie. One of the very first things he said to her was a deception. "It's that easy then?"

He shook his head, debating with himself whether he should simply leave her standing there at the gates or not. That gorgeous, spiteful woman conjured far too many confusing feelings in his chest. His morals were one of the few things he'd retained from growing up with his family, before the Knights and his father had beaten the rest of his mother's lessons out of him.

Always do what's right and always do what's kind, even if it angers him.

A shudder ran through him at the memory of his mother's words. They had been whispered against his ear as she'd dabbed at his face with a cloth, wiping the dirt out of his blackened eye. Perhaps that should've been the day he forgot those lessons, but he couldn't stomach the idea.

His smile was bitter and broken as he started to walk away from her. He brought his cloak a little closer to his chest, as though worried that the brewing early-autumn would freeze his heart solid. "I don't think showing kindness in the face of anger has ever been easy."

He left her with those words and marched on into the night.

THE KEEPER'S CREED

The mark of a Keeper is a heavy burden
But one we carry all the same
To bare witness to the crimes
Of our neighbors in Midgard
Least our forefathers died for naught
When they forged The Divide for our keeping
To save the elves from further torment
We serve our kin and the All-Father only
For the rest of our newly mortal days.

7

MENTORING A MENACE

SKALD: ADELAIDE AYLARA

Humans are so confusing.

Adelaide was quick to shred her dirty clothes and step into the natural hot springs inside the bathhouse after her conversation with Knight Strom. She'd only made a brief stop at her cabin to grab a fresh set of clothes before making a dash for the warm waters. The sweat clinging to her skin made each blow of air coming down from the mountains feel ice cold. Elves were more accustomed to freezing temperatures than humans but, after such a long day of training, even she had her limits.

The day weighed on her like a heavy coat in the dead of summer. Doubt smothered her as the Commander's words ran rampant through her mind. He seemed remorseful for his time spent in the Brotherhood, she could tell that much, but did it really matter in the end? Did his sorrow over his choices make those decisions any less relevant? Did it absolve him of the crimes he no doubt committed in the Brotherhood?

And why in all the realms do I care so much?

Perhaps she was reluctant to admit that he reminded her of herself. After the Knights upended her life, she'd made her own mistakes. She'd killed members of his Brotherhood without a second, fleeting thought to whether they were truly responsible for the death and destruction she witnessed or not. Their Order was large, spanning across The North, with numbers in the thousands. Still, she'd blanketed them all as murderers for the act of a few. She hadn't stopped to think of them as good people who smiled and felt real, genuine emotions just like her.

All I saw was red, red rage.

It had blinded her. It was that anger which led her to curse the very names of the people she'd lost. The old her, from those days right after she'd lost everything the first time, would've killed the commander merely on principle. Simply because she felt she had a right to.

How was that fair to the people she killed? To Karsten, whom she tried to shun at every chance, when all he showed her was kindness?

Perhaps her hesitance in admitting he was a real, good person was because it meant she'd killed real, good people just like him. Admitting that was far more difficult than just turning her anger on him for simply existing and contradicting everything she'd ever known.

"A look like that always means trouble, my dear," a woman said, her voice carrying softly on the light breeze, wafting through the hot spring caverns.

She tensed, goosebumps raising on her neck, until the stranger stepped out of the shadows and made herself known. By all appearances, she was just an old woman with a sad smile and a large robe covering her wrinkled body.

"What did you say?" she asked, relaxing back into the water. Whoever the human was, Adelaide had no doubt she could strike the other woman down at a moment's notice if she had ill intentions. She was simply that old and frail.

"Your face," the woman said as she sat on the lip of the pool, dipping one foot into the water and sighing as heat rose to touch the surface of her pale skin. "You seem anxious, and those who feel troubled typically *cause* trouble in my experience."

Adelaide sunk under the water until her shoulders were fully immersed. She was used to bathing naked in far more public areas than the bathhouse, which was enclosed on all sides and separated into three by gender. One for men, one for women, and one for those who didn't fully fit into the prior categories. She found the whole idea foolish though. If one were trying to provide modesty, that should've been provided by basic decorum and respect, not by the presumption of who found whom attractive. She could just as easily ogle any woman in the lady's side of the house as a man could, but she didn't, as any decent person wouldn't.

No, she sank into the water not to preserve her modesty but to instead conceal her nervousness. There were so few times she'd been alone with a human, and it sent her nerves alight with fear. "I promise I'm not trying to cause any issues."

The other woman thought her words over as she stared at the ceiling above them. It glowed in some sections with blue algae that continued down into the pool where the water also shimmered. The light painted them in tinges of sapphire and teal instead of the harsh, warm shadows of the lantern just outside the bathhouse doors. There were nights when she was young and slept beneath the stars, chasing light bugs through the woods, when the opposing cool and warm lights bled together just like the bathhouse.

Those days are long gone now, and I can't get them back.

"In that case, I will give you one clear piece of advice," the woman said, focusing her faded blue gaze on her. "Stay away from the Commander, Adelaide Aylara."

She rolled her eyes. "Believe me, I'm trying to."

"Good," the old woman said as she removed her foot from

the water and stood. "You've already been made aware of his previous title. He reached high ranks in the Brotherhood, and that never comes without bloodshed. As an elf, I'm sure you understand what that means."

She suspected that much, but her thoughts from before crept back up. She'd done the same, hadn't she? Plenty of Knights had fallen beneath her arrow and blade, and she didn't feel nearly as much remorse as Commander Strom seemed to. In the end, did it really matter?

If she could truly perform the magic they claimed she could, she would hold the spirits back like she promised. The Commander would find her family like he swore or she would do it herself. The Blood Oath he had no idea was forged between them would ensure their discovery one way or another. When everything was said and done, she would go back home. They'd rebuild their cabin in the woods, she would replant her garden, and her kin would forever be safe from the Knights of Rannadal because of the spell combining their blood.

It made her a little sick to have lied and bewitched him under false pretenses, but it was too late to go back. She'd wiped their blood off the blade when they'd demanded it be returned to Zareen, ensuring no one would ever know unless she loosened her lips.

She sunk into the water and stared at the glowing ceiling with a sigh. Yes, it didn't matter all that much if she got along with anyone in Rannadal. If they could work together and ensure the bargain was fulfilled, she could return to her normal life.

I could go home.

The woman was slowly making her way out of the bathhouse, but Adelaide was quick to stop her. "I didn't catch your name," she said, watching closely as the woman froze at the threshold. "You know mine. It only seems fair that I know yours as well."

She peered at her over her shoulder, the fluffy white robe obscuring her lips so Adelaide couldn't tell if she was smiling or scowling under her focused gaze.

"Jill," she said. "Sister Jill Gorm, but you can simply call me Jill."

The door closed behind her and a cold burst of fresh night air swooshed inside, making Adelaide shiver and sink deeper into the water.

These are strange times indeed. I never thought I'd end up bathing naked with a nun.

IT WAS in the light of a waxing moon that Adelaide stumbled, just a *little* tipsy, out of The Gilded Raven earlier than she expected.

With a belly full of the long since chilled dinner the Commander saved her, drinking her pain away was less appealing. Still, she drank a few horns of mead to take the edge off the loss clawing at her attention whenever the world around her was too silent and still. She'd tried to meander, drinking in the sights of the first large town she ever stepped foot in, but the piercing stares of the locals grated on her nerves. There was also too great a chance she'd bump into a patrolling Knight and panic would lance her heart so fiercely she couldn't move.

At least in the tavern, everyone is too drunk to notice my pointed ears.

She kept them hidden behind her hair and hooded cloak whenever possible, but that didn't help as much as she'd hoped. Humans apparently didn't have white hair unless they were older, so her youthful face paired with snowy strands gave her away to anyone who paid attention. The drunkards at the bar didn't care as long as she didn't get between them and the ale, and the drink dulled the sorrow threatening to eat her alive. She appreciated the reprieve The Gilded Raven gave her from everything wrong around her, even if it led her to sway on her walk and made her dizzy.

"*Shit*," she grumbled as her boot got stuck in an upturned root. She yanked it free, spraying dirt across the path and her pants in one go. "Odin, blast it."

"I don't think the All-Father spends his time cursing trees, Keeper," a man said, his voice soft against the bitterly cold night.

She squinted in the dim light to make out his face in the shadows. Elves had better eyesight in the dark than humans, but the drink made seeing clearly a little harder than normal.

Okay, maybe I did drink a bit more than I intended.

The man finally stepped into the warm light filtering out from the bustling tavern and gave her a small, sheepish grin. His thick, black hair was braided in parts and adorned with small jewels and runes carved from stones. He had grey eyes that reflected the light of the moon back at her and, most importantly, there were two pointed ears on either side of his face.

"Kinship," she gasped in greeting the way her mother always taught her to greet other Keepers. She wouldn't use that for elves who lived among humans, but with the many layers of pelts he wore, the runes hidden in every piece of fabric on his body, and the scent of herbs wafting from him, she knew everything she needed to know.

He was a Keeper, just like her. At least, she *thought* he must be. Elves who joined the rest of the humans across Midgard usually didn't keep in touch with their heritage and often weren't as dedicated to The Old Gods as he appeared to be.

Still, he waved a dismissive hand and moved closer to her. "I haven't been one with the mountains in a long time, Keeper Aylara. There's no need for such formalities."

"Then why are you here?" she asked, feeling more stable on her own two feet and more sober than she had been in days. She didn't know how to handle humans. She could keep up with their language, Common, but speaking to another elf? Her native tongue flew naturally from her lips and she felt a missing piece of herself slot back into place in her aching heart. "Rannadal seems an odd place for any of our kind."

He grinned, the smile teetering back and forth between smug and playful. "I imagine I'm doing the same as you, trying to find a way to steady the flow of spirits into our world. It's wreaking havoc on the natural balance of Midgard."

She nodded, watching as he rounded her to face the hill leading further to the longhouse in the center of town. She learned the humans called it The Great Hall. That was where most people dined, but she usually took her meal in the tavern or her cabin, so she was rarely there. Lights from cabins and longhouses scattered around the village flickered before them, the townsfolk turning in for the night as she should have done.

But it's felt like so long since I've seen one of my own.

"You will need to learn your new powers and the ways of the spirits themselves," he said, his moon eyes swallowing the town before him whole. "Jarl Lefa Thurston requested my presence specifically for the task."

"Do you have the same magic?" she asked, hope stirring in her chest.

He chuckled, the sound warm but a little tilted. Like his laughter was out of practice. "I assure you: my powers are not so grand that the humans have deemed them divine in nature." He peeled back one of his thicker pelts that was almost large enough to be a cloak, revealing a pack of supplies strapped to his back and a carved staff of white birch attached to his hip. "I will show you another time. For now, it's late. We'll begin your training at first light. I suggest you rest."

She folded her arms and turned her face towards the sky. The stars twinkled back at her, but she knew they'd soon be washed out by an endless sea of autumn clouds.

"And what is my new mentor's name?"

When she didn't get a response, she peered back to where he was standing only to find the space empty. The place where he'd once stood as a dark shadow, nearly blending into the night, was bare.

The only sign she hadn't imagined his presence was the upturned root that remained mangled against the earth.

"YOU WEREN'T JOKING when you said *first light*," Adelaide muttered between heaving breaths as she sucked in every ounce of air into her battered lungs as she could. Her mysterious mentor summoned her before dawn broke over the world and it was only when they reached their intended destination atop a steep hill that the first sparks of daylight dared to grace the skies. "Didn't Odin say something about rest being wise?"

He gave a small snort. "No, but he did say to rise early."

"No, no. I *specifically* recall sleep being important. Something about it being foolish to wake a woman before the sunrise. It can lead to one's early demise," she said, her sarcasm as dry as the early morning air as she folded her arms. "Are you testing such wisdom?"

"Of course not, Adelaide," he said with a laugh as he stabbed the end of his staff into the ground so it stood straight up. "'*A fool stays awake all night, worrying about everything. He's fatigued when morning comes, and his problems remain unsolved,*'" he said, quoting the Havamal, a text of lessons given to elves straight from Odin.

Her lips screwed into a scowl. "'*A stupid man thinks he knows everything if he gets himself in a tough corner. But he doesn't even know what he'll answer if men ask him questions*,'" she replied with an irritated click of her tongue as she quoted a different stanza of the same text. "I've asked you several questions this morning, none of which you've answered, including your very name. Answers would be appreciated, especially if you're waking me before the rooster's call."

The wind atop the hill changed, whipping around their heads so the man's hair tangled around his face. The runes and beads in his hair knocked, their sound almost like a windchime as he stared back at her. "My name is Sander Erling," he finally responded as the wind calmed and his hair settled back over his shoulder.

"I don't recall any Keeper clan with the surname *Erling*."

He shrugged. "I'm not from this region, and the mountains are vast. The Divide stretches far past The North. I'm certain there's much you don't know about who and *what* survives there," he said, motioning to the distant expanse of the mountains on the horizon. "Including the spirits your magic can control."

A retort was on the edge of her lips, but someone cleared their throat behind her and made the words slip away. They turned at the sound, watching as the culprit shifted uncomfortably at the awkward silence.

The Commander wore a blush beneath his tired eyes. "Apologies for interrupting, but what are you saying?"

Between the exhausting effort of hauling her tired limbs up the hill so early in the morning and the sheer confusing nature of the elf in front of her, she forgot who was following them. He'd already been awake, or perhaps never slept if that was the same tunic she saw him in the day before, and offered to be their guard out of the gates. A chaperone was the only way she was allowed to exit town, so they'd agreed to his company.

"'*A foolish man misuses his mouth—he talks too much,*'" she quoted one last time in her mother tongue. It earned her a chuckle from Sander before she switched back to Common for the Commander's benefit. "We're speaking of the Havamal. You wouldn't understand it even if we spoke it in your language."

"*Oh,*" he mumbled. "Then continue."

Sander arched a dark brow. "Suspicious of the two elves, Commander?" he questioned with a smirk. "You wouldn't be the first in Rannadal to do so. I met with your Jarl last night and she told me there have already been a hundred complaints about Adelaide's presence in town. It's why I insisted on meeting beyond their prying eyes and *ears*," he said, emphasizing the last word with a pointed look.

The blush on his cheeks darkened and his shoulders slumped. "I meant no disrespect. It's merely a protocol that someone accompany Lady Ayalra, and I was already awake. If you wish to speak in your language, you're free to do so. You needn't include me."

Sander's upper lip curled, and she was certain there would be more biting remarks from his lips, so she held her hand up to stop him. "While I appreciate your desire to defend another elf, it's not necessary," she said, slipping back into the language she was more familiar with. "I don't need to hear about their complaints either. I already know some of them don't trust me; I can feel it when they stare at me as I walk by."

"That is exactly the problem," Sander said as he shifted, blocking her from seeing the Commander. "The Jarl spoke about how you believe you don't possess any magic and that you never did. This is, of course, *impossible* for an elf. However, your magic may be stunted by your emotions. Knowing you're being watched or judged may prevent you from accessing your power. I'm uncertain how we can practice with such an *audience*."

She nodded and stepped around him. "Commander, I'm afraid Sander has a point," she began but, upon seeing his confused stare, realized she hadn't switched back to Common. She groaned and started again. "My mentor believes I won't be able to access my magic if I'm worried about being watched. I admit, I've rarely tried to harness magic while alone, so he may be correct."

Out of the corner of her eye, she saw Sander give a smug smile and wanted to slap it off his face.

New rule: don't ever tell Sander he's right. His ego won't fit in the door.

The Commander hesitated, shifting back and forth as he stared down the hill. Its peak was still in eyesight of the training fields he spent most of his days on. He would still be able to keep an eye on them from there to ensure she didn't flee, but catching up with her if she ran would be a difficult task.

She moved closer and hesitated when they were an arm's length apart. From a distance, his fatigue wasn't as noticeable, but up close it was obvious. His amber eyes were dull and ringed with dark purple, almost like he'd been punched in both eyes. He was a bit ashen and clammy, and he wasn't nearly as steady on his feet as he first appeared to be.

When was the last time he slept?

"Knight Strom," she began, but she didn't seem to be reaching him as he continued staring down at the fields. "*Commander Strom*," she said, trying again. That seemed to shake him into consciousness, and he looked back at her as though she was a dream he could barely see beyond his heavy eyelids. She dropped her voice so her words were only for his ears, even with Sander's keen, pointed ears not far away. "You're obviously exhausted. Send another guard to watch us down the hill and we'll return by the midday meal. Hopefully by then, I'll be able to tap into this miraculous magic you all claim I have."

He nodded, but the movement was sluggish as he forced his eyes open a bit wider. "Alright," he said before stifling a yawn. "Good luck with your training."

"You needn't worry, Commander," Sander said as he strode to her side. "I promise we will return to town."

He didn't respond, which Adelaide suspected was further proof of just how tired he was. If it weren't for that, there was no way in all the realms he would've left the two elves *alone* on the edge of their line of sight before most of Rannadal even woke up.

There's no better time to run and find my kin.

She smothered her devilish grin as she tried to pay attention to the beginning of her lesson, her gaze pinned on the swirling magic the other elf created even as her mind drifted to the mountains.

I just need to get past Sander first.

ADELAIDE'S TRAINING with hand-to-hand combat, daggers, and even the heavy sword Commander Strom instructed her with went smoothly. She was familiar with her bow, which she still fiercely longed for whenever she recalled its golden edges lost somewhere either in Rannadal or in the mountains, so she never bothered to strengthen that skill. It was her deadliest tool and a skill she'd honed from the moment she could nock an arrow to the string.

Magic on the other hand? That seemed like an impossible feat.

"This is pointless," she snapped when she failed for the

twentieth time to do even the most mundane spell Sander instructed her to try. "I've spent the past twenty-six years of my life without a single ounce of magic in my blood. My mother already determined that I didn't possess any after rigorous tests and trials. The humans were wrong."

All I ever did was disappoint her.

Sander didn't respond. He merely sat before her in quiet contemplation, staring at her with moon-like eyes even as the sun shone brightly above the horizon. Her stomach was growling, her legs were weak from sitting cross-legged on the earth for so long, and she still hadn't found a single way to manipulate the other elf so she could run.

Pleading her case to him hadn't worked. He'd sworn to Jarl Lefa he would do everything in his power to coach her magic from her. His failure meant the mountains would continue bleeding spirits into Midgard, which he also seemed to detest the very idea of, so she imagined he had some sort of personal stake in the matter if he was so determined to ensure their success. His eyes were also too sharp and he watched her every move like a hawk.

"The magic is within you. I can sense it, even if you cannot," he assured her, his willowy hand reaching out to feel the air around her as though he could see the aura of power lingering there. "I was once certain my magic was a weak, feeble thing unworthy of notice. Nothing when compared to my brother's, anyway." He paused, a dark chuckle rippling from his chest. "He was the eldest and most powerful of our kin. Wicked smart with a sharp tongue and sharper wit. His magic was fierce and untamed—something I was always jealous of since I had to study so hard for even the most meager spark of magic."

He snapped his fingers, a few specks of fire licking at the tips of his hand before they flickered and died.

"What happened to him?" she asked, watching the sparks of magic drift onto the grass and char the turf with a small sizzle.

"I'm certain he's still around—*somewhere*. I admit, I'm not close to any of my family anymore," he said with a shrug. "Not like you were, I'm sure."

She swallowed hard, her saliva hitting the rising bile in her gut like a sinking stone. "I still am," she corrected with a voice so soft the wind threatened to take it. "They're alive, so we're still close."

His smile was polite but strained as he nodded. "Yes, of course." He coughed, the sound breaking up the awkward tension before he returned to his lesson. "My point is that I understand what it's like to feel inadequate with magic. It's nothing to be ashamed of. Besides, if I can accomplish grand feats of healing and dream walking after years of study, then you should have no real issue accomplishing the magic you've already performed." He winked, and for a moment it was like seeing the crescent moon in one of his eyes before he smirked and broke the illusion. "Think of it this way, you're already ten steps ahead of me."

A devilish idea uncurled in her subconscious, but she clamped down on her delight. "Dream walking?" she questioned with a curious tilt of her head and a naïve pout. It was a look she used as bait for men who thought themselves smarter than they really were and wished to impart their knowledge on a pretty face. "How does that work?"

"It's a rare talent, but fascinating to those who master it," he said, his eyes lighting up as he began to spin the tales of its origin and the knowledge it could conjure. She listened until she was certain he was so far gone in his passions he wouldn't notice her mind straying.

Then, she formed her plan.

"Adelaide, are you listening?" he asked, an accusative quality to his tone that snapped her out of her thoughts.

She blinked, fluttering her lashes at him as she reined in on her rapid thoughts. "Of course I am," she replied as she moved her hand away from where it was holding up her chin.

"Then what's the last thing I said?" he challenged.

Mentally, she reversed his speech and picked up on the few words her mind managed to process in his lecture. "You were describing the ways spirits of Sorrow, Terror, and Lust can create nightmares, which are also things you can access with dream walking."

He pursed his lips and the sparkle re-entered his eyes. It almost made her feel bad for what she was about to do. "Yes, I was. That is a crucial piece of knowledge for dream walkers to understand and, should you find yourself able to access such an ability as well, it's paramount for you to understand. Accidentally stumbling into someone's worst dreams is no laughing matter."

She pulled on the very few other pieces of information she retained from his long-winded speech. "Didn't you say it's wrong to enter someone's dreams without permission?"

He nodded, the proud tilt of his grin doing nothing to disguise the way his gaze snapped to her lips before darting away again. "Yes, exactly."

"How would I know if I can tap into dreams if no one ever consents? How would I even know what it feels like?" Adelaide secured her pouting lips back into place. "It sounds so fascinating. I'd love to try it."

Sander huffed, propping up his head on his knee that was pulled to his chest. "You've complained about every type of magic I've tried to teach you, but you want to try one of the most difficult forms?" She gave an eager nod of her head and sat a little straighter like the perfect student her mother always wanted. "Fine, but first we'll start with me entering your dreams so I can guide you through the process. Do I have your consent?"

"Yes."

"Good," he replied as he lay down on the grass and patted the space beside him for her to join. She did so, but a bit further away than he indicated. "Close your eyes and let the winds take you. Ease yourself into the realm of dreams and leave your mind open to the possibilities."

She did the exact opposite, allowing her thoughts to run rampant and preventing her from sleeping as she heard Sander's breathing slowly even out beside her. He fell into a deep, meditative slumber a few minutes in.

That's when her plan began.

Quickly, she rolled away from him with the grass cushioning her movements. It tangled blades of green into her hair and sent the smell of wet earth into her nose, but it worked to soften the sound of her leaving the hill altogether. Once she reached the stones further away, she pulled herself up and peeked across to the training fields.

The guards weren't paying attention to where she was, their focus instead pinned on Sander's sleeping form and where they probably still assumed she was lying. As quietly as possible, she tip-toed down the stones and dropped onto the flat plains, the large hill blocking the human's visibility.

She ran.

THE SUN WAS bright above her head by the time she breached the first layer of trees back into The Wild Woods. It wasn't the same section of forest she called home, but it was the closest entrance into the mountains from Rannadal. The twisted birches and towering pines would act as cover, allowing her to slip into their shadows and disappear.

That was the plan anyway.

Her heart beat violently in her throat as she struggled to catch her breath, her knees threatening to give out on her as she propped herself against a tree. Its bark dug into her palms, slicing them open and tugging at the flesh. She bit her lip to stifle the hiss of pain and pushed away, continuing her expedition into the steep mountains she loved.

I must find them. If I'm the one to discover my kin, the Commander will never be able to fulfil his Blood Oath. He will forever be bound to protect them and we'll have decades where we'll never fear a Knight. They'll never hurt us. Not again.

She hacked at a thicket in her way, one of the kitchen knives she'd stolen finally useful for *something* even if it wasn't the best tool for the job. If she were never planning to return to Rannadal, she would've been more concerned about not leaving a trail for them to follow. Her life was bound by the same oath. She would have no choice but to return with her family in tow behind her, probably complaining about having to join the humans the whole time.

A laugh bubbled up in her chest unbidden and, with no one around to hear, she let it slip free and echo off the trees. The sound danced in the air, changing form each time it reverberated back to her. It almost made her feel like her sisters were right there around the nearest turn in her winding path, waiting for her to come home.

Nissa is going to tackle me outright, she thought with a smile. *Her wild red hair will stick out on all sides from her running into my arms. I can practically feel my ears ache from her squeals of delight already.*

A stream trickled in the distance, the water hitting the stones like a melody as she rushed towards it. Her kin would stay by a source of water, especially after the fires parched their throats, and so her sister could practice her affinity for elemental magic. When she reached the river, she ran her blistered palms into the water and sighed as it soothed the ache from the biting bark. With her gaze, she followed its winding path and checked her position with the risen sun.

It's the same river from the homestead, just further downstream. I can follow it.

Distant memories flowed to the forefront of her mind. She was young, barely initiated as an official Keeper, and floating on the river with her family. A spiral of water lifted into the air, Nissa's arms shaking as she tried to control it, before it splashed back into the swirling pools.

"Careful, Issa!" Birgitta cried out as the water fell across her curly hair. It took ages for the tight coils to dry, and she was always the first to leave the water to let it warm up in the sun. "You'll ruin my braids." She raised one of the long ends, showing off her hard work.

"Sorry," Issa said with a sheepish look and a blush marring her freckled cheeks.

Their mother sighed as she lounged on a nearby stone, waist deep in the water but her torso bared to the sun and hair laid flat across the rocks to dry. "Darling, your sister barely gets to practice with her magic. Why don't you let her try to pull the water from your hair instead of admonishing her for trying?"

Bir covered her hair with both hands, her umber skin somehow paling at the thought. "Absolutely not," she said, her voice holding its usual dry and stubborn tone even though it held a slightly grave nature. "Need I remind you of the last time anyone tried to help with my hair."

Adelaide shivered at the memory and how enraged Bir was when she had to chop it shorter because of their so-called help. That's when they'd learned that just because Issa and Bir both had curly hair didn't mean their curls could be treated the same way.

A male voice called from behind a row of bushes, "If you all are finished with your beauty routines, us men would like to bathe!"

Mother rolled her eyes. "You can join at any time!"

Another man, though perhaps he was just a boy then, responded in a frail and croaking tone. "No, we're alright!"

"Yeah, I'll stay with V over here until you're done!"

A smile fought its way onto her lips at the memory, and her heart ached with both nostalgia and the bitter sense of loneliness.

Dwelling on the past won't help me find them.

She began to stand but froze as something drifted across the water. It bobbed, churning in the mild waves until there was no mistaking what it was. Its face was waterlogged, bloated and purple, with what little remained of its dark hair dragging behind its oblong shape. Veins and stark white bone hung from where its neck used to be, and its pointed ear was chewed off.

Bile rose quick and fierce, and she puked into the nearest bush.

I need to find them—now.

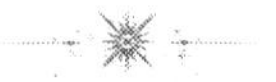

THE MEMORY of the Keeper's head, detached from the rest of its body, haunted her journey through the mountains. She knew every elf in their section of The Divide, but the corpse was so decayed she couldn't place who they may have once been. With each step beside the river which flowed back home, she caught more chunks of flesh floating on the water or stuck to the rocks where the ravens pecked at them.

She tried not to look or smell its stench, but it invaded her senses.

Any remaining hesitation to rejoin the humans in Rannadal vanished on her trek. She couldn't protect her mountains on her own, even if her family was found. They weren't enough to hold back the spirits, and the warriors in town might not have been enough either. Not when the spirits could destroy a body like that. She wondered what kind of spirit could tear someone limb from limb, but decided it was best to never know.

Darkening shades of sunset blues and pinks bathed the mountains as the sun descended, the shadows elongating and reaching for her with greedy fingers. The humans would have sent people to find her hours ago, but she still wasn't close to home. Her ribs ached fiercely and her legs shook from the exertion, slowing her pace to a crawl.

Guess I'm not as healed as I thought.

She grasped her left eye, her fingers idly rubbing at the sore edges of her scar as the skin burned. It started sometime during her hike, but the pain grew the further she went. With one eye watering, full of tears and closed in pain, and the darkness growing, she could hardly see. Her good eye scanned what little she could make out of the path, but her stomach rolled in anxious waves.

Someone could sneak up on her and attack far too easily. The thought forced the hair on the back of her neck to stand straight.

"I wish Bir was here," she said to herself just to hear her own voice instead of the too still and silent woods she blindly traversed. "She could hold the shadows back."

There were many times when she was young that her older sister used her magic to peel back the shadows in the corners of the room, proving to her overactive imagination that there weren't any beasts hiding where she couldn't see. On the long winter nights, when the sun never showed itself, her magic was a blessing that brought their kin safety on the hunt.

Odin, where are they?

As far as she'd seen on her return to the mountains, the Commander's reports were correct. There were no signs of elves, aside from the dead Keeper floating in the water. No bonfires or chimneys lit up the horizon with flames or smoke.

There was an absence of bird calls that sounded just a bit too much like a voice. Branches above her head didn't creak beneath the weight of hidden archers, like herself.

There was no one except the trees and the damned.

In the distance, there were the flickering lights of dancing spirits whose size grew with each step she took closer to home. She passed a few spirits, but they were all the helpful variety her mother trained her to spot on color alone.

They shine brighter when they are kind spirits who help mortals, her mother told her during one of her first lessons on spirits when she was little.

Throughout her years of training as a Keeper, she had met plenty of spirits who aided her during hunts or training. It had been a spirit of Mercy who taught her how to kill a deer so the creature felt the least amount of pain and fear. A spirit of Rest often drifted around their home when she was just a baby, rocking her crib to help her sleep.

But the one she saw most often was the canary-yellow glow of a Muse spirit. It had helped her hone her skills with a bow, its invisible hand urging her to pull her arrow farther back and give her strike more power than she ever thought she could. It had danced in the garden, showing her where her vegetables were ready for harvest and where she needed to prune the tomato vines.

It was her friend.

She saw that friend again as she tripped through the mountains, its golden essence shimmering as it tried to dodge around a tree but couldn't make the turn in time. It slammed against the trunk, collapsing into a pile of leaves on the forest floor. She ran and quickly dug it out. Its light flickered as it slowly lifted back into the air, its shape morphing and shimmering before her burning eye.

"Muse," she said, relief forcing her shoulders to fall as she sank to the earth in front of it. Her limbs were weak, her eyes heavy with sleep and unshed tears. "Have you seen my kin? Do you know where they are?"

It flickered like a dying fire, churning in on itself like a tidepool ready to collapse. In her scarred eye, she almost pictured the outline of its greater form: arms that shook as it ran nervous hands through tangled hair, and legs that paced before they gave out entirely.

'I have not,' it whispered in her head, its voice ricocheting in her skull. *'The mountains are wrong. So wrong. I cannot find anything that brings joy. No muse for a creative soul. No creative souls at all.'*

She swallowed, terror souring her tongue. "Does that mean everyone in The Divide is—"

Adelaide couldn't say it. Couldn't stomach the words refusing to leave.

'No. They are gone but not gone. I do not know,' it said as it rose to continue its rapid pacing around the tree. *'What is a muse with no one to inspire?'* It crashed into the tree and fell into the leaves before lifting itself up to repeat the same cycle again and again. *'What is a spirit without someone seeing it? How do I be without being?'*

Tears burned down her cheeks as she rose to leave it. The spirit went mad, and there was nothing she could do to save it. It merely cycled through the same questions, never forming an answer which could halt its rapid decay.

Her friend would die like that, tangled up in the leaves, and it would not be the only spirit to meet such a fate.

ADELAIDE HAD no idea when she fell asleep, but she woke with a start to a chorus of blackbirds and skylarks greeting the early morning dawn. She was resting on the grass, the earth softer than she expected as she stifled a yawn.

"Good morning to you too, Adelaide."

She sat up and stared at Sander. His dry tone and pointed brow caused a blush to burn across her cheeks. He was leaning against a tree, his arms folded over his chest and not a hair of his perfectly braided hair out of place.

"How did you catch up to me so fast?" she asked, forcing herself to stand. "And how long have you been watching me sleep on the floor?"

He snorted at her aggravated voice and pushed off the tree. "How about you answer my question first?" he began as he rounded her, circling her like a vulture. "After I've already sworn to Commander Strom to bring you back to town in one piece, how could you betray that trust to gallivant off in the woods?"

"I was looking for my kin."

"Doesn't answer my question," he snapped back as he stopped in front of her, and she caught just the smallest passing look of hurt in his eyes before they cooled to steel. "I gave my word and you made me break it." He tapped her on the chest with a sharp, precise finger. "The human's claim that you are their Promised savior keeps you safe from any who would harm you. I have no such protection, but you risked my life anyways. For what? The slightest chance you'd find your family in just a few hours?"

Guilt burned in her blood, and she struggled to meet his gaze. "I was going to come back once I found them."

"Would that be before or after they had my head?"

Adelaide looked away, guilty tears welling hot and heavy in her eyes. She'd been so focused on finding her family that Sander's fate, left vulnerable and alone on the hill, hadn't even crossed her mind.

"I'm sorry," she whispered, her chest tight. "I just saw the opportunity and took it. I didn't think—" She stopped, unable to continue speaking past the lump in her throat.

"Which is exactly the problem," he sighed as he pulled back, a hand running through his hair and pushing his black hair away from his face. "You overthink this magic of yours until you've convinced yourself it's not real, even when faced with the evidence of its power in every warrior whose life you saved that night. Yet, you cannot spare a thought for your teacher." He shook his head, a tired smile tugging at his lips. "What am I to do with you?"

An embarrassed grin fought its way onto her face. "Forgive me and move on?"

A harsh, barked laugh slipped out of his lips. "We'll see about that." He returned to his spot against the tree, which appeared to be the largest birch she'd ever seen. "For now, I will stop admonishing you. I'm certain the Commander will have enough choice words for you when he fetches you."

She squinted at him, suddenly dizzy as the trees above them seemed to stretch so tall they disappeared into the cloudy skies. "What do you mean?"

His smirk was firmly back in place as he inspected his nails. "Horses move faster than you can run, Adelaide. I merely waited until you passed out from exhaustion to let them know where you were," he chuckled, and she felt the blood drain from her face. "You did give me your consent after all."

"Son-of-a—"

"*Wake up.*"

Adelaide woke with a start, but that time it was due to the gallop of hooves against the forest floor as it rumbled beneath her. It was still night, and the shadows crept around her like the tendrils of dark spirits until the light of torches broke through the bushes, blinding her.

She squinted against the light and the pain in her eye that still fiercely ached. Three horses skid to a halt, their riders wearing matching, furious gazes that somehow still held the smallest vestiges of concern.

Well, two of them seem concerned. Zareen just looks like she wants to kill me.

The other woman leapt from her horse and strode to her in two giant steps. Adelaide couldn't even get a word out before Zareen hauled her to her feet by the collar, choking her as she brought them face to face.

"What in all the realms is wrong with you?" she screamed, spit flying out of her mouth and dotting Adelaide's face. "Fleeing into a spirit-infested mountainside when we haven't even discovered the culprit behind the explosion? If you perish, we're *all* dead!"

Zamir sneaked to his sister's side and yanked her hands away, forcing Adelaide to drop back to the earth from the few inches she'd been lifted to meet the other woman's height. "I know you're angry, but I need to make sure she's not injured," he muttered as he got to work, poking and prodding at her limbs to search for any wounds.

"I was going to come back, but I *need* my family." Her last word was morphed by a hiss of pain as Zamir touched her sore ribs. He scowled up at her as he bent over to weave his healing magic into the muscles and bones she'd overworked. "I can handle myself."

"Oh, is that why you're hurt and sleeping on the floor without any provisions?" she scoffed. "Any number of beasts, spirits, or demented humans could've killed you and we never would've found you. If Sander told anyone else that you escaped or if the news spread through town, there would be calls for your head. Who do you think they would've sent then?"

Knights.

She paled at the idea. It was another thing she hadn't considered. All she'd pictured was reuniting with her family. All other consequences be damned.

"I'm sorry," she said, though the words struggled on their way out from between her clenched teeth. "I was reckless and short-sighted, but what would you do if Zamir were missing?"

"Do *not* bring my brother into this," Zareen snarled as a vein protruded in her forehead. "We already have warriors searching for them, and Karsten swore to find them so long as you helped us. You cannot aid our efforts against the damned if you're dead."

"This is my *home*," she said, throwing her arms out wide and ignoring the way her chest burned from the rapid movement. "I know it better than anyone. I can find my kin and protect my mountains better than anyone. I do not need your warriors to do what I would have already accomplished on my own."

"Then why haven't you?"

The Commander's quiet question caught her off guard, and she froze under his scrutiny. He stood by the horses, their leads in his gloved fists, flexing in his silent anger. His gaze, which was once so warm, was closed off and distant. The cool look he settled her with was enough to silence her aggravation and felt like a cold bucket of water dumped over her head.

"If you could find your family, why aren't they here?" he asked, peering around the clearing she'd collapsed in. "If you could protect the mountains better than our army, why didn't you when The Divide was attacked in the first place?"

Her heart hammered in her ears, and a chill entered her veins like a blizzard. It was an honest question. If she were the great protector she claimed to be, why couldn't she protect the very people and things that mattered most to her?

"Because I'm a *failure*," she answered, her throat closing around the words. "It's what I do." Her eyes drifted between each of them, but she couldn't hold any of their gazes for long, so she stared at the ground instead. "I couldn't protect my home from whoever blew it to pieces. I can't find my kin in the paths I've traveled my whole life, and I don't know if it's because I'm incompetent or because they're *dead*." She tried to blink back the silent tears welling up in her eyes, but that simply freed them to rain down her cheeks. "I'm an elf who can't harness magic for Odin's sake. I'm a Keeper who can't protect those I love from the Knight, even when—"

Her gaze fell on the Commander again, and her words died under his piercing observation of her rambling words.

Silence stretched between them as Zamir finished healing the bruised sections of the ribs she reinjured. There was only the wind and the lapping of water against flesh-ridden stones.

ZAREEN'S DIARY

"My affinity for detecting lies has never failed me before, and yet here I stand—unsure if the slight magic in my veins is even real. I witnessed the aurora that day, but the tales of the Promised were always too grand for me. The Codex claimed so much, it can't all be true.

That doubt made me certain Keeper Aylara was a charlatan and the real culprit behind The Divide's destruction. When we spoke, my magic told me she only told the truth. Does that mean she believes she is innocent but her memory was wiped? Or that my magic is simply waning even from the meager thing it once was? I cannot cast spells or heal like Zamir. I've only had this one thing and it has always been enough. Until now.

Who else would be responsible? No one else survived. Perhaps her family, should they live, will be the ones to blame or have the knowledge we seek. After her escape, my belief that she wasn't who she claimed to be was strong. However, when she cried for her kin, I found myself changed. I do not believe Adelaide Aylara had anything to do with the destruction we witnessed. My magic was right, and real. But if all of that is true, that leaves two questions:

Who really tore the mountains apart? What do they want with the spirits they released from within?"

8

INTO THE DIVIDE

SKALD: KARSTEN STROM

"You'll ride with me," Karsten ordered as he released the other horses to Zamir and Zareen. They went without complaint to their masters, seemingly overjoyed to leave Finn, his black stallion, alone.

The damned horse was his sole companion for years. It was a parting gift from his mother and was just a feeble, sick thing when he left for the Brotherhood. Its weak legs were the only reason his father allowed him to take off with a prized stallion from the stables in the first place.

It was weak, just like him.

Finn thrived under the attention of Rannadal's stablemaster and left the fragility of youthful sickness behind before Karsten was even an adult and formal initiate of the Knights. On that fateful trip, when he dared to return home, his father even tried stealing the horse back from him since he'd grown into such a force on the battlefield.

As if Finn would ever allow that, he thought as he ran absent fingers through the horse's mane to calm its aggravated stomps against the earth.

On their journey to Rannadal, when Karsten was just fourteen years old and never even stepped foot outside his village before, the two struck an accord. Their bond was the envy of all his brothers-in-arms, but it came with its downsides as well.

Like the damn animal feeling everything I do, but he has no boundaries in expressing himself.

If Karsten was angry, Finn would be furious. If his master was sick, the horse nudged his hands until he was forced to pet him or throw a blanket around them both. It was sweet, except for when it gave away his emotions to anyone who knew about their bond.

"You're sure that horse won't just eat me alive the moment I step near?" Keeper Aylara asked as she hesitated, frozen in the same spot they discovered her in The Wild Woods. Grass was tangled in her white hair, and her face was pale in the juxtaposed light of the cool moon and roaring flame of Zamir's torch. "Or that you won't?" she clarified as she gave him a pointed look.

'Oh, we could eat her anytime,' a whispered voice echoed in the back of his mind.

He shook off the annoying thought and set his jaw. "Get on the damn horse, Keeper," he snapped, motioning to the saddle and hating the way she bristled under the command. "*Please,*" he added, hoping his tone sounded softer than it felt leaving his haggard throat.

She took tentative steps towards the stallion, allowing it to sniff her hand before she dared haul herself into the seat. Finn huffed at her weight, throwing his head back in stubborn annoyance even as he allowed her to get comfortable on his back. Over the horse's head, he caught Zamir arching a brow at him in surprise.

Finn doesn't let anyone but me ride him without throwing a tantrum, and that was the least resistance he's ever had to a new rider.

"Not a word," he warned his friend before hoisting himself

into the saddle behind the elf. She froze in front of him, her back so straight he could tell she struggled to maintain her posture, and goosebumps raised across her exposed arms. "Let's just get this over with."

She nodded but barely shifted into a more comfortable position. They weren't touching at all except for the briefest brush of calves, and it prevented him from seeing over her head. He tried to maneuver the horse's reins without touching her, but it was damn near impossible. The others were continuing back to town without them, and he couldn't even get a grip on the lead in the darkness without his brain threatening to burst at every flicker of light from the torch.

His migraine had only worsened with rest, and his self-deprecating thoughts just made the pain worse. He had woken after leaving Sander and Lady Aylara alone to Zareen's frantic shouts that the elf had disappeared.

I'm a fucking idiot, he thought as he massaged his forehead from the building stress and headache making his eyes burn. *Leaving the two elves alone was a foolish idea, but I'd been awake for two days. I wasn't thinking straight.*

"If you wish to yell at me, you might as well do it now like the others already have," Lady Aylara said once they were following the siblings on the path back to Rannadal. "No reason to keep us up once we reach town or start our day tomorrow with a screaming match."

He swallowed the growl trying to well up in his throat at the raging pain her voice conjured. Even the trickling of the distant stream grated on his nerves and pierced into his skull. "Oh, my apologies. I didn't know that I needed to schedule my anger so it was shared at a convenient time for you. Where are my manners?" he snarked back in the same agitated tone she carried.

Her shoulders rose to her pointed ears. "Looks like you *can* show anger! Here I thought the Brotherhood trained all the emotion out of your body. My mistake."

"Would my anger be easier for you to handle?" he questioned, the bite never leaving his voice as his fists tightened on the leather lead. "That way you can paint me in your mind as the evil Knight you wish I was?"

"Yes, actually it would be," she snapped back, her green eye piercing him as she peered at him over her shoulder.

"Fine, have it your way!"

He released the reins and grabbed her hips instead, sliding her on the saddle so her back was flush with his chest. Her scent, lavender and snow, invaded his senses where her hair brushed his lips. She gasped and he sucked in a deep breath as he flexed his fingers, trying to force his bruising grip to lighten their hold. Even if she wished it, he couldn't hurt her.

"Now," he began between his heavy gulps of air. "I can finally see the damn road."

"Oh," she whispered, her body frozen against him in the silence stretching between them. It wasn't until they reached the main road winding through the lowest levels of the mountains that her tense back softened against him. "For what it's worth," she began, her voice so quiet he almost didn't hear it. "I truly am sorry."

He sighed, his migraine still beating at his temples and causing the flame of Zamir's torch in the distance to swim before his eyes. "I'm the fool who didn't see it coming," he grumbled. "You don't wish to be here, I know that. I'm sure you could find your family if given the chance, but this is the hand fate has dealt us. Our only choice is to work together."

"A curse for you, I'm certain." He could practically feel the roll of her eyes.

"Actually, it's not," he said, earning a confused glare as she turned back to look at him as much as the saddle would allow.

"You haven't been cruel or unreasonable. You only asked us to find your family, even when we've asked so much of you. Thus far, I've failed to uphold my end of our bargain." He searched her gaze, his amber pinning her emerald in place. "You could've demanded far more, and we would have agreed. You could be cruel, using people's faith against them. You've done none of that." He tightened his hands on the reins to stop his urge to brush a strand of white hair from its place stuck on her cheek. "If you're a failure, perhaps we both are."

He could feel her stare at him, but he couldn't meet her gaze as he directed Finn through the mountains. It was only once the ground grew steep beneath them that she turned around, gripping the saddle between her legs to stay in place. The cliffside stood to their right, and Finn's hooves were unstable on the stones.

A few rocks slipped out from beneath them, cascading down the mountains and breaking apart on the journey.

His hand fell on her waist instinctually, holding her in place as Finn shared his fear with a scared neigh. "I've got you," he murmured as they descended, although he wasn't sure if he was speaking to the woman in his grasp or the horse beneath them.

Once they landed back on flat earth, all three of them seemed to sigh in relief. He went to release his grasp of her and return it to the reins, but something cut him. He hissed in pain and pulled back, staring in the dim light as a trickle of blood welled up on his exposed wrist.

Some half-formed excuse tried to fall from her lips, but she couldn't get it out before his instincts kicked in. His hand returned to the same spot, sneaking beneath her tunic and finding the shape of the blade hidden there. She sucked in a harsh breath, no doubt from the cold texture of his gloves, as he pulled it free and stared at it in the moonlight.

"Is this a *kitchen knife*?" he questioned as he blinked dumbly at the serrated edges.

"Uh, *no*?" she lied.

He huffed and bit his lip to hide his bemused grin as he turned the blade around so he held it by the handle. "What am I going to do with you?" he asked as he sent the blade careening through the air. It landed in the trunk of a tree, sticking out like a dart on a board.

"Let me go so I can find my family in peace?" she asked with a pretty flutter of her lashes. When he questioned Sander about how the other elf escaped, he imagined she manipulated the man with the same technique. He'd thought Sander was a dense fool for falling for such tricks.

But by the Gods, if I were in Sander's shoes, it would've worked on me too.

"Nice try."

KARSTEN BARELY SLEPT between their return to Rannadal in the middle of the night and the call from the Jarl to gather their leadership as soon as dawn broke, but that was nothing new to him. He would rather remain awake, battling the real spirits of the damned, than fight off the ones lingering in his dreams.

"She's not strong enough yet," he said, his fist slamming into the table in the center of the longhouse. It shook the tankards littering its surface, and he just hoped they would hide the trembling of his own palms. "If you want our only hope of controlling these spirits to die for your foolish impatience, then be my guest. Throw her life away on a whim, a mere *hunch*."

Lefa sighed, holding her elegantly adorned arms across her

chest. "She seemed fine enough to escape yesterday, did she not?"

Zamir scoffed, "And reinjure herself in the process."

The Jarl arched a brow. "Sander assures me he can train her to use her powers whilst traveling to the epicenter of The Divide's destruction. There's no use coddling her. Our village will not give her strength any more than the road to the mountains will." She sighed as her fingers moved to massage her temples. "Besides, if that is where she wishes to be, we should give her a taste of what we're protecting her from. Perhaps then she'll understand why we're having such an issue tracking down her family."

"I can attest that her strength has greatly improved," Zareen said, her arms carefully folded behind her back. "And my brother will be accompanying us. Should she need further medical attention, he won't be far, so I see no reason to delay."

Sister Ylwa scribbled something down on a piece of parchment and peered at Karsten from under her lashes. "One would think *you* of all people would be insistent on her entering the fray. Is it not your men who are dying in troves while we wait for her to gain her strength?"

The Jarl grinned. "Yes, that's curious."

Someone cleared their throat from the doorway, making him jump as they turned their attention to the intruder.

Lady Aylara stood at the threshold, the early dawn's light giving her an unearthly glow. It haloed her white, freshly washed hair lying in wet curls around her face. Despite himself, he couldn't deny how stunning she appeared even as the light outside burned his eyes. He had to look away even when everything screamed at him to keep drinking in her gorgeous form that was too close, yet not close enough. He pinched the bridge of his nose, taking a heavy breath to calm the racing thoughts and searing pain rampaging his head.

"If people are still dying, there's no reason to delay," she said, striding into the longhouse and stopping once she reached the table.

Between them, spread across the wood, was a crude map of the valley below the mountains. It stretched from the farmland to the seas, over the vast fjords and twisting lands dotted with other kingdoms and villages of all sizes. Then it reached the distant islands off the coast and all the way in the opposite direction, meeting the deserts of The South, where he'd only ever heard about from Zamir and Zareen.

She touched the place on the map where her home once was, the same area they had watched her float from the heavens. A black star smudged the page, marking where the destruction lay.

Karsten couldn't imagine what was going on behind her eyes, which wavered on every bend in the marked roads and sketch of twirling birches on the parchment. The way she spoke of her family, the few times she dared, hinted at a home full of warmth and love that was gone forever: broken at the bottom of the mountains. He hadn't been back to the front lines since that night and he was so disoriented by the blood, smoke, and heat of the fires that he hardly remembered what it looked like in person.

But if she went, what would she see? Where he saw burning trees, would she see the branches she climbed as a child? Where his men hadn't found any bodies in the charred remnants of her home, would she discover the evidence of their demise that only she could discern?

Had his men made a mistake in their identification of the dead, and would she find them all tangled up in the muck, hidden beneath the decaying carcasses of all the brave souls who held the spirits back? Or would she discover nothing but the ash-filled winds, with no evidence her clan ever existed?

And which outcome would be worse?

"The destruction of The Divide has already taken too much from too many," Lefa said, breaking up the silence settling across the grand hall as Lady Aylara inspected the map. "Sander believes that, with the proper training, you should be able to heal the tear in the mountains entirely and pause the influx of spirits escaping. He doubts you can accomplish such a feat now, but there's still a chance you could slow the tide—as you did the night we found you."

"How exactly did I do it last time?" she asked, removing her finger from where it was delicately tracing the star. Her fingertip came back black with ink—*tainted.*

"That's what we would all like to know," she said with a shrug. "Sander claims to have ideas, but nothing that can be solidified until your training resumes."

"Without interruptions from you fleeing," Zareen said with a glare.

The elf's upper lip curled back into a sneer. "That's your entire plan then? I train on the way to the mountains and hope for the best once I get there?"

Ylwa snickered. "According to the stories, you were practically unconscious when you stopped the flow of spirits the first time. I imagine with training and a good night's rest, this shouldn't be too difficult for you."

Zamir rolled his eyes. "If you fully believe those stories, then you know she was also possessed by Olena when that happened. Unless you're planning to mastermind further divine intervention, we shouldn't expect anything to be so easy."

"Of course not," Karsten murmured before he cleared his throat, his faith in his Goddess mixing with the unease he felt whenever he dared to meet Lady Aylara's piercing gaze. He'd asked for a sign to renew the faith he felt when he saw her descend the mountains, lit by the aurora, and it had been granted to him on the training field. He wouldn't let that falter, even after her escape. "However, there are signs something divine has interfered with our mission. No matter what Gods you follow, something desires our success. We should take care to remember that."

Her silver brows rose in surprise, her pink lips parting to release a sudden breath, and she nodded in agreement. "Yes, well—" She stopped to clear her throat too. "After The Divide is sealed and my kin are found, what *is* your mission exactly?"

The Jarl arched a brow. "I thought you had no intention of staying beyond your agreement?"

She shrugged. "I need to know if my family will be safe when we return home. We cannot allow what happened at The Divide to transpire again."

Ylwa grinned. "*We*, hm?"

The elf glared at the other woman. "*Silence*."

"If you must know," Lefa hummed as she tapped a sharp nail against her painted red lips, "we've heard whispers of strange happenings across The North. People of every faction acting strangely."

"The spirits," Lady Aylara whispered.

The other woman shared a grim smile. "We've been focused on the spirits in their physical form since that's the only time a blade can hurt them. We don't have many magic users in Rannadal and they're needed as our last line of defense, so we've been allowing the others to slip through the cracks. They could be possessing anyone, anywhere. Even here."

They stood in silence for a long, heavy moment. With so many spirits spilling forth, the number of possessions reported by the Brotherhood grew tenfold. The proof was strewn across his desk between lists of the dead, missives from scouts discovering the possessed running rampant in the woods, and letters from other Jarls across The North who sought aid for their citizens who succumbed to the whispers of the spirits.

Was that the goal of whomever caused The Divide to crumble? To sow disorder across the map as Saint Zelmar, the patron of the Chaos God Cismir, once did.

Such mayhem led to Alfheim's fall. We cannot allow history to repeat itself.

"Rannadal's Vikings should be returning soon," Karsten said as he shook off the dark turn of his thoughts. "Hopefully, only a few remained to start the new settlement and the majority believe you were sent by The Old Gods. Their faith in Odin could make them your greatest ally or your worst nightmare," he explained as he suppressed a slight shudder at the mere idea of the Vikings turning their blades against her. "Once they've returned, I can arrange for our full forces to investigate these cities with rumors of possessions. Hopefully, we can free anyone from corruption. If not—" He trailed off, his eyes pinned on the floor.

"Then that's what the Vikings are for," Ylwa finished, a little too cheerfully.

"You'll organize the Vikings and the Knights into one force?" Lady Aylara wondered with an uneasy shift of her weight from foot to foot. She was putting on a brave face, but he could still sense her fear from across the table.

When our people are blended into one army, she won't be able to tell the difference between a Viking and a Knight.

He gave a brisk nod. "I organize all forces within our land and three, soon to be four, settlements. Whether that be Vikings, Shieldmaidens" — he paused to nod at Zareen — "Berserkers, Knights, guards, witches" — he paused again to motion to Zamir — "or our newly recruited warriors. They each have their own individual leaders but they all report to me —at least to some degree. It ensures we don't accidentally settle the same area or commit violence against our own."

"It also strengthens our town tenfold," Lefa continued. "If we are attacked, we have several armies at our disposal blended into one singular force. No others in The North operate like we do. That difference allows us to remain independent from larger kingdoms. We may be small, but we aren't easily defeated."

"Which is why we've been tasked by the surrounding towns with protecting everyone in the valley from the spirits," Ylwa added. "We are the only ones who can," she said, her voice far softer and sadder than Karsten expected from her.

When said aloud, the weight of their monumental task bore down on his shoulders. If Rannadal fell beneath the onslaught of the spirits, they would be the first of many. The damned would start with the small farming villages, much like the one he grew up in, and the possessed would spread their chaos further into neighboring kingdoms until it conquered the entire north.

Perhaps that was when it would be stopped. Other regions of the world were more developed, with stronger armies and ancient magic, but what would remain of The North? Not much, if the local völva's visions were to be believed.

He peered around at their faces, all worn, except for Lady Aylara's. She had yet to review the reports of the dead or see the bodies lining the mountains she once called home. There was still a sense of hope she radiated that was thoroughly beat out of him years ago, long before The Divide was torn asunder.

"Well then," she began with a smirk. "Let's get started."

As Lady Aylara's personal guard, Karsten was dragged on the journey to The Divide alongside the bickering siblings, the fascinating but strange elf named Sander, and the woman who, unbeknownst to her, captivated him.

Adelaide.

In the weeks since he'd first dragged her limp and bloodied body out of the mountains, she had healed to the point where it seemed like she was never injured in the first place. Except for the scar puckering the skin over her left eye anyway. Zamir swore it would heal, with time, but wouldn't ever truly fade.

She hid it with her hair most days while in town, her white locks obscuring the damage whenever she passed a watchful gaze or any reflective surface. He wondered if she thought it hideous. Although the idea of anything about her, aside from her attitude towards him, being *hideous* seemed outrageous to him. Even when she was caked in blood or muck, she still drew his eye like no other could.

He tried to resist his admiration for her in the days leading into autumn—he truly did. At every corner of his vision, he seemed to find her white hair shining bright in the fading sunlight or the color of her piercing eyes transforming from a grassy field into hardened emerald. He told himself it was merely concern for her wellbeing, since she was so recently bedridden and on the edge of death, but he could taste the lie before he ever even said the words.

Karsten found her irresistibly beautiful.

From the pucker of her cherry-colored lips to the sway of her wide hips beneath her smaller waist, she was stunning. Even with her scowl permanently in place at the mere sight of him or any other inconvenience, she remained a sight for sore, tired eyes like his. Maybe he was a masochist for enjoying her displeasure at his company when he was still so thrilled to see her every time, but somehow their back-and-forth routine soothed him. It was an expected part of his day. He could rely on it when he relied on so little else.

But she *hated* him.

He imagined that, if she knew of such thoughts circling his mind, she would pluck them out and squash them right before his eyes. He knew that. So, he kept them tucked close to his chest where no one could see them. If he wished to see her, he allowed himself to scan the horizon instead of picking her out of their caravan on their trek to the mountains. He would not make her uncomfortable with affections or sentiments she surely didn't share.

Besides, there's no future there. She'll be gone soon, back home where she'll be safe.

As much as he admired her strength and found her a pretty sight to behold, there was far too much animosity on her end, too much damage on his, and years of history as Keeper and Knight that would forever divide them. He would be lucky if she even considered him a friend.

Yes, a friend. That, I might be able to do.

Their brief moments of calm and—dare he say *pleasant*—exchanges made him believe at least that could be possible. He could be an excellent advisor on battle tactics, an extra sword between her and danger, and a person to converse with when the day weighed too heavy. That was all he could ever be. It was more than he deserved. More than he could ask of her.

So, why does it still not feel like enough?

"DIG DEEP INTO YOUR CORE. Imagine the spirit beckoning forward," Sander said, his cool and collected voice carrying on the wind until Karsten could hear it.

The two elves were huddled together, perched on two stones beside the river flowing downstream towards Rannadal from the mountains. Briefly, he wondered if Lady Aylara's fierce gaze pinned on the rippling water was just her considering sending a rescue note downstream to Lefa.

Her training sessions certainly haven't been smooth sailing.

"You're almost there," Sander said, his fists clasped in anticipation, his knuckles turning white as he leaned closer to her.

Karsten turned to continue readjusting Finn's saddle, but froze when he heard her splash an angry boot through the water. "Enough!" she snapped.

He resisted the urge to turn at the venom in her voice. It was as if he expected any malice-filled words that fell from her lips to be meant for him.

At least someone else is finally feeling her wrath.

"This clearly isn't working," she grumbled.

The noise brought Zamir and Zareen from the clearing they camped in for the night. They were on the third day of their trip back to The Divide, having taken longer so the larger group of Knights and guards trailing behind them could keep up. They'd be exchanged with the warriors already posted at The Divide.

Normally, they'd have ridden with them, but Lady Aylara refused to be surrounded by so many of the Brotherhood. He'd agreed with the sentiment since she'd be training with her newfound abilities and already understood having such a large, curious audience wouldn't help matters. If it weren't for that, it would've only been a day and a half's ride to the decimated region of the mountains.

No, instead they had three *long* days of continuous effort that remained fruitless.

"Is everything alright?" Zamir asked, the man having the audacity to seem genuinely concerned for the first time in the many years Karsten knew him. Concern wasn't an emotion either of the siblings bore well. They didn't seem to be built for it, unless it was for one another.

"Adelaide is merely frustrated at her progress, which is understandable given the time constraint and pressure she's under," Sander answered, making Adelaide's lips screw down into a scowl as her eyes sank daggers into the back of his head.

You shouldn't have answered for her. She hates that.

A harsh laugh ripped from her chest. She wore a deep, long pit into the moist earth as she paced. "You say that like you're explaining why a child is throwing a tantrum. As if I don't fully know what I am and am *not* capable of, and I *know* I don't have magic."

Zamir held up a placating hand. "I can see how you still have doubts, but you cannot disavow the testimony of hundreds of people who saw what you did."

"They also claim it's some holy intervention." Her voice was getting louder and her face redder with each word. Karsten hadn't seen her that mad before, not even at him. "So, which is it? Do I have some never-before-seen abilities so elusive even *I* can't feel them or did your Goddess use me to save your warriors in a once-in-a-lifetime opportunity? Because it cannot be both."

"And why is that?" Zareen asked with a curious tilt to her head.

"Because that would make me someone holy in your eyes, and that's clearly something I'm not. If I'm not a vessel for your Goddess or a witch with an incredible, hidden power, then what am I?" They were all silent at that question, none of them seeming to have an answer for her. None that would pacify her, at least. "You were all wrong about me. There's no magic. There *never* was."

She choked on the last few words and turned her back on them before she rushed down the edge of the bank, splattering mud around her as she took off in the opposite direction.

"We cannot afford any delays in her training. We're only a day's ride from the mountains," Sander said, his thick brows pinched tight over his hazy grey eyes. Sometimes, they seemed to have the whole world hidden in that foggy gaze. Other times, it felt empty, like a barren landscape begging for life. "Shall I speak with her?"

Zamir shook his head. "She yelled at all of us and you in particular. Let Golden Boy take care of it this time."

Karsten cringed at the nickname.

His sister scoffed. "As if she doesn't already spend most of her time yelling at him anyway."

Zamir smirked back. "Hopefully that means she'll be too worn out from screaming at him and will be too tired to continue her tirade on us."

Karsten finally finished adjusting Finn's harness. He hoped that would keep the poor horse from chaffing for the last leg of their ride. "I don't like being used as a pawn," he said with a frustrated huff.

"And yet you always do as I ask anyways," Zamir said, his lips pulled back in a too-wide grin as he intently watched his friend cross the river in the direction the elf disappeared in.

Karsten elected to ignore the others as he descended into the small gorge the river carved out of the hills. Water seeped into his boots until he made his way onto the other side, back on damp land that was moist and fertile so near to the stream. Even with the early freeze threatening the land, tiny sprigs popped to life as if it were spring.

"Keeper Aylara?" he called into the forest, his own voice the only answer he received as it echoed back to him. The tall trees shadowed the worn path before him, blanketing the woods in shadows even under the rising sun. "Lady Aylara?"

Still, nothing.

Panic rose in him as he spun to check each diverging path in the woods. She was a Keeper; she knew how to survive in the woods better than anyone. But even a skilled traveler could get lost in unfamiliar lands when in distress. They weren't in The Wild Woods yet. She might not know her way.

If they lost her now, what would they do?

His warriors would keep dying. When the Vikings returned, they would fall just the same. All those brothers- and sisters-in-arms would be fodder for the spirits until a real solution was found. With her gone, what other option was there? They'd be picked off one by one unless another mysterious woman with the same ability to challenge the spirits dropped into their hands.

He knew his Goddess Olena was giving, but not that much.

If one was presented with a miracle, proof of divinity wrapped in a rather beautiful package, it needed to be treasured. It needed to be protected. He'd done that so far, to the best of his ability, but had he done enough? He'd warned Sister Gorm to stay away from her, defended her name against the citizens of Rannadal who questioned her innocence, trained her so she could protect herself when he could not, but would it ever be enough?

Would there ever be a time when he didn't fear for her?

And if he were ever lucky enough to call her a friend, would the fear only grow? Would it devour him? He couldn't afford such distractions when so many lives were at stake.

But a selfish part of him wanted to be consumed by her entirely.

"Get lost?" she suddenly asked from his right side.

He nearly jumped but held himself still at the last moment.

Best not to let her think Rannadal's Commander is a complete fool.

"I was more worried for your sake," he said. In response, she settled him with an expression he was fully aware meant that she thought him an idiot regardless. "I know it's foolish, but there is a lot at stake. I wouldn't blame you for being so distracted you got lost or running away again."

She leaned against the nearest pine and crossed her arms over her chest. "I know now that I cannot leave until your men find my family. I was just searching for them again myself, but I couldn't see anything even from atop the trees." A flash of that heartbroken expression she'd worn when her voice broke returned before she tucked it away. "And if these powers don't exist and I cannot help, I know our deal is off. On my own, it's unlikely I would find them with the mountains so infested by spirits."

Her gaze turned to steel as she pinned her attention across the path, on a rotting stump that couldn't be as interesting as her focused eyes made it appear. That's when he realized she wasn't angry, not truly. She was overflowing with sorrow and refused to show even an ounce of it. If she took her focus away from her anger, her eyes would turn from hardened steel to a watery pool of heavy tears. She loved her family more than anything. That was abundantly clear.

But he didn't think she loved herself at all and he thought that was a shame.

"Our deal will remain, even if your part in it is altered," he said, earning a confused glance from her that snapped the steel of her gaze in half. If he looked hard enough, he could start to see the cracks in the armor she'd built around herself. "So long as you try your hardest, you will continue to receive assistance in the search for your family. You have my word."

Her lip trembled slightly as it lifted into a smile. "Thank you, Commander."

He shrugged off her thanks and gestured back to the path he'd taken to find her. "Shall we head back? I wouldn't want them to fret."

"I need a moment if that's alright. If you must, you may stay to keep watch. I simply don't want to—" She trailed off, seeming puzzled by her own reluctance to return.

"You don't want to return to their expectations yet," he said, a fond smile tugging at his lips as understanding dawned in her eyes. "I understand that far too well, but I imagine your situation to be more troubling. After being thrown into this conflict by no fault of your own and being hailed as a messenger from a religion you don't belong to, it must weigh on you."

"Yes, it's exactly that," she sighed and mussed her hair, her fingers curling in the white strands until she could massage the scalp beneath. "But it's also the magic. I was the only elf my mother ever knew without a single drop of magical blood." She paused and pinned her gaze on the forest floor. "I *disappointed* her."

He shook his head. "I may not know the head of the Aylara clan, but I don't see how you could be a disappointment to anyone, least of all a family you obviously care for more than anything. But, regardless, her expectations for you seem to be just as troublesome as the ones Lefa has placed on your shoulders."

She nodded. "She always said she waited eons for me, whatever that's supposed to mean. Even though I was one of the youngest, I was always meant to inherit the homestead and full duties of Keeper. It was never fair to my siblings, but they didn't seem bothered by it. When I see them again, I'll need to ask if they ever felt the lack of expectations to be just as burdensome."

He huffed a quiet laugh as he thought back to his own childhood. "I can assure you it's not a kind place to be. It feels as though no one believes in you. For some, that's a blessing. For others, a curse." He coughed to cover the thick feeling building in his throat and sat atop the chopped tree trunk, his feet pointed towards the rays of sun slipping through the trees to dry his boots. "Do your siblings and mother have magic?"

"Of course," she scoffed. "They were all incredibly talented with magic and specialized in the most wonderful practices: water weaving, shadow work, healing, and shapeshifting." She bit her lip, and he tried not to stare too hard at the puckering of pink beneath her teeth. "I admit, I was always jealous. When everyone said I had abilities that controlled the spirits and manifested the Bifrost, I wanted to believe it."

"*Adelaide*," he said, his warm voice tripping over her name leaving his lips for the first time and forcing the full weight of her gaze onto him. "The magic lies within you. I know it."

A sigh of relief slipped free as she closed her eyes and let her head fall back against the tree. Her neck was long and exposed as she stared at the canopy above. "So much of me wants to believe, but even more of me wants to call you a liar." She swallowed and clenched her jaw, allowing him to follow the trail of veins caressing either side of her neck. "Why can't you be a horrid person? Why can't you still be a liar? It would make it so much easier to hate you."

He huffed. "Or you can simply *not* hate me."

"I fear that may be even harder."

"And why is that?" he dared to ask. As soon as the words left his mouth, he held his breath and froze, as if any movement or sound would scare her off. That afternoon, she seemed resolute in her swaying back and forth between tolerating his presence and wishing him dead.

Karsten had no idea which version of her those words would conjure.

Her eyes peeled open and drank him in. At the same time, he swam in their endless depths like a man drowning in an emerald sea. Her brows furrowed and, for the first time, he noticed how they were a touch darker than the hair on her head. Her lashes grew out even darker, bold against the sun-kissed, reddish hue spreading across her cheeks throughout their march.

He imagined how burned she'd be in the valley during summer and briefly wondered if she'd ever even been sunburned before. In the mountains, under the thick entwined branches, it was hard to imagine much sunlight reaching the forest floor at all.

"Because hating you is easier than admitting I may be wrong," she said, her voice feather-light against the growing, cool breeze settling over the woods. If he didn't provide her with his full attention, he felt as though she would drift off into the fading light and never return. "But if I've been wrong about your kind for so long, then I cannot justify my own actions. That would mean my guilt would only grow until it's a monster consuming me, bit by bit, until there is nothing left for my kin to find." She finally dropped her gaze and it was like she'd lifted a spell on him. "I cannot allow that."

"You've killed Knights before, haven't you?" he asked, his words slowly falling out as he worked to render each syllable without any ounce of judgment. She was finally opening up to him, finally being honest about why she'd changed her opinion of him so swiftly.

He would *not* hinder that progress.

Besides, he had plenty of blood on his hands he wasn't proud of—blood belonging to her people no less. She could sense it; he was sure of that. It was a wedge between them that could never be properly dissolved. They'd both grown and realized the error of their ways, had they not? If they hadn't, they wouldn't be speaking so quietly to one another, alone in strange woods.

Right?

"Yes," she admitted with her eyes pinched closed. "And now all I can think of is the kindness you've shown me whenever I imagine their bodies crumbled up in the dirt. You show me how to wield a sword and I think, what if the others were like him? What if they didn't deserve death? It's tearing me apart." She snapped her eyes open and pinned them on him, her fierceness returning to its full glory. "I must hate you and pretend your kindness is a charade. If I don't, I will falter. We cannot afford that kind of mistake."

If she were uttering such words to him a decade prior, he

would've loathed her. If he were still chained by the Brotherhood's indoctrination, he would've been honor-bound to kill her for slaying his brothers. If he were still under the influence of everything they'd done, said, and *given* him, he would've cut her down of his own volition.

He should've hated her, but he didn't.

Useless words he knew held no meaning clawed their way up his throat. He wanted to tell her things would be okay and she did what she needed to do. He knew the Brotherhood was corrupt, he just hadn't seen it until it was too late.

Most probably died by her hand for good reason,, but there was still enough guilt in her eyes that he knew that wasn't the full story. She'd killed good people just for wearing the armor of a faction he once belonged to. He couldn't lie to her and pretend otherwise.

She's right. It would be so much easier to hate her.

Goddess, why can't I hate her?

His fingers twitched as he held them out towards her, arching his brow in question. She hesitated before placing her hand over his. He clasped his other hand on top, caging it in.

"Thank you for telling me, Keeper Aylara. I had to go through a similar journey not long ago when I left the Brotherhood," he explained, and her eyes lit up with realization. With those simple words, she knew for certain that Keeper blood covered his hands, and yet she didn't pull her own away. "I do not fault you for it. If hating me makes any of this easier on you, then so be it. But that doesn't mean I won't stop showing you the kindness you deserve."

No, he couldn't hate her. Not even if he tried.

But he'd let her hate him if that's what she needed.

Her mouth opened and he remained glued to whatever would pass from her mesmerizing lips. The words she planned to say were stolen by the crunching of boots behind them. He dropped her hands and stood, a blush burning across his cheeks as he realized just how close they'd been.

She grabbed at yet another kitchen knife stored beneath her tunic, and he rolled his eyes as he plucked it from her hand. "I know the sound of that fool tripping through the woods."

Zamir popped out from around the bend in the path and scowled. "I take offense to that."

"What's more offensive is you feeling the need to spy—and doing it so poorly too. I trained you better than this," he responded.

The other man scoffed as he leaned heavily against an oak. "Spying isn't in my arsenal, my dear friend. Eavesdropping? Perhaps, but that's for me and the trees to decide."

She sighed as she pushed past Zamir, returning to the worn path weaving back to their camp. "Humans are so strange," she grumbled under her breath.

"You know we can hear you, right?" Karsten asked.

"Oh, I know," she said, a grin in her voice that she didn't bless him with a view of.

That woman shall be the death of me.

It was Zareen's turn to prepare supper that evening, and Karsten thanked his Goddess out loud when her attempt at a stew came out edible. After traveling on horseback for days, their only reprieve the occasional meal and magical training session for the elves, his stomach growled fiercely and his temples throbbed.

He grabbed a bowl from his friend and passed it to Lady Aylara, who stared at the stew with a sneer. "She didn't poison it, right?"

Zareen scoffed as she filled another bowl full of brown sludge barely passing for food but remained one of her better dishes. "Don't tempt me, Keeper."

She took the food with a grimace.

Evening was already settling over the world, the moon and campfire the only sources of light beating back the shadows. Their bedrolls were laid out, the horses tended to, and the rotations for night watch were already set. It was a quiet night, as were most of their evenings on the trip once their bellies were full, but something still itched beneath his skin.

Out of the corner of his eye, he caught the faintest glint of silver.

Lady Aylara carved at a loaf of bread, shearing off a piece before slathering it in butter and popping a chunk into her mouth. That glint of metal remained in hand even after she was done with it. He pretended like he wasn't paying attention, just to see what would happen.

She shoved the knife up her sleeve.

"You've got to be—" He cut himself off with a groan as he forced himself to his feet and strode to where she sat on the other side of the fire. She innocently peered up at him as if she had no idea why he was holding his hand out. "Knife, *now*."

"Fine," she sighed as the knife slid back out of her sleeve. How she didn't cut herself with the countless kitchen knives she'd managed to sneak into her clothes, he would never know. "You all will have to trust me with a weapon eventually."

Zamir snorted around a mouthful of stew. "Might've done that earlier if you hadn't stolen my sister's dagger."

The other woman grunted in agreement.

She opened her mouth, no doubt to give her own snark retort, but a rumble in the earth silenced their banter and sent his heart lodging into his throat. They stilled, and his gaze focused on the road they'd come from. Torches lined the path as horses beat their hooves into the dirt.

"It's our warriors," Zareen said as she stood, dinner long forgotten.

His gaze dropped to the elf before him as her face paled and her grip on her bowl tightened until her knuckles were white. There was a reason he had their small group travel in front of the others. It ensured the Knights in their numbers stayed far away from her and didn't bring that panicked look to her eyes.

"Here," he said, offering the knife back to her. "Just for now."

She nodded and silently accepted the meager weapon she hid back in her sleeve.

"Report, now," he ordered as he marched to the first riders who stopped in their clearing. His third in command, Sir Beiner, dismounted and removed his helmet to reveal his ashen expression covered in sweat and blood. "What happened?"

"A fear spirit surprised us on the road," he explained as he waved at the back of their group. A few men stepped forward, hauling a cart with the injured. No order needed to be given, they knew the procedure already, and he saw out of the corner of his eye as Zamir rushed to begin healing. "I know we were ordered to keep our distance, but none of the men feel confident traveling separately after that."

He ran a hand through his hair, guilt swimming in his gut as the cries of the three on the cart reached his ears. If he hadn't separated from them, perhaps he could've made a difference. "Understood, you made the right call," he said as he clamped the man on the shoulder. "Let's do what we can for them now. Did you kill the spirit?"

"Of course," he said with a nod. "But that spirit shouldn't have been there, sir. Our scouts said the manifested entities were heading west instead."

"Clearly, our intelligence isn't as accurate as we'd like." He pointed to the far side of the clearing. It was big enough for the additional warriors to rest, but it would be a tight fit. "Set up camp and do what you can to get some rest. This is only the beginning. The closer we get to The Divide, the worse it will be."

A shout tore his attention to the cart of injured warriors. There were three of them, two men and a woman, covered in blood and blindly flailing their arms at monsters that weren't real. Zamir was above one of them, his hands pressing on a wound to stop the steady flow of blood seeping between his fingers.

But that shout wasn't from any of the injured.

"Back away," one of his warriors screamed in warning at Sander, who stood frozen by the cart. "We don't want your help, elf!"

Sander blew out a harsh, heavy breath as his gaze flitted back and forth between the man and the injured woman on the cart. "I can help and she obviously needs it."

"No one asked for you, so step away," the warrior warned, his teeth bared and his grip on his sword shaking.

Karsten stepped between them, his hand on the man's shoulder to keep him at bay as someone else squeezed in close at the same moment. He blinked in surprise as Lady Aylara gripped Sander's arm to pull him back.

"Enough!" Karsten snapped at his man, who bristled and stood straight at the admonishment. "You are in no position to deny someone else's medical treatment because of your own asinine ideas about who is worthy of delivering aid." He nodded at Sander. "Please, do what you can."

He gave no response but immediately went to work. His magic ebbed and flowed behind him, pulsing white beside the flowing green energy of Zamir's power. It glowed through the night, stinging his eyes.

"Why are you still here?" the man asked, his dark tone dragging Karsten's attention back to the warrior as he hovered over

Lady Aylara. "If you can't save us, return to the mountains where you belong."

She snorted up at him. "Believe me, I've tried."

He spit on the ground at her feet. "Some Promised you are."

"I've never claimed such a title, and I have no idea if I can help, but it seems like you wouldn't even accept it if I could," she said with a shrug before her gaze drifted across the man's pristine armor, not a drop of blood in sight. "Now, are you going to keep being as useless as you seem to be in a fight or are you going to fetch the water they'll need to clean those wounds like a good boy?"

"You son-of-a-bitch."

Karsten caught his fist before it could strike, his hand on his other shoulder forcing him to turn away from the woman whom he towered over and was almost twice the size of. "You heard The Promised, get to work," he ordered as he shoved him in the opposite direction.

He gawked, his large eyes darting back and forth between him and the elf before he shrunk under Karsten's murderous glare.

"I'm surprised, Commander," Lady Aylara murmured at his side, forcing his gaze to pin back on her as she stared up at him with those large emerald eyes that could swallow the whole world. "That you would stand between me and your men, all for my benefit," she explained in a quiet voice.

"Ignore him," he said with a sigh, relief coursing through him as he heard the cries of the injured begin to slow as the healing magic took hold. "If I remember correctly, he's a Knight with a track record of cruel words without any follow through." He leaned over a bit, a grin tugging on his lips. "You assessed him perfectly. Good with unimportant tasks but horrid on the battlefield. I once caught him crying in the barracks after a poor first date."

She bit her lip to subdue the laugh trying to escape. "I

suppose Knights aren't as scary as I thought they'd be," she said as she peered back up at him.

His grin fell and something dark, old, and horrid twisted in his gut. "They can be," he whispered, his words earning him a confused glance from the elf in front of him. "Never forget that, Lady Aylara." He couldn't stomach the puzzled, anxious look in her eyes, so he marched across camp to ensure each of his warriors knew to keep their distance.

The next time someone threatens her, I will not be so kind.

SETTLEMENTS OF JARL LEFA THURSTAN

Rannadal: Headquarters of The Covenant and old refuge of The Knights of The Divide.

Krossdalr: City across The Northern Sea, near The Isles, settled by Thurstan the Cruel.

Skagi: Trading village beside The Divide, known for The Whispering Maiden Tavern.

Thuralla: The newest settlement, connecting The North to The Southern Kingdoms.

9

A HOME SO BROKEN

SKALD: ADELAIDE AYLARA

Despite her ceaseless attempts, not a single flicker of magic coursed through Adelaide's veins on their final day of travel.

The others believed she could do it. She could tell by their hopeful expressions before they uttered a single word of encouragement. That should've filled her with resolve, but it only made her feel worse. She was failing them, just as she'd done with her own kin. If the threats at The Divide continued to grow, perhaps she'd let the entirety of The North down in the process.

Knowing how the spirits worked, that would most certainly be the case.

They made their final stop at the small village of Skagi just below the mountain. According to Zareen, they'd forged the town into their primary post to rotate out their warriors who kept the spirits at bay. Some still slipped through the cracks, so most of the townspeople fled, and it was primarily occupied by warriors instead of the usual citizens. Still, a few brave souls remained.

As soon as they entered the gates into town, the

Commander barked orders at the nearest warriors and received updates on the forces stationed in the mountains. She could tell by the color sinking away from his cheeks that whatever news he'd gained from the parchment in his gloved hands wasn't promising.

"Five more people dead in a fortnight." His voice was forged from steel, unyielding in its rage and slicing straight through the air like a knife. She knew he wasn't directing such a venomous tone at her, but it still raised the hair on the back of her neck.

His gaze slipped from the parchment to her, and his eyes softened. Normally, a look like that from anyone would assure her that she wasn't the intended target of someone's ire. His pinched eyes dropped to the earth, and his shoulders fell. No, he wasn't angry with her.

He was *disappointed.*

Somehow, that felt far worse.

A childish part of her wanted to throw her hands in the air and inform everyone who could hear that she was right. There was no way in all nine realms she could stop the pending deaths, which would grow past the five lost prior to their arrival. Most of her just felt as he did: *disappointed* she wasn't what they needed.

The bitter churning of guilt forced bile to rise in her throat. She coughed it back down but still couldn't rid the ache traveling from her stomach straight up to her heart.

Mother was always disappointed. If she's already dead, did I disappoint her then too? Was she hoping I'd come save her and I never did? Is that my legacy in the Aylara clan? To be expected for so much only to always fall short?

Zamir laid a heavy hand on her shoulder as he passed, dragging her from the morbid turn of her thoughts. He beckoned her deeper into town with the smallest smile. "Let's get you settled before they throw you to the wolves."

He led her down a side street that opened into what once must've been a beautiful, sprawling garden overflowing with roses. In the quickly approaching winter that brought crisp air and bloodshed, it was a wasteland of dried potential shifting beneath their feet. Long tables and a hearth were placed in the center, a makeshift kitchen for the many warriors taking rest before returning to the torment awaiting them up the mountain.

The Whispering Maiden tavern rested in the far corner and bled warmth from its chimneys into the dirt road. It beckoned them inside like moths to the flame. Zamir planted her at a small table by the fogged windows while he searched for a hot meal. Outside, she could see the warriors hunched low to the dirt around the smoldering hearth.

Exhaustion and sorrow weighed heavy on their shoulders, dragging them into the depths of despair and nearly into the earth itself. There was no joy to be shared around the fire, unlike the many nights she had with her family in the dead of winter. They used to pass around stories and bread to dip into Mother's famed lamb stew.

Well, *"famed"* was a strong word for a meal only their small family ever tasted. For her, it was a flavor from childhood that brought with it every tear and laugh shared in all the years of their youth. It was prominent for them, a famed minstrel to their taste buds that, when paired with Nissa's freshly baked rolls, were an opportunity they would never pass up.

A bowl of lukewarm sludge was tossed in front of her as Zamir gobbled down his own so-called meal from across the table.

She'd never wanted to cry over a stew before but her eyes filled anyway.

Will I ever taste that stew again? Will I ever share another meal with my kin? Will the recipe die with Mother? She tried to teach me so many times but it was never the same. Did I let her down in such a simple way too?

"Don't offend the cook, dearest Adelaide," he said, stirring both her soup and her thoughts as he rotated her spoon around the edge of the bowl. "They're trying their best given the circumstances."

She shook her dark thoughts away and gulped some of the liquid down without really tasting it. She was famished when they rode up that final hill into town, but the horrors of the mountains mixed fiercely in her gut with the memories of home, quelling any hunger pains she may have once had.

"We're so close to my home," she whispered into the bowl before letting her eyes drift back out the foggy windows and straight up to the billowing smoke continuing to burst from the mountainside. "And yet I've never felt further away."

They didn't speak again until the bowls were empty and every spilled tear was dried.

"HERE'S YOUR ROOM, MISS AYLARA," the innkeeper said as she unlocked the heavy wooden door with an iron key attached to a ring on her hip. "I did my best to clean it up from the last warriors who stayed here, but pardon if there's any mess still. Running things on my own has been—" She stopped, her throat bobbing on unsaid words as she wrenched the door open, a cloud of dust rising into the air around them. "It hasn't been easy."

She nodded and gave her as kind of a smile as she could muster. The poor woman was running both the inn on the top floor and the tavern below it, and Adelaide wasn't certain if that was normal or not. Either way, it wore on the woman's shoulders and formed dark purple bruises beneath her exhausted eyes.

"Thank you for allowing me to stay here," she murmured. The woman busied herself around the room, opening a few windows to remove the stuffy air and lighting candles along her way to beat back the shadows. "I know the warriors have kept to the tents outside, but—" She stopped, unsure of how to continue without letting a stranger know all her fears.

She scoffed and waved a dismissive hand at her. "You needn't explain, Miss. You're a Keeper. That's all I or anyone else needs to know to understand." She rushed into the hallway where Adelaide continued standing, her bag over her shoulder full of the few meager belongings Jarl Lefa gave her. It was all she owned aside from the raven pendant hidden beneath her tunic, her only reminder of home. "No elf in their right mind would camp alongside the Knights."

Her gut twisted into knots. Had she not done that before? On those days of travel between Rannadal and Skagi, had she not slept at the same campsite as the Commander? Yet, as soon as the other Knights joined with the rest of the warriors, she couldn't stomach the idea of being so exposed.

"You've lived in Skagi for a while, I take it?" she asked, to which the woman nodded as she grabbed a few quilts out of the cabinet in the hallway. "You're so close to the mountains here. Have you known many elves then?"

She shrugged as she reentered the room and began making the bed. "A few here and there. Usually, your lot sticks by each other and don't trust the likes of me. Until they see this of course." She paused to reach beneath her shirt and tug on a chain, bringing it into the light to reveal a carved pendant.

"Mjölnir," Adelaide said, understanding slowly entering her heart and steeling her nerves. The innkeeper wore an emblem of Thor's hammer, marking her as a pagan follower of The Old Gods. "Most humans in these parts follow Olena."

"There is enough room in my heart for all the heavens," she explained as she straightened the final quilt across the bed. "At least, there used to be before all of this." She froze, her hand on her pendant, and her eyes cast to the window and the mountains towering outside. "Tell me, are their claims about you real? Were you truly sent to us by Odin or Olena?" she asked as she stole a glance back at her, her cedar brown eyes swimming with confusion. "I care not which God it was, only that you can help us."

She swallowed the tight ball in her throat threatening to choke her. "I'm going to try."

"That's all I ask."

The woman headed for the door as Adelaide entered, dropping her bag on the floor and waving away the dust rising from her movement across the creaking floorboards. When they passed each other, something clawed at her senses. It ripped at her skin and burrowed into her soul like a maggot beneath the flesh. Her eye stung, hot and fierce, and she hissed in pain at the protruding ache she desperately tried to ignore the moment it began at the entrance into Skagi.

"Are you alright?" the innkeeper asked, her willowy hand barely brushing the surface of her arm.

"Yes," she gasped, her hand covering her eye until she shut it to stave off the pain. "It just hurts sometimes." She tapped the scar over her left eye for emphasis and struggled to meet the woman's gaze as it scrutinized the puckered flesh. "I know it's ugly. You needn't look at it if it displeases you so."

The innkeeper blinked, still staring, but also didn't back away as Adelaide expected she would at the aggravation in her tone. Usually, humans were incredibly uncomfortable or outright enraged by even the slightest show of anger from her kind. It wasn't until she was older that she learned it was because they believed they'd be cursed or otherwise harmed by an elf's magic in some irreversible way.

It always made her laugh when the humans feared her and shrunk away from her anger. They never had a clue that their fear was unwarranted. Not because she wouldn't harm or kill them, but because she would use a bow or blade instead of magic.

They were always so busy watching for magic that they never noticed my arrow until it was too late.

"I heard that you received your scar when you saved our lives," the woman said, pulling Adelaide from her thoughts. "Nothing that marks a warrior for their bravery can ever be ugly."

With that, the stranger left the key to her room on a table by the door and began to leave.

"Wait," she called, peeking at her from over her shoulder. "What's your name?"

The innkeeper's smile didn't meet her eyes, and her tone was a bit too hollow as she paused in the threshold. "My name is Embla Hagg," she said, before frowning at the floorboards and drifting down the hallway. "At least, that's who I used to be."

THERE WAS a spark dancing on her palm, but it wasn't her magic lingering against her skin. Sander held his hand in hers, passing his magic across her skin in soft waves.

"This is how magic feels, although everyone's is different depending on their abilities, feelings, histories, and bloodlines," he explained as they waited on the others to gather by the horses for their final journey directly into the heart of the mountains. "It all mixes together to create their own personal flavor of magic. Focus on mine and see if you can describe it. If you cannot call on your own magic, at the very least you'll be able to recognize mine and perhaps siphon some of it for your own abilities. You should do the same with Zamir."

She focused on the occasional surge of power pulsing from his skin, but it felt the same as her siblings' and mother's always had. An indescribable force to be reckoned with that lacked any shape, texture, or temperature. It was simply *there*, a pressure rising from elsewhere, but never from within her.

"You're allowing your frustration to cloud your intentions," he said, reprimanding her as his magic zapped her, biting into the flesh like it was trying to teach her a lesson about not listening to its master. "If you focus on what you believe is your lack of magic, you will never allow yourself to feel the magic of others."

"Silence, Sander," she growled under her breath as she shook out her tense shoulders and refocused on the magical pulse. She did as he instructed, emptying her mind of the bitterness she felt each time the topic of magic got involved.

Adelaide was so jealous of Nissa's control over the small waves within the cascading rivers running like veins across the mountainside. She watched her sister for days on end, weaving water into the mimicked shapes of the lynxes and foxes frequenting their home, envy clawing at her core.

She let it go.

On the longest winter nights of their youth, when her sisters were still freshly born into their powers, Birgitta would drag her into the shadows and forge them into something more. Those shadows danced around the yule fires with their mother, the partner she never had. A perfect mirror to the powers that never graced Adelaide's palms outside her dances with the darkness.

She let it go.

Every scratch and bruise of childhood was healed by the sibling closest in age to her, always followed by a hug or kiss on the forehead. Some days, in her youngest years, she'd fall on purpose just to receive that love. She wondered if that's why they left to travel beyond the mountains, bringing home a distance she didn't recognize and more stories than she could name. Had her love been too much for them? Had she needed them too deeply?

She let it go.

She endlessly coveted her mother's ability to shapeshift into any manner of creature she or the others desired. A bear, to tell them stories of strength. A raven for Birgitta, who always fancied the darkness they cast as a foreboding omen of death. A salmon for Issa, who would just as easily slink from your grasp and all responsibilities like a fish.

It would've been a bunny for Adelaide, if her mother ever transformed for her. It was her favorite animal as a child and there was even a stuffed one in her bed for years. She saved it, even though it made her bitter to look at. Mother never did turn into a rabbit for her, even when she begged. Her mother promised that, once Adelaide's magic formed, she'd show her as many shapes as she liked.

Still, Adelaide saved that stuffed little bunny for the youngest of their clan. In the same bed with the same toy, Sophie truly was the best of all her kin. A perfect blend of Nissa's brains, Birgitta's stealth, all her siblings' charisma, and her mother's beauty.

She would've been the best of us. No, she still will be. She's alive damn it, she's alive.

Odin, please let her be alive.

Let it go.

All at once, her shoulders lightened and the magic beneath her palm tingled in time with her racing heart. She could feel Sander's magic and his very essence crowding around her, sinking into her pores.

She hated that he was right, but she'd never tell him that.

Despite his youthful appearance, something ancient lingered under his skin, like a wild oak tree refusing to bow to the weight of time. Instead, it merely grew taller and wider, its branches dancing towards the sky in unimaginable shapes, touching every cloud and star on its way. Like the Yggdrasil, the Tree of Life, bending through the realms with a mind of its own.

There was something unsettling about that untamed nature but she still found solace in it. It was the comfort of her Gods lying hidden in the very essence of his powers.

"You're not doing anything creepy with your magic, are you?" Zamir asked, pulling her out of touch with Sander and lessening her hold on his abilities altogether. It ran in the background: a presence she sensed the familiarity of but no longer felt attached to.

Sander scowled at the other man as he strolled towards them, no care in the world for having ripped the connection of magic between them so utterly and completely with a single sentence. "What exactly are you accusing me of?"

He shrugged and stopped beside Adelaide, who immediately felt his magic when their shoulders brushed. It was warm and inviting, like a hug from her siblings or a roaring fire in the dead of winter. It was young, like a baby just starting to stretch from a swaddle and learn how to crawl. She wondered if that meant he was new to magic or if his bloodline was new to the magical arts entirely.

"Not accusing you of anything, though it *is* interesting how defensive you got," Zamir mused as he fully turned to Adelaide, blocking her view of the other man. "I'm glad you can sense the magic around you now. Hopefully that means you can sense us nearby and know you're not alone."

A smile fought its way onto her lips. "Thanks, to the both of you."

The thunder of boots against the packed earth stole their

attention. Several warriors followed the Commander and Zareen, who both wore stony expressions as their gazes focused upward, pinned on the mountains.

Back towards home.

"I guess we'll have to pause the fun for now," Zamir grumbled.

"Are you ready for the final trek?" the Commander asked once he was near.

Zamir scoffed. "We've been ready. Where have you lot been?"

His sister scowled. "You try organizing twenty weary warriors in a camp of the dying."

"I'd honestly rather not. That's your area of expertise, not mine. All I'm saying is you could do it better."

Zareen raised her fist, agitation forcing the veins on her neck and forehead to bulge, but the Commander laid a heavy hand on her shoulder, freezing her in place. "You know this is just his way. Let your brother be." He paused, looking Zamir up and down. "*For now*."

Her fist lowered and she rolled her shoulders back, although the pulsing vein in her forehead remained. "You survive today, little brother." Her eyes trailed up the serpentine path into the mountains. "At least, I hope so."

What little levity Zamir managed to conjure vanished as they mounted their horses and followed each other up the mountain path. It wound across a hill littered with bloodstains and opened into one final field before taking a steep turn skyward. Once in that final line of trees, the terrain would be predominately forged from rocks and ash until they reached the levels of the mountains Adelaide knew best. But, before that, there was a large field to cross.

She saw that region plenty of times. It was where the hot springs emptied out, fueling the intense brush growth making the hill such a vibrant green. She urged many lost human souls back to that space when she discovered them in her woods. However, she'd only ever seen it in its intense beauty. Even in the dead of winter, buried in several yards of snow, it was a stunning spot nestled between the space where two forests met.

But on that day, she'd never seen such death.

Bodies were strewn across the once lush yard, coloring the greenery into red, muddy patches. Limbs lay in hacked pieces, hidden in the underbrush tangled around their mounts' ankles. The blooming flowers lay dead, their scent gone with them, and replaced by the tang of soot and taste of iron on her tongue. Swirls of grey ash thickened to black with each step they took closer to the crevice where spirits continued to descend into Midgard.

When she had the stomach for it, she snuck a glance at the tear in The Divide. It split the mountain open from the gut, spilling its innards in every direction she could see. Black, charred remains of its once gorgeous self were laid bare for the birds to peck both its and the warriors' festering skin. A few warriors tried to recover the remains, but their bodies were embedded in the dirt—forgotten by the earth, which refused to reclaim that which was touched by the spirits bleeding into the world.

In the distance, she could already see them. Wisps of spirits she'd only ever read about or seen the briefest, flickering shadows of coasted through the air, leaking like water from a dam.

Will I find their bodies if I travel far enough? Or will I simply join them among the dead?

They're alive, kill such thoughts.

Her stomach sank and she, too, felt like she was marching towards death with each crimson-drenched step. She held her breath, but the sting of ash and smell of corpses still invaded her senses. There was no blocking out the sickness, so she merely let it in and accepted the destruction around her.

It was only once they breached the threshold of the forest, *her forest*, that the Commander spoke. "We saw you descend from here," he said, motioning towards a ridgeline in the carved-out portion of the mountains. "As far as my men can tell, the tear cuts straight through to New Alfheim. If it was any deeper, there would nearly be a walking path straight through." He pointed towards the sky, where not a single tree rested over the gaping wound in the mountain. "The aurora shone on you from the opening here."

"No wonder you all assume I hold magic or were sent by some God," Adelaide mused. "No one could survive this."

My kin couldn't survive this.

"Yet you did," he said, his voice a little breathless as if he too were certain of her divinity.

As if a Knight would know anything of the divine.

"But my kin didn't, did they?" she asked, keeping her voice low so the others couldn't hear. She hated that she had to confide in *him* about her worry for her family, but he was the one leading the search for them. He was the only one she could go to.

He sighed, and suddenly he seemed ten years older and not an ounce wiser. "I truly don't know, but I wish I did. If anyone has news of them, good or bad, you will hear of it immediately. I won't have you fighting by our side for our people when you don't know the truth of what happened to yours."

She wanted to give him thanks, but her throat closed too much to speak, so she moved to blend in with the others instead. Perhaps Zamir's ability to lighten the mood would wash over her if she kept close to his side. With thick tears already stinging her eyes, she was willing to give anything a try.

The trees called her back home, even in their smoldering state. The breeze blew their ashen bark away, whipping it into their faces as they ascended the mountain. She never thought she'd walk in her woods like that: followed by human warriors with the familiar trees of her childhood burnt to ash around her.

The garden she'd tended for years wasn't far from them, she realized with a gut-wrenching punch that nearly made her double over. When she was young, she had tended it with the friends the Knights stole from her. She'd kept those plants alive for them. They had lived in their place, filling the void in her life and heart their deaths created. It had been a thin cloth against a wound desperately aching for stitches, but it was one of the only forms of healing she'd had.

She held her middle as they crested the final ascent, begging silently for her stomach to settle. The last thing she wished to do was hurl her meager breakfast into the burnt brushes of the lingonberries her family often foraged for. All that effort to contain herself broke when they settled on the flattened earth beside the crevice swallowing her home whole.

With the highest point of the sun streaming straight overhead, she could pick out the charred, crushed wood of her cottage's roof and the mangled limbs of her mother's rocking chair. In that seat, every member of their clan had been soothed to bed when they were young.

She vomited against the nearest tree.

For a moment, she smelled burnt flesh and decaying corpses, the same scent that had haunted her for years, but it was just a foggy memory floating away in the breeze. A phantom scent of the past, not a reality of what happened to her family.

Not, not them. Never them.

Zamir patted her on the back before wiping a few damp strands of white hair stuck to her forehead back. "If it's any consolation, Karsten assured me your family isn't down there. They've found no bodies in this part of the tear."

Between gasping breaths, she thanked him and dried her

tears on the heels of her palms. "Allow me to collect myself." When he hesitated, she waved him away. "Just for a moment."

He nodded and left her alone with only her own bile at her feet as company. Partially, she was grateful he did as she asked but, more so, she simply felt the hole inside her chest grow bigger and wider. That gaping wound in her heart bled onto the ground between her feet.

Once her shaking settled and her steady breaths returned, she looked up from her feet and focused on the tree line leading away from the horrors she turned her back on. Further into the woods, towards the path she had been traveling on that day her life changed forever, she could see rays of sunlight beating back the smoke. Small creatures lived and breathed in the greenery surviving not too far from where she stood.

If they could live, why not my clan?

I will *find them.*

She ran towards the light.

COMMANDER STROM'S CASUALTY LOGS FROM THE DIVIDE

Day One:

Fifty-three deceased. Seventy-five injured.

Day Two:

One hundred lost souls. Fifteen succumbed to their wounds. Two lost their minds.

Week One:

Two hundred bodies were counted. Only twenty have been recovered.

Week Two:

Of those identified, eighty of the dead were from our forces. The rest belong to Skagi.

Week Three:

Thirty letters written to the families. Five personally delivered in Rannadal.

Week Four:

Twenty new letters to write. I'll add them to the list. I need to buy more handkerchiefs.

10

THE DEAD FIELDS

SKALD: KARSTEN STROM

Twenty-two fresh recruits who were civilians less than a month prior weren't nearly enough manpower to do sufficient damage to the spirits pouring from The Divide.

Still, he'd survived worse odds with less men before.

And back then, they didn't have Adelaide.

If she could figure out those mysterious powers of hers, Karsten had no doubt they could turn the tide in their favor. If she continued to doubt the very existence of her abilities, he wasn't sure what would happen. His men would die, that was certain, but what would become of the rest of their world?

When their line of defense between the mountains and the rest of Midgard fell, who would pick up the pieces in a realm ruled by the damned?

They were on the precipice of a greater change than he could fathom. He knew it in his very bones that a shift was waiting to occur—the tide begging to break. They were in a land torn between the spirits of the underworld clawing for their souls and the intense magic that would rupture hope into every beating heart if only they could see it.

They were between the shadows and the dawn, waiting to see which side broke first.

He hoped, for all their sakes, Adelaide would bring that dawn of hope with her wherever she went. He'd sensed that about her from the moment they first met. She was meant for great, beautiful things. He merely hoped he lived long enough to witness it.

With a jolt, he realized just how true that sentiment was as his hand shook against the pommel of his axe. He gripped it tighter, trying to hide the primary sign of his pending deterioration when Zareen's voice cut through the air.

"Where is Adelaide?"

He froze.

Shit.

He spun away from the destroyed section of the mountain and fixed his gaze on the tree where he saw last, hunched over with Zamir. He wanted to comfort her, let her know her family didn't reside somewhere in the darkness beneath the cliffs, but he knew his words wouldn't be of any assurance to her.

As much as he found hope and comfort in Adelaide, he could never provide that for her. His past was too tainted in darkness to ever let her see past it. Even when her light shone on him, it couldn't wash the stains of sin from him. She could see that; it was why she stayed away.

She has good reasons to.

"Her tracks go this way," Sander said, motioning to where her boots marred the blackened earth. Those steps took her away from the destruction and towards the sun-drenched region where life still thrived, or so it would seem from afar.

But he knew what truly rested on that part of the mountain. He knew what she would find if they didn't catch her in time.

"With haste," he called as he bolted into the tree line, the heavy footfalls behind him giving little comfort as he rushed to find her white hair among the birch trees. With the start of autumn painting the mountains in earthen tones, finding her shouldn't have been difficult.

He hoped they were quick enough.

Karsten ran hard, unable to pause for breath until he found her. Even with his hands still shaking, the tremble traveling up his arms and weakening him, he couldn't stop. It just made him run faster, determined to reach her before—

He skidded to a halt as they reached the very place he'd dreaded finding her. He had no idea how she knew it was there. His only explanation was that she'd somehow been drawn to it.

Adelaide stood at the threshold of a clearing deep in the forest. They were her woods, so it wasn't shocking she knew it existed, but what that space was transformed into wasn't something she'd recognize. He was sure she'd expected tall grass beaten by the winds and budding wildflowers dancing in the sunlight.

The burials were anything but that.

Those who perished were brought back to Skagi, the village below the mountain, for funeral rights. It was impossible to bring the many other corpses down the sheer mountains. Especially while they were still in the heat of battle with the spirits flooding the lands from every crack in its surface. So, his men collected those they could and transported them to the hills below for proper burial and identification whenever there was a break in the surges of the spirits. That was normal in war, but what wasn't normal was *who* exactly lay in the clearing before them: the bodies they had left in the mountains.

Since his men didn't often travel up the mountain paths, the bodies they'd discovered this high up weren't of their brothers- and sisters-in-arms.

They weren't human.

The corpses belonged to other Keepers and their clans who were slaughtered after the mountain was torn in two. He'd already confirmed her family wasn't among them using the descriptions Adelaide provided, but they were still her people in more ways than one.

They were *elves*, and their bodies were being tended to by *humans.*

He was sure she'd be furious. No one had told her about the countless number of dead in the mountains—in her *home.* Would she find her friends or distant relatives among the bodies? She'd rage at him for hours, maybe even try to kill him.

He had sent his men to gather their dead and hadn't consulted her like he should've. He could have asked what he should do and sought her counsel on the matter, sent his men to perform burials the way her people would've wanted. He made sure they were prepped for pyre burning but also had a few items from their lives, just in case they were to be buried instead. He remembered both methods were used by those who followed The Old Gods, but he wasn't sure if those practices had changed since his youth.

Truly, asking for her opinion on the matter was exactly what he'd wanted to do, but Jarl Lefa's word was final on the matter. Her words still chilled him to his very bones.

"If she discovers so many of her people dead, aside from her missing family, what will she suspect? That we hid their remains? That we killed her people ourselves? Perhaps even that we're responsible? In her emotional state, we haven't the slightest idea what she would believe. We need her to quell these spirits before we all end up just like those elves. Under no circumstances is anyone allowed to tell her."

And that was that.

Without thinking, he rushed forward and covered her eyes with his gloved palms. Even through the leather, he could feel the rivers of tears that made her face slick. She was shaking, her body shifting with each swift breeze or heaved breath from her lungs.

I touched her. I'm a dead man.

And I deserve it.

"I wish you didn't see this. You didn't have to see it. You shouldn't have to see this. I'm so sorry. You don't deserve this. We did what we could for their burial preparations. If I did something wrong, I'm sorry." He was rambling and he knew it, but he couldn't stop himself.

I've barely admitted to myself that this woman truly was sent to us by Olena, and I've already failed my Goddess' most important task: to protect what is hers.

Her hands slowly rose to cover the ones shielding her face. He expected her to shove him away or downright bite him, but she held his hands in place instead as her sobs grew.

And, most unexpectedly of all, she whispered, "*Thank you.*"

He almost jumped back in shock, but her grip on his hand held him in place. He peered back at the others, who seemed just as surprised as him. Sander, especially, seemed perplexed by her reaction. Karsten nodded and was relieved when they sank back into the shadows of the forest with the rest of their warriors. He knew they wouldn't travel far but he knew even some semblance of privacy was better than being stared at so openly amid her grief.

"You shouldn't thank me," he said, as his hand shook along with her. He could only hope she believed it was her trembling instead of him. "I should've asked you what to do. I should've told you. I'm a coward for not."

"No," she said with a shockingly firm tone. "You did what you could for them. You tried to spare me from what I'm feeling now. I understand that. I've done the same for others." She took a deep, soul-achingly long breath that almost deflated her. "I've *seen* the same before, so others wouldn't have to." She finally lowered their hands, but her fingers lingered on his gloves, barely grazing the edges for something sturdy to hold onto. "But someone must witness these things. History can't forget them and their sacrifice, so neither will I."

He didn't have the heart to tell her she was wrong. That he hadn't kept the many dead surrounding her a secret from a misguided effort to protect her, but out of a sense of duty to his Jarl's orders.

She was furious with me for being a liar, and here I am lying to her again.

Karsten couldn't stomach telling her the truth. He could already imagine the hurt and the rage in her eyes at hearing what Lefa ordered them to conceal. In the face of so much death, he wouldn't add to her pain, and he also couldn't bear the thought of lying to her again the moment she put her trust back in him.

"That isn't the reason why," he murmured, and he sensed her freeze. "Lefa ordered us to conceal them from you for no other reason than to ensure your assistance." He couldn't even look at the back of her head as the truth spilled forth. "Please, *don't* thank me."

Silence stretched between them, and not even the birds fluttering from branch to branch overhead seemed to make any noise in the stillness of The Dead Fields. In that disquiet, he cursed his honesty and the rage it would conjure, but he couldn't take it back. Nor would he want to. She deserved the truth, even if it made her hate him.

"Did the Jarl also order you to prepare them for their journeys to Valhalla?" she asked, pulling away from him and leaving his world a little colder from the distance. "Did she demand you find their personal effects and place the families beside each other?"

He shook his head, unsure of what she was saying. "No. She only ordered for our secrecy. The rest was left to me."

She stopped at the first row of bodies and kneeled in the earth beside them. "Then thank you," she said again, bowing her head. "You could've thrown them in a ditch or left them to rot. Instead, they've been cared for—*lovingly* so. It's more than most would do."

He had no words to convey the mangled emotions in his gut, so he remained silent.

There were thirty-three elves in total waiting for burial or pyre, each laid in rows according to which corpses were found closest to one another. Ten were children under the age of fourteen, and the rest ranged from eighteen to sixty by his men's estimations. Ages were hard to tell with elves since their lifespans varied so widely from humans. Either way, those numbers were burned into his mind. He only wished they didn't grow.

Or expand to include her family.

"You found these four by the Eastern Ridges, right?" she asked, her voice wobbly as she peered over the blue, distorted faces of the fallen.

The first four they suspected to be a family, discovered massacred by a chaos spirit slashing ruthlessly through their bodies. There were two women and two children, a little boy and a girl of crawling age. They'd wrapped their bodies in linen, a few items from their destroyed home lying atop each of them. A toy carriage for the boy, a stuffed cat for the girl, a worn book for one woman, and a half-finished quilt for the other.

"Yes, why?" he asked as he followed her to the first row of bodies.

She danced her fingers over the little boy's head of curly locks. "That red hair is so specific for the Arud clan. I could see their family for miles." She peered over the rest of the field. "But no others are here. The rest may yet live. Small blessings, I suppose." She tucked the infant in to hide the slashes cut across her tiny body. "If my memory serves me right, they named her Emma." She touched the boy's hair. "Fredrick." She motioned to the women. "Ingrid and Damira."

He placed his shaking hands back on the grip of his axe, took a deep breath to steady his nerves, and murmured, "Beautiful names for a beautiful family."

She closed her eyes to fight back the silent, growing tears. "Odin, guide them into blissful havens meant for only the strongest warriors. Welcome them to Valhalla with open arms. For while they didn't ask to be fighters or know of the battle they fought, they died with honor." She placed two hands on the children's foreheads and opened her eyes, allowing herself to stare into the frozen pupils of the small bodies before her. "Freya, let them know the greatest peace and play forever in your fields of glory. They are your smallest warriors."

THEY DIDN'T STOP THERE.

Adelaide and Karsten directed each other through the remaining twenty-nine bodies in the field. He would tell her where they were found and she would do her best to guess who they were in life.

When she figured out their origins, she jotted their names down. Back in Rannadal, she planned to write each of their families to inform them of their loved ones passing and their resting places. Sometimes, she knew them by heart from passing interactions or letters shared between their families. Others, she couldn't conjure their names or clans no matter how hard she tried.

Those seemed to upset her the most.

When all she could were identified and wished safe travels

into the afterlife, she finally seemed to settle. She rested in the grass, paying no mind to the blood seeping into her trousers where she kneeled.

"I know I didn't have to thank you," she said, her eyes closed as she turned her face to the last lingering rays of warmth from the sun. "I shouldn't need to thank people for doing the bare minimum, of treating people with respect. It should be a given." She peeked out at him from one eye. "But, sadly, it's not. So, thank you for preparing them in the old ways. It's what they would've wanted."

She stood and turned away, but he couldn't look away from her even if he tried. She was haloed by the sun, her silhouette so like that night she couldn't remember—the night he'd never forget.

The night she saved all our lives.

But, for just a moment, he questioned if she could do it again. If she could truly tap into the power he'd seen before. He didn't doubt her abilities or her strength, nor the divine intervention that had brought her to them in their hour of need; he merely questioned if her own self-doubt would be their collective undoing.

"Are you alright?" he asked, feeling stupid for even asking the question in the first place. Of course she wasn't *okay*. She found a massacre of her people, unidentified and so dangerously close to being forgotten.

There was no way to be okay with that.

"I will withstand it," she said, her voice a little raw until she cleared it and faced him, fully blocking his view of the sun until all he could see was her shadowed silhouette. "I'm done being so full of sorrow I can barely breathe." Her face changed then, her expression distorted by more anger than he could fathom. "Now, I'm full of rage."

Any remaining doubt Karsten had in her vanished.

THERE WERE several wayward spirits they encountered on their journey back to Skagi: a misery spirit sank its sad songs into a few of the more downtrodden warriors, and a spirit of sorrow caused another to break down in tears before it was slain.

The physical spirits were easy to contend with. A few slashes from their swords or a well-timed arrow did them in with efficiency. Spirits that maintained their astral forms were far more dangerous. Briefly, he was grateful they hadn't encountered one.

A misery spirit could cause a depression so expansive that one's mind could never cross fully over into happiness again. The physical manifestations of them could as well, but it was easier to tell it was the effects of a spirit when they were nearby. Their physical forms made them more bold and brash, so they didn't play mind games like their astral siblings did.

All spirits fed on the living through the emotion they forced them to feel. Misery fed on the downtrodden, loneliness fed on widows and the elderly, jealousy on insecure partners, and the list went on. In their physical shells, they were a burst of sudden emotion one could recognize as a spirit's influence.

The astral variants of those same spirits were far more subtle. They'd fester and linger in homes and under one's skin, swaying the mind until one forgot what it was ever like to be untouched by the damned.

Karsten shivered at the thought and the memories conjured by his musing. He'd killed countless spirits in his life, starting at the ripe age of thirteen when a vanity spirit had corrupted his neighbor. In the end, the prideful old woman had begged for death, and he'd been the hand to relieve her of the pain. That was the day he'd decided to become a Knight, to go to the source of all those horrors and protect those most affected by them.

What a fool I was.

The Knights were corrupt themselves, and they had been long before he'd joined. He'd just been too young and naive to see it. He'd done things he regretted in the name of their Brotherhood, and they'd forever keep him awake at night, struggling to find peace. When he wasn't bombarded with his own regret, he was mentally fighting off the effects of the many spirits who had sought to feed on his emotions.

It was tireless work, but he'd endured far worse.

Like the Lust spirit.

He shivered again and, when a warrior eyed him oddly, he brushed him off as if his cloak slipped from his neck and let a draft in.

Karsten hadn't been the same man after Lust tormented him, and he never thought he would be that man again. The first lust spirit had stolen every ounce of innocence his sixteen-year-old self had had left. It was years since the encounter, but it still left his heart and mind scarred more than he cared to admit.

So, for Adelaide's sake, he truly hoped she wouldn't face anything similar. She'd lived in The Divide all her life after all. Perhaps she knew a few secret ways to avoid the spirits' ire.

Maybe she could teach him.

But then a sickening feeling twisted in his gut.

What if there was no secret to any of it? What if she constantly fought off the spirits in her mind, day after day, from the time she was a babe? What if it wasn't that hard after all, and he was simply *weak*?

The next opportunity he had, he would ask her. As much as the potential answer pained him, he needed to know.

SKAGI WAS SETTLING in for the night by the time they arrived back at the village.

Each building was lit from within by warm flames that fogged the windows, acting as perfect canvases for the few children who remained in town. The lingering scent of The Whispering Maiden's beef stew flooded the streets, guiding him and his men to the tavern.

He couldn't fully express how grateful he was for the civilians who remained in Skagi. They deserved every ounce of peace they could find for the remainder of their—*hopefully*—long lives. They risked everything by staying so close to the destruction, and all to help his warriors. They washed their clothes, filled their bellies, and kept life going in the face of endless streams of death. Even in the quaint evening after a ceaseless day of work, they wouldn't rest until the last man made it down the mountain and had a bowl of stew in front of them.

He held the door to the tavern open, allowing the others to file in before he planned to shut the door firmly closed to help block out the growing winds. Adelaide paused at the threshold, her hair whipped into a frenzy by the breeze as her emerald gaze focused elsewhere, deeper in town.

"Something doesn't feel right," she murmured, her words sent adrift on the brisk air that was plummeting in temperature.

His hunger pains turned to a sick ache as he took in her uneasy expression. With his focus not solely pinned on the aroma leaking from the tavern, the one he craved when morale was at its lowest and the nights stretched out too long, he could sense it too.

His training as a Knight made his senses attuned to the ebb and flow of spiritual energy and he imagined, as a Keeper, she was the same. There hadn't been much time in the mountains for sensing spirits; they were embedded in the land, even with part of it ruptured. It became a dull thrum of energy under their skin, so connected to their being that it was the sheer lack of spiritual energy giving them pause.

But outside The Divide, where they were used to that absence, a single presence felt like a million spirits cramming to the surface—begging to be noticed.

Pleading to feed.

Not that the spirits truly wished to be acknowledged, except for perhaps vanity since it was within its nature. Usually, they preferred to subtly bleed into the world so they could travel unnoticed by mortals.

Unless they were about to kill the human they were feeding on. In those times, they didn't care for subtlety. Their only focus was on the final sip of their human's worst emotions. The sweetest drink of them all.

Adelaide drifted away and he followed, forsaking the warmth of the tavern's hearth for her fiery expression instead. He didn't have to ask why her fury was bubbling under the surface. He understood, better than most, what it was like to return from battle only to find another waiting at home.

They slunk through the shadows, following the sense of unease tugging at their guts and the intuition guiding them through town towards whichever spirit dared to linger. Perhaps they'd be lucky and it would only be a physical manifestation of a spirit, something he'd killed with relative ease all day. His gut told him that was wishful thinking. He knew the spirit they'd find would be latched onto someone in town, feeding on their emotions like a leech.

Muffled crying reached her ears before his, the pointed tips twitching towards the noise before he turned his head to listen better. "A woman," Adelaide said as she hastened her step towards the sound. "It's coming from here."

They snuck around to the side entrance of what was once the local brewery. It had since run dry from his warriors needing the strong drink after their trials in the mountain. What hadn't been used for drinking was poured on wounds before they received their first shipment of medical supplies. That was when Adelaide was practically a corpse, pale as the snow and as still as the summer wind.

But at that moment, as he unsheathed his sword and she readied yet another stolen kitchen knife hidden in her boot, she'd never seemed more alive.

They slid into the brewery and snuck to the back wall as the cries grew louder, higher pitched as someone rustled around by the empty wine barrels in the center of the room. Between the cracks in the towers of emptied wine, he could make out the shape of a pacing woman. But there wasn't a single spirit in sight.

She was either being fed on by one or possessed by one. Either option wasn't pleasant. If she were simply being drained by a spirit, they could try to expel it with some convincing, even without Adelaide's abilities. Some spirits could be talked down from their murderous endeavors, but that wasn't accomplished often. As for full possessions, those ran too deep. Even her abilities couldn't help then. He'd never heard of someone being unpossessed, except through a swift and clean death—like his neighbor when he was young.

When they rounded the final stack of barrels, he recognized the woman and the spirit attached to her in the same moment. It was Embla, the tavern owner who served his men during their daytime meals. She didn't work evenings, so she wouldn't be noticed missing until everyone broke their fast.

That was just how the spirit intended it.

Embla sobbed, her hair a wild mess standing at all ends around her head. Tears stained her cheeks ruby red and her chapped, torn lips bled down her chin in crimson rivers. Her hands were tangled in her shirt and her hair with equal measure and ferocity. She paced in front of a chair, which held a simple dagger on its top.

She was fighting the spirit, murmuring between her sobs.

"He wouldn't want me to die," she cried. "But you're right, he wouldn't want me to suffer like this without him either. What do I do? Why don't I do it? I should do it. No, that's wrong."

He sheathed his sword and Adelaide returned the knife to her boot as he led the way, moving as quietly as possible. Embla was always so kind, but she'd never been the same after The Divide fell. Her husband had been killed in the first wave of spirits while trying to protect her. Karsten wondered if her guilt over that ever weighed on her, even if she never showed it, but it wasn't a spirit of regret which fed on her.

It was a spirit of suicide.

"I shouldn't h-have to live like t-this," Embla wailed. "I m-miss him too much. I miss him more than a-anything. I-I can't do this alone."

"Embla, yes you can," Karsten said, breaking up her weeping. He spoke in the softest voice he could manage when fear gripped his heart so soundly. "You're stronger than you know and b-braver than most. Torvald would want you to keep going for him, not to give in."

"How would you know, Commander Strom?" she snapped, her voice hoarse and brass as it rang out around the room. "You weren't even here until he was already dead. You were too damned late!"

He squared his shoulders as she inched back towards the chair, her fingers reaching towards the dagger. "Because I-I know what it means to l-love someone," he admitted. "To let my family know to press on should the worst befall me. I would n-not want them to fall on their sword in my name."

"But it isn't *your* name!" she screeched as she wrenched the dagger from the chair and held it to her throat, the edge already drawing a thin line of blood across her skin. "Torvald was *everything* to me. We were soulmates. You don't know what that's like! To have love in your arms that's ripped away in an instant by no fault of your own." She grabbed her stomach with her free hand. "We were with child," she sobbed, her words echoing around the room and coating them in her sorrow. "That's why he jumped in front of that rage spirit—to protect us both. And I was so ruined by his death that I *destroyed* it." Her fingers looked like claws as they dug at her belly. "I destroy *everything*, even the most innocent things like our love and our baby. It's all my fault."

The blade moved to slice clean across her neck, and he was powerless to stop it. He was still too far, and his words hadn't been enough. It would never be enough when the spirits tangled themselves too deeply in their victims. He'd simply have to watch another good person die before him like so many others before. If he were a lesser man, he'd close his eyes to prevent the visage of her final moments from burning themselves into the back of his eyelids.

But he wasn't a coward. If Embla were to face death, she would not do so alone.

He was ready for it, prepared to write a letter to her family and arrange a funeral for another lost soul. The need for those things never came. Instead of slicing through to the bone, the blade sat, taunt as a bow string, in her trembling grasp as her gaze pinned on the woman at his side.

Hesitating, not wanting to look away from Embla should the blade suddenly run deep, he turned to Adelaide and froze at the sight of her glowing beside him.

Her expression was fierce but pained. Tears slid down her face from her red-ringed, glowing eyes. She trembled with the momentous effort of holding the spirit in place. Her hands held the very aurora he'd seen the night she'd saved his life and, as he followed the path of the light from her hands, he watched it ebb at Embla's hand holding the shaking blade.

"Spirit of suicide," Adelaide called, her voice not her own. It was deeper and held a certainty he knew she didn't possess when it came to her magical abilities. "Leave this woman's fate in her own hands. Return to your original form."

A screech tore through the air as a shadow peeled away from the woman, its hand latched around the blade until the last possible moment. Then, it was blown into the air by the light in Adelaide's hands and flew out the window, glowing a brighter color than when it leeched from the woman's pain.

As soon as it was gone, Embla tossed the blade to the floor and crumbled before their eyes, her sobs more wretched than before. She shook, her bloodied neck dripping onto her woven skirt. Adelaide ran to her, dropping to her knees and holding her to her chest.

"The spirit is gone, but why do I still feel like I want to die?" Embla asked, her words barely audible above her cries piercing both the air and his heart.

"It's not a wish to die," Adelaide said, and he could hear it in her voice as she choked back her own tears. "It's a wish to be where they are. *Wherever* they are."

The two women held each other until Embla fell asleep in her arms. Karsten called for a few of his people to take her to her room above the tavern—the one she'd once shared with Torvald—and stood in silence in the darkened road with Adelaide until her limp form disappeared around a corner.

"You did an incredible job, Lady Aylara," he whispered, although there was no reason to lower his voice, but the moment felt so fragile in the darkness that he didn't wish to break it.

"I tried so hard for the last few days to train but it didn't matter in the end," she said, her voice just as low. "I didn't need practice. I needed someone to truly help, not just some random spirit to kill."

He shrugged. "While I agree your powers are impressive, as I've told you before, that's not what I meant." She arched a brow at him in question. "Your words helped her when mine could not. That's no easy task when someone is on the brink of destruction, whether it be aided by a spirit or not."

She pinned her eyes on the moon, allowing it to wash away the pains of the day. It lit her emerald eyes in shades of silver, the beauty woven within threatening to drag him under. "That was easy. I know her pain." She began walking away, her shoulders slumping and eyes turning to the wet earth. "I think that's all she needed: to know she's not alone."

Karsten waited for Adelaide to be out of sight before he dared to turn his attention to the moon as well. It sat elegantly in the sky as a shining crescent, watching the world and lighting the shadows riddling it. It was an untouchable beauty stirring hope in his heart like nothing else.

Almost nothing else.

"O-Olena," he began in a hushed voice that was for his goddess, the moon, and him alone. "Your servant has taken away the pain of another. I pray you will do the same for her. She deserves it more than anyone." He walked to his room, hoping the heavens would heed his words.

And, even if his Goddess wasn't listening, he hoped Adelaide knew she wasn't alone either.

CASUALTIES OF THE DEAD FIELDS, WITH NOTES FROM THE PROMISED

Thirty-three bodies were recovered from inside the mountains of The Divide. All elves. Ten children under fourteen. ~~Twenty-three between the ages of eighteen and sixty.~~ *(Elves have longer life spans and age slower than humans. Correct age range: twenty-three between the ages of fourteen and three hundred and eighty. – A)*

Family 1: ~~Two women and two children, a boy and girl.~~ *(Arud Clan. Ingrid, 170. Damira, 156. Fredrick, 10. Emma, 3. – A)*

Family 2: ~~Two men, one child.~~ *(Ferne Clan. Vragi, 18. Braith, 20. Wenda, 1. – A)*

Family 3: ~~Eight women, seven men, three girls, two boys.~~ *(The Odran Clan. I will write to their relatives and see how many of them can be identified. – A)*

Family 4: ~~Three women, two men.~~ *(Tor Clan. Kirsi, 380, and her children.)*

Family 5: ~~Three women, one boy, one girl.~~ *(The girl ~~is~~ was Gwen. She visited my gardens during Ostara. I don't remember anything else. I'm sorry. – A)*

Singles: ~~Two women, two men, one boy.~~ *(Unidentifiable. Claudia Erikkson, 100. Soren Barrius, 25. Jon Berry, 59. Unidentifiable. – A)*

PART II

THESE WHISPERED WALLS SHALL FALL

EMBERS OF THE PAST | SIX YEARS PRIOR

It wasn't supposed to end like this.

Adelaide's throat was raw from her screams as she cursed his name to the All Father. He was a dense, stubborn fool for leaving her on his so-called *short* family visit that turned into months of absence. Her heart grew colder with the passing of autumn and, when winter loomed overhead, it finally sought answers.

The chill of the biting snow couldn't compete with the numb feeling gnawing on her chest. She'd been so bitter, so angry at the prospect of the man who'd vied for her heart since they were children leaving her for another. She'd thought them inseparable, even when they were merely friends and not lovers.

They could've been more—if only he'd stayed.

As her resentment lessened, her curiosity piqued. Eventually, it led her to pack a bag and venture into the first rays of moonlight illuminating the snow-drenched paths leading her back to him.

Regardless of the biting cold, she would find Vanentin and bring him home.

It was two weeks of travel from her home to his clan's, and she crossed every steep snow drift and frozen riverbed to get there. Only when the mountain began to descend and the snow lightened did she realize she was close to where his kin resided. As she came upon his family's home, a foreboding dread settled in her stomach and her heart stuttered in her chest.

When she last visited, the horizon was blocked by a two-story cabin forged from oak and white birch, allowing the clan to blend into the tree line. On that day, it was a smoldering pile of ruins drenched by the seasonal rainstorms and endless snow. It sat heavy and limp, barely holding onto the side of the mountain. If she'd waited any longer, it would've been washed away with the next downpour.

"Vane!" she called, as she stumbled through the damp earth scattered with debris. If there was a fire, they would've started rebuilding nearby. She was sure he'd be around the next bush or riverbank. He had to be. "Vanentin!"

She almost called out again when her words, and her breath, were ripped from her lungs as she teetered on the edge of a ravine gouged out of the mountains. What once was a beautiful field of cornflower was tarnished by black soot and decay. Bones twisted out of the muck; limbs locked up in the positions people died in. Maggots squirmed in and out of the rotting bodies whose flesh hung off the twenty-one corpses littering the field she'd once danced in with Vane.

The polluted smell of death and a new, fresh wave of pain wracked through her until her chest nearly tore itself open and tears leaked heavy down her cheeks. Every nerve in her body told her to run—to pretend she hadn't seen a thing so she could continue lying to herself that Vane, her oldest friend and closest confidant, was still alive.

But that would dishonor his memory.

She fell to her knees and gripped the damp earth between her fingers. Sobs wracked through her, her pain soul-deep and aching with each escaping tear. They dripped, mixing with the blood-soaked and fire-touched earth, which would become Vane and his family's burials.

Twenty-one lives were cut so short, and she loved them all. Vane had been her warmth during the winters. His grandparents had been the gran and pa she never had. His siblings had been her own, all six of them, and his nieces and nephews had been her joy and tiny—*so tiny*—helpers.

When she peered into the pit, she could pick each of them out. Children as young as three still grasped their mothers' arms and, on the edge closest to her, was Vane. His eye sockets were empty, birds having long ago picked anything away that once remained of his handsome face. All his light brown, fluffy hair and big hazel eyes she knew far too well were gone. She could see him, still frozen in his last moments. His skeleton hand clutched the edge of the pit, trying to claw his way out.

If he'd made it only a few more feet, he would've come home.

But he didn't. He *couldn't.* Because some barbaric bastard stole him and his entire family from her. All she had left of him was the raven necklace she carefully removed from his body.

She tore her gaze away from the corpses and searched the surrounding forest for any trace of his killers. Trails veered in every direction, but with so many months passed, it was hard to discern what was recent and which prints in the mud and snow belonged to the culprits she searched for.

Finally, a glint atop a nearby knoll drew her in.

A sword was struck into the earth, standing straight towards the sky. On its pommel was the entwining ribbons of the Cislenian religion. She knew of only one group to wear such a symbol atop their weapons. With it perched like a calling card atop the highest peak, she knew what that sword was meant for.

It was a call for bloodshed and, if the Knights wanted a war, she would be more than willing to provide one. But first, she held onto the hilt of the sword and wept to her Gods.

"Odin, why him?"

The All Father did not answer. She was certain even he didn't have words for such cruelty. Humans cursed her with an agony that tore at her chest, and a rage burning like wildfire in her core.

And Keeper Adelaide Aylara was left alone to pick out what little remained of her heart from the ashes.

THE LOST ASTROM CLAN

"Bea and Otto Astrom, known lovingly to their clan as Gran and Pa, died at the ages of six-hundred and thirty and six-hundred and fifty-two. They perished alongside the rest of their kin, including their two children, eight grandchildren, and five great grandchildren.

Their children, Penelope and Joni, are survived by none. Penelope and her wife Thea died honorable deaths fighting for their children Airi and Darian. All four are welcomed into Valhalla.

Joni and her husband Lauritz are buried along with their six children, Gerda, Eleanora, Markus, Klara, Arabella, and Vanentin, on the homestead. Klara and her husband Kenton are still holding their children, Dimka, Carina, and baby Fallon. Arabella and her husband Niklas rest with Andrey, for their daughter Raniya's body was never recovered.

I ask no Keepers to be mistaken. This was an act of violence by the Brotherhood. Treat it as such."

- Keeper Adelaide Aylara

11

TO BIND ONESELF

SKALD: ADELAIDE AYLARA

Adelaide once believed she'd be happy if she ever discovered a single ounce of magic in her veins.

She'd expected to shout with joy and prance into the nearest fields to tell The Old Gods her blood was magic too. She'd imagined doing it thousands of times as a child: how excited her family, her mother especially, would be.

Some days, it seemed her mother's only desire in life was to find her pale-haired daughter finally attuned to the magical arts that seemed one and the same with her. She was no longer a child who daydreamed of such things.

No, she simply felt *empty*.

The small room she was assigned in The Whispering Maiden had a draft under its door that allowed every slight breeze to cut straight through her. She huddled in on herself as the emptiness grew.

The woman she saved, Embla, hadn't deserved what befell her husband and child. As she pulled out her necklace, the mangled raven pendant gleaming in the dim, she supposed she understood her pain far too well. She lost Vane six years prior, and it was only her kin that got her through it. Embla didn't have that. She only had a tavern full of warriors and an inn with creaking floorboards letting the drafts and spirits in.

If I'd known about my abilities earlier, could I have saved them?

What good was she if her powers were only useful after something horrible happened? If she couldn't prevent the terror of the spirits, what was her purpose? Was she born with lingering abilities that never awoke simply because nothing destroyed The Divide yet?

Or were her powers gifted in the accident? Did some God truly intervene on the humans' behalf and bestow her as their savior? Or was it sheer, dumb luck that her powers manifested and were necessary at that exact moment? What would happen after?

When the world wasn't in chaos and the spirits returned to a mended mountainside—*what then*? When every person responsible for the destruction was held accountable in the cruelest ways she could fathom—*what then*?

Would she be tossed aside by the humans she was still desperately trying not to view as allies? Would her powers become dormant once more? Or would they force her to travel to the edges of every realm, hunting spirits just to feel useful after she'd already failed at so much?

None of her questions had answers. All they accomplished was keeping her awake through the night, just a few winks of sleep between her and the nightmares of the corpses in The Dead Fields.

"EMBLA HAS SWORN A BLOOD DEBT," Zareen said, no hesitation in her blunt words and matching tone. "I would recommend you accept and use her as a handmaiden or attendant."

Adelaide bristled. It was true that she'd saved her life the prior night, but she had saved many lives and never asked for repayment. She just let people part ways from her. They'd sometimes insist on giving her a few silvers for her trouble, but certainly not *that.*

Except for the pact she'd struck with the Commander, unbeknownst to him, and in secret.

The more I get to know him, the more that makes me sick.

"I don't accept Blood Debts," Adelaide said, suddenly queasy at the mere sight of her breakfast. "If I save a life, it is theirs. I have no claim on it, and I won't hang it over someone's head to make them my *slave.*"

Liar.

Zareen blinked, long and slow, as if she hardly understood the words leaving the other woman's mouth. "I assure you, Blood Debts in these parts don't start or end in slavery. In some places, like where my brother and I come from and perhaps in New Alfheim, but not here."

Oh.

Speaking of Zareen's brother seemed to summon Zamir from elsewhere in the bustling tavern. He slid into a chair beside Adelaide and, behind him and off to the right, she could just make out Embla's frame in a distant corner. She'd nearly ended her life the night before and, come the dawn, she was working like nothing happened.

It was almost admirable, if it weren't so concerning.

"I've spoken to Embla plenty in the past few years. She's headstrong, like someone else I know." Zamir coughed on those words and Adelaide shot him a heavy glare. "She wouldn't offer this to anyone. She feels indebted, that's true, but it goes beyond that."

"And where exactly does it go?" the elf scoffed but halted mid-dismissal when Embla stopped beside their table.

"You have been promised to us, my lady," Embla said, her

resolute tone stirring further wariness into Adelaide's heart. "I don't know which Gods sent you, but I know this to be true. You've saved many lives, mine included. Even if I didn't owe you my life, I would still want to assist in your efforts in any small way possible." She kneeled and the other woman froze, horrified at the gesture of a human on their knees for her. "Olena, or perhaps Odin, gave me a vision after you saved me. They told me to stay by your side and help you rest so you may heal the world." She looked up with tears in her eyes. "Calling forth a Blood Debt is merely so I remain strong and do not falter in the face of my own fear." She squared her shoulders and clenched her jaw. "Never again shall I cower before a spirit."

Adelaide hesitated as she felt every single eye in the room fall on her. Many lifted their goblets of wine or horns of mead in her direction while others laid a heavy fist over their chests in respect. She knew Embla told other people about what happened the night prior, but she never expected her words to have already traveled through the town so quickly.

With all those eyes on her, how could she refuse? How could she shun someone who, only a few hours earlier, was on the brink of death by her own hand? If believing in her gave Embla a reason to stay alive and *try*, who was she to deny her?

Adelaide only hoped that she'd keep her own resolve if the worst passed and her kin truly were dead like the others in the fields. She knew herself well enough—recognized enough of herself in Embla—to know that she wouldn't need a spirit to manipulate her into dying.

She'd do it herself, somewhere on the battlefield, in increasingly dire circumstances. She'd take out as many Knights and demented spirits as possible to ensure her place in Valhalla, with her kin.

"I accept your Blood Debt," she said before she truly realized the words were leaving her tongue. "We'll take you with us back to Rannadal as my lady-in-waiting but only for the time

I'm there. No one shall claim your debt in my name or force you to stay past what we decide, *together*. I won't remain in Midgard forever and, when I return to the mountains, you will *not* follow."

She straightened and held her chin high, shoulders back. Somehow *proud* to be the servant of an *elf*. "I will not let you down, Promised."

What in the realms is a Promised?

The dagger Adelaide saw, trembling in the woman's grasp, was suddenly on the table before her. She eyed the other woman as her throat bobbed nervously. As her savior in the pact, she could demand any amount of blood necessary. She could slit her open, letting her bleed out on the tavern floor, and no one could stop her if that's what she decided was necessary for the oath.

Her lady-in-waiting was giving her the first sign of her devotion and trust. She wouldn't forsake that.

She grabbed the dagger and pricked her finger, allowing the smallest bubble of blood to coat the surface—the same spot she'd punctured when she bound the Commander to her secret pact. A shiver ran through her at the thought as she passed the blade back.

Embla copied her movements, the two drops of their blood meeting with a spark of magic sealing their fates together. The human's shoulders seemed to fall in relief once the oath was sealed, tying their lives together.

Adelaide pushed her empty tankard towards Embla. "As your first act, *please* get me another drink." Those last few words came out as a stressed sigh, forcing the tavern folk to collectively laugh and return to their drinks as if nothing happened.

Embla chuckled and bowed as she took her jug towards the bar. Adelaide was certain it would be one of the many necessary refills she'd need until the world around her fell away, leaving her numb to the nightmares that continued to haunt her.

The dreams of her family lay out forgotten in The Dead Fields.

UNDER ZAREEN'S DIRECT ORDERS, Embla cut off Adelaide's supply of mead after the fourth tankard. The world was only slightly blurry, and her emotions were still sharp beneath the surface of her aching heart.

In that moment, she decided she hated them both.

"If I'm not even allowed to have a weapon, I don't understand why I must be sober," she complained as they readied their horses for another trek into the mountains. The day prior, they'd spent most of their time in The Dead Fields, and it left little time for any real attempts at quelling the spirits. Their goal was to try again, but Adelaide's only focus was on forgetting everything she'd seen the day before. "If this magic is as divine as you say, it should work even if I'm inebriated."

She knew she sounded like a spoiled child, but she simply couldn't help herself.

Perhaps I did drink more than I thought.

The Commander growled under his breath; his brows furrowed over tired eyes. His face was ashen, his eyes pinched until the crow's feet showed on what should've been a young face, and the purple bruises beneath his gaze seemed darker than before. Whatever ailed him, it was clearly grating on his nerves.

"Here," he snapped as he yanked a sword out of the nearest warrior's sheath and shoved it in her hands. The other man balked as he stared between them, his hands outstretched in surprise. "Will this get you to remain *silent*?"

She pursed her lips, the bratty child in her rearing its ugly head. "You know I can barely use this," she scoffed as she held the weapon back out to him. "Where is a bow and some arrows?" She paused as he took the sword and returned it to the warrior he'd stolen it from. "In fact, where is *my* bow and arrows?" she asked, the memory of their lost, golden edges infiltrating her drunken mind. "I assume you took them when you found me. If we're traveling back into the mountains, it would be best if I had those returned."

The Commander pinched the bridge of his nose and released a strained breath. "You didn't have any weapons on your person when we found you, but I'll arrange for a bow," he said each word carefully between gritted teeth as he waved over a scout. All that effort to remain calm would've been admirable if it weren't so obvious he was struggling to control his temper. "Retrieve a bow, quiver, and a bundle of arrows for The Promised," he ordered the scout, who was quick on her feet as she rushed to do as she was told.

There's that term again, The Promised, what does it mean?

The bow was thrust into her arms and the quiver hooked over her shoulder. The Commander wore a deep scowl the entire time, and it only worsened when Zareen arched a brow at him. "Karsten, are you certain it's wise to give her a weapon?"

"Don't care," he replied, before he turned on his heel and stalked to the horses. "We're wasting daylight and my men are dying. If she wishes to shoot us in the back, that's her choice."

"I'm right here, you know," Adelaide replied under her breath as her white knuckled grip on the bow tightened, the wood creaking beneath her grasp.

Zamir sighed as he clamped her on the shoulder and gave her a friendly shake. "Don't mind those two. I'm certain something just crawled up Karsten's trousers and died," he laughed, the sound infectious. "As for my sister..." He paused, the grin disappearing. "She's been like that for a long time. Not forever, but long enough to forget how things were before." He forced his smile back in place, but it didn't reach his warm brown eyes. "Let's move before they rip both our heads off."

Her thoughts scattered as they mounted their horses, her heart in her throat as she faced the mountains once more, and an uneasy feeling rotting in her gut at the solemn resignation and quiet anger in Karsten and Zareen's faces.

What happened to make Zareen so cold? And why does the Commander seem . . . sick?

THE EARTH SLIPPED between Adelaide's fingers, somehow moist and charred at the same time. As she let it drift back to the forest floor, its residue stained her palm black and left the stench of magic and death behind. In the deep crevice torn from the mountains, the sounds of The Wild Woods were distant, and no other signs of life remained.

Nothing would grow in that spot in the mountains again, even if it was once the lush garden she'd tended all her life. The rose bush Vane had planted was a dried heap crunching beneath her boots, and the linnaea flowers, her mother's namesake which once overtook the hillsides, were dead and buried in the ash.

The sight of her home in the distance, shattered at the bottom of the fissure, sobered her immediately.

"The magic here is *odd*," Sander noted as he tilted his face to the breeze and shifted his boots through the soot. "Can you feel it, Adelaide?"

She nodded, licking her lips as the tang of dreadful power assaulted her senses. "It's a wild thing. Untamed and untampered. Rage and wine spilled on a fur rug. Winter and wet like the first spring rainstorm, but it floods instead of heals," she said, struggling to piece together what she sensed thrumming from within the dirt. "But there's something else. Something more powerful and ancient beating at the doors of the ages. Fleeting form on the edges of my vision. It's angry, *so angry*. Its claws and blood and ash and death all combined in a stroke of—"

His hand on her back, softly weaving a calming wave of magic over her, lulled her words and severed her connection to the magic once in her grasp. It was a dull, distant thing then. Only a whisper of fear against her skin.

"Don't let it consume you," he warned softly as he helped her to her feet. "Whatever this is, it's not like Embla's spirit. It is not bound by flesh and blood, and it will swallow you whole if you let it."

She nodded and wiped her hands off on her trousers before she dared to take her stained palms to her face to rub at the stress building in her temples. "Do you have any idea who or what could've done this to my home, Sander?" she asked, hating herself for the way her voice shook.

"I'm sorry," he said with a shake of his head. "This is beyond even my understanding. However, I do believe I have a theory on how you can halt the spirits."

Zareen folded her arms from her spot a few feet away, by the first wooden beams of what remained of her home. "Last time I asked you about that, you claimed to have no ideas on the matter."

"That was in Rannadal," he began, folding his arms behind his back. Adelaide trained with him enough to recognize him preparing for one of his lectures, so she leaned against the stone walls of the cliffs they'd scaled to get into the crack within the earth. "Now that we're here, I believe I can sense the being causing this mayhem."

"You just said you didn't know what caused this," Adelaide pointed out.

He furrowed his brows at her interruption. "I did, but what caused the destruction in the first place is not the same being ushering forth the damned. Whether the two are working together remains unclear, but I know a few things with certainty." He paused to stomp his boot against the ground, kicking ash around him. "This fissure was caused by a person. Who they are and what allegiances they have, I do not know. Their magic is but a remnant, so they are no longer here, nor are they dead. They live on elsewhere and are probably planning their next move against The Divide."

"And against *us*," the Commander surmised, his gloved hands rubbing at the veins protruding from his temples. During their trek into The Divide, his sickly appearance hadn't improved, and neither had his growing temper. "Sander, how are you able to discern this?"

Adelaide rolled her eyes. "Are you suspicious of the elf, Commander?"

His lips screwed into a nasty scowl, and something harsh was about to cross his lips, but Zamir cleared his throat, loudly cutting him off. "Of course not. My sister already interrogated Sander when he first arrived and her ability to detect lies determined his innocence," he explained with his usual polite grace, but then he shifted uncomfortably. "But even I'm curious about how he can tell so much just by standing here. My magic can't do any of that."

Sander smirked, a proud tilt to his chin as he regarded the humans in front of them. "We're *elves*, Zamir," he explained with a warm chuckle. "We are the original creatures that held dominion over magic and brought it to Midgard from our realm. Even though your bloodline has a distant elf ancestor granting you magic, our kind will always have abilities beyond your comprehension."

Zareen bristled at the mention of their bloodline, and Adelaide scrutinized the movement.

"Please, continue," Adelaide said, steering the conversation back to the matter at hand.

The other elf smiled, seemingly pleased he could continue his impromptu lesson. "Like I was saying, there are three veins of magic coursing around us." He tapped his boot against the ground again. "The one who destroyed The Divide." He laid his palm across the crevice's walls, lithe fingers wiping black soot away from the silver stones. "The spirits who naturally reside within the mountains." He motioned forward, past her destroyed cabin and deeper into the bowels of the earth. "And the one who controls them, coaching them to escape through this tear."

"So, we kill whatever is encouraging the spirits to flee, and that should stop them from flooding the world?" Adelaide asked as she pushed herself off the wall.

He nodded, the wind traveling through the fissure whipping his long dark hair into a frenzy and sending a chill down Adelaide's spine. "Spirits don't normally enjoy entering this realm. It's an unnatural state for them and can be painful. They often prefer their home beneath us. Some may still escape, but it should considerably slow the tide. Until your magic is strong enough to heal the mountain entirely, this will be our best option."

The Commander gave a brisk nod and unsheathed his sword. "Then let's get started."

They marched deeper into the fissure, stepping over what little remained of her childhood home shattered against the rocks. Logs and fabric were strewn across the blackened earth, tangled with the plants and soot until she could hardly tell a charred quilt apart from the smoldered remains of her mother's rocking chair.

The bricks that used to be part of their cabin's hearth poked out of the ground, red against the shadows stretched across them with every step deeper into the earth. They lit lanterns and torches to beat back the darkness, even as the sun rested high above. Between the towering cliffs gouged out of the earth and the canopy of pines above, little light could reach them at all. All the flames did was send her heart racing, their own shadows stretching across the stones until they were giant monsters soaring overhead.

"None of our scouts have traveled further than this," the Commander said as he paused at the ledge of a cliff. The rift traveled deeper, but they would need to carefully maneuver across a ridge to get any lower. "Are you ready?" he asked, his voice just a bit softer.

My family could be down there, rotting, and no one would know.

She nodded, so they descended into the dark.

"It's too quiet," Zareen noted when her boots finally settled on flat ground again. They were so deep into the fissure that they ended up inside the cave systems fueling the hot springs. Water trickled from the stones above their heads, and large cracks threatened to take the entire roof down. "Our scouts said spirits were leaving this place every few minutes. We haven't seen any of them."

Zamir snorted. "Perhaps they're terrified of Adelaide's magnificent power?"

Adelaide sighed as she absently rubbed at her sore, scarred left eye. "That would be a nice fantasy, would it not?"

The Commander grunted in agreement as he led their way across the cave, his boots splashing through the trickling water. The sound echoed back to them on all sides, whispering against the stones. "If that were the case, we would simply keep you in the mountains like you desired and have Sander train you here until we could seal the tear," he said, pausing at a split in the path, and his pinched expression deepened in the harsh lantern light. "Sadly, I've never known us to be *that* lucky."

Some small part of her bristled at his words. They were the ones who insisted on her remaining in Rannadal and dragged her from the mountains when she escaped, but at the slightest convenience the Commander would toss her aside? Even if it was her desire to leave and return to her home, the rejection vexed her.

'Of course they would act that way. They don't truly want a Keeper in their ranks. That's why he mentioned leaving Sander here as well, to abandon the elves in the rubble.'

She shook those childish thoughts away. The spirits wouldn't kneel to a mortal's mere presence, so the possibility of her staying wasn't real. It shouldn't bother her so much that she would be left behind so easily.

But it does. It sours something within me that once could've been so sweet.

She followed the others deeper into the mountains, where the land was still and even the water was silenced as it veered into different regions carved into the stone. There was just the brushing of fabric and the clank of their swords scraping the rocks. Their breaths painted the air with white clouds as the cold settled in around them, creeping down their spines.

"It feels like something is watching us," Zareen noted as she peered with wide eyes at every darkened corner.

"*Something* is," Sander said as he kept his gaze focused straight ahead. "But what is it?"

In the quiet following the question, her thoughts returned

to the harsh words the Commander had allowed to spill from his lips.

'He said they'd be lucky to get rid of me. I disappointed them when I couldn't use my magic. I'm only worth what I can do. That's why Mother looked at me that way. I let her down even before I let her die.'

No, no. That's wrong. They're not dead. They can't be dead.

'It's a possibility, and I haven't even been searching this cave to see where they are. I don't want to know, so I'm not looking. I'd rather delude myself than face the truth.'

What is wrong with me? Why can't I shake this feeling? It's eating me alive.

'This is why I frequent the tavern. It dulls the thoughts and helps me forget who I am—the failure *of the Ayalra Clan. The one who let her kin die. The only elf who never had magic. The heathen masquerading as their savior. No wonder they want me to leave as soon as possible. All I bring is death.*

'Just like Vane.'

Adelaide gasped, her hand clutching her chest as she doubled over. Her left eye burned, the world in that part of her vision dimming. Something frigid and bitter latched onto her heart, squeezing it from the inside out as her body went cold, its warmth leeched away by an unknown force.

Yet, it was somehow *familiar.*

Zamir coughed, and when she dared to meet his gaze, it glittered with tears. "Something is wrong," he murmured from between gasps for breath. "I haven't thought like this in years."

Sander kneeled, bracing himself on one knee beside her. Tears he refused to acknowledge trailed down his cheeks as he grasped at his own chest. "Whatever spirit this is has infected our minds. Don't listen to it."

Zareen leaned against one of the walls, her head in her hands. "How can we not?"

The Commander was the only one who remained standing,

his focus darting to each of them in panic. "What's wrong?" he asked, his gold eyes blazing through the shadows as the torch in his hand flickered in the growing cave breeze. "What's happening to all of you?"

The winds picked up speed, pushing the hair away from Adelaide's face and cutting through every flame until they were left with only the pitch darkness. Elves could see better than humans in the dark, but even she found herself blindly reaching out into the void for something to keep her grounded. Her hands landed on Zamir's arm and Sander's shoulder as she braced herself against the tunnel of air blasting over them.

"What's happening to them should also befall you, and yet your mind remains a maze I cannot travel," a voice murmured, its gloomy tone carried on the air until it seemed to caress their very skin. *"Tell me, Karsten Strom, are you truly so broken even the damned would lose their minds if they dared to breach yours?"*

Unbidden, the memory of when she first met the Commander infiltrated her thoughts. A spirit clamored for control, feeding on her emotions, and he was the one to sever the tie.

"Sorrow," she panted, struggling to regain her breath as the heartache in her chest threatened to crush her from the inside out. "I didn't expect to hear your lies again."

She sensed the spirit twist around her, tightening its hold like a coiled snake ready to strike, and its words were suddenly both in her head and echoing around her. *"Are they truly lies, Adelaide?"* it asked, its voice slithering across her spine and leaving a wet trail behind. *"I am not of mortal flesh and blood, so I have no reason to omit the truth. I'm not like you or Karsten. I need not hide what I am or what I've* done."

Bile rose in her throat from the sour pit in her core. Would the spirit tell the Commander about the Blood Oath she forced upon him? Would that truth be laid bare and ensure her demise by his sword? A spirit could convince any of them to act against their nature and turn against each other in their sadness. It would be the easiest way to tear them apart and ensure the greatest amount of sorrow for it to feed on.

It chuckled in her ear and said for only her to hear, *'Oh, don't worry about that. There is so much else I can torment you with. Why start there?'*

The spirit's voice boomed over their heads, its timber rattling in their bones. *"Sander, what a fool you've been,"* it began as it lessened its hold on her only to fiercely grasp the man beside her. *"Your love is gone, and yet you cannot help falling again. Isn't that your fate? To always fall from grace."* It snapped to the side, feeding on Zamir next. *"What a horrible brother you are. If it weren't for your stain on the family line, neither of you would've run away."*

Zareen snarled from somewhere else in the cave. "Do not speak to him!"

It unfurled itself, growing larger until she could feel its form built from their tears soaking her tunic. *"Nothing you can say or do will make up for it now. You're already too lost and far away from home. No one will be there when you break, but you already knew that."*

The glint of a flame tore her attention away from where she believed the spirit was, pushing back the darkness and highlighting the Commander's tormented expression as he coached the tiny light to life. The glint of his sword caught in the firelight, but they still couldn't pinpoint where the spirit was exactly.

Then, it was atop him.

Karsten fell, the air pushed from his lungs as he kept his hands outstretched, ensuring the fire didn't die. Crouched over him was the sodden, indigo form of the spirit digging its astral claws into his back. He cried out, his hands shaking around the fire flickering in his grasp.

Its shape morphed, its nonexistent face forging itself with

every tear they shed. Its back, once serpentine in nature, shuddered as it curved into hunched legs that bent backwards at the knees to point towards the cave ceiling.

"What do you think your father will say when he sees you next? Will he remind you that you aren't really his son, or will you have accepted your place already?" Sorrow demanded, his claws gouging deeper and forcing a scream to fall from his lips before he cut it off, biting his lip until it bled to contain the sound. *"I herald the spirits from these depths, harkening them to our master's bidding in your realm. Even I know my place, and yet you always fall short of doing so. Always reaching for more than you deserve—and you know it."*

"Get off of him!" she shouted as she finally caught her breath, her hand stabilizing just enough for her to tug her bow free from her back. "You don't know us. You only know our greatest sorrows: the things that bring us the most pain. That doesn't mean they're real."

"Oh," the spirit said, its empty eye sockets meeting her gaze. *"But yours are, Adelaide."*

It skittered closer, its back legs keeping Karsten pinned, his face pressed onto the floor, and the dying fire glowing beneath its belly. She needed to free her arrows and land a shot before the flame died, but her hands trembled around the quiver and she dropped it.

"You remember how it hurt, don't you?" it asked, its face twisting as dark, moist hair sprouted from its head and lay thick across its paling expression. *"That delicious despair you felt when he died ravaged your heart."* Her finger twisted around the fletching of an arrow she lost in the shadows, her heart hammering in her throat. *"It nearly ended you, left you sobbing and screaming to Gods who do not answer."* The memories of those days after she discovered Vane and his family massacred crossed her vision, blurring the world around her. She was broken then, and it was only her kin who had managed to put

her back together. *"How much worse will this feel, when you finally accept that your family is dead?"*

She placed her arrow on the notch in her bow, but her strength waned when she tried to pull the bowstring taunt. With the light dimming, she only had one chance before they were cast in darkness and she could no longer see the target, but she was weak.

That was all she'd ever been—too weak to save the people she cared about.

The sorrow spirit's face contorted, lines and pores taking shape. Brown, kind eyes she knew like the back of her hand formed above a demented smile. Vane's face was staring back at her, tormenting her with his memory even as the rest of its materialized body continued contorting in misshapen shapes.

"They all died because of your failure," it said, its voice taking on the honeysuckle sweet tone of the man she'd once loved. *"That's all you ever do. Fail and disappoint the people who depend on you."*

"No." The Commander's voice, sure and strong, broke through the spell the spirit weaved around her heart. His face was still pressed against the ground, and he spoke without seeing her as he struggled to speak from where the spirit continued holding him in place. "Adelaide, you saved my life. You saved all of us that night. I know you don't remember, but you didn't fail us."

A harsh, choked laugh spilled from her lips as her fingers trembled on the bowstring. "Haven't I though?" she questioned, her breath rattling in her aching lungs.

He shook his head, struggling against the spirit's grasp on his skull to meet her gaze. It danced with the light of the dying fire, burning straight through her and searing his words into her heart.

"You could *never* disappoint us or your family," he said between clenched teeth as the spirit's clawed foot dug into his hair. "All you've done is try to find them and keep your word to protect us when you had no reason to trust us at all." A self-deprecating laugh ripped from his chest. "I'm a former Knight, and you've *still* decided to help us. You could've killed me, but you haven't."

"He's a liar," the spirit hissed. *"You already know it's within his nature to deceive you."*

"No, he's right," Zamir said from his place beside her, lying on the ground where the weight of the spirit's whispers kept him pinned and lost in his fraying mind. "You only fail when you give up, and you haven't yet. It's why you're still here—why we're all still here."

Something in those words rocked her, unfurling the spirit's claws from within her chest.

I'm still here. I didn't lay down and die beside Vane when I discovered his body, even when that was the only thing I wanted to do. I didn't leap from the cliffs when my home was destroyed, I went to find my kin. I never stopped trying.

Her gaze slipped back to Karsten as he struggled beneath the weight of the spirit. He uttered nothing more, but something in her gaze took her back to that night they trained together. She was relentless in the fight, even using a sword she barely began practicing with.

"Your grip on the hilt is wrong. You're holding on so tight you're not allowing movement," he'd said, his words conjuring an immediate, stubborn response from her gut.

I'm holding on too tight and refusing to let go of what I think about myself. It's what Sorrow is feeding off, what this spirit has been draining me of since I first encountered it in the chapel. Dulling my emotions with ale and running away into the woods has never been my nature. I've only been feeling this way because of its influence that's devouring me from within.

Adelaide couldn't move on if she kept holding on so tightly to her past—to Vane and her kin. She wouldn't be able to save anyone, least of all her own family, if she kept allowing the sorrow and doubt to eat her alive.

She let it go.

Her arrow flew from the taut bowstring, piercing the spirit wearing Vane's face. It caught the creature between the eyes, warping its expression into a replica of the corpse she found six years prior, before the body burst into a bright show of indigo light.

The fire died, whisked away in the blast of magic.

"NO FURTHER SIGHTINGS of the damned to report," a scout said, his growing smile lightening her heart. "Whatever you did, Promised, thank you."

She still wasn't sure how to respond to that title, so she simply nodded.

"We don't know how long this reprieve will last and the mountains aren't sealed entirely," the Commander responded as he scribbled something down on a parchment and handed it to the other man. "Ensure we use this time to further search for the Aylara Clan, tend to our wounded, and replenish supplies."

The scout gave a quick salute before running to deliver his orders. Once the man was out of sight, he crumbled to the side and barely caught himself on the table covered in reports that was arranged right at the path into the mountains. Her hands reached out to help, but she pulled back at the last second.

"Commander, you don't look well," she said as her gaze focused on the smearing of blood staining his back from where the spirit had dug its claws in.

He waved off her worry and rearranged the reports littering his desk. "Don't worry about me. You saved us yet again. The least I can do is not complain about the wounds I have in the aftermath."

She couldn't bring herself to mention that she had noticed he was unwell before they ever entered the mountains, so she started to drift away. A hot meal was calling her name from the tavern, and she was obliged to answer that call, but something made her pause.

"For what it's worth, I could only do it because of you," she admitted into the quiet. He didn't turn around, his hands still rifling through the parchment. "You're an excellent teacher." Still, he didn't respond. "Commander—" She stopped, his title suddenly feeling like lead in her mouth. "*Karsten*," she began, and that time he did stop to listen. "Thank you."

He returned to his reports. "It was nothing."

She wanted to tell him it was *everything*, but her throat closed around that admittance.

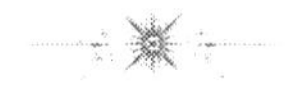

THE FIRST GOOD piece of news they had received since Adelaide woke, broken and battered after falling down the mountain, arrived shortly after she woke the next day.

The spirits remained distant, no longer flooding the realm even after the warriors evacuated the mountains. There was still a chance another spirit could take Sorrow's place and lead the damned into their realm, but the mountains felt peaceful again for the first time in weeks.

The few spirits still daring to trickle out into their world were typically in their physical forms and were done away with by an efficient sword. Until she was strong enough to seal the tear, that was the most they could do to aid Skagi and their warriors on the border.

Yes, because I will *be strong enough eventually. Not if.*

With those reports, they quickly decided they would leave for Rannadal the following day. That left Adelaide to explore the few remaining shops in town, the humans there so grateful that they seemed to forget she was an elf at all and welcomed her with open arms.

In the evening, she ended up in Embla's bedroom across from hers at the inn. She helped her pack what meager belongings she had, including a painting of her and her husband, Torvald, that was commissioned by a local artist on their wedding day.

"Poor girl is gone now," Embla murmured as she packed the portrait in her bag. "Most of Skagi is, but they can rebuild thanks to you."

Adelaide recoiled. "Embla, *please*, I've received enough thanks for one day."

She clucked her tongue, a small admonishment, as she took the quilt from the other woman's hands to fold it properly and shove it into her bag. "Then you should stop doing things deserving of praise, my dear," she said with a laugh. "Everyone here talks, you know. I've already heard whispers about you helping the townsfolk today."

A blush burned across her cheeks as she looked away. "I just did what I could."

"Which is still more than most," Embla countered as she closed her bag. "And it's exactly that reason which made it easy to aid you. Someone must look out for you when you're busy looking out for all of us." Her eyes darkened just a fraction, and she bit her lip. "Besides, I don't think Odin or Olena would be pleased with me if I disobeyed their instructions."

She raised a brow. "What do you mean?"

"The night you saved me," she began as she clasped her hands in front of her. "I had a vision. I don't know what God sent it to me, but it was the most vivid dream I've ever had."

"What did you dream about?" she asked, her heart thundering in her ears. She wasn't certain why, but she knew whatever Embla's vision was, it would come to pass.

She shrugged, a blush crossing her cheeks instead. "I will save your life in return, not so far in the future from now." She motioned to her own face, her finger dancing along the left side. "Your scar still wasn't fully healed. It looked the same in my vision."

"Well, thank you in advance," she said, earning a grin from the other woman. "May I ask what exactly you're going to save me from?"

Embla's smile disappeared, and an uneasy tension filled the air. "It's better you don't know."

With that, they parted ways for the night.

THE NEXT MORNING, they swapped forces with those stationed in Skagi, taking the more weary and injured warriors back with them. Despite the horrors they'd witnessed in The Divide, there was a lightness to their march growing with each step further from the mountains.

Their journey back to Rannadal was a far more joyous one than the trek to the mountains. They wore hope like a banner before them on their march towards what they deemed home.

For now, I guess it's my home too.

But home was more than where she slept, it was the people: *her* people.

Begrudgingly, she admitted the humans around her *were* her people, at least for the time being. They relied on each other and, with a heavy burden weighing on her shoulders, she admitted to herself that she did like them well enough. And, with deep regret, she realized she was rather fond of one man in particular.

Karsten.

She found herself staring at the back of his head as he led from the front, his blond curls shining in the early morning light. It was as if he and the sun were one. They rose together, retired in tandem with one another, and were the same matching gold. He'd shown her patience and kindness, like the first light after the ever-winters freezing her mountains, even though he was obviously in pain. It woke something in her that hibernated throughout the coldest, darkest months of the year.

Like that first morning of spring after Vane died.

Something in her chest shuddered and shrank away at the thought. Vane and his entire kin were murdered by Knights. He'd be furious at the idea of her comparing them, even by simply saying the Commander brought her comfort like the first rays of sun did. She needed to stay strong and far away from any remaining appreciation for his kindness. It was a slippery slope.

Especially with how handsome he is.

Her cheeks burned as she tore her gaze away, focusing on the trees instead.

Damn me. I must be desperate to eye a human Knight in such a way.

Well, it has been a while.

By "*a while*", she regrettably noted that she hadn't lain with another since long before Vane died. Their union had been friendly but lacked the passion of the previous one-off encounters she'd had on the few trips she'd taken beyond their borders. It had been more of a marriage of convenience, of what was expected of them, but her love had still been true.

Still, their lovemaking had never fully satisfied and they hadn't partaken in it often. Once to consummate the marriage, their first time together, and a few moments between that and his death. A year and a half of marriage while living with her entire family inside one small cabin hadn't lent itself to passionate thralls.

Maybe, if they'd been given enough time and resources to build a home of their own like they dreamed of, it would've been different.

She buried the regret as far as it would go but it twisted, knotting with her breakfast and turning her stomach sour. That sick feeling only made her determination rise.

No more thoughts of handsome Knights. No more visions of a future with Vane that could never be. No more traitorous thoughts about curled blond hair gripped tight in her hands, warm lips trailing down her neck, leaving pure heat behind in its wake—

Oh, for Odin's fucking sake.

She physically shook herself and played it off to any prying eye like it was merely a chill.

"An elf feeling cold?" Zamir asked from atop his horse as he trotted closer. "The world truly is ending."

"Not if I can help it," she said with a roll of her eyes and a sharp squaring of her shoulders. "Besides, Ragnarök says nothing of spirits ending the world. This will merely be a small blip in history: a moment most will forget."

It was his turn to roll his eyes and pin her with a stubborn glare. "Hardly, dearest Adelaide. At the very least, it will be remembered as the time humans uplifted an elf as Promised. That will not be forgotten."

"Embla called me that," she said, just as confused as when she'd first heard the word. With only Zamir as company, she finally felt like she could voice her confusion. "What in all the realms does it mean?"

He sputtered and brought his horse to a halt. She followed suit as the rest of their caravan moved on without them. His brows lifted until they were hidden behind his shaggy hairline.

She found a strange sort of satisfaction in her ability to silence the boisterous man, even as she found his shocked expression unbecoming on his handsome face.

Stop seeing these humans as beautiful, you fool.

She could hardly help it though. Even Zareen, as grumpy as she was, shone so brightly with her sharp cheekbones and plump lips that rivaled any Goddess. She had, most unfortunately, found herself in the company of the most stunning humans she'd ever encountered. Even the casual dalliances of her youth were of no comparison. Perhaps because her memories of them were blurred with time and drink.

Or she'd simply been unlucky—*or lucky*—enough to find herself among Gods and Goddesses made flesh and blood.

With golden hair melted by sun rays and fire-forged amber eyes.

Silence, you absolute dumbass.

"No one told you?" The silence that met Zamir's question was his answer. He slapped a hand over his eyes and sighed so hard the breath ruffled the ties of his loose, open top. "Of course not, they're all absolutely useless." He lowered his palm to meet her gaze and almost seemed pained as he spoke. "Do you have any knowledge of Cislenians? Of whom and what they follow?"

She shrugged as she nudged her horse, urging him to continue down the worn path ahead. "I simply know it overtook The Old Gods in Midgard—made them *old* in the first place rather than just *The Gods*. Humans have bastardized the temples of those who still follow the ancient path, much like the chapel in Rannadal that was once ours."

He grimaced at her words. "Besides that, what do you know?"

"Not a damn thing and I don't care to."

"Well, you might want to change your attitude on the matter fast," he said, earning him a firm glare. "Don't look at me, I still follow the old path. But most of Rannadal, and their forces for that matter, are Cislenian." She suppressed her surprise and pinned her gaze on the road ahead. *Zamir is a follower just like me, even in these strange lands? Even in a town which stole our temples? And he made peace with it?* "The Great Conversion hit this region hard, but there are still those of us who pushed back from the waves of religious zealots and held true to our faith. We just aren't doing it as openly as before. Jarl Lefa does what she can to maintain the peace and allow us to practice openly, but it gets harder every season." He sighed, deep and low in his chest. "But that's beside the point."

"And what is your point exactly?"

He shook off whatever bothered him and took his horse a few paces ahead, forcing her to meet his gaze. "The dual gods of Order and Chaos, the Divine and the Dread, are Olena and Cismir. They maintain the balance of right and wrong in the world. When humans destroyed Alfheim, Midgard was under the command of Saint Zelmer, a patron of Cismir. It has been foreseen through prophecy for over a millennia that his opposite, a prophet sent by Olena, would right the balance of the world back to one of Order and sway the tides away from Chaos." She pinched the bridge of her nose, hoping to block out what she knew to be coming. "They call that prophet The Divine Promise."

She felt like screaming and bit her tongue until it bled, coating her mouth in copper. Those humans believed her not just to be a miracle but to be *divine*? To be part of a prophecy set by Gods she didn't even believe in? To be promised to them, as if she were not a person but a *thing* to be shared?

What a bunch of fanatics.

"Anyone who believes that is a fool," she snapped, although she made sure to keep her voice low enough so no one nearby could hear. The last thing she needed was to offend any of them and lose the fake title ensuring her safety. "I am no more blessed by a false religion than that rock or tree. I was simply unfortunate enough to be at the wrong place at the worst of times. You should see to it that your Jarl quiets such rumors."

He smirked. "You're not curious about what would send so many to believe in an elf's divinity?"

"Not in the slightest," she grumbled as she urged her horse to move faster, hoping it would dissuade Zamir from following.

Fools, the whole lot of them.

But, by the Gods, what would Mother think if she caught wind of such falsities? She'd tug my pointed ear off and hang me from a tree by it. Nissa and Birgitta would have a grand time at my expense, no doubt. But what of the youngest of them? She would be proud of me just because she was too young to know any better.

She swallowed her rising bile as the girl's face flashed through her mind.

Adelaide tried her hardest not to think of her since her memory brought the most pain. At the very least, the rest of her kin were old enough that their deaths were unfortunate but not an entire tragedy. They'd lived full lives. Their mother, in particular, was ancient and lived every story imaginable—except for perhaps one of romantic love. She could bury them, if they were truly dead, and comfort herself with the knowledge that, at the very least, they'd *lived.* But the youngest in their clan? If they perished, they'd hardly even had a chance to live.

That, she knew, she couldn't bury.

She swallowed her fears, focusing instead on Zamir's words. She hated her curiosity about why the humans thought of her as a prophetic idol from their holiest of Gods, but how could she not? She'd been despised by so many humans for so long, how was she supposed to feel being revered or even *worshiped* by them?

With her thoughts finally focused on matters far removed from her deepest sorrows and regrets, she felt relaxed enough to look forward and pin her gaze on the horizon.

Only to meet the sweetest honey-colored gaze and fall down a slippery slope once more that was a blissful distraction from where her dark thoughts once were.

Gods, I'm completely screwed.

AT THE HALFWAY point between Skagi and Rannadal, they made camp closer to the mountains and further from the streams carving themselves through the hills.

It put her at ease, being closer to the only home she'd ever known. The small creatures and foliage were the same as what she'd always hunted and foraged for. Rannadal wasn't so far removed from her mountains, but the small differences set her on edge.

The foxes were reddish instead of white, the winds didn't howl and merely whispered, and she was always surrounded by humans instead of her clan and neighbors. She was outnumbered by the humans she once chased far from those very knolls. Her purpose was to stick with her clan, guard her kin, and protect her mountains from the same humans she broke bread with.

Zamir passed her a bowl of a steaming broth that made her mouth water, even when she couldn't name the exact spices tickling her nose.

"After our previous conversation today, it's come to my attention that I might not be fully aware of who or *what* I've aligned myself with," she said, hardly able to meet the man's eyes as she admitted to her own ignorance. "I would appreciate being better informed."

"For starters, you should know that I'm the most handsome bachelor in the entirety of Rannadal, so you shouldn't set your standards any higher," he mused, tapping his spoon against his lips.

She resisted the urge to push him off the bench they shared by gripping her bowl tighter. "Zamir, *please*." He sighed and motioned for her to continue, so she took a deep breath and asked, "What type of army is this? I thought Rannadal was just a training ground for Knights, not a fully-fledged infantry needing command."

She hated admitting that she was so unaware. It felt like acknowledging she was poor at her job and hadn't kept close enough attention on her human neighbors. Was it that same folly which caused her home to fall? She could hardly bear the thought.

"That's what Rannadal once was, not too long ago," he said with a smirk that fell on the kinder side, rather than having its usual smug edge. "Three years ago, Jarl Lefa fell deathly ill. The healers, both magic bound and medicinal in nature, knew she wouldn't make it through the winter. Perhaps not even through the night. At the same time, Rannadal was famished with blighted crops and stolen coins. She prayed to Olena to grant life to herself and the town. As the stories go, her prayers were answered in the form of a vision."

"A vision of what exactly?" she asked as she blew on the hot steam rising from her next bite of food.

He motioned out to the region before them: the grassy knolls burdened by the boots and bedrolls of their warriors. "An army fighting in Olena's name for the good and fair. To bring justice to those who need it and vengeance upon those who deserve it." He paused to sip the broth, color returning to his cheeks with each warm gulp. "Lefa made a promise to the Goddess that night. She would ready ten thousand men for any war which called upon their need. Many believe you were the shepherd of Olena's message, that it was time for the army to fight for peace. Thus, The Covenant was born," he explained, finishing with a dramatic bow before he returned to his brew with a shrug. "Or so the story goes. Could be a load of horseshit."

A harsh laugh ripped through her chest at his quick shift in demeanor. "Beautiful story, Zamir, but I fear you've only confirmed my worst fears." He arched a brow as she leaned in, lowered her voice, and said, "I've joined a human cult."

It was his turn for a gut-deep laugh as he clanked their bowls together. "As have I!"

They drank until warmth filled their bellies which echoed with the cold only minutes before. The roaring fires around camp cast a hazy glow, filling her with a comfort she'd thought lost along with her home. If she hadn't been so bone-deep tired, she would've laughed at the sheer irony of finding peace in the humans who she once hunted and in the fires which claimed her home.

"If I'm understanding you correctly," she began, her voice cutting through the tranquility lying like a heavy blanket over them. "Your Jarl created an army of ten thousand warriors for a fight that hadn't started yet?"

He scooted onto the floor and rested his neck on the log Adelaide continued perching on. "Not exactly. Karsten has been attempting to increase our numbers for the past year, but it wasn't until The Divide was torn that fresh recruits truly appeared. Before, it was primarily retirees seeking a cause to change up their mundane existence, the Knights whom Lefa conscripted into service, and Rannadal's Vikings who naturally followed Karsten's lead after obeying his orders when he was among their ranks."

She felt small, jagged pieces of what she knew about the Commander's life begin to unfold before her. He was a Knight *and* a Viking? He couldn't have been much older than she was, and she'd barely celebrated her twenty-sixth name's day. By elf standards, she was hardly an adult. Old enough for marriage, but not old enough to sit in a tribunal of elders or claim any title. She hadn't yet proved herself to her clan, let alone to her people as a whole.

She hadn't even made her pilgrimage to New Alfheim. Her whole world was the mountains and her family. She hadn't lived long enough to know anything else. Human lives were shorter and, to many elves, less important for that very reason. They were too rash and quick to jump into action. They wouldn't live to see the two-hundred-year eclipse or the rise and fall of empires like her kin would. They would simply live and die and be forgotten: a nameless spirit of what once was without any real consequence to the realms.

So, how has Karsten known and seen so much?

She stood and brushed the sleep from her eyes even as her body cried out in protest. The day of travel wore on her, but she knew she couldn't rest until she had answers.

"I have further questions I think the Commander would be more suited to answering. Where can I find him?"

Zamir stifled a yawn and pointed deeper into the camp where the tents grew closer together. A suffocating sight from her perspective, but the warriors seemed to enjoy themselves and the mead which heavily flowed between horns. It was a ruckus even from the great distance she and Zamir found peace in. For answers, she'd brave the drunken humans and all their obnoxious laughter.

Besides, if Karsten is half out of his mind with drink, he might be keen on answering my questions.

She weaved through the throng of bodies who pushed with earnest deeper into the camp. Cheering and laughter grew until her pointed ears hummed with the sound: an echoing crescendo that became one singular, booming voice of the fighters she was determined not to stay around for too long.

Regardless of what some of the people around her believed she was, she still didn't trust their motives. Rannadal's Knights were conscripted into the ranks of the other recruits, so most of them wore the same armor when traveling out of town. She couldn't tell who belonged to which faction in The Covenant's army and she didn't wish to find out the hard way that she'd bumped into the wrong sort of person.

Perhaps a few humans could be trusted, like Zamir. The rest remained unknown to her and she wasn't enthused about changing that.

Across the main fire roaring through the night, she found two men locked in arms with their teeth bared and fists covered in each other's blood. The crowd around her screamed louder in response to each fist connecting with a jaw or gut. She expected someone to jump in and break the fight up, but no one came.

She finally spotted Karsten at the back of the group circling the brawl, but he remained rooted in his spot like the towering trees in the distance—watching but never wavering.

Adelaide shoved through the horde and finally took her first full breath once she was on the outer edge, standing beside the Commander who gave her a passing nod before returning to watch the thickening mob. The heavy weight on her shoulders from being surrounded lessened with the free wind to her back and the glimmer of the fire lighting up the shadows.

A different force burdened her as she followed the flickers of flames as they danced across Karsten's face.

He looked worn, like a man dragged under a carriage and spat back out into the streets. Dark bags hung heavy below his tired eyes that creased with each resounding yelp of the men locked in battle and every shout from the enthusiastic audience. He was ashen and his shoulders sagged where they were normally firmly frozen at attention.

Perhaps he was watching and wavering all at once, like a branch threatening to snap under the mounting pressure of a blizzard.

"You look like shit."

He sighed, and his shoulders sank deeper. "*Thanks.*"

She shook off her initial surprise and composed herself by staring at the fight again. "I didn't mean it like that," she said as she struggled to find the right words. She wasn't *worried.* That would imply she cared about his wellbeing. No, it couldn't be that. So, why did she feel so mangled on the inside at the slightest downward turn of his lips?

Don't think about his lips.

He hummed in thought and she hated herself for noticing the way his chapped lips trembled against the sound. "Lady Aylara, was that *truly* your best attempt at showing concern?"

"Don't make a fit about it," she said as she looked anywhere but at him.

"That was honestly quite pathetic on your part, but I'll accept it nonetheless."

She pierced him with a scowl that could rival her mother's, but he didn't seem to notice as his weary gaze remained pinned on the fire that's heat barely reached them. She braced herself against the nearest tent post and dug her heels into the ground, rooting herself in place so she could get the answers she sought without running away.

Yes, running away. Not moving closer to him.

"Zamir brought to my attention that I'm not familiar with your ways in Rannadal and other human customs. Like whatever display is happening before us. I figured you may be best suited to give me answers." She paused as he peered at her from the corner of his gaze, the weariness never leaving him. "If you're feeling up for it," she challenged with a grin.

He scoffed and shook his shoulders, firmly righting their once-fallen position. "I think that's a good idea. It's best if we all understand each other. Perhaps we could trade: a question for an answer?"

She hesitated, unsure of what in all the realms he could

possibly want to know about her, elves, or her life before. "If it's within reason, yes."

He gave a small bow, just the tilt of his head towards the earth, and she noticed how his curls bobbed out of their usual places and danced across his forehead. "Ask away, my lady." She jutted her chin out towards the fight to indicate her first question of the night. "They're simply letting off some steam. Those two are like brothers, so this is for fun and not due to any actual disagreements. They'll stop before they seriously injure each other. If they did, they'd never be able to live with themselves."

"You humans are incredibly strange."

He chuckled and the sound twisted something painful inside her gut. "Believe it or not, you're not the first person to tell me that." He scratched at the stubble lining his jaw, which she remembered was far lighter that morning. "I'll give you another answer," he said, pausing to motion to his face. "I look like *'shit'* because I'm staying awake to keep watch. Wouldn't want any accidents or godless deeds committed while I slept peacefully. If they know I'm watching, they'll keep themselves more in line than if I was away. Many of the fresh recruits are still incredibly young, hardly in their sixteenth turn around the sun. They'll need more guidance than the seasoned members here."

"How old are you anyways?" she asked. "I can never tell with humans."

It took him a moment to remember and the fact that such a simple question seemed to perplex him more than the others piqued her interest. "I suppose my twenty-eighth name's day will be shortly before Yule, but I haven't celebrated that in years." He said the last part as if it were an afterthought, as if one's day of birth or naming was inconsequential.

If she'd ever gone without a celebration for her name's day, her mother would've wrung her pointed ears straight off her skull.

"But I believe I've earned more than one question, three if I'm not mistaken," he said, his words causing the hair on her neck to stand straight towards the sky. Would he ask about her watch rotations in The Divide? How many Knights she slaughtered and could be put on trial for?

"I suppose you have," she said, feeling as though she were resigning herself to a burning at the stake.

He thought for a moment as they watched one of the men finally give into the fight before he was replaced by Zareen. She seemed to be seeking her own pound of flesh for the night as she shrugged off her cloak, weapon, and tunic to ready herself for the brawl. Her top half was bare aside from a linen wrapped around her chest did little to hide the scars littering her torso.

"If The Divide hadn't fallen, what would you be doing right now?"

Her heart hammered in her chest and she struggled to find an acceptable answer to his question that wouldn't see her dead and buried. If she were back home and saw so many humans a few yards from her borders, she'd be bathed in their blood. That was the simple truth of it. There was no way to describe that to the leader of those very same warriors.

Especially not when the guilt of it all made her sick, forcing the broth back up her throat.

"I said any question within reason."

"I think that's a fairly reasonable question," he said with a scoff. "For example, I'd be back in Rannadal readying for our next day of training. Perhaps actually getting to enjoy a pint of mead by the fire myself."

Right. Simple answers about home would do. Nothing about protecting it.

She swallowed the bile and bit her lip, her gaze forever

pinned on the dancing flames so she had any excuse not to look at his face and break under her own growing guilt.

"Don't ever feel guilty about doing what you must to survive," her mother had once told her when she was the ripe age of thirteen and made her first kill of something other than an animal. *"They would've gutted you and left your body for us to find. Don't ever hesitate to do what's needed to come back home to me."*

"I'd be helping mother and Nissa clean up after supper," she said, the words soothing both her guilt and the ache she felt at her family's continued absence. "Haustblot is approaching, so the others would be plucking the ripest options from the garden and we'd have food to last us weeks. We'd be preserving vegetables, trading with nearby towns for fruit, and drying out the meats from my hunts. In a good year, it would last us through Ostara." She shivered as a chill crept up her spine. "But even if the garden was still standing, it doesn't seem like a good year for harvest."

"Can you remind me what Haustblot and Ostara are?" he asked, his tongue tripping over the words as he tried to repeat them.

"If your kind still followed the old ways, you'd know them." She grinned and finally allowed her gaze to be stolen by his instead of remaining captivated by the flames. "Ostara is our celebration of the start of spring. Haustblot is our harvest during the autumn equinox. I suppose the closest thing your kind still celebrates is Winter Nights, which we call Vetrnaetr—the day of the last harvest where the veil between us and the spirits is thinnest."

He settled his hand on the battle axe strapped to his side. "Yes, we'll need to be well prepared for that day this year. We don't know what could happen with The Divide during that period while it's torn open."

That hazy feeling of nostalgia for a time with her family she may never have again was washed away by cold dread. "You're right. I hadn't even thought of that."

They lapsed into a heavy silence for a time and she found herself glancing in his direction more than once. There was still one more question for him to ask, and she was both worried and looking forward to what it might be. She also still had her most important question to ask: the very one that brought her to his side that night. What made him become a Knight, then a Viking, and, finally, a Commander? And in such a short amount of time?

"Before all of this," he said, waving to the torn mountain and the warriors around them. "How did you handle the spirits?"

She arched a brow. "What do you mean?"

He sighed and his shoulders fell once more, the exhaustion returning to his gaze. "You lived atop the very home of the spirits. They must've come to you in both physical and astral form throughout your life. You claim you didn't have magic prior to this, which many have found suspicious since we've always heard that all elves have magic. So, how did you handle them? Whole armies have fallen over the ages from a single spirit possession, but it's almost like they've left the Keepers alone for some reason."

Usually, she'd hear those words as an accusation—an assumption she and her people were hiding some great knowledge from humankind. But Karsten appeared genuinely confused and, if she was honest, *upset*. She supposed that was to be expected when he'd lost so many people fighting the very beings her kind seemed to shrug off. It wasn't frustration over the deaths around him that shook him so.

No, it seems far too personal for that.

"I suppose I always lived with that evil, so I knew how to recognize it in the air and in the people around me," she said as she turned her back on the diminishing crowds. After Zareen's fight ended in the fractured nose of her opponent, it didn't seem like anyone else wanted to risk their necks against her. Most were heading to their bedrolls and tents for the night. "The rest of my family had magic, which they used to keep me safe, but I was always the outlier. The *disappointment* to Mother. She swore I'd be the most powerful elf to ever live, but I couldn't even heal a single cut or alter the elements." She struggled to go on for a moment, hating the voicing of her own failure.

"She'll be proud of you."

That ache echoed deeper into her core, but she smiled anyway. He spoke in present terms, as if he was certain her mother still breathed the same air as them.

Of course, Mother lives. They all do. They must.

"My childhood woes are beside the point," she said, waving off her melancholy and focusing back on his question. "Our homestead was covered in protection runes, so they didn't bother us. When I was a child, I struggled with some of the spirits in their astral forms when they used to tease me. At that point, Mother stitched the runes into my clothes. Eventually, she told me I needed to face them on my own as all Keepers must."

He hummed in thought. "The Iniquity, right?"

"Our rite of passage into adulthood," she said with a nod. "At the age of ten, we're taken deep into the forest where no light shines and given only a small dagger to survive through the midwinter's night. Spirits in all forms tempt us and try to maim us. But, when the dawn breaks and we've made our way back home, we're adults."

"That still troubles me, even after hearing about it so long ago," he said with a shake of his head. "To have a child left alone with only a knife to defend themselves in one of the harshest seasons and environments in the realm? It feels too cruel."

She swallowed, her saliva hitting the bubbling bile in her gut. "The dagger isn't for the spirits or animals. It's to ensure no elf returns home possessed."

In the fading firelight, he grew pale. "I suppose that makes sense."

"The life of the Keepers is not gentle, Commander, but I wouldn't trade it for all the realms," she said as she looked out into the pitch-black woods. "But to answer your question—runes, a magical family, and the skill of a hunter trained since they could walk is how I've survived the spirits this long. I will not lie and say temptation has never clawed at me, but I am stronger than any lingering essence of sorrow, rage, or loneliness that has ever tried to claim my soul. I think our battle against Sorrow proved that."

Those days after Vane died were the worst she'd fought. She'd been too old for the runes stitched into cloth and so far from the protection of her home and family. She had traveled through The Divide, her boots frozen in icy blood, for days without food or water. She had been too sick to drink or eat and was snow-blind for hours in the ravaging storms.

The spirits had been loudest then, when she'd felt like all was lost. She'd wished she had that small dagger on her hip from when she was young, but she had still made it home for them.

I simply hope they make it back home to me this time.

When she peered back at Karsten, he seemed lost in tormenting thoughts dragging him realms away. He tried to conceal it, but she saw his palm tremble on the axe and his body shiver when there wasn't a breeze for miles. She wasn't sure how she hadn't seen or sensed it before, but it was clear as she looked at him—*really* looked at him—that he was a man ravaged by spirits no one else cared enough to see.

Whether they were truly spirits of The Divide or merely a

conjuring of a broken man's mind mattered little. He was suffering and no one noticed.

Was that why Sorrow couldn't manipulate him? He already has too many spirits to contend with?

With a hesitant hand, she tugged on his cloak and met his gaze even as it remained incredibly distant. "Mother showed me how to stitch the runes. I could do it, if you'd like a layer of protection for yourself."

He tried to shake off the trembling and square his shoulders, but it all seemed *wrong*. Like the confidence of a commander was a mask he wore instead of ingrained into his very being after the many years he spent leading others into battle. "I wasn't asking for me," he lied. "But it might be a good idea for the warriors."

She pinned him with what Birgitta called her *"no-nonsense bitch stare"*.

"Karsten," she said, her voice softer than she expected it to sound. He jumped at the sound of her using his first name instead of his title. "Let me help."

Still, he hesitated. It took a full minute before he gave in, unclasping the cloak from his shoulder bracers and neatly folded it into her arms, never meeting her gaze. "Just be careful with it. It's one of the only things I have left from my family." He admitted the last part in a whisper as he ran his hand across the fur mantle attached to it.

"Then I will treat it as if it were from my own kin," she said, holding it close to her chest. "I did have more questions for you, so perhaps we can continue this game another time?"

He nodded eagerly. "Yes, I'd like that."

Something fluttered in her core, creating a sickening twist with the bubbling cauldron within her stomach that had yet to rest. "Then I will bid you goodnight and return this to you when it's complete."

She turned on her heel and forced herself to put one foot in front of the other. There was a desperate part of her crying out to move closer to him, to see deeper into every wound he dared to share with her. She loathed to admit it, but he'd captured her curiosity completely.

"Adelaide?" She froze at the sound of her name on his lips. He hadn't said Keeper or Lady Aylara, but *her name.* "Thank you, truly."

A smile fought its way onto her face even as she tried to squash it. "It's not a problem."

She brought the cloak a little closer as she walked against the growing winds threatening to blow her over. But, in doing so, she caught a whiff of his cloak and drew it nearer for a deep breath of the intoxicating scent. Oak moss, wild berry, and smoke nestled in each fiber alongside the underpinnings of something subtle and medicinal she couldn't name.

With every part of her being, Adelaide hated herself the more and more she leaned into that smell. If anyone asked, she did *not* sleep curled up around it.

REPORT FROM COMMANDER STROM

Dear Jarl Thurstan,

You'll be pleased to hear Lady Aylara has successfully secured The Divide and harnessed more of her magic. It was no small feat, as she destroyed a spirit of suicide and a spirit of sorrow to accomplish the task. Before we departed, you briefly mentioned getting her a gift in thanks—something imported from our neighbors in Odivammer. Upon our return, I believe that would be appropriate. She accomplished much in Skagi, even if she won't admit it.

I heard whispers while I rotated our warriors. Not only did they sing her praise for slowing the tide of spirits, but for her genuine kindness to the citizens who remained in town. She assisted Embla with cooking supper for the men and helped her pack. A rumor claimed she gathered herbs in the woods for the healers and returned of her own accord. I even witnessed her playing with the children so their parents could sleep for the first time in weeks.

Miraculously, she has even extended that kindness to me. I would give her something myself, but I fear it would be unwanted and I would test the fragile truce we've come to. So, please, feel free to order one of those luxury items you were considering that's worth more than my yearly salary. After everything she's been through and done for us, she deserves it.

- Commander Karsten Strom

12

FOUL DREAMS FOR GENTLE HEARTS

SKALD: KARSTEN STROM

Sleep evaded Karsten that night.

Between the tension building behind his eyes and the image of Adelaide wrapped in his cloak, her features softened by the firelight and her gentle voice offering to help him, he was too fearful to rest. What dreams would haunt him the moment he put his head down, when she was all he could think about?

He knew the answer, and they were too improper to *ever* give into, so he stayed awake.

When the guards rotated to relieve him of his watch, he walked the perimeter of their camp to avoid his tent. He'd spent weeks trying to regain her trust, and it was only when he was cruel to her, allowing his frustration at his illness—his *weakness*—that she dared to soften in his presence and show the kind, gentle side of her he'd met in her cabin the first day she awoke.

That woman makes no sense to me, yet she's captured my thoughts all the same.

With sleep a distant, impossible commodity, he sent a raven to Lefa to ask her to provide *something* to Adelaide for all her efforts. How little he could offer her gnawed at his spine. Even if she wasn't outright screaming at him, that didn't make a possibility of more with her any more real.

I am forever a poor farmer's weakest son and a former Knight. No one would desire that, least of all her.

Still, he could do *something* and be of use to her. But he only had one thing to offer: the very thing he swore to do.

Find her family.

With a lantern and a tired guard in tow, he breached the mountain again and combed the lands for any signs of people living in The Wild Woods. They were on the border of her forest, probably too far from her home and the site of destruction to truly find anything, but his skin itched with the urge to move, and the fact he had yet to join his men in their search ate at him.

I can't keep telling her we're doing all we can to find them if I've never gone out on my own to try.

But he understood why his warriors were struggling. The Wild Woods were a stunning section of the mountains, but it had *changed* since the Divide was torn apart. Everything was charred beyond recognition, and the earth fell away in steep craters and cliffs that gave no warning of their presence.

His legs trembled with the exertion of every incline, his breath short from the altitude as the first rays of sunlight beamed across the world in the early morning dawn. He'd found nothing, and his search hadn't eased the ache in his chest nor the tension in his skull.

But then, an echo bounced off the stones and tore his attention to a thicket of fallen trees.

He readied his sword, the guard who he brought with him slow to do the same as exhaustion weighed him down, and they crept towards the noise with a wary uncertainty riddling the air between them. The noise came again, a soft whine piercing the sky in a sorrowful lament.

"It's a horse," the warrior murmured as he helped Karsten

push a fallen tree off it. It was a white, spotted stallion covered in muck and ash that clouded its eyes and stole its breath. Its malnourished state and the strange bend of its legs gave him little hope it would survive, but the sight of its pathetic neighs still ravaged his heart. "Should we ease its pain?" the other man asked as he offered his blade.

Karsten nearly agreed, but a soft chime stole his attention back to the creature. Something was braided in its long white mane, and he crouched to wipe the filth from the decorations to see them better. They were golden runes, carefully knotted into the hair, and they rippled with magic.

He checked the parchment in his pocket listing the descriptions of Adelaide's family, but a horse wasn't named. Still, the creature obviously belonged to a Keeper—perhaps one of the many in The Dead Fields.

"No," Karsten said as he forced his warrior to lower his weapon. "This beast still has a chance. Send for a few healers and let's see if we can get her on her feet."

The warrior nodded and disappeared in an instant.

A sigh slipped through his lips as he emptied his water onto a handkerchief, one of the many he carried just in case he had to physically deliver news to a family about a loved one's passing, and dabbed it across the beast's eyes. It neighed in protest, the fight in it alive once again as it shook its head.

"I don't like this anymore than you do," he said as he redirected its face to reach the filth better. It gave a feeble fight until it could blink one bleary eye open and, with its sight restored, allowed him to reach its other eye. "But if you can survive out here, so can the Aylara Clan."

The creature looked at him as though it understood, its soulful brown eyes boring into his as he freshened its fur and coached it into resting its large head on his lap. If the mare could make it while pinned against the earth, he knew its survival would bring Adelaide some semblance of hope for her own family. He simply wouldn't share his discovery with her until its survival was certain.

Yes. If I cannot give her some grand gesture of appreciation, perhaps I can return to her the very thing she's given me.

Hope.

THAT AFTERNOON WELCOMED the songs of wild goldcrests, fresh dew across the sagging pines, and a brand-new migraine beating like a war drum against Karsten's skull.

He tried not to snap at the slightest sharp sound or raise his voice more than normal when being reported to by seemingly *every* messenger in the realm, but each attempt grew more profoundly difficult. His brain screamed back at him for every breath he took and his skin felt like it was burning beneath the surface, just out of reach.

There was a slight comfort in the idea that Adelaide's rune-stitching might ease his burdens and, by extension, the pounding in his head. It did little to lessen the endless daggers pressing into his temples.

"The world seems to weigh heavy on your shoulders today," Zareen said, keeping her voice surprisingly soft as she laid a firm hand on his shoulder. "Let me know if there's anything I can do to ease your struggles."

He patted her hand and fought the fond smile pushing its way to the surface. "I appreciate it, my friend, but you know as well as I that if I cannot handle this on my own, there's no kinder future waiting for me up ahead."

She sneered and dug her nails into his shoulder. Without his thick cloak in the way, he could truly feel the bite of her fierce grip, but he still refused to let the pain show on his face.

"Your stubborn nature will see you dead." She shoved his shoulder and rounded him, her softness from before vanishing. "Commander Strom, you have a duty to show up for our warriors as your best self. I cannot have your obvious illness affect their morale." She spoke quietly, so no others could hear, but her voice was firm and unyielding. "As your lieutenant, I'm highly *suggesting* you seek the assistance of a healer."

"Sounds more like a command to me," he said with a roll of his eyes as he moved to return to work.

Her firm grasp on his arm kept him in place and, when he peered back at her, he saw through all the layers she hid behind. The bravado and anger were stripped away, revealing true fear hidden in her hazel eyes.

"*Karsten*," she hissed, her stubbornness matching his own. "Please, get some rest. Let me handle the march back to Rannadal."

When he sighed, it felt as though his entire chest deflated, and his hands unfurled from around the reports his tired eyes tried and failed to read a dozen times. She was right, and he was deeply troubled to make such a confession, but that didn't stop it from being true. He'd heard similar sentiments the day before, with Adelaide's *"you look like shit"* comment standing out from the bunch.

His warriors could tell he was sick but, thankfully, none were bold enough to ask about his health outright. For the time being, many simply thought his constitution was frail during the transition from summer into autumn. He'd let them think that if they so desired, but once spring bloomed, he knew that excuse would fade. Then, people beyond Lefa, Ylwa, Zareen, and Zamir would have to know about his condition if it hadn't improved. If it didn't, he'd have to find a replacement and step down from his post.

After all, it would make The Covenant's forces look weak if their commander died from sickness instead of in battle.

He placed his hand over hers once more, gaining strength in her death-grip on his arm and in the tight knitted friendship they shared. In the face of all the doubt and pain, Zareen and her brother kept his secret and earned his loyalty beyond all measures. He would treasure it always, no matter what fate befell him in the end.

"Thank you," he said, his words prompting her to peel her fingers off his bracers. "I'll just reply to these reports, send them by raven, and then I'll seek out Zamir for assistance."

She groaned in frustration as she ripped the reports from his hands. A protest was already halfway out of his mouth, but it was silenced by a different, rolled parchment being thrust into his hands. "No," she said simply. "If you insist on sending letters, you will respond to your sister and then go to my brother." When he didn't respond, his focus pinned on the paper instead of on her narrowed gaze, she gave a long sigh. "You can't avoid answering her forever."

He gave a silent nod and pointed at a scout who was returning from the road up ahead. "In that case, this one will be all yours," he said as he turned away.

She huffed, her warm breath forming a white cloud in the air that blew a strand of her black hair away from her face. "I suppose that's an improvement, coming from you."

He grinned, feeling a little better already. "I do what I can."

"Which is always too much," she shouted back as she turned to take the next report.

Karsten did as he said he would, but by the time he finally forced his eyes to fully adjust to the letter, his hands were shaking.

They trembled over the parchment intended for his response, making his words illegible. He just hoped his sister, Caroline, wouldn't notice or care about the many ink splotches decorating the page. He gave the letters to the lead messenger, knowing his fingers wouldn't cooperate long enough to tie the letters to a raven's twitchy leg.

Despite being relieved of duty for the day, his body refused to listen to Zareen's orders for rest. Spasms racked up his spine and his chest tightened with every intake of air. He couldn't stop himself from standing firm and straight, even as his back protested and wished to hunch over in pain. He had to look strong, for all of them.

They would not see him *weak*. Not if he could help it.

The flap to Zamir's tent blew open in the wind before he ever touched it. Inside, he spotted his friend listening intently to some story Sander was spinning about the greatness of Alfheim that was lost when the humans tried to conquer the realm. Karsten wasn't sure if the stories were as true as the elves claimed them to be. They always spoke as if they were historical facts and not entangled with their faith. But he also couldn't help believing the stories when the elf spoke about it with such conviction.

"Apologies, am I boring you with stories of my people's history?" Sander drawled, catching Karsten off guard as he looked up from where he'd been pinching the bridge of his nose, still fighting off the growing migraine dancing at the edges of his vision. Before he could respond, Sander gave him a once over and his expression softened. "Or perhaps not?"

Zamir recognized the pain shooting across his face, even as he desperately tried to hide it. He was on his feet and at his side before any other words could be uttered.

"Thank you for the lovely stories, Sander, but we'll continue them another time," he said, ushering the other man outside before directing Karsten to sit, tightly tugging his tent flaps closed behind them. "Zareen sent you to me hours ago," he snapped once Sander was out of earshot as he rifled through his many trinkets of medical supplies. "You can't disappear when you get like this or I'll fear you're dead in the woods somewhere."

"S-sorry," he said, humming when the first dose of healing magic washed through him. "I just wanted t-to send a letter before—" He stopped talking and instead showed him the ceaseless trembling in his hands.

Zamir froze, elbow deep in his chest of supplies as he stared intently at the other man's gloved hands shaking in the air. "It's getting worse, Karsten."

"I-I know."

His fist met the top of his trunk as he forced it closed and pinned him with his fiercest glare. "You do realize it will only continue to get worse if you don't treat it *before* it gets like this, right?" He stood and placed the regular potions he'd prescribed him into his lap, not trusting Karsten's hands to remain steady on the glass. "My sister and I stood by you when you told us what you wanted to do, but you agreed to let us help." He pointed at the bottles as Karsten began downing them one after the other. "When you come to me this desperate, it doesn't feel like helping."

He wiped the excess healing potion, lavender in color, off his lips. "And what does it feel like exactly?" he asked, detesting how much hate seeped into his voice. But he was unable to control it as Zamir's words wracked around in his brain, searing pain deeper into every crevice of his mind.

"It feels like signing your death warrant."

Zamir didn't give him room to object as he stormed out of the tent and back into the throng of people ready and waiting to make the final push back to Rannadal.

They'd be back soon and, for many, he imagined returning home brought them a sense of comfort. But it wasn't truly a home for him, despite all his efforts to make it so. His cabin was barren except for his desk and bed. Almost no personal effects were hidden in his drawers nestled between missives and reports. He had no family to dine with inside the hall. All he had was Zamir and Zareen, and he just couldn't help himself each time he pushed them away.

He would've loved to find the spirits tormenting him at fault for his actions. To lay the blame on their astral shoulders instead of his. But he wasn't that far gone—not yet possessed by any entity of sinful nature. Even with his illness eating away at him day by day, he remained strong in the face of every reprieve the spirits promised if only he gave into their pleas.

'Go back home,' Loneliness cried into the long nights of his mind. *'You haven't seen your family in years. Give up on The Covenant and all your men. They're not your real family.'*

Fear chattered on the outskirts of his brain, begging for entry to corrupt every ounce of courage he had. *'You'll die for them, truly? What have they done to earn such a sacrifice?'*

'I miss mama and papa and my siblings,' sobbed Sorrow, its voice breaking.

'No, we must stay and kill everyone responsible for tearing The Divide in two. Murder, torch, pillage, and torture every living being who stole Adelaide's family from her,' Revenge and Wrath demanded day after day after *blessed fucking day.*

'Adelaide,' the spirit of Lust moaned, its hot breath caressing his ear and sending shivers down his spine. *'Oh, what fun the two of you could have. Her breathy voice calling your name in the dark. Her skin, so soft, pressed against yours. Can you imagine how she'd feel with her thighs wrapped around your waist? Imagine the sounds you could pull from those decadent lips. Who needs any sweet mead when you could simply have a taste of the honey between her legs?'*

He shot to his feet, his face warm and his palms slick with sweat. *'Enough,'* he mentally shouted back at the spirits as he felt them skitter into the darkest reaches of his mind. *'I will not use her image in such a manner.'*

Disgust coiled and rotted in his gut, turning his breakfast sour and worsening the migraine beating on his skull. She was far too good for a man like him. What truly ruined him was that he couldn't blame Lust for all his thoughts of her either. It wasn't just a spirit playing with his mind because he found her beautiful. That happened before, when he was a Viking, with other people he'd fancied for a single night as he traveled the realm.

He knew he was developing true affection for her. A fondness she would never return, which made his thoughts of her worse and gave the spirit more strength to torture him with every detail about her.

From the soft waves in her white hair, to the scar across her lovely emerald eyes, to the curves of her waist, to the lilt of her voice when she said his name. It all tortured him even without the spirit's influence.

If only she had never shown him her gentle, kind side in the brief moments she decided not to hate him. If only she never let him see beyond her stony exterior in the moments of weakness she shared. Then perhaps he wouldn't be so enthralled by her.

'You're lying to yourself,' Lust whispered. *'Can you imagine if she hated you like she truly claimed? She'd have a knife at your throat at this very moment.'* His heart broke at the mere idea. *'Oh, but what fun things you can do with a knife.'*

A vision of that very scenario played in his mind, projected onto the back of his eyes whenever he blinked. He and Adelaide were back in the temple where they'd first met, a blade pressed firm against his neck.

"Are you hurt?" he asked, both in reality and in the dreamscape Lust played for him. Instead of allowing him to help her stand, she grabbed his hand and yanked him forward, tugging him off his feet.

He collapsed on the stone chapel floor, the breath pulled straight from his lungs and pain ricocheting up his back as he was rolled onto his side. She climbed over him, straddling his hips as she grabbed the dagger hidden in his boots and pressed it to his neck.

And he was helpless to stop her.

"You honestly think I'd trust a human warrior in a temple stolen from my people?" Adelaide scoffed as she pressed the dagger closer, drawing a thin line of crimson and causing goosebumps to break out across his skin. "I can practically smell the essence of the Brotherhood in your blood. You must think me a fool."

The sharp pain of the blade digging into his skin blended with the firm feeling of her body above his, their cores aligned to build the slightest friction between them with each hard breath they took. Somehow, he enjoyed the push and pull between pleasure and pain as it traced down his spine and pooled heat into his veins.

"I don't think you're a fool," he said, his voice breathy and strained.

"And what exactly do you think of me? That I'm a scared, defenseless elf who'll play willing captive for a Knight?"

His fingers brushed the tops of her knees braced on either side of him and, when she didn't stop him, he continued moving them up her body. "I only think of your beauty," he whispered, entranced by how her eyes grew large under his attentive hands gripping her thighs, dwarfing them in size. "Your mouth," he said, leaning forward until their lips nearly touched, just out of reach as the blade held him a single breath away. "And how I wish to be captivated by you instead."

Beneath his palms, he felt her tremble on the edge of giving in to the pleasure he promised. So close, he could see her pupils blown wide, turning her once green eyes jet black. She was panting with the effort of holding back, her breath coasting over his lips, and practically begging him to breach the distance between them.

A small smirk played on her lips and, by the Goddess, he wanted to feel those lips everywhere.

"Then prove it, Knight."

He lunged for her waist, his grip unyielding as he dragged her down while thrusting to meet her. She gasped at the feeling of his straining member pulsing against her core, only a few layers of thin fabric separating them. Her hold on the blade loosened and he knocked it out of her hands so he could bring her whole body closer and turn them in one fluid motion.

Her back hit the floor far softer than he had, and he was looming over her instead, his hands pinning her wrists above her head. She was smiling wider then, her lips pulled between her teeth as she arched against his hold. It was a feeble attempt to break away; she didn't truly mean to if her legs wrapping around his waist, her core grinding against him, was any indication.

"What happened to not trying to capture me?" she asked, her voice strained under the pressure of his armor digging into her breasts.

He leaned forward, his mouth hovering over her tantalizing lips he wished to pluck between his teeth. If she let him, he'd devour her whole. He'd worship her in the place of his Goddess and sin in the holiest of chapels again and again if only it made her stay by his side. There was no force, divine or otherwise, that would keep his hands off her except for her direct plea.

If she let him, he'd taste every inch of her and leave his mark on the most intimate parts of her. He'd call her name into the long nights until she was the one crying his name, begging for more until they both broke under the spell of exhaustion in the early mornings. Every inch of her body and being called to him like a song, stronger than any quest or dream he had in his entire life. Still, all she needed to do was say no and he'd stop the world for her.

"Tell me to release you and I will," he said, his voice hoarse as he strained to control himself from claiming her lips and body right there.

Her legs tightened around his waist, forcing him to press harder against her until he could feel the heat radiating from her center and the moisture of her already soaking core. His breath left him in a rush as she turned her head to the side, her lips at his ear, her breath ghosting over his neck and sending a shiver down his spine.

"Why would I ever ask you to stop?"

A call from Zareen that they'd be marching soon broke him from his trance.

He gasped as the vision cleared and shook his head to erase the last visages, but the physical effects remained. He was hard and throbbing beneath his armor to the point that each movement was painful.

He collapsed on the cot with his head in his hands, waiting for his body to calm.

Adelaide, please have that cloak ready soon.

And, by the grace of Olena, don't look so attractive when you give it back to me.

"T-THANK THE GODDESS," Karsten murmured as Zareen pushed him towards a waiting carriage. He dropped onto the bench inside and sat the stack of reports in his hands beside him.

"I know the potions usually have a sleep tonic added," she whispered, and he hoped none of their nearby warriors could hear her. "You typically don't ride in the carriage but, when they asked, I told them you'll be finishing reports and aren't to be disturbed. You should be able to get some real rest now."

"You're a blessing, Zareen."

She smirked. "Remember that the next time I ask for a drink, Commander."

"You have my word." He laughed for the first time that day as she firmly closed the door.

He waited, somewhat impatiently, for the carriage and all

his men to begin the trek back to town before he began unbuckling each strap to his armor. The moment his breastplate loosened, he felt like he could breathe again. The bracers clattered to the floor and relief echoed through him, saddling up alongside the ever-present pain.

In just his plain tunic and black trousers, he felt exposed when he knew his warriors were just outside the carriage doors. Without the cloak he always wore, the bitter air snapped at his flesh and left him feeling completely out of his element.

Still, the walls of the carriage soothed him. At the very least, there was something between him, the elements, and the warriors he led who, above all else, could *never* see him so weak.

He carefully arranged his discarded armor on the opposite bench and leaned back in his seat, finally resting his eyes as the carriage rocked over a patchy spot on the road. He swayed side to side with each turn in their path, but it wasn't enough to deter his eyes from being glued shut and his thoughts from slipping out of reach. Sleep descended upon him like a wide, warm blanket.

Often, sleep gave little reprieve whenever he finally allowed it to consume him. The spirits would always find him, no matter how deep in slumber he went. That's when they ensured his sleep was anything but peaceful. For that reason, sometimes the moments he remained lingering between realms eased him more than the sleep itself did. Despite his uncertainty and the soreness he was bound to have after slumbering upright in a moving wagon, he knew he needed real sleep more than he let the others know.

He struggled to remember when exactly he'd gotten more than three hours of shut eye, but he knew it was long before The Divide fell into the deepest crevices of the earth. If only he could get a few more hours of sleep, just one more time, without the spirits dogging him. Then perhaps he could finally fight the sickness off. He could give The Covenant every bit of effort it deserved. It would have all his energy and time, if only he could rest for just a few more moments.

Maybe then I could be a man worthy of her—I mean, The Covenant.

Yes. That's what I mean.

Before sleep claimed him, Lust sang in his ear once more.

'Stop lying.'

THE CARRIAGE DOOR burst open and was slammed shut behind whoever barged inside.

In an instant, he was awake and had his sword in hand, pressing it to the throat of the invader before his mind was fully awake. All he felt was a heavy gasp, sweet as strawberries, grace his face as the person froze, as if patiently waiting for their undoing.

After a few deep breaths that cleared the muddled fear from Karsten's mind, he refocused on the intruder and felt the air in his lungs freeze.

"Just because you're dead asleep doesn't mean you get to make me dead too, Commander," Adelaide jested as she tapped the blade securely pinning her in place.

The vision Lust placed in his mind came back full force. Goosebumps ran up his spine as the blade caressed her pretty skin. The memories ran through him. The way he'd itched for more as she'd drawn crimson from his neck and the way her eyes had dilated when he'd grabbed her by the chin, begging for a taste of her lips on his.

The noises she made.

In real life, he'd never been so close to her before. He'd

never smelled the sweet scent of her breath nor the ever-winter tangled in her hair. He shook the last of the images away and managed to pull his blade back after another few beats of his racing heart. She gave him a quick thanks and plopped down in the seat beside his armor. All he could do was swallow a low groan and turn away to hide his reddened face from her view.

Embarrassment compelled him to apologize, but he couldn't meet her gaze as he mumbled the words. "Apologies, Keeper. I meant no offense and would never threaten to harm you in my right state of mind."

"No need for formalities and apologies," she said, waving his words away even as her gaze grew distant. "I understand not being in one's right mind in such a compromising state." Whatever thoughts haunted her were shaken away and replaced with a timid glance. "I shouldn't have barged in, but I was attempting to sneak past Zareen. She was adamant I leave you alone."

He arched his brow. "And why didn't you listen to her?"

Her hands disappeared into her bag and produced his cloak from the farthest depths. Its black fabric and matching fur were as familiar to him as his own hands. She'd given it a firm washing if the scent of lavender was any indication, but that wasn't what caught his attention.

Gold thread was woven throughout the edges to accompany the plain stitching. It elevated the design from a regular cloak into something almost *regal.* Runes decorated the trim, a nostalgic familiarity hidden within each curve and line. If he focused hard enough, he was sure he could remember some of their names and purposes. With his mind still distorted by the brimming migraine which sleep hadn't cured, he couldn't recall what they meant.

He fingered the nearest rune, rubbing his thumb across the longest edge. Once, in his childhood, he knew each rune by name and revered them as she did. Those days were dulled by years far removed from such traditions and overshadowed by his devotion to Olena, her cause, and those who trained beside him in her name.

"Courage," she began, pointing to the rune he held before following the trim. "Protection, health, strength, and *healing*." She said the last one pointedly before showing him the final blank edge. "I have a few more: luck, joy, power, wealth, and hope. I thought we could continue our question game while I sew."

"I'd like that," he whispered, hating how soft and gruff his voice sounded to his own ears. He was supposed to be a leader commanding masses with nothing but strength in his tone, but none of that was present when he spoke to her.

With her so close, the visages of Lust dancing at the corners of his mind, and his armor tucked out of reach, he didn't feel like a commander under her watchful gaze. He felt totally exposed.

I'm not sure if I love this feeling or loathe it.

Nodding to the stitching, he asked, "Why all the other runes? I thought I'd only need protective ones if I wished to fend off the spirits."

She pinned him with a stubborn but playful glare. "It was technically my turn to ask a question, but I'll allow this one." He blushed again and was glad she was focused on stitching instead of the burning weakness filtering across his expression. "Protection helps, of course, but fending off the spirits is most effective when they have nothing to feed on." She pointed to the first rune again. "If you have a rune of courage guiding you, Fear cannot feed on you. If you have runes of health, strength, and healing it will give Sorrow, Loneliness, Regret, and Misery less to devour." She gave a quick stab at the cloak and thrust the thread through. "Luck, joy, power, wealth, and hope are all things every living creature wishes for, so in having it, the spirits cannot tempt you with wishes for anything more."

"What about Lust?" he blurted, regretting the words as soon as they left his lips.

That time, it was her turn to blush as she re-focused on the cloak. "To be honest, I hadn't thought of that one," she admitted, her voice quivering slightly. "I was a child when mother sewed these for me. Spirits such as Lust, Wrath, Revenge, Obsession, Vanity, and Suicide don't often mark children as prey."

Oh, by Olena's grace, of course. She can't arm me with defenses against my main terrors—the spirits of Lust, Wrath, and Revenge. I should just be thankful Obsession and Vanity aren't on the table.

At least, thanks to Olena's guidance, Suicide hadn't played with his mind in years. Not since he was a part of the Brotherhood anyways.

"Why?" she asked, stopping mid-stitch to peek up at him. "Does our dear Commander fancy someone back in town?" His cheeks burned as he sputtered out half-baked answers that didn't seem to satisfy her. "Remember the rules of our game, a question for an answer."

His throat ran dry, making him mute until he cleared it and looked away, peering anywhere but at her piercing gaze. "Not in town."

She hummed as she returned to her stitching, lost in thought. "A warrior among us then? Never expected a good Cislenian man like you to break such ranks."

"*Not quite*," he murmured, catching her gaze for just a moment and watching her eyes widen before he switched topics. "I've heard plenty of Knights, Vikings, and townsfolk complain about the spirits haunting them, like Embla with Suicide. When you were young, did any specific spirit cling to you?"

The slight blush on her cheeks vanished, replaced by a pale sheen as she kept her eyes trained on the cloak in her lap. "Loneliness was my friend before any living thing was," she answered, her voice barely above a whisper. "Once I passed my Iniquity, I grew closer to my kin and the other Keepers. Loneliness left me alone after that, but I've been entangled with Sorrow and Revenge for years." She seemed to shudder, but not from the cold wafting in from cracks in the wood of the carriage. "I suppose that's why the sorrow spirit in The Divide was so strong. It had plenty to feed on."

He nodded as his heart rattled with the memory of her tear-stained cheeks that day in the chapel. Even when they first met, he'd felt for her. After knowing her a little better each day, the memory of her pain echoed deeper and deeper into his heart, forever staining it. She was still suffering without the very people who'd wiped Loneliness from her mind. He was meant to help, and yet he failed her each day she didn't learn what became of her family.

"Has Loneliness returned?" he asked. "Without your family, has it made any reappearance or did you manage to shake it for good?"

She scowled at her hands frozen over the fabric. "I believe it was my turn to ask something," she said, effectively dodging his question and giving him an answer all at once. She closed her eyes and took a deep breath before forcing her hands back to work. When she opened them again, she seemed to have calmed the troublesome storm raging through her. "What of your kin? You must have family somewhere. In Rannadal perhaps?"

Sorrow of a different kind, the type without a spirit and mixed with seeds of regret, pulled at his heartstrings. "I'm afraid not," he said, planning to leave it at that and move on. When her pointed ear twitched in annoyance, he knew she'd want a better answer. "My family lives deeper inland, in the small farming village of Birkson. I haven't seen them in—" He paused, mentally doing the math. "Goddess, it's been years."

"Why'd you become so distant?" she asked.

He nearly dodged her question the same way she did before. It was technically his turn to ask after all, but he couldn't think of one fast enough. "I left home to join the Knights when I was still young," he said, carefully watching as her shoulders stiffened at the reminder of who he once was. "We exchanged letters during my training, but I didn't really see them again until I left the Order." He pinned his gaze on the small stream of light shining from beneath the curtains blocking the carriage's window. "I fear I wasn't myself during that visit and I only made things worse for them."

"You're ashamed," she said, her tone lacking any indication she was asking a question. She didn't need to ask; she could read the regret written all over him. "But are you ashamed of being a Knight or for how you acted with your kin?"

He huffed at the dark memories her words conjured. They were all covered in blood and filled his ears with the sounds of harsh words he wished he could take back.

If I could, I'd take everything back.

"Both," he said.

Her eyes pierced through him, even as he refused to meet her gaze. He found a loose thread on his tunic to tug at, attempting to avoid her scrutiny. Under her heavy stare, he fought the urge to shrink into his seat with each passing second. He almost filled the silence with any half-baked, awkward response he could manage simply to change the subject to something other than his family but decided not to at the last second.

For a moment, he decided he hated her. He hated the way she saw right through him. Hated the firm grasp her eyes held him in. Hated the way she said *Commander* or, on an extremely rare occasion, *his name*. Hated the way her nimble fingers moved blindly across his cloak, still sewing the runes. Hated how she thought to help him, even as she claimed to hate him right back. More than all of that, he hated himself for every thought of her that his mind obsessed over, playing it on repeat whenever he pulled away.

The shifting of her hips as she bent to grab firewood at camp.

The dancing of her fingers on her too-thin shirt.

The changing color of her eyes as she gazed at the flames.

The arch of her back in the vision Lust spun.

The way she cared about his wellbeing, even when she hated him for being a Knight.

The way she bit her lip when he found himself transfixed by them.

Her lips were moving, but he could hardly hear her over the blood rushing in his ears.

"So, how did you do it?"

He shook his head and tried to remember what she said. "Do what?"

Those same bewitching lips quirked into a grin. "How have you managed to go from being a farmer's son, to a devoted youth-recruit for the Knights, to a Rannadal Viking, and finally to a Commander in a Cislenian cult's army?"

The word *cult* caught him off guard, but not enough to tear his gaze from the tantalizing sight of her lips pinched between her teeth. "We're a devoted group honoring our most holy Goddess in battle. Not too different from the Keepers who defend their lands or Vikings who fight for their place in Valhalla. We merely plan to do the same for Olena." He finally broke the spell her lips had on him and leaned back in his seat, not having noticed until then how he'd been leaning towards her as he spoke. "So, if we're a cult, you're in two."

She rolled her eyes and pointed the needle at him, as if threatening him with a prick from its sharp end. "Just answer the question, Commander."

He sighed as he shifted through memories he tried not to recall in his waking hours. They already haunted him enough at night, he didn't need them tainting his mind during the day too.

But for their game, he'd try.

"My family was *complicated.*" He started there, figuring his life from the beginning would be the best place to start. "If my father heard you call me his son, he'd—" He stopped, feeling the blood drain from his face at the mere thought of the two of them in a room together.

That can never be. I would never let him near her.

"As for the Knights," he said, changing the direction of the conversation, "I foolishly believed in their cause. I thought they were actually protecting people. Both humans and elves." He swallowed the bile rising in his throat. He'd wanted so badly to save his family from his father and, in the end, *failed.* It made perfect sense to him to try to protect others and, as a bonus, he'd get to leave home and never return. That was the plan, at least. "It wasn't until I'd finished training and begun my patrols without the watchful gaze of my mentors that the reality of who I'd aligned myself with hit me."

Goddess, what a fool I was.

Those first few years, he'd been so devout to Olena and the Knights who worshiped her that he couldn't see the cracks in the walls. His mentors were strict and the lessons long, with the physical training growing more and more brutal as he aged. But it was for a purpose. At least that's what he told himself. He could protect elves and humans. He could keep them apart, safe from harming each other.

He'd prevent any spirits from leaving The Divide, lower the chance for possession across Midgard, and proudly return home one day. He'd earn the right to tell his father he was wrong about him and save his family, once and for all, from that cruel man's clutches.

Yes, a fool indeed.

"The patrols weren't anything like training," he said,

fighting the nausea rolling in his gut. "My brothers-in-arms who were so kind to me were brutes to the elves as soon as our mentors' backs were turned. I saw through it eventually, but not quick enough." He could barely hear his own voice since it became so small, but he knew her pointed ears were stronger than his. "I-I left, abandoning what I'd trained years for and tried to go home." He laughed, the sound bitter and soiling his tongue like the lies from the Knights once had. "But just like when I was a Knight, I couldn't save anyone."

She was quiet for a time as she finished his cloak, letting the air sit heavy between them as he glared into the wood above her head. He suddenly wished it would break and free him from the stiff confines of the carriage.

"You became a Viking after that, I take it?" she asked as she folded his cloak.

He nodded. "With Birkson behind me, Rannadal was the only home I'd known during all those years of training. I returned to try and sort the Knights out myself. I couldn't weed out every bastard in their ranks, but many of the worst offenders left when they knew they couldn't beat me in combat. I made examples of a few, which led to many leaving of their own accord. The Vikings took notice of my efforts. I could lead and fight, they liked that." He chuckled to himself, the sound dark and bitter. "I suppose they saw a man who had nothing left to lose and they liked that too, so I quickly rose up the ranks. When Jarl Lefa decided to form The Covenant, I'd just come back from my first raid as captain. I was perfectly poised to train, lead, and prepare the two opposing fighting forces Rannadal has under a single banner."

"And how has that been going for you?"

"How do you think?" he scoffed. "I'd already culled the Knights, and my Viking brothers were worried the same fate would befall them. Of course, the Knights also feel threatened by their dwindling numbers. To lessen tensions, we sent our

Vikings on several raids so they've been gone for some time. I hope being welcomed so readily and with enough gold and mead to drown in will make them thankful to be back, ready to defend their homes. But I haven't been able to weed out any bad apples from the bunch, which worries me." He settled his heavy gaze back on her and sat forward, reaching out for her hand before he stopped himself. "I don't know how many of them will welcome a Keeper as The Promised of Olena."

"As if all the townsfolk of Rannadal already have?" She huffed as she stood, brushing stray sewing threads off her lap. "I don't need people to like me, I just need them to do their jobs so we can save my home."

That time, he did grab her hand as she tried for the door. She froze, a murderous look on her face until she saw the genuine fear cross his. "A random citizen in town doesn't have years of militarized training from me, dozens of Berserkers, and access to an arsenal of weapons forged for war."

"You truly believe they'd defy their Jarl's orders and try to kill me simply because they don't believe in the miracle you all claim I performed?" she asked with a scoff.

He shook her arm, hoping to hammer his words straight into her head. "Their faith in The Old Gods is stronger than any orders by a mere mortal. Rannadal is their home, where all their families are. They will not allow anything to corrupt or endanger them, and their numbers double that of our current army."

"Or split your forces in half," she said, realization dawning on her face.

He nodded, his tone growing a bit more frantic as he let some of his growing fears slip free. "If we are united, few forces could stop us, but if we are divided, we stand to lose everything. We won't have enough warriors to defend our borders if the spirits decide to continue escaping, despite you stopping Sorrow. We won't have the men necessary to fight whoever tore through your home or the people to spare to find your kin." Her face twisted, her shoulders hunching until they nearly touched her ears. He continued,"If they don't believe you were sent by Odin as we believe you were sent by Olena, they *will* try to kill you. With their numbers and training, n-no one will be able to stop them, and it will be *my fault.*"

Adelaide stood there, frozen and staring transfixed into his eyes as his words died, filling the carriage with silence. She didn't seem to move or breathe as his fears washed through him. His hands trembled with a mixture of true ailments and a deeply rooted sickness at the mere idea of her being harmed. Just the thought made his heart shatter again and again in his chest.

"What's one more dead elf on your record?"

He ripped his hands away, as if burned by her words, and his body felt like it was scorched from the inside out. Part of him wished he could be enraged. He wanted to be angry she'd say such a thing after he was open and honest with all the questions she'd asked. She'd known what answers she'd receive, but she still asked. And why did she? Simply to torture him with his regrets? As if the spirits weren't already?

'She hates you. She's told you as much. Why are you still surprised?' Sorrow whispered.

He knew she had every right to hate him for what he'd done —and not done—while bound to the very Order causing her people so much suffering. He deserved her ire and wrath, but that didn't stop the painful gap opening wide in his chest, threatening to swallow him whole.

A look flashed across her face and she finally seemed to breathe as she took a small step towards him, her lips moving over silent words that refused to reveal themselves.

He grabbed the cloak off the bench and moved to the farthest corner of the carriage. "Thank you for the sewing. I'll see you're properly compensated for your time when we return to town." With his back to her, he focused on bringing the cloak over his shoulders and holding it in place since he wasn't wearing the armor he'd normally clasp it to.

"I didn't do it for coin," she said, her voice somehow too large for the tight space and too small for his ears all at once.

"I must return to my reports," he said, dismissing her as he gathered the once-abandoned parchment in his gloved palms and hating the way they shook the whole time.

The door opened and firmly closed as she left. He waited for her footsteps to meld into the crowd of warriors outside before he dropped the papers and let his trembling hands comb through his tangled curls.

His father was right, all those years ago when he left home.

"You break everything you touch, boy."

He curled on his side on the small bench, bringing the cloak around him to block out any traces of sunlight. If the runes worked to protect him, perhaps he'd finally get to fall into a blissful sleep where nothing else existed except for the void: a darkness where nothing he'd broken existed. It was a place where he couldn't hurt anything or be hurt in return.

Karsten drifted between realms, so exhausted that his own thoughts and the spirits couldn't catch him. He took a long, deep breath of the fur mantle he used as a pillow. It no longer smelled familiar, like the medicinal herbs Zamir made him and the oak trees that forged his cabin.

No, it smelled sweet—like lavender and winter.

It smelled like *her*.

Despite everything, that still somehow brought him enough comfort to sleep.

KARSTEN WAS JOLTED awake as the carriage came to a dead stop, the voices beyond rising to a crescendo that pierced a brand-new headache through his skull. He hardly thought as he grabbed his sword, noticed how well rested he was, and barged out of the carriage, ready for whatever bandit met them on the road.

Instead, he found the townsfolk of Rannadal cheering as they stopped on the outskirts of town, the gates only a short distance away. Confusion warped his mind until he rounded the carriage and saw a second caravan of people advancing from an opposing path.

Horror curdled in his core.

He met Adelaide's gaze across the throng of people and watched as the light and warmth from her face vanished into an expression of pure fear.

The Vikings had returned.

A LETTER FROM KARSTEN STROM, RIDDLED WITH INK SPLOTCHES

Dear Caroline,

Zareen finally forced my hand to write you back after your latest correspondence, so I've thanked her for us both. I would feel terrible if I didn't congratulate Roland in a timely manner on the big news. So, please send my congrats to our brother and his wife. I'm thrilled to be an uncle again and wish I could be there to meet my nieces and nephews. The Covenant and the destruction on Rannadal's borders will keep me away for some time. Please, do not wait for me to celebrate.

No, I do not require any more gifts from Birkson but thank you for thinking of me. The cloak Mother sent years ago is pristine. I still cannot believe it was a family heirloom. It's held up well, even in battle, despite its age. Speaking of which, someone has been kind enough to sew runes onto it. If they serve to fend off the spirits we're fighting, I may commission a seamstress to add them to the armor of all our warriors.

As for your questions regarding the whispers and rumors you've heard about our Promised, that will take an entirely different letter to respond with and I am running out of time. ~~In so many ways.~~ Simply know this: Her magic is remarkable, and we are lucky to have her.

- Karsten

13

CHAINS SO DEEP

SKALD: ADELAIDE AYLARA

I*'ve truly, royally, and undeniably fucked up.*

That was the only thought running through Adelaide's head as she followed the massive surge of people into town.

The townsfolk were ecstatic their families in both ranks of warriors, mostly former Knights and Vikings, had returned. People were already planning festivities to celebrate the seemingly divine arrival of both parties on the same day, but Adelaide could feel the tension between the two factions without a single word uttered between them.

"Stay close to me," Karsten whispered as he appeared at her side, his grip on her sleeve unyielding as he directed them through the crowds. He'd donned his armor once more, so she knew there was no wrenching her hand out of his grasp without tearing the fabric of her sleeves beneath his thick gloves.

When she peered at him, he looked better in terms of the bags under his eyes and the exhaustion that plagued him before, but all emotion was wiped clean from his expression. His jaw was locked firmly around his down-turned lips, and his gaze was focused on the path leading to the great hall in the center of town.

"I'm sorry," she said, the words escaping her in a rush before she had time to properly think of a real apology.

A bitter chuckle rumbled out of his chest. "You realize I'm right about you being in danger, so now you're sorry?" He shook his head, and a vein twitched in his brow. "Figures."

She pulled at him, hoping to halt his quick approach to the longhouse, but she only managed to slightly slow him down. "I was going to apologize either way," she snapped under her breath. "I was an ass and I didn't mean it." It took a moment for the words to settle in his mind and, once they did, he finally started to slow his rapid steps. "I tried to before you kicked me out of the carriage, which you were right to do, but I wanted to apologize anyways. I just—" She stopped, unable to find the right words. "I'm not comfortable with the idea that I can't defend myself on my own. I've never needed to. I've always had my kin and I was usually the one saving them, not the other way around."

He didn't look at her, instead scanning the army of people around them. Thankfully, they weren't drawing attention to themselves just yet. Everyone was too preoccupied by reconnecting with their families and reaching the longhouse in time for supper. The warm embraces and gleeful laughter sent a sharp pang of loneliness through her chest that echoed in the empty space her kin once held in her heart.

Odin, please let that be me one day.

When Karsten seemed certain no one was looking their way, he pushed Adelaide inside the nearest building and locked the door behind him.

"What are you doing?" she asked, but no answer came as he silently moved to the back of the herbalist shop they sneaked into. He peeked into the back rooms and nodded to himself when he confirmed the building was vacant.

"There's a trapdoor here," he said, stomping on a rug in the center of the room. It echoed back, hollow, unlike the floorboards beneath her own feet. "Should anything happen to you, use this to escape. It leads to a t-tunnel system out of town." He paced to a window facing the gates: the only visible entrance or exit in Rannadal. "Don't run for the front. Most of our men are camped outside, waiting for us to f-finish building the new barracks for our growing numbers."

She huffed in frustration, blowing a stray strand of white hair out of her face in the process. "Commander, you're not making any sense. If something is amiss, I trust you'll tell me all of this when you or Zamir are helping me escape."

When he looked at her next, his face was pale and sweat dotted his brow. "And i-if something h-happens to me?" he asked, the stutter in his frantic words slowly growing. "If I'm not f-fit for duty, least of all w-well enough to f-fight off my own people? They'll know to incapacitate m-me first, if I'm n-not already." She stayed silent, unsure of what to say in the face of the panicked look in his eyes. "No, y-you need to know this n-now while I have my w-wits about me." He stomped the trap door again. "I'll personally m-move weapons and provisions into the t-tunnels. Preserved r-rations, w-water, and changes of clothes. Some mead to k-keep you w-warm if it's cold out. A bedroll and plenty of a-arrows."

The way he spoke, fast paced and erratic as if he forgot she was in the room, set off alarm bells in the back of her mind. He wasn't well, that much was certain. He had been fine only a few minutes before, but his paranoia only grew with each backup plan to a backup plan he crafted aloud, weaving ideas into formulated steps to keep her safe. If it were written out and sealed with wax, she'd think it all expertly crafted by a talented strategist. It was a different story altogether when it was spewed from a tongue heavy with dread.

He sounds like a mad man.

"Commander," she said, hating the quiver in her voice. "Commander," she said, trying again. Still, he didn't respond. "*Karsten*!" He finally froze in front of her, his hands tangled into the curls at the back of his neck. "What are you doing?" she repeated as she took a careful step away, her back hitting the door.

His throat bobbed as he turned to look at her, meeting her gaze for the first time since he'd ushered them into the building. Clarity slowly filled his eyes even as the anxiety remained, his lips moving over unspoken words until he placed both hands on either side of the door, hovering above her.

She was pressed between him and the locked exit but, to her own surprise, she didn't feel trapped. Worry for him ate at her heart and, regrettably, she noted how comfortable being so close to him truly felt. Even if he'd just been rambling quicker than she could follow, she had the sense that he wouldn't hurt her. His body radiated a warmth that drew her in, and she couldn't help herself from brushing her fingers over his forehead, wiping the sweat from his brow and melting the tension from his expression in the same breath.

Despair clamored for a grip on her heart. It was a familiar feeling, often sent from Loneliness, her oldest friend, but she dismissed it. No spirit would distract her from whatever Karsten was going through; her feelings could wait until she banished whatever was hurting him.

"I just want to keep you safe," he whispered, his voice strained as he closed his eyes and rested his forehead against the door.

The Commander had promised to protect her not long ago, but she hadn't believed him. How could she? He was a force to be reckoned with between his imposing stature and his skill with a blade. The Brotherhood was carved into his skin and he had yet to break every habit the Knights had beaten into him. At that moment, tucked into a secluded herbalist shop, the human wishing to protect her wasn't the Commander she thought she knew.

The man before her, trembling with a mix of whatever troubled him and his own fear for her safety, was Karsten Strom. She truly did believe he would protect her with all he had.

Whatever may come, it's only fair I do the same for him.

Adelaide could no longer see the visages of the Brotherhood in his expression or the commanding presence his warriors followed into battle in his body language. All she could see was a man hurting beyond words from things he wouldn't speak of. She didn't expect to fix him, only he could do that, but she could help.

"Cold sweats, paranoia," she said as she took in the trembling of his hands beside her head. "The cloak worked, it's why you look rested, so this isn't a spirit's doing. This is some sort of illness."

He sighed, his shoulders slumping as he pushed himself away. "It's nothing for you to concern yourself with."

"Of course it is," she snapped. He furrowed his brow, her fierce tone surprising him. "You're the Commander of the forces who will find my kin and save my home. You're one of the only people who have offered to protect me from the army of people in this town who would sooner see me dead than labeled a Promise from any God. Besides all of that—" She stopped, astonishing even herself with the sincerity she felt when she admitted, "I find myself caring for your wellbeing and I'd like for us to try to be friends."

A small, stunned chuckle left his lips. "*Try* being the most crucial word here."

She grinned back, hating and loving the way her heart lit up at the stabilizing of his hands and the return of his usual, collected manner. "I know it's my fault such a concept seems foreign, but I'm willing to try if you're willing to let me help." She motioned to an empty chair by the window. He stared at it, hesitating. "Please, Karsten." She met his gaze, heated amber pinning her in place as his watchful eyes cleared. "Let me help."

After a few agonizing, slow moments, he nodded and finally sat. She promptly busied herself around the shop, searching for ingredients that could help. Eucalyptus, feverfew, and mossroot were added to a mortar she ground into part paste, part powder in the minutes of silence stretching between them.

In that time, his cheeks reddened, and his grasp on the back of his neck turned his knuckles white. "I'm sorry," he mumbled, breaking the silence. "This is all beneath me. It won't happen again."

"You're sick," she said, ignoring his apology as she handed him a teacup rimmed with the paste, the water infused with the powder. "You needn't ever apologize for being ill." He sipped the room-temp tea and grimaced. "Even if I had time to heat the water, it would still taste like the bottom of a dirty pond." She tapped the bottom of the cup, urging it back to his lips and the scar there she desperately tried not to be distracted by. "Finish it regardless."

He took the last few sips down like they were strong whiskey and wiped any residue off his tongue with the back of his glove, looking like a cat prepping itself for a grooming. She stifled a laugh at the image and wiped the paste off the edge of the cup, painting her fingers green.

"What's that for?" he asked.

She used her clean hand to push the hair back from his neck and he froze at her touch. She closed the distance between them to slather the paste behind his ears. "It's a trick my mother taught me when I was young." She could feel his heart beating faster under her palm twisting in his hair. The green mixture was smoothed over his pulse points, the skin surprisingly soft given the many years he spent training and fighting. "It eases pain and relaxes the body."

His tired eyes tried to find hers, but she refused to meet his gaze. Staring into their firelight depths would only drag her in further. "I'm trying to—" He paused, and she felt his throat bob under her touch. "*I am*," he said, correcting himself, "removing myself of a crutch. Something I used as a Knight to maintain my strength." His gaze fell to his hands as they finally stabilized. "It's been hard not to give in, but this is something I must do to fully sever myself from the Brotherhood: to rely on my own strength instead of something granted by magic."

An addiction.

Adelaide had never heard of a substance like that: something granting strength but taking so much from those who dared to quit. She'd met plenty of people who gave into drinks or mushrooms that took them into other realms, but nothing like what Karsten described. She was tempted to ask more, but some things were best left unsaid. He was holding back, only telling her as much as she needed to know, and she thought that was for a good reason.

"Paranoia, anxiety, shaking, and sweats are all symptoms of withdrawal, but what I just made you should help. I'll make sure you have a surplus," she said, holding up a finger when it seemed like he was about to object. "Just accept the help or I'll be sneaking it into your food, ensuring every meal you have tastes like a horse's ass for weeks to come." His mouth snapped closed. Satisfied, she began cleaning up the mess she'd made around the shop. "You haven't had any delusions from the withdrawals, right?"

When he didn't answer, she turned back towards him only to see his gaze pinned on the ground, his cheeks five shades of red and his hand gripping the back of his neck like a lifeline.

"Uhm, no," he finally said, the blush spreading down his neck. "None from the withdrawals but, since I quit, the spirits' visions have gotten stronger."

Their conversation in the carriage drifted to the forefront of her mind.

"Luck, joy, power, wealth, and hope are all things every living creature wishes for so, in having it, the spirits cannot tempt you with wishes for anything more."

"What about Lust?" he'd asked, making them both blush.

"I hadn't thought of that one, to be honest."

She thought her cheeks must have matched his as she busied herself with straightening potion bottles on a nearby table she never even touched. "I see," she mumbled as she fought not to think about the very thing he alluded to. Intense visions from the spirits could convince people reality was fake and the visions were real. She could imagine it would be disorientating to have a vision of something so intimate only to wake up, aching and alone.

Would he be alone when those visions plagued him? Or would Lust find it more amusing to torture him with visions of sex while he was surrounded by his warriors? In the middle of a meal with his friends? Had he been fighting those thoughts off around me?

Were those visions about me?

No, she determined quickly. *He said he has eyes for someone out of town. Besides, how could a former Knight ever see a Keeper that way?*

Still, she couldn't deny how intriguing the idea was. She'd never lain with a human before, even when she considered it in her rebellious youth. Her only partners had been elves. Her first had been a girl a little older than she was, so they'd had a similar build and shared the same aches to be touched after a drink. The few partners between her and Vane had been inconsequential dalliances that hardly satisfied, and most of her kind were lithe in build, rarely as *big* as human men.

Karsten was especially large for a human, standing over a head taller than she was when she'd already been considered tall for an elf. His shoulders were broad and as strong as steel.

His hands dwarfed hers, and she'd felt the strength in them when they trained together.

She wondered if that height and power translated to the size of *other* things.

Her face burned at the thoughts tugging at the back of her mind. His hands could easily pin her in place, like his arms did when he hovered above her by the door. She remembered the way his heart, strong and steady, thrummed under her touch but stuttered whenever her breath ghosted over his skin as she applied the healing paste.

A touch grazed her hip, and she jumped, pulling away instead of moving closer to him like she desperately wanted to. His brows were drawn as he stepped back into her space, his warmth radiating out of him like the sun to her frostbitten skin.

"Are you alright?"

Absolutely not. I'm daydreaming about fucking the Commander of a human cult in this abandoned shop before anyone in town notices we're gone. I must be mad.

She nodded and tucked the same errant strand of hair behind her ear as she pivoted her body away from his comforting heat. "While I agree your paranoia was brought on by the withdrawal, you unfortunately still have a point. We should be prepared if the Vikings decide I'm some sort of charlatan."

He grunted in agreement as he pulled out his coin pouch and left a few silvers on the table for the items they used. "The captain of Rannadal's Vikings is Fillip. I trust him with my life, but he's not a particularly devout pagan. I doubt he'd care either way. So long as his men do their jobs, he'll be content." He ripped a piece of parchment off a board in the back of the room and scribbled a note for the shop owner. "However, his second-in-command is a Berserker named Njal Magunusson. He has a tight leash on the rest of the Berserkers, and they're all dedicated followers of The Old Gods. We were never able to prove it, but I'm certain they killed one of the clergywomen responsible for converting the Rannadal chapel to our faith. He's the one you really need to convince."

Her heart stuttered in her chest. Her faith in her Gods was just as strong and she'd felt just as murderous when she'd discovered the temple stolen in another's name. If she had been ordered by her mother to follow a Knight who claimed to be sent by Odin, she wouldn't believe it for a second.

Before The Divide was torn apart, perhaps she would've even killed them on principle.

"And how do I accomplish that?" she asked as she nervously gnawed on her lip.

He folded the note with the silver tucked inside it. "I honestly have no idea," he said, pinching his brow. "I've hardly seen or talked to the man in recent years. He and his Berserkers stay outside town, beyond the gates and knolls. They only enter town for the tavern, brothel, and their next assignments."

She rubbed at the stress building behind her eyes. "I knew an elf who left for the Vikings once. He told me the Berserkers use some of the strongest herbs and mushrooms to obtain God-like powers on the battlefield. It would make sense they'd stay far away from towns if they're protecting something so powerful."

"That's why we wouldn't be able to protect you if Njarl set his sights on you," he admitted. "I was stronger when I took what the Knights gave me, but even then, I couldn't best Njarl in a real fight. If he's taken The Bane, no one in Rannadal could stop him. That's not even considering the five other Berserkers he commands."

The door to the shop rattled, and a feminine voice cursed on the other side.

"It's time to leave," he said, beckoning her to the door and unlatching it. "Whatever you do, act as if you don't know anything." He opened the door, apologized to the shopkeeper, and directed Adelaide back to the road leading to the great hall. "You're not well versed enough in our religion to pretend otherwise, and if you show preference to the pagan faith, it will sow doubt in everyone else's minds. We'll have to hope Njal's curiosity stills his blade. If he has doubts, he'll listen to Fillip."

She nodded as they neared the entrance, her heart beating against her ribs and her breath coming up short. It felt like marching towards certain death, but she trusted Karsten. Despite everything, she knew he wouldn't see her dead if he could help it. Neither would their Jarl, Zamir, or even Zareen for that matter. She was the only one who could control the spirits bleeding out of the mountains.

Adelaide just hoped that was enough to save her skin.

VIKINGS, Knights, warriors, and townsfolk alike were all crammed into the longhouse side by side. The great hall was built to fit hundreds but, already, it was bursting at the seams. Many were seated outside to try to get a glance at the heart of the building, the hearth where the leaders of Rannadal gathered.

Karsten's grip on her arm was firm as the crowds parted for them to join the others in the center. Panic continued to swell in her chest with each step, the lack of room between her and the next person heightening her desire to run away.

He tugged her in front of the fire and let go once she was placed between Zamir and Zareen. With him behind her, the flames before her, and the siblings on either side, she was boxed in. She was sure Karsten intended it that way and, to her own surprise, it brought her a sense of comfort. Even though she and Zareen weren't exactly on friendly terms, she still thought the other woman wouldn't stand idly by if someone tried to take her life.

From the outside, she'd thought every group was combined: forced into each other's spheres of influence by the sheer lack of room. From the middle, she could clearly see the separation of the two primary groups. The Knights were mixed with The Covenant's recruited warriors on one side of the fire pit. On the other, the Vikings sized up the other's numbers.

Still, neither group was the ten-thousand strong army their Jarl had visions of.

Their numbers were perhaps three hundred in total. Impressive for such a small town, but nowhere near what was necessary for any grand feat against a spirit horde and whomever was powerful enough to destroy the mountains she loved.

Karsten had a lot of work to do if he planned to make the two factions one monumental force under a single banner worthy of a Goddess's blessing. Unless he'd already done ceaseless amounts of work gathering men- and women-at-arms, only for their lives to be cut short by the spirits. Truthfully, she had no idea how many they'd lost or continued to lose to the damned.

"Where's Fillip?" Karsten asked Zareen as he leaned towards her, his body curving over Adelaide's shoulder so he wouldn't have to raise his voice.

"He was killed in their last raid," Zareen whispered back. "They performed his burials on The Southern Seas before they returned. Njal is captain now."

Her blood ran cold and, beneath her cloak, Karsten's fingers gripped the edge of her tunic, tugging her a bit into his chest. It wasn't enough for anyone in the busy room to notice, but it still made her cheeks heat before she followed his piercing gaze across the room.

By sheer size alone, she could pick out the man who frightened Karsten so. Njarl was a hulking figure towering above the heads of every man around him. He needed to bend his neck to duck into the doorways and he blocked the fire from any who dared to stand at his back. His long brown hair was braided with leather chords and tangled with gold ornaments that dripped down his back and chest. His dark eyes were narrowed right back at Karsten.

Njal's eyes flickered down, drank her in, and focused on the hand Karsten was holding her with. His lips tilted into a smirk and he arched his brow, which simply made her blush harder. To her surprise, Karsten's cheeks didn't darken, but his gaze certainly did as his hand tightened on her hip.

"Welcome," the Jarl began, her booming voice echoing across the room and silencing the chatter. "All of our esteemed warriors have returned," she continued, motioning to either party separated by the fire. "Now, there is much work to be done. Thanks to our Vikings, we have the gold to arm The Covenant with every weapon possible to defeat whoever is responsible for the destruction on our borders." She turned to the other warriors, bowing her head in respect. "And thanks to our army, we have protected and trained the only person in this realm with the power to hold the spirits at bay."

Adelaide felt the blood drain from her face as every gaze in the room shifted to her.

"Our Promised and messenger of many Gods," she said, lifting her hands to the ceiling. "Keeper Adelaide Aylara, Daughter of The Divide, Summoner of Spirits."

The room was silent save for the thrumming of blood rushing in her ears. She could see people talking, some seeming overjoyed and others angered by Lefa's words, but none of their voices truly reached her. The room stilled again, but not from the Jarl speaking. Instead, it was from Njal shifting in her direction.

His heavy footfall as he crossed the room was all that

pierced through her senses before she was pulled flush against Karsten's chest, his sword between her and Njal's approaching form. She could feel his chest moving quickly behind her, his breathing just as labored as hers.

The scraping of unsheathing steel weapons rang through the room until Njarl stopped, barely a pace away on the other side of the fire. His eyes, as dark as night, pinned her in place beneath his stare, and she was unable to break free. That was the man whom Karsten knew he couldn't defeat. Yet he still drew his weapon in her defense. It warmed a part of her, buried deep beneath her fear, that he would risk his life to even try.

"Can you truly control the spirits?" Njal asked, his voice so deep that it vibrated straight into her bones.

She nodded, but staying quiet like Karsten instructed no longer felt right. Would a messenger of the Gods truly cower in silence? She doubted that, so she cleared her throat to hide the fear and said, "Yes, I can."

He jerked his head in a quick nod. "Then you have my arm in battle," he said, easing her worry slightly. "But you do not have my faith." He took one more step forward, causing Karsten to drag them both another pace backwards. If he moved any closer, his beard would catch fire. "*That* is unshakable. You will need to prove your divinity not just to me, but to the people of Rannadal, and at least half of these warriors," he said, nodding to the opposing groups. "Are you prepared to do so?"

Am I?

Would she willingly endanger herself for their cause? Would she fight beside those humans as a sister-in-arms? Would she make them believe in her magic that she was barely able to conjure? Would she allow them to have faith in her divinity, something she didn't even believe in?

But, if Karsten was willing to do the very same things—believe in her, have faith in her magic, fight for her life in a battle that would see him dead just to protect her—how could she let him down?

Cowering behind Karsten's sword won't prove anything.

She pushed his weapon away and rounded the fire so she was standing right in front of the Berserker, their noses nearly touching from how far he bent down and how straight she stood.

"Your faith is your own and I cannot dictate whom your beliefs reside in," she said, loud enough for the entire room to hear. "All I know is that I have the power to do something *good*, to save the people of this realm from an army of spirits, and I will not stop until the spirits are banished, The Divide is fully sealed, and whoever destroyed my home is dead at my feet."

I did not *agree to do all of that, but now that I've said it, there's no taking it back.*

Fuck.

"That's all I ask of you," he said, pulling back, and peered between her and Karsten, who returned to his place at her back. "I will answer to your command, the directive of Jarl Lefa, and the wisdom of this Omen sent by the All-Father." His gaze fell back on her. "But should I doubt your intentions, you will find my blade at your throat."

"And you will find the same," she snapped.

The room froze, tension nearly snapping it in two as he glared down at her. Slowly, a smirk ripped across his face and he laughed, the sound echoing across the ceiling and bouncing back to them in the quiet.

"I'd love to see you try, little elf," he said, still chuckling as he lumbered back to his spot at the fire. "Jarl, I believe this calls for a celebration!"

Lefa rolled her eyes. "Yes, we'll make further preparations when we're more focused. You're all dismissed and free of duty for the night unless Commander Strom has stated otherwise. Enjoy your debauchery."

Njal's excited roar broke the tense spell on the room as everyone rushed out towards the tavern, the kitchens, or the fire pits outside where music was already lifting into the air.

Adelaide slumped. Karsten caught her on one side and Zamir propped her up on the other. "That was fucking terrifying," she mumbled as she straightened herself.

"You think?" Zamir laughed, the nervousness in his voice not lost on her. "You went toe-to-toe with the craziest Berserker this side of the seas."

Karsten patted her on the back. "But you did well."

Zareen nodded. "He wouldn't have respected you if you backed down."

She pushed away from them and sighed, finally feeling the day catch up to her. "That was thrilling, but I think I'll be retiring," she admitted, wariness eating away at her spine. She would collapse right there on the floor if she truly thought it was safe. "I hate to miss out on the festivities but—"

Zamir scoffed. "Oh, trust me when I say you won't miss anything. These lot go for days when one group returns. You can get a full night's worth of rest, and there will probably still be fun to be had when you wake. Best to get it done now."

She turned to get confirmation from Karsten and he nodded. "They're *Vikings*."

"Oh, yes, of course," she said, blushing. "I'll join everyone later then."

"I'll post guards at your doors as well, just in case. You deserve some rest," he said.

She mouthed a quick thank you as she left the great hall since she doubted he would be able to hear her over the drumming rising into the air. With all the noise, she wouldn't get much rest, but she hoped her cabin was far enough away, nestled on the edge of town, that the music wouldn't hinder her sleep.

The heart of town was already transformed into a celebration larger than any she'd seen before. Although, that wasn't surprising since she'd only been to her siblings' name days with less than a dozen people over the years.

Her mother used to spin stories of grand balls to rival the feasts of Valhalla she'd attended in New Alfheim before she joined the Keepers. Adelaide imagined the gathering before her had to be similar, although not as elegant. Her mother had described grand affairs in glittering halls carved from stone, not the sloshing of mead across the earth until it was caked in mud. Still, it seemed *fun*. If her head wasn't throbbing from the long day of travel and her skin still didn't prickle at the idea of being surrounded by humans she didn't know, she would've joined.

She locked the door to her cabin behind her before she realized she should've just gone to the festivities.

A scream was already half-way out of her throat before a heavy hand was laid across her mouth. She was pinned in place against the door, her heart hammering in her chest until it threatened to burst. Njal's giant form held her perfectly still, his hand that wasn't wrapped around her shoulder was pinned to his lips, forcing her into silence.

"I just want to talk, but we can't if you yell," he said, giving her a pointed look until she relaxed under his hand.

He must think I'm a fool.

As soon as his hand relaxed, she wrenched her chin out of his grasp. "*Karsten—*" The rest of her plea was cut off again and she was secured back into the same position as before. Only that time, Njal's patience was thinned.

"Gods damned it, woman!" he snapped, his nostrils flaring at her disobedience. "If I wanted to kill you, I'd have done it by now."

She supposed he was right, but it didn't slow the panicked racing of her heart as it beat with bloody fists against her chest. After a few more moments of glaring into each other's eyes, he finally relented and lowered his hand again. She met him halfway by remaining silent instead of screaming, but she was fully prepared to run or shout at a moment's notice. If even Karsten doubted his ability to defeat Njarl, she knew she wouldn't stand a chance.

He cursed under his breath and stepped further into the room, his voice quieter. "The Commander's guards are moving towards your door. Luckily, I beat them here. My men will be expecting me at the fire and those warriors will expect you to be asleep, so we should make this quick."

"And what exactly are we—" Her words were cut short as she froze, the air stolen from her lungs and her heart halting its once rapid pace at the sight in front of her.

Njal fell to his knees, the giant of a man bent until his hair obscured his face and the only thing she could see was the offering he held up to her. There was no denying the obvious worship stance he dropped into and, if she had any doubts, his mumbled words were further confirmation.

"All-Father, forgive any transgressions I've made against your chosen," he said, his voice hushed but full of conviction. "I cannot let them see the truth."

Confusion replaced her shock as she moved deeper into the room, stopping before his outstretched hands. He was holding a dagger, its sheath covered in silver runes and the pommel carved to resemble Thor's hammer. "What are you doing?"

He picked his head up, his thick brows scrunching as if *he* were the confused one. "You were beckoned by the lights, were you not?" She nodded even though she was unsure of what exactly he was implying. He straightened, his height dwarfing her instantly. "The others claim it was the aurora of Olena bringing you to their aid. Those of us who follow The Old Gods know better. It was the Bifrost, welcoming you into the battle as if Freya herself were riding into war."

"That's what they're claiming, yes. Truthfully, I don't remember that night at all," she explained as the dagger was carefully placed into her hand, its weight and intricate designs capturing her attention. It was worth a small fortune, and that's when a realization struck her.

Njarl was making an offering, not to Odin, but to *her.*

"Of course you wouldn't recall the might of the Gods. It would devour your mortal mind," he said with a snort. "Us Vikings have stayed true to the old ways, and we have no such reservations about Odin's choice in an elf as his messenger—unlike the Brotherhood." He rapped his knuckles on the blade in her hands. "Consider this a sign of our devotion, even if we must keep it secret from the likes of the Jarl and Commander."

She nodded as she unfurled the strap on the sheath and fastened it as a belt around her waist. It fit perfectly, as though it were made for her. "Why in all the realms must this be secret?"

"The Great Conversion corrupted many in The North to the Cislenian's perverse ways, but our Vikings struck an accord with the church to remain faithful to the All-Father decades ago. The method we chose to do so sickens me," he explained, his voice growing quiet. "We agreed to uphold their *distaste* for elves and never hinder the Brotherhood's dominion over The Divide. If we refused the treaty the religion of the Jarls offered us, we would've been disbanded and the days of raids would end. Then, the only protectors left would be the Knights." His eyes grew sorrowful as he peered at the tips of her pointed ears. "Neither humans nor elves wish that to be so, so we've remained silent. Our silence after this long has been mistaken for acceptance of their hatred for your kind. To maintain that charade, I could not publicly accept an elf being sent by Odin. You are an omen of The Old Gods: one I cannot ignore but also cannot embrace before the others lest the chapel discovers our deception and disbands us entirely."

She nodded, her unease and fear quieting into a hushed murmur in the back of her mind. Despite her initial reservations about him, there was something in the way he spoke with so much fire and conviction that it set her mind at ease. There was even a way he spoke that settled the subtle, dull ache behind her scarred eye. When she blinked, she almost swore she could see the vague outline of a white light burning around him. As though his faith were a tangible spirit she could sense lingering around his heart.

Besides that, she had a gut feeling he was rarely allowed to show such passion outside the battlefield. She couldn't imagine what it was like, constantly hiding who you were and what you believed to pacify the very same clergy decimating your home.

"I understand," she said, watching as his shoulders slumped in relief. "But why are you telling me this? Why are you here?"

"To prove my devotion and explain why I couldn't show that in front of the others," he explained, his hand scrubbing through the thick hairs running across his jaw. "If I immediately believed in your divinity, they would question why a human Viking would believe an *elf* was sent by his Gods when I hadn't seen it with my own eyes. The others have witnessed your holiness and I have not, but any true follower of The Old Gods understands how Odin works. We are not all-seeing like the All-Father is." He curled his palm into a fist and slammed it over his heart. "I cannot speak for all the Vikings in Rannadal, for some are true converts to the new faith and others non-believers, but my Berserkers and I have all come to an agreement." He grabbed her hand and held it in his far larger ones. "We will follow you to Valhalla and beyond. For Rannadal, for our people, and for the Gods themselves."

In that moment, all her lingering doubt about Njarl's intentions vanished.

He would die for her, for the town, and for their Gods. That's how much he believed in her and their pantheon. Despite her own misgivings about the divinity everyone claimed she had, she couldn't find it within herself to turn that devotion away. He truly thought she was divine, and she couldn't dissuade him. He was too certain and focused, with an intensity in his gaze screaming of his faith. If he believed in her ability to cull the spirits and repair the mountains, who was she to argue?

"Thank you, Njal," she said, patting his rough hand with her far gentler one. "I admit, it's nice to see the love of The Old Gods in someone's eyes again."

He chuckled, the sound deep and guttural. "Don't get used to it, I need to return to my stone-cold exterior the moment I leave. My people will have your back regardless." Then, he leaned in. "Also, *Karsten*?" She fought the heat rising to her cheeks as he grinned. "Didn't realize the Commander let anyone in on a first name basis." His grip on her hand tightened. "How did you manage that, you minx? One of my men swears there's something called a love potion. Did you try that on him? He could use the tension release."

Their hands parted, and an annoyed scoff passed from her lips. She folded her arms, a snarky retort half-way out of her mouth that was stolen by a sharp crash as her cabin door slammed open. The force rocked the entire room as a shadow rushed past her. It moved between her and Njarl with such extreme force that the towering man crashed to the ground. She recognized the head of curly blond hair as the sound of his snarls pierced the air.

"Karsten," she gasped, part horrified and part amazed that he had a man twice his size knocked off his feet and pinned to the floor.

"Stay back, Adelaide!" he shouted as he pinned his blade against Njal's throat.

The other man arched a brow at the Commander and turned to look at her out of the corner of his eye. "Seriously, *this* is the effects of a potion, right?" The blade dug deeper, drawing a line of blood across his tan skin. "Regardless, can you rein in your guard dog?"

Karsten hesitated, the blade lifting slightly. "What is he talking about?"

She tugged at his arm, urging him to remove himself and his weapon from the other man. "Ignore him. He thinks he's funny." Once he was standing again, she noticed the two guards flanking the door who'd been useless in the scuffle. "Help the man up, will you?" They rushed inside to help Njal's lumbering form back to his feet as she turned to the Commander. "We were simply coming to an agreement regarding his Berserkers and the other Vikings." Then, she stopped and squinted at him. "But what were *you* doing here?"

He huffed as he pushed a few curls from his face. "I was checking on the guards I stationed when I heard his voice in your room." He grabbed the nearest warrior by the collar and hauled him forward. The other man quivered in his boots as he stared up into Karsten's vicious, rage-filled eyes. "Good thing I did since these two already partook in the mead and were half-asleep at their post."

Njal, finally back on his feet, laughed and clapped one of the men on their backs. "Don't worry so much, Commander. I'll have two of mine stationed instead. Unlike these new recruits, Vikings know how to fight while drunk!"

"Absolutely not."

"Thank you, Njal."

Adelaide and Karsten met each other's gazes, having spoken at the same time and quickly finding themselves at a stalemate.

Again, Njal broke the silence. "I'll have Kare and Thora guard her cabin." He moved towards the door, stopping to wrench Karsten's fingers off the poor guard's collar. "You'll like those two! Good warriors."

Karsten pinched the bridge of his nose. "Fine, Njal. Do as you wish."

"I always do."

The failed guards exited behind Njarl, leaving just the two of them in the middle of her cabin with the door creaking back and forth in the wind. She was no longer tired, the thrill that came with finding Njal in her quarters having given her a second burst of energy, but Karsten looked nearly dead on his feet.

"You should get some rest," she said, making him grin as she parroted the words he'd said to her only a short time before.

"You know I can't." He nodded outside where the festivities were growing. "They need at least one sober man among them."

She knew his words were deeper than that though. He'd looked better rested after she stitched the runes into his cloak, but one good nap wouldn't undo however many years of tormented sleep he'd gotten while dealing with the spirits.

"A walk then?" she suggested, heading to the door and giving him an expectant look. When he hesitated, she put her hand on her hip and narrowed her gaze at him. "If you're not going to sleep, you might as well get a little peace before the party truly begins."

He seemed to concede her point as he followed, softly closing the door behind them and looking apologetically at the broken lock. "What of your rest? I thought you were tired."

She shrugged as they walked down the path winding throughout the village. The roaring of laughter and merriment grew until they were outside the gates, where the noise lessened with each step around the encampments where the warriors slept. They were barren, their typical inhabitants no doubt enjoying the drinks and stories around the many bonfires lighting the town anew, their warmth bled through the shadowed night.

Out of the corner of her eye, she saw Karsten pace beside

her. While everyone else was brimming with happiness and hope, she wondered if any of that filtered through the exhaustion weighing on his shoulders. Outside the gates to Rannadal, he no longer seemed like an imposing Commander of a growing army.

Then again, she always found him to be a different man depending on the time, as if he transformed when bathed in sunlight or soaked in the moonlight.

In the daytime, he shone like a distracting and handsome beacon on their long trek to and from the mountains. Karsten was different after the sun fell behind the broken Divide. It was as if the moonlight illuminated the darkest parts of him, making them more bearable so long as the moon graced him with its soft glow.

Adelaide always loved the night and the way it played with the shadows, casting things askew and highlighting the flurries of falling snow when the winters approached her home. Sure, daylight was a blessing when the dark months took over the lands, but there was something intimate and magical about the night.

He seemed to bask in that magic, tilting his head towards the moon and letting it fill up the darkest corners of his usually grim expression. When he caught her staring, he stopped and his brows pinched together, hiding the light that was once present.

"Is there something on my face?" he asked, his large hand running across his jaw, scratching the stubble on his chin and pulling at the scar skipping over his lip.

"No, not anymore." She turned back to the night and let Mani, the moon, fill her with its cool light as they sat on the cold earth by the lake.

The moon's reflection glistened in the gradually freezing water, its watery form morphing when a golden leaf floated its way. Unbidden, a memory of her life before The Divide was destroyed crashed down around her. It replaced the unfamiliar forest with the trees of her home. Even the earth morphed into the snow-drenched incline she'd known her whole life.

While bathed in the light of the dimming campfire, the youngest of them was curled into Mother's side, her tiny hands leeching the warmth from her. "If the moon is called Mani, what is the name of the sun?" she asked, her voice small and soft and her curiosity for the Gods as constant as the energy of her youth.

"Her name is Sol," Mother told her. "Mani is her brother. Together, they bring us light, even in the darkest of times."

She considered those words with what seemed like a heavy heart. "Sol doesn't visit us often. Does she not like us?"

Mother's laughter echoed through the birches. "No, sweetling. She loves us very much. In Alfheim, we saw her all the time but here—" She paused to stare out at the wilds. "The humans get her attention more than us, but they need her light far more than we do. I don't think it's that hard to share her love with those who need it."

She shivered as she stared at the reflection of the moon on the lake, unable to move. It was as if she was worried that, if she dared to look away, the water would reach out, choking her as it pulled her under and forever damned her to a world without Mani's light.

"You have that look on your face again." Karsten's abrupt words pulled her away from her memories and back to the edge of the village where they'd been sitting for Gods only knew how long. "You were remembering your family, weren't you?"

She nodded instead of speaking, fearing her words would be soaked by a sorrow she couldn't bring herself to share.

His attention slipped away and focused on the stones lying on a bed of sand, blocking their path to the edge of the lake. He pulled himself up, his joints popping with the effort of moving a stiff body in the cold, and he offered her his hand, his face silhouetted by the moon.

When she took it, he eagerly pulled her to her feet. When they stopped in front of the stones, his hand lingered beside hers. She wondered if all humans ran hot like him, since she could feel his warmth even through his thick gloves. Before she could ask, he pulled away.

"The top stone has been smoothed by the constant brush of the waves," he said, kneeling to run his fingers over its even surface. "Or maybe it was purposefully smoothed by followers of The Old Gods." There was a hint of teasing in his tone, something she never thought she'd hear from him.

What he suggested hit her a few moments later.

"Won't someone see me?" she asked, wariness creeping down her spine as she eyed the path back to the village they'd taken to find their secluded spot.

He shrugged, his mantle rising with his shoulders until the fur tickled his exposed, flat ears turning red from the wind. "I'll keep watch." His hand clamped down on her shoulder, a comforting weight as his warmth bled through her tunic. "You should at least get to pray for their safety in your own way."

Then he was gone, his form slipping into the shadows until she couldn't see him in the darkness. Still, she could feel his gaze occasionally as she busied herself around the clearing, searching for materials to make an altar.

She used the gifted dagger to carve a protection rune into a piece of bark she pried from the nearest tree and surrounded it with lingonberries harvested from the nearby bushes. It was a humble offering but it was all she could give—all she had to show her devotion and desperation.

Adelaide sat in silence with the Gods, hoping they knew what was in her heart, and remembered a tale her mother told her of Freyr, the God of peace and pleasure, who was lovestruck by a giantess. The tale came back to her in parts, and she recited them as if she were telling the night a bedtime story.

"'How shall I tell thee, thou hero young, of all my grief so great?'"

The words came suddenly, choking her on their way out. "'*More famed shalt thou grow, than the watchman of the Gods. Peer forth, then, from thy prison. Rage and longing, fetters and wrath, tears and torment are thine; where thou sittest down, my doom is on thee of heavy heart and double dole.*'" The words broke off and sounded pathetic to her own ears. There were no tears left for her to shed, but sorrow felt like a tangible weight on her chest. "'*Grief shalt thou get, instead of gladness, and sorrow to suffer with tears.*'"

The soft breaking of twigs behind her was the only indicator Karsten gave of his presence before he finished the story. "'*Long is one night, longer are two; how then shall I bear three? Often to me has a month seemed less than half a night of desire.*'"

The tale sounded beautiful and some of the lines resonated with how she felt, but the story itself was horrendous. Freyr had asked his friend Skirnir to bid a giantess to rendezvous with him and, when she'd refused, Skirnir had attempted to bribe her. Then he'd threatened her with curses and the blade. She'd eventually agreed, for how could she not? Even though Freyr's love had been true, the lengths Skirnir had gone to to make her comply had tainted any future they had together.

"Skirnir is an ass," she said. A small huff left Karsten's chest, and she almost believed it to be a chuckle. Then it struck her, how odd it was that he, a devout Cislenian, could recite a tale of The Old Gods. "How do you know that story?"

His expression darkened until not even the loving moon could brighten the cold look in his eyes. His mind was too far gone, pulled back into memories that were better left forgotten.

"Not all of us converted by choice, Adelaide."

Her name rolled off his tongue, the sound heavy and dull. Even with her name spoken with such sadness, she'd give anything for him to say it again. To paint her name with his tongue and soothe the parts of her aching to have him near. If only he'd speak her name when his mind wasn't clouded by the horrors of his past.

"Does that mean—" She stopped, unsure how to ask the question burning in her mind.

Still, he understood her. "They stripped us of our traditions, punished us for sneaking them into their own customs, and eventually we stopped trying," he said, his amber eyes a million yards away. "They called our loss in our own faith *proof* theirs was true and that we willingly converted. Eventually, my younger siblings weren't even told of the old ways and didn't remember the Gods' names." He stopped to sigh, his words sending a shudder through him. "But I remember. I always will."

He offered his hand again, and she used it to pull herself off the forest floor. Their trek back to the village was silent save for the rushing of wind through the trees and the growing uproar of the festivities, but Adelaide's mind rang loud with a million swirling thoughts.

Daydreams of his hand back on her, running over her skin without his damned gloves in the way. Of his tongue, sounding out her name and then morphing into sounds of pleasure. Of the million and one things she could do with a body built as sturdy as his. Of the way none of those thoughts made her feel guilty anymore.

She merely relished them instead, even if their reality was an impossible dream.

THE GREAT CONVERSION DOCTRINE

The proclamation of the clergy is threefold.
One: Never ask permission for what is Promised by Olena,
For Midgard is our home and Her word our greatest quest.
Two: Never forsake the visions ordained by the most holy,
For our Gods speak to us through our Lines of Divinity.
Three: Never allow a pagan to suffer a life without The Divine,
For death is a lesser tragedy than a life without Olena's grace.

14

A SHIFT IN DESIRES

SKALD: KARSTEN STROM

They lingered outside Adelaide's door, on the porch where the guards normally stood.

The Vikings Thora and Kare were posted outside like Njal promised, but Karsten gave them a brief reprieve to grab food for both themselves and Adelaide. He planned to watch her door in the meantime, ensuring she wouldn't have further interruptions or unwanted guests for the night, but she seemed determined to stay outside in the cold with him.

"You really should rest," he said for what felt like the hundredth time as he leaned against the wall of her cabin. The wood dug into his back in a pleasant way, grounding him and releasing some of the tension in his shoulders. "It's getting cold. You'll catch ill."

She shook her head, her white hair lying heavy on her sinking shoulders. She was obviously exhausted, but she still wore a brave face. He understood why she'd want to hide her pain. After all, he did the same, but he was nothing if not a hypocrite.

"Elves don't get cold," she said it as if it were well-known fact, although he knew she was exaggerating. They were more acclimatized to the winter temperatures than humans, but they still felt the cold and could get sick. In Midgard and New Alfhiem, they were made mortal just like humans. "Besides, my cabin is lovely but—" She swallowed, and he tried to hold himself back from watching the bob of her throat. "I'm used to sharing a home this size with my family. It's rather imposing for just one person."

"So, you're going to wait until you're dead on your feet to sleep?" he asked, earning him a glare and a pointed look that told him he had no room to talk. "Fair point."

They were silent for a time, listening to the drumming and distant voices from the celebration. He wished he could join as a regular man and she as a regular woman, each unburdened by darkness and duty. But that wasn't the hand they'd been dealt. Besides, he couldn't picture her *ever* entertaining a dance with him.

Even though he could feel a shift in the dynamic between them that night, it wouldn't undo the years of resentment she'd felt towards his previous title. It also wouldn't wash his mind of the horrors he'd dealt to her people in the Brotherhood's name. There was less tension between them, but something new replaced it.

The prior tension was filled with animosity, as if she could decide he wasn't worth the trouble and end his life at any moment. That all vanished and, instead, there was a pulsing beat attracting them into each other's orbit. It burned in his blood, unsettling him. He wanted her, all of her, and there was no denying that.

Even without the lust spirit's influence, he longed to be by her side.

He just needed to accept she'd never return such affection or his desires. Maybe if he'd never become a Knight or was an elf like her, they could've been *something.*

There was just too much pulling them apart. There was no

point in trying to woo or court her. It would only end in pain for him and a return to that uncomfortable tension when she inevitably rejected him. The last thing he wanted was to make her feel more pressure due to his own foolish heart.

"The others are back," he said, breaking the silence as he noted the Berserker and shieldmaiden heading their way with food in hand. "You should really try to rest after you eat."

She sighed, her breath coming out as a white cloud around her tempting lips. "You'll eat and rest eventually too, right?"

He froze on his way down the short steps leading off the porch. "I'll try."

Once her cabin was out of sight and all that lay before him was the frenzied celebrations overtaking the village, he repeated their night by the lake in his mind.

The way she'd let him protect her from Njal, and yet still held him back from making a mistake by slitting the other man's throat. The sound in her shaky voice as she'd asked for his forgiveness earlier in the day. The sorrowful story she'd cried out to the lake. The warmth of her hand through his gloves.

Despite everything between them, he thought she might truly care for his wellbeing. She wouldn't ask him to rest and eat otherwise. She wouldn't sew protection runes into his cloak if she didn't care even just a little. She laughed with him, let him see her cry, and trusted him to keep her safe. That might not have been enough for romance, but there was something just as important blooming between them.

Friendship.

He couldn't stop the smile forming on his lips at the thought.

Yes, if nothing else, we can be friends. What an honor.

THE NIGHT STRETCHED IMPOSSIBLY LONG before him, and it felt like ages before the guards relieved him and switched stations. By that time, the world flickered in front of him like a dying candle and his thoughts were sluggish, like he was swimming through molten tar to conjure a single coherent sentence.

But when he found himself alone in his cabin, the barren space impossibly large, his mind ran to Adelaide's words without issue.

"It's rather imposing for just one person."

Karsten was never bothered by the empty space. After growing up with five siblings who all shared one bedroom, having something to call his own was a blessing. He'd never felt lonely while staying there, but suddenly the feeling clawed up in his chest unbidden. There was just a bed with standard issue quilts and pelts every warrior was granted, his desk that never ceased to be overflowing with reports, and the typically unused hearth. Outside, there was an old rocking chair on his porch: a gift from the local carpenter's guild when he found one of their missing apprentices lost in The Wild Woods before the Keepers did.

Would Adelaide have really killed the boy if she found him? It's hard to picture that now, but I'd been so certain then.

He tried to rest, as she'd requested, but he tossed and turned even as his head screamed at him for each movement. His only reprieve was further work, so he strapped his armor on again and went back out into the pre-dawn light.

The mead was still flowing, although several people had already retired, and the laughter and bonfires pierced at his brain. There was only one light that didn't hurt him, and that was the soft glow of Adelaide's cabin lit from within by candles and the hearth bleeding warmth into the roads. Mindlessly, he drifted towards it like a lost ship seeking shelter from the storms.

But then he heard it. The softest hum of a melody he almost knew. It drifted through the cold air, turning his attention to the bonfire nearest to her cabin.

There she sat, back to him so her white hair was haloed by the flames. Zamir, Sander, and Embla sat around her, laughing and sharing stories he'd heard a thousand times but were brand new to her pointed ears. Her laughter lit up the night, slicing through her humming before she resumed it again, swaying to the urges of the mead in her goblet.

Memories, distant and dark, filtered through his mind. His training as a Knight seared into his mind, as did that song. He'd been warned of it by his mentors: told how the mountains echoed with it right before you died. It was the calling of a Keeper, signaling for their clan to come to their location and deliver a swift end to any human they set their sights on.

Karsten had only heard the melody a few times. One of which he'd never forget for all his days. He had no longer been a Knight then, but his former brothers-in-arms had begged him to help search for a missing recruit. Unlike the carpenter's apprentice, that recruit hadn't been found alive. He'd discovered his body, bloodied and beaten, at the bottom of a ravine.

That melody had echoed above his head before he'd run for his life.

His stomach rolled, and he turned away from the bonfires to seek the reprieve of the shadowed alleyways nearby. He doubted the Keeper who had killed that recruit was the same woman who held his hard so strongly and unknowingly in her grasp, but the possibility was still there and it weighed on him.

Perhaps there's too much between us for even a timid friendship.

He shook his head, but it didn't help clear the shadows at the edge of his vision as he stumbled down the alley. It opened to a secluded area by the tree line inside Rannadal's walls. There were voices shouting and laughing close by, but he couldn't discern one word from another as he blearily viewed the men in the shadows.

Their forms swam like ink in the rain, their faces featureless in his mind's eye. The only noticeable things about them were the shining emblem of the Knights on their shoulders and their sheer strength as they competed with one another for who could throw a large log the furthest into the woods. They still weren't as powerful as a Berserker who'd taken The Bane, but that strength still wasn't natural.

He saw it then, the sly pass of a shimmering blue bottle between gauntleted hands.

Vow.

He threw up in the nearest bush.

In the morning, Karsten was hungover without ever having taken a single sip of mead.

His head throbbed with blood and pain, his vision swam, and his back ached. All those feelings were made worse by the bitter chill biting into his skin. A groan escaped him as he sat up, surprised by the amount of light filtering into his room.

That's when he realized he *wasn't* in his room.

He'd passed out around the main bonfire sometime after

stumbling upon a few Knights taking Vow, but the rest of his night slipped from memory. He smacked his dry lips and was relieved to discover there wasn't any residue of that vile elixir on his tongue.

Someone had been kind enough to drape his cloak around him as a makeshift blanket, but many around the fire weren't as lucky. Drunk villagers, warriors, Vikings, and Knights alike were bundled up or sprawled freely around the dying embers of the fire. The scent of mead and body odor filled the air, making his stomach roll. He figured they'd pace themselves, dragging out the party for days on end like usual, but it seemed like the town collectively decided to wrap things up in a single, frantic night of debauchery.

His body protested with each move he made to his feet. He rolled out as much tightness in his shoulders as he could manage. At the very least, he wasn't the only person who had fallen asleep outside that night. If he was, he would've simply crawled under a rock to die.

He blushed at the thought, and the heat in his face only grew at the idea of Adelaide finding him in such a state. Even if all they could ever be was defined by a timid friendship resting on a tightrope where one wrong word could send them toppling into uneasy tension once more, he would not want to be seen in such a state by *her* of all people.

He jogged to the bathhouse and stripped to clean the scent of alcohol and sweat off his body. The hot water washed away the ache in his bones and woke him until the feeling of sickness eased from his stomach. Still, it did little to lessen the wariness he felt about where in the world he'd slept.

Was he truly so unwell that he'd collapsed just before first light? Worse yet, had he truly fallen and no one had noticed?

The thought wove a deep, sorrowful feeling into his heart that made him claw at his tightening chest. He quickly exited the steaming baths, dried with the provided linen, and started dressing in the same clothes from the day before. His hands shook with each tie and button of the trousers and tunic he wore under his armor, making him feel just as worthless as his father did. He could hardly dress himself; how could he lead an army for his Goddess?

How could he protect *her?*

Adelaide truly showed that she cared about him, but how long would it last? If she'd been the one to find him sleeping in the dirt, his face in the ash of the fire, that would've already ended it. She would've returned to the feelings of disgust she no doubt had felt for him before, after she'd found out he'd once been a Knight: another thing he failed at.

Adelaide wouldn't be there if he fell and, if she were, she'd cast him aside for certain. He couldn't rely on his men for such things. He couldn't even confide to his warriors about the illness plaguing him or the spirits dogging him.

None of the others he called friends had found him, passed out in the dirt, and taken him back to his bed. The Vikings he'd fought alongside, the warriors he led, and the Knights he'd bettered were all the same. He outranked most. He couldn't rely on any of them. He couldn't ask for help or find solace in their friendship. There was no way he could find romance or *love.*

Not when he only wanted one person who was sure to despise him when she realized his weakness. He was completely alone.

"Begone," a voice suddenly snapped as a shadow passed over Karsten.

His cloak was thrown over his shoulders, the runes glowing golden as it dispelled the spirit feeding off him. He gasped as the tight dread clawing at his chest vanished and his shoulders shook beneath the thick, black fabric. In the glowing light, he made out Zamir's deep frown as he waved his hands around him, as if he could dispel the spirit with a simple gesture.

Zamir hummed when he turned back to the other man.

"Looks like Adelaide's not the only one who can control the spirits, huh?" he joked, his humor and smile as infectious as ever.

That's when Karsten realized those feelings for what they were, compulsions of Loneliness. He hadn't faced that spirit in a long time, not since his trip between his childhood home and back to Rannadal with his tail between his legs after his father had kicked him out. With people like Zamir and Zareen around, he hadn't been tempted to fall into such beliefs in years.

He grabbed Zamir by the collar and yanked him forward into a fierce hug, the smaller man crushed against his tunic before he could fully process what he was doing. "Thank you," he mumbled, still feeling breathless from the whispers of the spirit in his ear.

And thank you, Adelaide, for the runes.

Zamir pushed on his chest until his friend released his firm hold. "Ugh, you beast of a man! You wrinkled my tunic." He huffed as he stepped back and brushed off the light blue fabric on his chest. Then he stopped and met his gaze. "But you're welcome."

Karsten sighed as he reached for his bracers and strapped them on. "You're a good friend, truly."

"You needn't butter me up, Karsten. I'll always be here," he said, patting him on the arm as he picked up the next piece of his armor and held it out for him. "Even if you're hilariously passed out in the dirt like a ruffian." He fought off his blush, but it still burned its way across his cheeks. "What, need that much mead after your late-night rendezvous with our Promised?" he asked, wiggling his brows.

The blush deepened. "I didn't drink anything. I passed out," he said with a roll of his eyes. "And for your information, nothing happened. She simply needed a walk after finding Njal waiting in the shadows of her room. However, he claims to be on our side, so we'll see."

The other man's face paled. "Go back for a moment, you passed out not from the mead but from—" He stopped, his face souring in annoyance. "Now I feel like an ass for leaving you."

He shrugged as he adjusted his chest plate and settled into the familiar weight of his armor. "It wasn't the withdrawals exactly. I was just exhausted," he said, the lie slipping from his lips too easily for his own comfort. "Although, I'm sure my sobriety helped in my embarrassing demise last night."

"Still," Zamir said with a sigh. "No Knight has ever safely quit Vow. I'll always support your choice to be the first, but you promised my sister and me that you'd be careful." He locked a hand firmly onto the taller man's shoulder. "That you'd tell us how you were doing, truthfully, and rest when you needed to."

"I know. Your sister already gave me a lecture," he assured him, patting his hand until it loosened. "But like you said, no one has attempted this before. I don't know what to expect from my day or what will push me too far until I'm already on the edge of breaking apart." He braced his shoulders until Zamir's hand fully fell to his side. "The runes Lady Aylara sewed are helping so I'm not fighting on two fronts. I'm feeling better overall as long as I wear this." When he still seemed doubtful, Karsten huffed in annoyance. "See it this way: I haven't taken a single sip in eight months. That's farther than any Knight has gone before."

Zamir folded his arms. "Yeah, and who cleaned your puke for the first two months?" His blush returned in full force until the other man's shoulders seemed to fall in defeat. "You're doing well, that's good, but you'd do better if you relied on your friends. That's all I'm saying."

"You're right," he admitted, wrapping his arm over the other man's shoulders as he led them out of the bathhouse. "I'll do better, and I already have a task I need help with."

He arched a brow. "What would that be?"

Down the hill from the bathhouse, the main fire Karsten had slept at was starting to busy with people just waking up.

Among them, Njal was untangling himself from bodies and mead horns.

Karsten motioned at the hulking figure. "Keep an eye on Njal and his Berserkers. I want to make sure they don't have any ill intentions with Adelaide."

"*Adelaide*, hm?" he asked with a sly purse of his lips.

Karsten glared at his friend, but it only served to widen Zamir's smug grin.

"This doesn't have to do with any jealous feelings, right?" At the confused twist of his expression, Zamir went on. "You found another man in Adelaide's chambers. That doesn't lend to your distrust of him?"

"That's exactly why I don't trust him," Karsten clarified. "He snuck into her cabin, uninvited, in the middle of the night!"

"Uninvited from what you know," he corrected, making the Commander's face turn red from anger rather than embarrassment. "I'm just saying, you can't be jealous of another man acting first if you refuse to take the initiative."

He pinched the bridge of his nose. "I'm asking you to spy on Njal, not give me courting advice."

"I can do both at the same time, my friend." He laughed as he descended the stairs towards the fires. "But keep my words close to heart!"

That's the last thing I'm going to do.

After breaking his fast with a plain bowl of oatmeal he hoped would steel his turning stomach, he headed out the front gates to see which of his men would be sober enough to train for the day. He stopped at the threshold, peering out at the fields, and found a sight for sore eyes.

Adelaide was training, swinging wildly around her opponent who was blocking her practice sword with their staff at every turn. Sander was practically dancing around her, long black hair waving in the breeze behind him. He shifted and a zap of electricity shot out of his staff. It hit her in the leg, catching her by surprise and knocking her off her feet.

On instinct, Karsten lunged forward as if he could help her from yards away.

Instead, Sander swept her up and set her back down as if she'd never fallen. She laughed, the lovely sound echoing towards him like a haunting melody as she grasped onto the man's chest for support before finding her footing again.

Unbidden, Zamir's words shot through his head.

"You can't be jealous of another man for acting first if you refuse to take the initiative."

Oh, he most certainly could.

His breakfast soured in his gut as he turned around to start his work.

If he was a bit harder on the warriors that day, no one commented on it.

THE DAYS PASSED and turned into weeks of ceaseless training for everyone in town.

Integrating the different factions within Rannadal into a single army was no easy task, but it was going surprisingly well. Karsten knew that was thanks to Njal keeping his word and ensuring his Vikings stayed in line.

But he would absolutely, under no circumstances, be thanking the man.

Similarly, Adelaide made a striking amount of progress in her sword fighting, hand-to-hand combat, and her ability to manipulate the spirits. She'd practiced with that last element the least, since few spirits ever made their way close enough to town thanks to their warriors stationed in Skagi. When they did, he made sure she was riding alongside his battalion to handle the matter so she could practice.

Sander was a great help with both her close combat and magic training, but Karsten knew most of the hard work was coming straight from her. She was relentless, constantly chipping away at practice dummies and anyone brave enough to fight her in the training ring. He had a feeling he knew why she was so focused and undeterred from her practices, and it had little to do with any spirits clamoring towards their doorstep.

She was distracting herself from her desire to find her family.

It was a cold morning with autumn around the corner, the leaves just beginning to change color, when he knew he was right in his observations. He was training his warriors as normal, and she was elbow-deep in the dirt with Zareen, who'd agreed to go toe-to-toe with her in the ring that day.

Zareen was one of their most seasoned fighters, and she was broad in size and muscular like a man. In the kingdom she hailed from, she'd been trained as a soldier and personal guard to their King. That showed in her ferocity and skill. Her deadly nature only grew under her newer mantle as a shieldmaiden and later as his lieutenant.

Her broad build ensured Adelaide knew all her weak points as she used her lithe body to her advantage. Bets were made in hushed whispers around the training fields, coins silently passing between sly hands.

Karsten noticed, but decided to let his warriors have their fun.

The women were drenched in sweat, their hair wild halos around their heads as blood steadily dripped from their mouths where they'd given each other matching split lips. The rigid nature of their relationship hadn't changed, even after weeks of working together. Zareen had accused Adelaide of destroying The Divide and, in those early days, truly believed the other woman was responsible. That initial interrogation created a tension between the two that was never resolved, and they tended to keep a professional distance between them.

That all dissolved in the training ring, when fully fledged aggression sparked between them. It showed in the brutality of their swings and each hard hit created a deeper divide.

He sent their newest recruits on a run, dismissing them so he could focus on the training that was quickly turning into a full-blown brawl.

Zareen gritted her teeth as she locked arms with Adelaide, trying to force the other woman to the ground as her knees trembled. "*Yield*," she ordered, her voice booming across the field as Karsten quickened his steps towards them.

"No!" Adelaide screamed as she pushed her away, the other woman's back slamming against the gate around the practice yard with a hard crack.

Zareen brushed it off as if it didn't hurt, but he knew there would be a large bruise hidden under her armor. She freed her practice sword, forcing Adelaide to grab her own, as they began circling each other.

"Why must you insist on training this hard, hm?" Zareen asked, pausing to spit out blood into the dirt. "To prove elves are stronger than us meek humans? Are you simply too prideful to submit?"

Adelaide didn't respond, but he knew her silence didn't indicate she agreed with those assumptions. She was desperate for the distraction pain brought. She'd admitted to him that she couldn't even stand being in her own room without her family, and none of those weeks she spent training brought any answers for their whereabouts. It only confirmed one truth in their minds: that her family was long dead and she couldn't even bury them.

That idea turned her cold and calculating.

"Or are you trying to prove you can truly be a protector to these people?" another woman asked from outside the ring, pulling all of their attention towards her. He hurried towards Sister Jill Gorm and her insistently running mouth. "After all, your track record for protecting people is rather poor, considering what happened to your kin."

Adelaide's expression distorted with rage, the practice sword creaking in her hands before she tossed it into the muck. A fury blazed in her eyes as she lunged for the gate, half-over the structure before Zareen yanked her backwards by the collar. He couldn't hear what she was hissing into Adelaide's ear, her hand pressed to the elf's chest to hold her back from attacking the clergywoman, but it didn't seem to lessen the anger in her eyes.

"That was uncalled for, Jill," Karsten snapped, grabbing the old woman by the arm and urging her towards the path leading into town.

"Just stating simple facts, Commander," the Sister said, her voice sounding far more innocent than he knew her intentions to be. "How are we, as a village, expected to rely on her assistance if she's already failed the people who mattered most to her?"

Jill was sure to speak loud enough for the crowd to hear every word. He refused to meet anyone's gaze as he escorted her away, but he could feel the tension rising around them. She'd planted the seed of doubt and, as a farmer's son, he knew that it took little for weeds to grow and fester.

"Are you trying to undermine her, purposefully, or are you just that senile?" he snapped as he released his death-grip on her, shoving her towards town. "Her ability to save Rannadal from these spirits is the only thing protecting her."

Jill straightened her robes and brushed the non-existent evidence of his touch from her arm. "I'm simply stating facts. If people doubt her after hearing the truth, that says more about her character than mine." She stopped to fix her sleeves over her wrinkled hands. "I told you that she had one chance, and she's been here for two months with almost nothing to show for it. How have you allowed that?" she questioned quietly as she arched a brow at him. Then, louder, she asked, "Does the Knight fancy himself an elf pet?"

It was his turn to nearly punch her before a hand on his shoulder stopped him, pulling him back from giving into his darker urges. Instead, he watched Jill return to town with her chin held high, before he turned to the person who held him back.

"She was kind to me before," Adelaide said, her brows pinched over her confused stare. "I don't understand why she'd —" She cut herself off and lowered her gaze.

Zareen stopped beside her and scoffed; her nose scrunched in disgust. "It's *Jill*, you must expect that with her conniving ass. She'll use her role in the chapel to convince others to open up to her, only to use those very same insecurities to tear them down."

He nodded. "Try to avoid her at all costs."

"And just know anyone with half a brain wouldn't believe a word she says," Zareen explained with a grimace of pain as she rotated her shoulder. "You can protect and fight incredibly well." She paused to glare at her. "*Too well*, in fact."

Adelaide gave her a sheepish grin. "Apologies, Zareen. I shouldn't have taken my frustration out on you." She held her hand out. "Can we start over?"

"Would've been lovely if you came to that conclusion earlier, but yes." Zareen took her hand and shook it. "Now, I need to visit the healer if you'll both excuse me."

She took her leave so only Adelaide and Karsten were left standing at the gates, watching as a few of the onlookers argued about who won the fight and, therefore, who among them won the bets. He almost chuckled at the sight, but her words stole every ounce of laughter from him.

"They're really gone, aren't they?"

A chill ran through him. "We don't know that."

She turned around to face him, her eyes glinting with tears as she bit her lip. "I've seen no evidence to say otherwise." She looked at the mountains, and both their hearts seemed to topple to the floor between them. "I never thought I'd have to start planning a funeral instead of a reunion."

He wracked his brain, struggling to find any small sliver of proof her family lived in all the reports he'd received: any sightings of elves who matched their descriptions. None came to mind. They'd been fruitless in their efforts over the months since The Divide was destroyed.

Except for one thing.

He grabbed her hand and tugged her to the left side of the gates, down a path often not taken unless one planned to leave for the towns and cities further in the mainland.

She arched a brow but allowed him to drag her along. "Where are we going?"

"The stables," he said, releasing her hand with a little reluctance once he was sure she was following. As far as he knew, she'd never been to the stables. Whenever they traveled beyond town, the horse she typically used was brought to her at the gates. "I was waiting until he was back on his feet to tell you."

"Tell me what?" she asked, wiping the drying blood on her split lip away with her sleeve.

"We found a horse that belonged to one of your people," he explained, pushing the door to the stables open. "Poor thing was malnourished and covered in ash when we found him, but he's been on the—"

As soon as the door opened, she gasped and rushed inside. "Enok!"

The white and speckled horse huffed and nodded as she

collapsed beside him, holding onto his neck like it was a lifeline. She buried her tear-stained face into his mane, using his battered body to muffle her cries as she clutched onto the wounded creature with all her might.

Surprise froze him to his spot. "I didn't realize," he said, forcing himself to take another step into the room. "You didn't describe any horses, so I never had my men look for one."

She sniffled as she peeked at him from behind the horse's hair. "I didn't expect him to be alive if my family perished. If he lived, I expected him to be by their side." She ran her fingers through his hair, untangling the matted ash and muck still present in the locks. "Thank the Gods for this miracle."

He moved to the horse, crouching on its other side to be eye level with her. The poor thing couldn't stand yet, but it seemed happy enough to just rest its head on her shoulder. He tried not to think about her family dying or in a similar state of pain, instead focusing on the blessing between them.

"More miracles will come and, with it, so will your family," he said with every ounce of conviction he could muster to ease her battered heart. "I don't care which Gods you follow, just have faith in them."

She nodded and hid her tear-stained face back in the horse's mane.

BURIED DEEP under the Cislenian chapel, opposite of the door which led to the hidden relics of The Old Gods, was an archive of literature from across Midgard. It was cherished by Karsten and all followers of Olena, for it told of her immortal life and all its glory. However, it became a chore for one rather beautiful and *stubborn* woman.

Adelaide groaned up at the ceiling for the tenth time that hour, ignoring the scroll in her hands that was older than Rannadal itself. "I can't make heads or tails of any of this!" She slumped against the stone wall. "Why are you humans so confusing?"

Karsten suppressed his annoyance as he lowered the book he was reading and settled her with a heavy look. He'd been struggling to read the same page for what felt like ages as he was continuously interrupted by her troubled noises.

Jarl Lefa insisted she studied their religion, since she was being anointed as their Promised but had very little knowledge of the faith outside campfire stories whispered by her family like scary tales. Not only would it improve her standing with those who doubted her divinity, but it would help legitimize the entire Covenant.

If only she could stop complaining about it.

He sighed and pinched the bridge of his nose, fighting off his rising irritation. He didn't mean to be so cruel, but her life was on the line. If anyone else heard her speak such a way about their sacred text, The Codex, they'd drag her behind the horses in an instant. They'd claim she was a false prophet.

Besides that, Sister Ylwa had finally organized a meeting between them and the clergy. Her hope was to mend the relationship between Rannadal and the church, which had been fractured when Lefa formed The Covenant against their directions. If their forces and belief in Adelaide were backed by the most faithful, they would gain an abundance of resources—enough to truly form a ten-thousand-men strong army to fight the spirits.

And she was whining about the same passage for an hour.

Groans and moans falling from her pretty lips wasn't helping his plight to be her friend—*and only her friend*—either. Every noise she made set off alarm bells in his mind, bringing forth tempting visions from Lust. He'd only accompanied her to the archives to ensure Sister Jill left her alone as she studied beneath the chapel, as was his duty as her guard, but Lust liked to play with the idea of them being *alone.*

'You two are unchaperoned, hidden away in a dark crevice of the most holy place in town. Doesn't that sound tempting?'

He shook off Lust's teasing and focused back on her, only to be teased once more. She pulled her plump lip between her teeth and sighed, slipping further down the wall so her stark white hair stood at all ends.

'Her hair always looks crazed, but can you imagine what it would look like if you took her on the cold stone ground?'

"What passage were you trying to understand?" he asked as he cleared his throat, hoping his cheeks weren't burning at the thoughts invading his mind.

She shrugged as she tapped the scroll. "Something about a holy blessing?"

"Let me see," he said, standing and adjusting himself when she wasn't looking. He peered over her shoulder, her hair wafting the heavy scent of lavender and snow—enticing him to get a bit closer than necessary. "It's the Chant of Order, otherwise known as Olena's prayer. It's straightforward. We learn it as children. Can you truly not understand it?"

She huffed, her breath ruffling the hairs on the back of his neck and sending goosebumps over his skin. "Human children must be geniuses."

He turned to her, their noses nearly touching before he leaned back even as Lust *begged* him to inch closer. "Adelaide, can you even read Common? I know you speak it and the language of the elves but—" He stopped himself when she turned red in the face and pointedly focused on the page. "If you know you can't read, then why—"

She threw the scroll down between them and folded her arms. "It's The Codex; you get credit for trying."

He couldn't help laughing at that point, his gut turning on

itself until he collapsed beside her against the stone wall. "That's not how this works!"

She huffed, blowing an errant strand of hair out of her face. "Well, how should I know? I'm not Cislenian, remember?" She grumbled something else under her breath before placing the scroll back on her lap and smoothing it out. "Besides, I can read Common. It's just—" She paused as her fingers ran over a few of the letters, making his laughter cease as her body turned rigid. "These letters change like magic. I can't keep up with the way they move."

He froze at that, wondering what in the realms she was saying, before he followed her piercing green gaze down to the parchment and back again. She was struggling over simple words: words anyone even slightly familiar with the language would know. Her eyes danced, never settling on one word until she squinted a little harder, focused a little more.

There was once a girl in his village, when he was young, who had read the same way. Every word had been a struggle for her. Her parents had thought her dull and ceased her tutoring, eventually assigning her to hard field work on their farm not built for her rather sickly body. It wasn't until he had returned as an adult, determined to fix his family, that he'd seen her again.

The years had weighed on her, but she'd seemed happy regardless. She'd left her family and discovered she wasn't alone in struggling to formulate letters into full words. She'd shown him some of the techniques she'd learned to read Common properly, and her life had turned around as a result.

What had she called it?

Karsten reached forward and placed his hand on the scroll, covering the lines before and after the sentence Adelaide was fighting with. Immediately, the tension in her shoulders lessened and she unclenched her jaw.

"That better?" he asked.

She nodded, surprise etched into her uplifted brow as she read a line, then the next one with greater ease. She still stumbled at times, but the improvement was instant.

"How did you know to do that?" she asked.

"A girl in my village was the same as you," he explained, finally finding the right word for it buried deep in his mind. "She called it dyslexia."

She tested the word on her tongue and he tried not to be mesmerized by it. "How strange." She hummed as she returned to reading the scroll. "The runic alphabet of my people would sometimes move, but the characters meant more words than one, so it was never a major problem for me. Common is so different. Every letter is singular. It takes so many to make one word and they all get twisted in my eyes."

He shifted his hands down to the next verse in the stanza. "I can get you some clean parchment to help separate the lines."

She shook her head as she pointed downward, indicating for him to move to the next line as she leaned back. Her head rested beside his on the wall so her chin was nearly on his shoulder.

"No, I think I like this better."

He chuckled as he stayed in place, moving his gloved hands to each new line as they read together the rest of The Codex. She sometimes stopped to ask what a specific word meant or how to pronounce it. Other than those small questions, the archive was silent for the rest of the night.

He thanked Olena that, despite their proximity, Lust was quiet too.

KARSTEN WOKE WITH A JOLT, forgetting where he was until the shifting of the scrolls at his feet echoed across the arched stone walls. He had fallen asleep, for the second time in such a short while, without realizing it.

It was against all his training, as both a Knight and a Viking, to do such childish things. It endangered not just himself, but all his warriors if he was on watch and fell asleep unexpectedly. He never had an issue keeping his eyes open before. Typically, sleep was a luxury he couldn't afford. Ever since Adelaide had stitched those runes into his cloak, he found rest to be within easy reach whenever night fell upon the village.

He jolted again when he realized exactly where the woman in mind was.

Adelaide was asleep beside him, her fingers still curled around the many books they'd browsed, with her head on his shoulder. She softly snored, her white hair a mess around her head where it wasn't braided into submission. Her lashes curled around her softened eyes and her plump red lips were parted, her breath ruffling the fur lining of his cloak with each exhale.

Even in sleep, she was a stunning vision.

"Hey," he murmured, brushing a white lock from her chin before he tucked it behind her ear. She shuddered against him when his gloved finger curled around the pointed tip, and he could feel a warm blush covering his cheeks. "We fell asleep, but we can't stay on the stone floor all night."

Her brows pinched over her heavy-lidded gaze as she blinked awake, her eyes foggy with sleep as she searched the room around them. That tired but dangerously captivating gaze fell on him, drinking him in until he feared he might drown in their depths.

"I can't believe I fell asleep," she said, her words muffled by a small yawn as she, to his deep regret, retreated from his side. "I have so much I still need to learn." She rifled around in the piles of notes and half-read scrolls. "Lefa wants me to meet with the clergy so soon."

A blush burned across her cheeks as she peered at him out of the corner of her eye, as if testing to see if he would judge her. When he didn't respond, she turned back to the piles of parchment and started organizing what she could in a half-asleep, half-frantic mess unfolding like a hurricane before his eyes.

"I know what you're doing," he said, his words only serving to further her anxious movements. "You can't work yourself to the bone every day just to distract yourself from your fears. It won't work. Trust me."

She stopped; her hands curled around a tome. "Then what do you suggest I do?" she snapped, angry tears mixing into her exhausted gaze. "I've seen you outside the village with your men. You work from sunup to sundown and, sometimes, past that. You're constantly exhausted and burning at both ends. If you haven't found a way to distract yourself from whatever haunts you, what luck do I have of doing the same?"

He huffed, equally annoyed at her observation and impressed she'd surmised so much about him. "I'm well aware that I'm a hypocrite."

She snorted, her movements slowing as a small, tired grin fought its way onto her lips. "So, what then?" she questioned as she dropped a book into her lap. "Am I expected to be better than you simply because I'm some holy being—a Promise from a Goddess I don't believe in?" Her eyes pleaded with him for answers he didn't have. "I cannot live up to those expectations."

"I don't expect anything from you," he said, hoping his honesty was plain on his face. When she still seemed to doubt his words, he gripped his right-hand glove between his teeth and pulled it free before moving to the next, leaving his hands bare. "We all have parts of ourselves we don't like to show," he said, holding up his palms between them and not meeting her gaze as they shook. "I don't expect better from you. I just think you *deserve* better. If that can't be provided for you, then you should take it for yourself." More words he wished to say lodged themselves into his throat, forcing him into silence.

I wish I could do more for you.

I wish I could be *more for you.*

You deserve so much better than the hand you were dealt.

You deserve so much better than me.

And yet I cannot help but want you all the same.

"If anyone deserves to be a little easier on themselves, it's you," she said, and his gaze snapped to hers in surprise. "I suppose I'm a hypocrite as well, wishing you'd be easier on yourself when we're both at our own throats." She reached out, her hands clasping his to steady his callused palms with her soft touch. "But I'm glad we're not at each other's throats instead, at least not anymore."

A half-formed chuckle rushed out of him, the sound interrupted only by a flash of Lust's wanton visions caressing the back of his mind before he shoved them away. "On that note, I think it's time for us both to properly retire before Sister Jill starts spreading rumors about us being down here so late into the night."

She rolled her eyes as she collected her notes, leaving the mess of scrolls and books to deal with later. "I grew up with two older sisters. I can handle whatever petty disagreements or rumors that old hag cooks up."

He properly laughed that time as he propped the door open for her, letting her squeeze through before he locked it behind them. "I'm certain you can hold your own against the likes of her, but I still detest the idea of anyone speaking ill about you."

They walked up the stairs to the main floor. "Why is that?"

His cheeks bloomed with shades of red as he mentally cursed her for constantly doing that to him. He was a grown man and hardened warrior. He shouldn't *blush.*

"You're the Promised of Olena, a prophet sent by her most holy. No one should speak ill of you," he said, forcing himself to focus on the steps beneath him instead of the curve of her ass as she ascended the stairs ahead of him.

She murmured something under her breath, and he could hear the smile in her voice when she asked, "Does that give me free rein to be a menace to the village? Because I was thinking, we could use some good pagan practices. Perhaps a few more that allow for day drinking and flashing the sisters all our intimate bits?"

His cheeks burned like he'd been lit aflame, and he quickened his steps until they were back in the central area of the chapel and exiting the doors. He silently prayed no one was around to hear such words uttered in those sacred walls.

Once the doors were firmly closed and he could breathe the fresh scent of the autumn night, he glared at her. "You're going to be the death of me."

She gave him a cheeky grin as she meandered down the path winding deeper into town. He thought he noticed her hips swaying a bit more than normal, but he must've been mistaken.

"What, the all-powerful Commander of The Covenant's army can't handle a talk about intimacy?" she gasped, the sound as mocking as it was enticing. "Whatever will the sisters say?"

"Of course I can." He shook his head as he pushed off the chapel doors to follow her. "I just don't think it's appropriate for those holy walls."

A devilish grin spread across her face as she spread her hands out around them. "We're not in the temple anymore. So, how does a return of our game sound? A question for an answer." She didn't wait for him to respond as she turned around, her cloak swinging around her until he could see the light blue color of whatever gown she wore beneath it. "Are you a virgin?"

"W-what? No," he choked out before hesitantly asking, "Are you?"

"Most certainly not." She laughed as she matched his slow pace, neither of them seeming to want their night to end. "If you're not a virgin, why do you act like one when the most basic of sexual topics comes up?"

"I don't—" She cut him off with a stern look that immediately silenced his protests. "It's my understanding that elves are freer with their sexuality. Humans aren't so ready to speak about such matters. You'll find a similar response from most in town." He couldn't stop himself from asking his next question, and it spilled from his lips unbidden. "However, I have a feeling you're not speaking like this to many in town, so why ask me such things in the first place?"

She stopped in front of him and put her hands on her hips, the pose forcing her cloak back so he could fully see what was hidden beneath. The blue fabric was too familiar. He'd seen it earlier that day when Lefa had given her the thin, fitted nightgown as a thank you gift for her efforts.

It was the very present she'd purchased after receiving his letter urging The Jarl to import something nice for her. It was a glorified negligee and not proper to wear like a dress, even if it was long and not as sheer as it could've been.

Damn it, that was the best letter I've ever written in my life.

"I like it when you blush," she admitted, a tinge of pink gracing her own cheeks. "Besides, if I can't overwork myself to forget my sorrows, then my new distraction method will be embarrassing you into submission."

His mouth was suddenly dry and he couldn't tell if it was from the sight of her in the nightgown caressing her skin *just so* or if it was from the idea of her being domineering to him in *any* manner.

"I think you'll find that I'm not so easily swayed, Lady Aylara."

"We'll see about that, Commander." She smirked as she turned around, concealing her form beneath the cloak once more. "For your information, I've had similar conversations with Zamir, and he's been far more forthcoming than you. Then again, we both enjoy the company of men, so that's led to some familiar ground."

He sighed as he moved to her side. "Zamir and his sister didn't grow up Cislenian. The lands they come from have yet to meet the missionaries which dominate this side of the realm. You'll find Zareen to be more conservative in manners of intimacy, but Zamir—" He chuckled as he rubbed the back of his neck in embarrassment. "He's always been *bolder*. He flirted with me endlessly when we first met, until I had to turn him down."

She rearranged some of the notes in her hands, seeming uninterested in their conversation even though her ear twitched in his direction. "You prefer the company of women then?"

He shrugged as he brought his cloak closer to beat back the growing chill. "I never really cared. Perhaps Zamir and I could've been lovers at one point, but I was too broken for romance, and he was looking for something temporary to mend his own heart. I preferred to keep him around as a friend rather than lose him for a quick dalliance."

"And are you still too broken for it?"

"Probably," he admitted as he looked into the shadows in shame. "Doesn't stop the *wanting* though."

He felt her move a little closer, but he wasn't brave enough to meet her gaze, so he kept his eyes pinned on their next steps. "You mentioned something weeks ago in the carriage. You said a spirit of Lust was haunting you," she said, making his veins run cold. "Is that why you feel broken?"

"I don't believe it was your turn to ask a question," he snapped, hating himself as soon as the harsh words and matching tone slipped free. He stopped, closing his eyes to take a long breath and face her. "I apologize. That was unbecoming of me." He swallowed, growing nervous under her watchful gaze that seemed to hold no judgment. "No, it's not," he said before he took the words back. "*Yes.*"

She nodded, as if she could see the evidence of Lust's torture written all over him. Maybe she could. Was he truly that obvious? He imagined himself from her point of view. Were his pupils blown wide with want? Could she sense the dryness of his mouth and the eager pounding of his heart whenever he dared to glance her way?

"Sander is teaching me how to sense them," she explained, her hand hovering around his shoulder, as if she could feel the pulse of the spirit constantly dogging him. "With the runes, there are less surrounding you, but there's still Lust. I have a feeling the wounds it's caused are old." Her hand moved forward, hovering over his lips only a breath away. "Like a scar."

Her fingers reached temptingly close to his lips and the scar running over its edge. He often forgot it rested there—the obvious failure permanently written into his skin.

"The Knights' Initiation isn't that different from a Keeper's Iniquity," he said, the words so quiet that he worried she couldn't hear him before the wind stole the sound, but her ears fluttered, as if leaning in to listen. "You leave your young to fend for themselves in the darkness of The Divide. The Brotherhood employs a witch to capture a manifested spirit and release it into an enclosure with a recruit looking to complete their first phase of training when they turn sixteen. They can leave once they've killed the spirit. Mine just happened to be Lust."

Her face paled as she let her hand fall. "They left *a child* locked in a room with a physical manifestation of Lust?"

"It's meant to be whichever spirit the recruit struggles with the most. I was the most devoted to Olena, whose word says to bind yourself in flesh only to your eternally beloved. I'd planned to do so, but a girl in town caught my eye," he said, sighing as he fought to remain as passive as possible, to not weep or rage at the memories. "She was an elf whose family long ago left New Alfheim. I knew there could be nothing real between us, but one of my mentors must've discovered us. She decided to make an example of me."

Adelaide looked shaken, her teasing and laughter vanishing completely under the weight of his words, and he hated himself for ruining the lightness she'd once shared with him. "She told them to bring a Lust spirit to you in the flesh?" she asked.

He nodded as he turned to look at the moon, its fullness bathing the shadows in light. It was easier to look at its beauty, which never wavered, than to see the crushed look on Adelaide's face.

"The spirit took the form of the girl, tempting and torturing me at every turn, and I was shamed for every single desire of mine she made reality. I was shamed for nearly giving in." He peered back down at her, but her gaze was pinned to the ground beneath them. "I killed it, eventually, and was a proper Knight reborn in the Brotherhood. But I could never look her in the eyes again. After that, it left me susceptible to any manner of Lust spirit, so a second one began haunting me shortly after I returned to Rannadal. Thankfully, it has remained in an astral form. In a way, that's far kinder."

When she looked up, he knew what he'd see. He'd seen it on the face of all his mentors in the Brotherhood—*disgust*. He'd been too weak. He'd desired too much when the purpose of the Knights was to serve and give. At least, that's what it was *supposed* to be. His desires were against all The Codex demanded. Some even claimed wanting sex at all was against Olena's demands, let alone desiring all the things he truly craved.

Because Lust wasn't wrong when it had given him that

vision of Adelaide holding a knife to his throat or the dozens of other positions it tempted him with. He desired to consume her entirely. To mark her body as his in every sense of the word. Every carnal pleasure of the flesh he could imagine, he wished to fulfill with her. The eternal love Olena wished for, where sex was only meant for procreation, be damned.

He wanted her all to himself, every aching second of the day.

But she would never want him.

She already couldn't desire him, not with everything between their people and the fact she'd barely looked his way with kindness the entire time they'd known each other. But with her knowing the truth? How could she look at him with *want* when every other person who knew what he'd gone through looked upon him with disgust, shame, or pity? When he met her gaze, he was shocked to see none of that on her face.

No, she was *enraged.*

"You were trained here, right?" she demanded. All he could do was nod dumbly in response. "Are your mentors still among the ranks?" She grabbed his hand and he could feel her racing pulse through his gloves. It hammered into him as he shook his head. "Then where did you send them when you cut them from the ranks?"

"Most of them ended up in Helkaro but—" He paused to pull her to a stop. "What are you saying?"

She peered back at him, her eyes full of blazing fury. "I'm going to find the bastards who did that to you and skin them alive," she said, her tone menacing and cold. She wasn't threatening anyone, she was stating a simple fact. If she found his mentors, she would kill them on sight.

He gripped both of her hands in his and brought them to his chest to keep her close, preventing her from slipping free. "Adelaide, you're not doing that." She began to argue, so he pulled on her wrist to bring her even closer. "It was years ago and I made sure to deal with them the way I saw fit when I took control of the forces here." He rubbed his thumb over the back of her hand, soothing the raging inferno in her gaze. "But I appreciate your willingness."

Her shoulders fell even though the angry crease between her eyes never left her expression. "None of that makes you broken, Karsten."

He could hardly stop himself from shuddering at her soft voice uttering his name.

"Perhaps not, but how I reacted to it does."

She arched a brow at that.

"I still finished my training and became a Knight, remember? Even enduring that, I believed it was for a purpose. Instead of healing from the trauma, I buried myself deeper into the Order. *That's* what broke me."

She pulled her hands from his and let them slip to her sides. "Right," she said, her tone heavy with disappointment before she cleared her throat and seemed to throw a mask over whatever she was truly feeling. "So, young Karsten Strom had a crush on an *elf*?"

He chuckled, thankful for the change in topic, even as it brought a new blush to his cheeks. "Yes, I suppose he did."

"Got a thing for pointed ears?" she teased, her effort to return to easier topics not lost on him, but perhaps he didn't want to return to lighter discussions and teasing.

He simply wanted all that he couldn't have.

"And if I do?" he asked, freezing her in place with his words and his hand which raised to the side of her head. He tucked the same errant strand of half-curled hair behind her ear, ghosting his finger across the tip. She shuddered, just as she had when he'd done it in the chapel, and he wondered if she'd truly been asleep at that moment. "What then?"

She licked her lips, and he couldn't help his gaze from following the movement. Her tongue played with the edge of her lip before darting back into her open mouth. A white cloud formed from her breath and he followed it up to her eyes, which were blown wide in surprise. He was certain he saw her pupils dilate as they ran across his face, settling for the scar on his lip.

Her demeanor changed then, her expression pained for a moment before the mask slipped back into place alongside a playful smirk. "Then no wonder you turned Zamir down," she said, flicking her ear. "He doesn't have the right parts."

He chuckled, and whatever spell that lay between them was broken. Still, another fierce blush broke out across his face. "Yes, I suppose you're right."

After that, they walked to her cabin in a comfortable silence. When the door closed between them and he turned to walk towards his home, he couldn't help feeling lost.

Some part of him screamed she wanted him too, but logic won every time. It was normal for a body to respond in such a way, but that didn't mean her heart or mind wanted him too. He'd have to accept that. He just hoped he hadn't made her uncomfortable with his blatant longing.

That was the last thing he desired.

THE CHANT OF ORDER AND SOMETHING BETTER LEFT FORGOTTEN

"Olena, grant me the strength of ten thousand men."

I just need Mother's cloak. Then I can run—run back home like the coward I am.

"For a broken blade can still cut, and I will forever bleed in your name."

They won't let me leave Rannadal alive, not after I reported them to the elders.

"I pray for your salvation in my darkest hour, so do not forsake your strongest warrior."

My leg is broken. I can feel it dragging behind me, limp, but they just won't stop.

"When all I desire is your name on heathen tongues, and to be your servant forevermore."

Everything burns and there's blood everywhere. I cannot move. Why can't I move?

"Do not turn from me when I cry your name."

My Goddess, where are you? It hurts, and it's getting dark.

"Olena, please grant me strength."

Please, Olena, make them stop.

15

CHANGING OF THE TIDES

SKALD: ADELAIDE AYLARA

Adelaide awoke to the pre-dawn light painting her cabin in cool shades of blue that warred with the red warmth of the burning hearth. It turned the foggy sight of her bed into a romantic violet burrowing into her dreams.

She was half awake, half in the realm of sleep as her skin prickled against the sheets. Warmth spread to her core as the vague memories of her fantasy reformed in her mind, urging her hand to slip between her legs to relieve the building pressure. She was already wet, and her fingers glided across her pearl with ease.

A soft hum escaped her as the vision took hold of her once more. Strong hands pinning her against the door, hot breath on her skin as lips trailed across her neck and teased at her breasts. Her breath caught, her fingers quickening as she imagined another hand where hers lay, teasing her entrance beneath her hiked-up skirt.

The mouth moved to her breast, those rough hands tugging her tunic out of the way to allow the figure before her to feast. The push of their tongue swirling around her nipple before it tugged on the flesh sent her reeling, and she dipped a finger into her core to feel something in her throbbing little hole begging to be filled. The figure shifted, their mouth sucking on her skin and the scar on the edge of their mouth sending another shiver down her spine. It urged her to fall apart, to shatter across their hand and allow their lips to swallow her moans of ecstasy.

Wait, scar?

Her hand froze, a burn searing her cheeks as she fully awoke to the reality of what she was doing and *who* she was thinking about while she did it. Years passed since she felt a need like that, so desperate for release it made her a fool. She removed her hand, her slick dampening her thighs as she forced them closed. She was still aching with want, but shame curled in her stomach at the same time.

If I invited Karsten inside last night like I wanted, could that have been us?

A former Knight desiring her was a foolish thought, especially after what he told her the night prior about his initiation. That she would use his image in her mind for such purposes after everything he said made her want to throw up.

Of course, she knew she was easy on the eyes by most people's standards and that the Commander basically admitted to finding her attractive, but that was where things ended. If he harbored any further feelings for her that could compel him to disregard everything standing between them for a night of passion, it was only because of the spirit of lust haunting him.

If we were together because of Lust, it wouldn't be real.

The last thing Adelaide desired was for something fake, like the devotion Karsten showed in his efforts to find her kin. It wasn't because he truly cared, it was because of the Blood Oath she had forced upon him and couldn't stomach admitting to. If she could undo it, freeing him of one of the many burdens his station required of him so he could finally rest, she would do it in a heartbeat.

The fact that she would risk never seeing her family again for a chance to rectify things with a *human* should've made her sick.

But it's the right thing to do.

THE DAY ADELAIDE needed to leave to meet with the Cislenian clergy arrived far too soon. She studied to the best of her abilities with Zamir, Sander, Karsten, and even Zareen assisted in her schooling until the day they left Rannadal.

But she was *distracted*.

The time she spent with Karsten took most of her focus that should've gone into memorizing The Codex, with a few moments sticking out from the rest: his gentle hands over the parchment, helping her read; the brush of his finger across the tips of her ears; the smirks and smiles they shared; the story he'd told her about his initiation.

It haunted her just as his touch did. She found herself craving the connection and finding small ways to attract his attention, but he was always wearing those damned gloves. She knew why they never seemed to leave his skin: he was hiding the shaking in his hands from prying eyes. But that didn't tell her why they trembled. Was it the trauma, his withdrawals, or something else?

She hated herself for all her wanting regardless.

To her own surprise, she didn't hate herself for wanting a human, or even a former Knight. She could no longer see the evidence of the Brotherhood marring his skin and could hardly picture him in the Brotherhood at all. No, she hated herself for wanting a man who so clearly wouldn't want her the same way.

She could tell he—or at least Lust—was attracted to her, but where could that lead them? He felt too broken for proper courting and already said he wouldn't ruin a friendship for a short dalliance, so where could her desire possibly lead?

Ruin, that's what.

She fought with herself as the days grew shorter, autumn's full power approaching as daylight began to disappear. Half of her wished to draw him closer, and the other half pushed him away. She wanted him near, despite all their differences, but she also couldn't bear the thought of losing him just so they could both give into one moment of lust.

Pathetic. I don't even need a spirit of Lust to haunt me. I can daydream about us together all on my own.

Would she even want more than that? She could begrudgingly admit to her attraction to him, but that didn't mean she desired a *relationship*. They were treading on a fragile friendship. They'd become allies in combat, comrades in The Covenant, and neighbors within Rannadal, but none of that would last if their oath wasn't forcing them together. Was any of that a solid foundation to build a relationship on?

Certainly not.

Even knowing all of that, she still found herself watching him when he passed by. His deep amber eyes studied the world around him at every moment, but they remained passive until they fell on her. Then, it was like the cracking of a mountainside as lava burned beneath his gaze.

Still, desiring his body wasn't the same as desiring *him*, as a person, and he deserved that much. Especially after all he'd been through. She was certain she couldn't give him that, so she made sure to keep at least some small distance between them for the remainder of their lessons together.

Pain burst from her arm and she hissed, jumping back as

she re-focused at the task ahead of her. She realized far too late that she'd lost herself in thoughts of him.

Again.

Zareen glared at her as she drew back her practice sword. "Adelaide, you mustn't let your thoughts wander in battle."

She shook the pain out and adjusted her grip on her weapon. "It won't happen again."

"*Enough,*" the other woman said, stabbing her blade into the ground and rounding it to stand beside her. "Your mind has been distant all week. We're leaving for the clergy shortly and, although they'll be battling with wits and words, that doesn't mean they won't be deadly. You must be clear of mind when you face them."

"I know," she snapped, throwing her sword away. "There's just been a lot going on—" She trailed off and looked away, hoping she wouldn't see the blush burning across her cheeks.

Zareen was silent for a moment, and Adelaide could feel her gaze raking over her, assessing her like one would seize up an enemy in combat. They'd amended their rocky start, and she understood that even if Zareen's words were short and her tone clipped, the warrior truly meant every word with the best of intentions. She simply always spoke with a cautious attitude that revealed only that she thought everyone could be a threat.

"You're truly feeling the loss of your family, hm?" Zareen asked.

Adelaide nodded as if her words were true, grateful she hadn't discovered what was truly distracting her.

Of course, she really did miss her kin, but she had been truthful when she spoke to Karsten: she'd stopped distracting herself from her family being missing by overworking. Instead, she obsessed over her growing attraction towards him as a means of deflecting her thoughts from ceaselessly focusing on her family's whereabouts. It was a far more enjoyable diversion than working herself to the bone every day only to wake up and do it again the following morning.

Zareen laid a heavy hand on her shoulder, dragging her attention back. "Your horse will be ready to ride again once we've returned. Perhaps he could lead you to wherever he came from? It might give you a new area to search."

She'd already thought of that and employed Sander's help in doing a tracking spell. It had traced Enok's horseshoe impressions through the wet earth until they disappeared somewhere deep in the mountains. Karsten's men had followed it until the trail ran cold. They'd searched but there was no evidence of her family or any other elves in the area. Zareen seemed so hopeful. She wasn't willing to wipe the confident and reassuring grin from her face, so she lied.

"Yes, I'll do that when we get back," she said, reaching into her back pocket. "That reminds me." She handed a note to Zareen. "I have a feeling this won't be my only trip out of the village. I might be away when my family is discovered. If I am, they may not believe I'll return. If that happens, this note will assure them that I'll see them again."

She hoped Zareen wouldn't question it and simply pass it to whomever needed access to it in their absence, but she must've sensed the deception on her tongue. She gave Adelaide a skeptical look before unfurling the note and scanning the unfamiliar words. She nodded and tucked it into her pocket.

"I may not read elven," she started, settling Adelaide with a solemn look. "But I know enough to tell what's a letter and what's a last testament." She folded her arms. "Are you expecting to die?"

She shrugged, hating that she didn't have a proper answer to the question. "I left it vague enough that it could be used for both. If my family appears while I'm gone, they'll know I will return. If I die before I'm reunited with them, I will see them in Valhalla."

"That assumes your whole family will also die in battle."

"That's what we decided long ago, Zareen," she said, picking up her sword and getting into position across the practice ring. "Whoever shall die first among our kin will set the standard for us all. If I'm taken to Valhalla, they are honor bound to fight and die just the same so we can be reunited. Should I live and die a peaceful death, I will find them once more in Hel."

There was hesitation in Zareen's words and movements, something uncommon for her, as she grabbed her own sword. "And what if they're already dead?" she asked, not meeting her gaze. "What will you do then?"

Adelaide swallowed, saliva hitting her gut like a stone. "Why do you think I wish to know their fate more than anything else?" she asked, as if Zareen should've known that all along. But, by the surprised lift to her dark brows and the sharp intake of breath, she hadn't thought of it. "My fate lies with theirs. If they are dead, I will die in this fight. If they live, I will do everything in my power to return to them." She leveled her sword with hers. "This has been my vow all my life: to live *and* die for my kin."

Their wooden weapons clashed, the sound echoing off the trees as they danced in familiar steps around each other, always hoping the other would falter first.

Yes, there was no point in desiring Karsten at all. Whenever he was healed from his past, he would want something *more*. Even if she wanted to give him that, she wouldn't dare do so when she didn't know what her own destiny would be at the end of their journey. She would not bind herself to him when her life lay in the hands of another.

It would be too cruel a fate for a man so kind.

It was a half week's trip, riding hard, to reach the center of Cislenian power.

The city of Lysafell was truly one giant, interconnected chapel, if Zareen's teachings were to be believed. The buildings were constructed with thin, shared walls spilling any manner of secrets between the white-painted stones. The streets were practically lined with gold and emeralds, which only grew closer to the heart of the city. At the very center, a looming cathedral foraged from crystals and mirrors reflected the light of the high-noon sun into their eyes, making the entire square difficult to digest without fearing complete blindness.

Blossoms danced on the wind, a welcome reprieve from the dazzling displays of wealth that made Adelaide feel so out of place. At the very least, squeezed between stones and rows of gold, there were touches of nature springing to the surface despite autumn's death grip.

Even those were manicured and polished to a perfection screaming of opulence, excess, and greed.

The entirety of Lysafell felt askew—as if it weren't real even though the citizens living there were. She could feel that with the growing pressure of their stares digging into her skin, making it itch with every caress of their probing gazes. Some undressed her with their eyes, others sneered, and still others paid her only a passing, wary curiosity.

There were elves among the throng of people in the square, but they weren't as familiar as she wished they were. Long ago, their kind had left the safety of The Divide and New Alfheim, having forgone their traditions to assimilate with humankind instead. She supposed, in a way, she could be seen as doing the same, but she wouldn't forget her roots like they did. She would return, as was her right as a Keeper, but they wouldn't be welcomed back to the mountains. They were barred by tradition from returning to the lands the elves claimed as their own.

She pitied them, truly. For what could've convinced their ancestors to forsake all they knew in favor of the gilded walls of Lysafell? Her emerald eyes, so like the jewels that the city used for cornerstones, fell on the back of Karsten's head, his curly locks glowing golden in the sunlight.

If she were an elf whose ancestors left New Alfheim behind, she could've had him. If she didn't have her vow to her family, she could've been with him. If she were a Keeper without any clan, she would have met him in secret.

Duty to her people would always come first. She could never be like the elves in the square or their ancestors, abandoning all they knew for humanity. Even if some humans came in rather gorgeous packaging, it would not dissuade her from her purpose of serving her people and her kin.

She lowered herself from her horse, and the others followed suit. For that journey, they'd forgone Karsten's usual selection of warriors in favor of a diplomatic party. Zamir, Zareen, and Sander joined to assist with her studies on the way to the city. Karsten joined as their leader in Lefa's absence, and, despite the Commander's complaints, Njarl accompanied them as their guard. As the head of Ranndal's clergy, Ylwa joined them with Sister Jill at her hip as well.

They'd ceaselessly argued over the necessity of bringing *that* Sister, but Lefa had had the final say. It would've been a deep offense to not allow the previous head of Rannadal's chapel to join her townsfolk in the city. Adelaide had decided then and there that she hated politics.

I'd rather stab something instead.

Karsten seemed to be of a similar mind as he watched Jill struggle to get her old bones aligned enough to get off her horse. He sighed after a few long moments and offered her his hand, which she took as if she expected nothing less of him.

She locked her jaw and looked away, her hatred of the woman only growing with each passing moment they were forced to travel together. When Jill wasn't intruding on Adelaide's lessons on the Cislenian faith, she was downright trying to *convert her*. Or was she just insulting her? She couldn't honestly tell.

"You know, Adelaide, you wouldn't have to study so hard if you were a true believer."

"You know, Adelaide, your studies would come more naturally if you relinquished your heathen nature."

"You know, Adelaide, Common isn't that hard to grasp—or are you simply daft?"

As she watched Jill say something to Karsten that made him shrink slightly, the Commander's facade falling in the face of whatever insecurity Jill brought to the forefront, she decided stabbing was indeed her preferred method of political negotiation.

"Careful, Little Elf," Njarl rumbled as he took his own horse to the stables, his eyes twinkling with mirth at her immediate scowl from that *damned* nickname he insisted upon using. "If you turn any redder, they might mistake you for a ruby and put you on a pillar in one of the monasteries."

Zamir slunk to her side, his gaze trailing Njarl until the giant man was out of earshot. "I hate to agree with the Berserker, but he's right."

She tore her gaze from the Sister and the Commander. "Why does he let her belittle him? She seems to get away with more than she's worth."

Zamir sighed as they handed their horses to the servants who rushed between their group and the waiting stables. "You must remember, Karsten joined the Knights in Rannadal at a young age. She was like a mother to him when he'd left his own family behind. Jill used that to her advantage; she still does." He narrowed his eyes on the cathedral towering above them. "As for her worth to our cause, she's yet to prove it. She knows she's on a timeline. That makes her more dangerous than we could possibly imagine."

She wanted to ask what in the realms he meant by that, but their conversation was cut short as a clergyman exited the chapel and made his way towards their group. He stopped in front of her, his long black robe billowing slightly in the breeze as he bowed at the waist.

"Keeper Adelaide Aylara, it is a pleasure to have you in our humble home," he said, his voice just as smooth as the wet, slicked back locks atop his head. Zamir scoffed at the word *humble* but otherwise remained silent. "I am Brother Knut, twenty-sixth in line for divinity."

She bowed back, but not as low as he. That was what Zareen told her to do, so she merely hoped she got it right. "It's a pleasure to meet you, Brother Knut."

His smile was small but seemed genuine enough. "You will find your party's accommodations at the Imperial Inn. The Inquiry will begin tomorrow morning." His grin grew just a bit, a small blush peppering his cheeks. "Truth be told, I'm hoping your claims of being our Promised ring true. I know myself and the other members of the clergy are looking forward to a display of your divine powers."

A display?

"You will not be disappointed. Olena wills it," she said, hoping the panic rising in her chest hadn't seeped into her voice.

The Brother's smile didn't falter, so she assumed she did well as they were ushered to the inn on the west side of the square. It wasn't until the doors were firmly closed behind them, blocking out the prying eyes and ears outside, that her shoulders slumped in defeat.

Jill hummed. "What display have you been practicing, exactly?"

"Silence, Jill," she sneered on pure instinct, only worrying afterwards that someone in the inn may have heard her disrespect the Sister. Luckily, the foyer seemed empty.

Ylwa sighed and glared at Jill. "Sadly, she's right. They won't risk bringing a spirit into the city walls, and that's the only magic you've practiced."

Zamir tapped his chin. "We will need to prepare something else. Only teaching you about Cislenian texts was a mistake. Anyone can recite stanzas of The Codex. A display of holy magic is the surest way to prove our claims."

"If only you'd thought of that sooner," Jill said, a sly grin marring her face. Clearly, she'd known they'd ask for such a thing. She just wanted to see Adelaide struggle at the last moment rather than having time to prepare.

Yes, stabbing seems like a great idea.

Karsten laid a heavy hand on her shoulder, tearing her fierce gaze away from the other woman to meet his honey-colored eyes instead. "This isn't something you agreed to when Jarl Lefa sent you here. If you wish to turn around now, that is within your right."

Relief washed through her, but she knew she couldn't risk it. If she did, they'd use that as proof she wasn't divine at all. She didn't believe she was, but so many others seemed to. According to Lefa, it was imperative the clergy did as well.

With the backing of the church, their numbers and resources would grow exponentially. They'd have more manpower to attack the spirits, more scouts to look for her family and whoever was responsible for destroying her home, and more coin than they could fathom.

Without their support, they would be heralded as a cult steering the faithful away. Recruits would be less willing to join a cause running against their teachings. Fewer would donate coins or resources to a rogue army.

Adelaide couldn't run from them, even if she wished to.

She shook her head. "No, we'll continue as if nothing has changed, but I'll study with Zamir and Sander until we find something of use."

"And if you can't come up with anything?" Jill asked as she picked at her nails, seemingly bored with their presence.

"Then we won't secure the clergy as a primary ally," Adelaide said, narrowing her gaze on the old woman. "Which makes your presence useless to us. So, I would pray to both of your Gods that we succeed."

Jill paused, considering her words before shrugging. "If that was meant to be a threat, I'll be praying for all our sakes and not simply my own. After all, a threat against me is a threat to the church itself. If you can't align with them and I show up dead, the war against the spirits won't be the only battle The Covenant will need to wage."

Odin, please let me stab this one woman—that is all I ask.

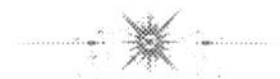

Adelaide pretended as if she needed a few minutes to compose herself before she joined the others for supper in the tavern portion of the inn.

Then she struck.

Her hands trembled as she rifled through Zareen's bags she'd left on her bed in their shared room. They were full of rolled up reports and far too many sharpening stones for one woman. She didn't find what she was looking for, so she hurried to her trunk instead.

The guilt of what she'd done was a slow disease, infecting her every waking thought, the more she admitted to herself that Karsten wasn't the horrible person she once believed. The more time she spent in his presence, the more that infection spread and threatened to eat her alive. If she could just find Zareen's dagger, the very one she used to gather both of their blood, she could try to reverse it—to give him back his autonomy when it came to aiding her search for her kin. It should've been his own choice, something she had *never* taken away from him.

This is why I never wanted to know him better, to rectify the image of him in my mind. Believing he was a cruel, evil Knight lying about his intentions was so much easier than admitting that I've made a mistake.

The Blood Oath binding them would only tighten the longer they didn't fulfill their ends of the bargain. She was at least having some results, like killing Sorrow and attending the Inquiry that brought her to Lysafell in the first place. Aside from finding Enok, Karsten had no such success, and she wasn't sure if the oath was just another compulsion driving him away from rest. Still, he was tireless in his attempts, and his dedication worried her to no uncertain ends.

If he gets desperate enough to search the mountains on his own, half mad from the blood tie, he'll get himself killed and it will be my fault. If I'd known his kindness was real, if I'd known what the Knights did to him, I never would have forced this upon him.

Most days, she could forget The Blood Oath was active at all. Karsten would smile at her and share reports of any activity that may have been linked to her family, and she could almost pretend he was doing it all from the kindness of his heart. Then there were nights when she peered out her cabin window and saw him pacing in the pitch darkness, unable to sleep until the last scouts returned without news.

It's not real. None of it can be real until he has a choice.

A throat cleared behind her, forcing her heart into her

throat as she spun to the source of the noise and froze under Njarl's watchful gaze. "Hey, Little Elf," he said with a smirk. "What are you up to?"

She slowly shut the trunk behind her and silently prayed to any Gods that would hear her he wouldn't realize the chest behind her wasn't her own. "Hm, nothing."

He folded his huge, thick arms over his broad chest and his grin vanished. "I'm not stupid. What are you looking for?" he asked as he shut the door closed behind him with his boot.

"One of Zareen's daggers," she sighed in defeat as she stood. "Don't worry about it and—" She paused, her blush hot across her cheeks as she looked at the ground. "Please don't mention this to her."

He chuckled, the sound warm and full of disbelief as he shook his head. "I didn't come here to shame you. I came to help." He strode past her, stopping briefly to ruffle her hair like she was a child. She was so relieved by his words she didn't even glare at him for ruining her braid. "I already told you: I shall follow you wherever you go, no matter how strange or dangerous, and to Valhalla and beyond," he explained as he snuck a finger and a curious glance into Zareen's bag. "Including into the undergarments of a shieldmaiden."

She slapped his hand loud enough for the hulking man to hiss, feigning true hurt as he yanked his reddened palm away. "While I appreciate your *help*," she said, glaring at him when she said that final word and causing him to look away in guilt, "if the dagger isn't in her bags or trunk, I doubt it's here at all." As she spoke, he walked to the head of the warrior's bed and peeked beneath it. "She might have left it back in town or kept it on her person. You know how paranoid she—"

The words died in her throat as Njarl pulled the dagger from beneath Zareen's pillow.

"You were saying?" he asked as he twirled the dagger between his fingers. "*Oh, Njarl, you have the eyesight of Odin!*

How ever did you find it?" he asked in a sing-song voice that was meant to be a mockery of her own. "What do we say when someone helps us, Little Elf?"

Her upper lip curled back in disgust as she yanked the dagger from his hand, blade side to catch him off guard, and didn't even flinch as it cut her palm. "*Piss off*," she snapped.

His roaring laughter took her off guard as he wiped tears from his eyes and pulled a handkerchief from his pocket, wrapping it around her palm even as his shoulders continued shaking. "I'm just giving you a hard time because I care," he explained as he patted her torn flesh, earning a pained wince in response.

Blood covered the rag, oozing along its pure white surface to forever stain it crimson. She stared at it, unable to tear her gaze away as the day she betrayed Karsten's trust filtered across her vision. It slammed through her again, stealing every bit of joy from her chest.

"What's your problem with the dagger anyways?" he asked, his voice a little gentler as he grazed the jeweled handle. When silence met his question, a sigh slipped between his lips. "A long time ago, I heard it was a gift from their father. The last thing they had of him before he passed." He pushed the hilt towards her so it rested against her chest. "Whatever you do with it, make sure to give it back."

What *would* she do with it? She had half a mind to melt it down and destroy The Blood Oath using any destructive means possible. After hearing that, how could she? Even if it was to free Karsten, she couldn't betray Zamir and Zareen like that either. They came from such a far away land, the dagger could never be replaced even if it didn't hold sentimental value.

She sniffed to hide the tremble in her voice as she slid the dagger back into place beneath the pillow. "Nothing. I just wanted to make sure it was here," she lied, and it convinced neither of them as they left her room in the inn.

It was only after they meandered down to the tavern on the ground floor of The Imperial Inn that Adelaide managed to gather her emotions and tuck them safely away. Njarl didn't mention her tears, and she wasn't sure if that was because he was kind enough to remain silent or unobservant enough to never notice it.

As soon as they set foot on the bottom of the stairs, she knew it was because of the former reason.

He stiffened beside her, his hulking form spinning so he blocked her view of the tavern. His hand fell upon the wall over her, forcing her to stumble back against it until he loomed above her. The slight panic in his gaze was the only reason she allowed it, and it froze her in place to see such an intimidating man brought to fear over *anything.* Then she heard it, that distinct click of metal boots against the cobblestone.

Njarl wasn't blocking her from seeing the tavern, he was preventing a group of Knights from seeing *her.*

"I heard they *actually* allowed one of their elf bitches into town." One of them laughed as they stumbled, drunk, into a table while following their comrades to the stairs they just left. "How long do you think until the novelty of her wears off and they let us play with her instead?"

Another man scoffed, his voice heavy with age. "These are no laughing matters, recruit. The Keepers are dangerous enemies of the clergy. That they would invite one and this charlatan Covenant into our walls is a sign of the dire times."

Their voices drifted away, and Njarl peeled back so she could breathe, but she remained pinned in fear regardless. She was in the shadows, unable to move and feel her own legs as she stared at the ground between them.

There was something in the air around those men that screamed violence and malice in a way that didn't reflect the Knights in Rannadal. Those within The Covenant were already vetted by Karsten as, at a bare minimum, not a danger to her or other elves. Of course, they could still spew insults and act aggressively, but it didn't feel the same as even those few simple words from the Lysafell Knights did.

It's been so long since I truly feared them, I almost forgot what they were like.

"You alright?" Njarl asked as he leaned against the wall beside her.

She huffed in annoyance. "That's a dumb question."

"Yeah, but it got you to say something," he mused as he stared back at her.

"I suppose it did," she said as she tore her gaze away and focused on the rest of the tavern. It was bursting with life but its sheer size allowed for plenty of darker corners where whispered words were shared and sly hands reached for more than the mead. In the center were the people she knew and trusted, including Zamir, who noticed their presence and kept looking over. When she caught his eye, he blushed and looked away. "Looks like someone has a crush, Njarl."

The giant hummed in acknowledgement and licked his lips. "Yeah, I've noticed that too." He groaned as he pushed his large body off the wall and sauntered forward a few steps. "He keeps watching me when he assumes I'm not looking. It's cute."

She smiled despite the fear still rattling around in her chest. "Probably best if we don't keep him waiting then."

THERE WAS a soft buzz dancing in the back of her scarred eye, like an itch she couldn't scratch without clawing her skin off. It made listening to Zamir even more difficult as he tried to explain the basic beginnings of magic to her, as if she were a *child.*

"When humanity attacked Alfheim in their vanity, supposedly waving the banner of the God of Chaos' patron, Saint Zelmer, they possessed no magic of their own outside their ties to the Gods themselves," he said, as if reciting an old scroll he memorized ages ago. "That's the story the Cislenians and your kind claim anyways: that humanity had no magic until they destroyed your realm and your people bred magic into humankind."

She propped her chin on her palm, her fingers idly rubbing at the bottom of her scar. "Mother said every witch, mage, seer, and völva only possess magic because they were gifted it by an elf ancestor."

"In my homeland, we have a different story," he said with a shrug. "We're told about the way the world used to stand still, no sunrises or sunsets to grace the skies. Still, magic was infused in every living thing in the lands. It was only after the stars and moon blessed two individuals with the powers of the cosmos that the earth began to turn. The beauty of our sunrise attracted the elves to our world, where they forged a new home for themselves in The North, which already overflowed with magic from dragons. It also attracted a few *charming* creatures of the night to our sunsets, but that's beside the point."

"What *is* your point exactly?" she asked, part curious about the folktales of his home and part appalled that anyone would disavow the atrocities committed against her people.

"You, my dear friend, are an *elf*!"

She pinched the bridge of her nose. "Shocking, I'm sure."

He folded his arms. "I mean that, no matter what mythology, religion, tale, or story you believe in, they all include the well-known fact all elves carry magic." He stabbed his finger at her chest, as if to physically ram the point in. "You had magic long before you stood at the threshold of The Divide with it burning behind you. No elf is born without that connection for as long as they've existed. The idea that you were the only magic-less elf in thousands of years of history until that very moment doesn't make sense."

"Unless you believe in my supreme divinity, of course." She snorted at the thought.

His expression flattened, all emotion wiped clean from the surface as if Embla scrubbed it raw herself. "Truthfully, I don't know what I believe. But neither of us will have a chance to find out if the church cuts you down for being a heretic all because you can't prove your magical abilities." He sighed as her shoulders slumped. "My point is that magic is naturally inside you and always has been. Perhaps we can't show them your divinely gifted abilities, but we can dazzle them with regular elven magic until we think of a better plan."

"We'll try," she said as she forced a smile, hoping she looked more relieved than she felt. Something in his words tugged at her thoughts and upturned the heavy weight in her heart. "You don't speak of your homeland often. Is there a reason—" She stopped at the sad turn of his lips. "Never mind, you needn't bring up old pains for my sake."

"No, it's fine," he said, the lie evident on his tongue as he shook his head. "I sometimes forget you haven't been in Rannadal long. Almost everyone else has been there since long before we arrived, all caked in dust and blood." He paused to card his fingers through the wavy wisps of dark hair at the nape of his neck. "Our father was a high ranking official and, as such, devoted *everything* to the empire." He bit his lip, his brows furrowing over pained eyes. "Everything except for us."

She leaned forward, her hand falling upon his for support, which he accepted with a grateful smile. "He sounds lovely," she whispered, her heart aching at the slight shine of tears in his eyes.

"He was," he said as he wrapped his fingers around hers. "Against Father's wishes, Zareen enlisted as a soldier to protect our lands. She was noticed by the emperor almost immediately and he conscripted her as his personal guard. He was furious with Father for hiding his child's skills, including her ability to detect lies. He received twenty lashes for it, and it was only then that we learned why our family tried to hide our prowess from him: to prevent us being used for his vanity and cruelty." He shuddered, and all she could do was hold onto him a bit tighter. "But they still didn't know about my magic. If the emperor found out that our father lied to him again, he'd kill him."

"He found out, didn't he?" she asked, the air stolen from her lungs as she clasped both her hands over his.

He nodded, and he couldn't look her in the eyes as the words spilled free. "It was my fault. If I couldn't be useful as a witch, I wanted to learn to fight like my sister. I overestimated my ability—not to fight but to watch someone die at my hand." He jerked his chin to the ceiling above them, where the rooms of the inn were located. "That dagger Zareen always carries is a reminder to us both. It's the blade I used to end a life, and it was my magic which saved that very same person only for them to reveal my powers to the emperor. She has always been okay with dealing death, and it was my inability to stomach it that led to our demise."

They sat in silence, Adelaide's thoughts swirling into a storm as she digested everything he'd said. Was that why

Zareen was so cold and distrusting? Even if she was a soldier before she took up the mantle of shieldmaiden and, later, Lieutenant for The Covenant, she never seemed glad to kill. It was a duty she bore, not for any faction or army, but so her brother never needed to pick up the blade again himself.

"Our only choice was to flee for a land where magic was free," he continued in a quiet voice she strained to hear. "Where we wouldn't be *used* for another's gains. There is still hatred for magic here, all because of a myth that our abilities come from elves so distant in our bloodlines we cannot trace them, but it was our only choice. In the Isles, people imprison witches without cause. Past The Southern Kingdoms, monsters have claimed the realm in shadows. Now, the only place in Midgard allowing us to be free is drowning in spirits."

"Not if we can stop it," she said.

His smile grew a little brighter as he nodded. "Exactly, which is why we must figure something out and *you* must embrace the magic that has always laid within you," he explained as he separated their entwined hands and forced himself to return to the easygoing veneer he often had. "You were lucky enough to be born in a land where magic thrives and your powers are encouraged instead of stifled. Never forget that."

"I'll try not to," she murmured as he continued formulating new ideas for how to coach her magic to life. Her mind continued to stray at each attempt that never brought results.

Zamir and Zareen are from a family who wished to quiet their magic. I am from a clan where my lack of magic was always a disappointment. We aren't the same, and yet our pain echoes in each other's hearts anyway.

Adelaide's stomach was growling by the time Sander interrupted their failed attempts at magic, insisting that he try to coach her instead. He dismissed Zamir, who seemed grateful to be relieved for a later supper.

They were midway through dinner when she lost her appetite, her irritation stealing all her focus and souring the empty feeling in her gut. She couldn't stomach another bite of bread or stew.

"The magic is within you," Sander said for what felt like the thousandth time. "You must only embrace it."

She slammed her fists on the table, her shoulders shaking with frustration as she struggled to keep her tone down. "I get it, I'm an *elf.* It's in my blood but it's never been as easy for me as it clearly was for you, okay?"

He blinked at her, long and slow like a cat trying to make heads or tails of a bug ramming itself repeatedly into a windowpane. "When one is attempting magic correctly, it should become easy with practice and as your power grows. If that is not the case, then we have been going about things all wrong."

An annoyed grunt was all she could offer as she turned away from him to look at the rest of the inn instead. From their small table on the upper level, she peered down at the bar and dinner tables scattered on the first floor. She wasn't sure what she was looking for as she searched the crowds, but she knew she'd recognize it whenever she found it.

"Zamir's magic was formed from a long lineage of witches hiding their talents," he said, continuing as if he couldn't tell she was trying to find a distraction. "Mine was developed over intense studying and passion for the art. Every magic user, elf or not, is different. You must find what anchors and inspires your magic to grow on its own."

"How exactly would I discover that?" she asked, hoping he could hear how little she truly cared for his thoughts on the matter in her dull tone.

As far as she was concerned—and was *always* concerned—her magic was to be written off—a fluke of genetics that granted her as little magic as an elf was allowed. Perhaps even none at all. Being able to bend the spirits to her will was an occasional blessing she was glad for since it served their cause, but nothing beyond that was needed.

Not until now, because of the damned clergy.

Sander touched her hand, pulling her attention away from the ruckus of the dining hall below. He smiled, his deep red lips set to a determined grin as his eyes sparkled in the candlelight with barely contained mirth. "Think back on what you were doing each time your magic manifested. What was it?"

She shrugged but still forced herself to pay attention to his line of questioning. She even allowed his hand to continue holding hers on the table. "The first time, I don't remember. After that, it was Embla. I just wanted her to live so badly and feel better, to get a chance to heal. Ever since then, it's always been when we're faced with a wayward spirit."

His smile grew, his excitement palatable and forcing her own nervous grin to the surface. His joy was just so infectious. "You were always *protecting* people, Adelaide." His grip on her hand tightened. "Your magic is motivated by your desire to care for others. That's why it was so strong the first time, so close to your home. You weren't protecting strange humans you hardly knew, you were trying to save your people."

Her eyes were glued to the half-eaten plates of food between them as she mulled over his words. Her powers were at their peak on that night she still couldn't recall. Afterwards, she'd truly felt for Embla. She suffered from the loss of her husband, just as she did when Vane was murdered. She understood how she felt in so many ways she dared not speak of.

Since then, it was as if her powers fluctuated whenever she attempted them. When she was riding with the warriors through the outskirts of Rannadal's lands, she could barely affect a spirit's actions. There were random times when her powers rushed to her with vengeance, morphing larger swaths of spirits to her will. With a jolt, she realized each of those times was when one of her companions joined her.

Whenever Zamir, Zareen, Sander, or Karsten was by her side, risking their lives to fend off the spirits, her doubts about her magic faded away. All she could focus on was keeping them safe from harm, and the magic manifested where uncertainty once was.

"What does that mean?" she asked, hating how small her voice sounded as her heart thrashed against her ribs. She was frightened by what his answer would be, but she wanted to hear it all the same.

His hand slipped from hers, but it lingered just so their fingertips brushed. "Your powers will be beyond comprehension once your family is within your grasp. Until then, you must find other things or people to motivate your magic into being. Find someone who shines light into your shadows and let that light radiate on us all; use it to prove all the clergy wrong."

She froze, staring right back into his hopeful grey eyes. Sander was kind, wasn't he? He was always wishing her the best and believing in her magic when she doubted its very existence. He was pleasing on the eyes, but that might've been too simple of words to describe his appearance. His braided black hair perfectly framed his chiseled, clean jaw and his eyes were two constant, swirling orbs wishing to drag her in and swallow her whole.

In another life, she could imagine it. How easily he could sweep her off her feet. How his sugar-sweet words mixed with his soothing voice would dampen her before his tongue ever touched her. His lengthy fingers would play in her white locks for hours and disappear for just as long under her skirts.

That other life, so far away from her reality, was just ahead of her. It was a breath away, yearning to be reached for just like his open hands on the table were.

Sander was someone she could take home to her mother. He was an elf she could share a future with, maybe even somewhere in the mountains she longed for. He'd please her, she was certain of that. He was far too earnest not to. Did he shine light into her darkest corners? Did he make her burn?

A rumbling laugh echoed up from the inn's lower level. On instinct, her gaze snapped to the sound.

Karsten had finally joined the others for dinner, long after the main courses were served and devoured. All that was left was the berry pie from dessert. It looked like Zamir had saved him a slice, something she had missed out on, and he was letting it serve as his final meal of the day.

His lips were coated in crumbs of sugar and his tongue was tinged blue from the treat in his hands. It crumbled slightly in his large palm, the juice running in languid streams down his arm, leaving lavender streaks behind. He took another bite and sucked at the trailing juice, his lips puckering before he laughed again at the mess he was making, the others teasing him for it.

The next bite caused the juice to spill past his lips and trail down his throat. She wanted to lick it off more than she wanted to breathe.

No, Sander didn't make her burn.

But Karsten did.

Sander's sigh forced her to turn back, a blush blazing across her cheeks even as her heart continued hammering in her chest. There was no denying what he'd seen in her expression, but she still felt like lying anyways. Sander was a friend to her and she couldn't lie to him, so she bit her lip to remain silent.

"I am not a jealous man, Adelaide," he said, propping his chin on his hand so his fingers could tap along his fierce jawline. "Nor am I a stupid one. If he is who lights up your heart, then give in to it."

"Sander, I—"

He held up a hand. "We are *elves*, Adelaide. We live ten times that of humans. I can wait a few decades for you to explore this affection for the human. We all have our forbidden desires; I will not deny you of yours." He arched a brow at her. "I feel like I've waited an eternity for you anyways, what's fifty or so more years? You're one of a kind and worth the test of my patience."

There was no way she could fathom an answer to that, so she decided to ignore as much of it as she could. "I hardly think I'm one of a kind."

He didn't seem convinced. "Believe me, you are a most rare creature indeed. I can sense how old your power is. It's a tether, an ancient thrum to the magic of a realm long since lost. You are divinity in the flesh, and there is no reality in which I do not crave to stay beside that holiness, whether we are romantically entangled or not."

"You truly believe in my divinity as well? Even as a fellow elf?"

He nodded. "Odin works in strange ways, but he has sent you to this realm for a reason. We cannot ignore that."

In that moment, all Adelaide wished was to want him as much as he clearly wanted her. His words were poetry and she was his muse, but guilt was the strongest emotion she could conjure when it came to him. Guilt that he believed in something inside of her that he was wrong about. Guilt that she could not return his affections, not when the person she truly desired was so close and yet not close enough.

So close and yet I can never have him. Yet, Sander is right. Karsten won't live as long as I will. Even if we were together, how much of a life would that truly be? To be with him and lose him when I'd still have ages left to live without him.

I already did that with Vane. I cannot live it again. To be with him, I slow to age, as wrinkles warp his features beyond recognition. I'd become an outcast from my homelands for eternity for only a mere fifty years of life with him.

As a Keeper, she could freely travel through the realms and always return home, but a longstanding relationship with a human would break her vows to the clan.

If Adelaide was with him and anyone discovered them, she wouldn't be welcomed back home. However, she could take Sander home. Even if he was an exiled elf, forbidden from returning to New Alfheim, perhaps she could make a plea with their elders to make him a Keeper instead. They could be together that way, but no such deal could be struck for Karsten.

She'd have to forsake her home to be with him. The choice should've been simple, and yet her heart could not fathom anything besides Karsten's lips on hers.

Sander hummed as he tapped his fingers against his lips, peering back down at where Karsten was finishing his pastry and wiping the evidence of its destruction from his tempting lips and neck. "Might be less than fifty years with that one though."

She furrowed her brows as her attention darted back and forth between the two men. "What do you mean?"

"The Commander was once a Knight," he said, as if that should clarify things for her. When she continued to stare back at him, waiting for an answer, he paled. "You don't know?"

"Know what?" she asked, her nails digging into her palms.

He worried his lip between his teeth before he dared to

utter another word. "All Knights partake in a drug called Vow. It grants them the ability to detect spirits, heightens their eyesight to see better in the shadows of The Divide, and grants them immense strength." She was about to ask what that had to do with his life expectancy, but the sad turn of his lips silenced her. "In exchange, it shortens one's life. Most Knights won't live into their fortieth year."

There was a cold grip wrapped around her heart, and she could hardly breathe around it.

Karsten is turning twenty-eight this year. He barely has a decade left compared to the hundreds I can expect.

"Are there any other symptoms from the drug?" she asked.

"Generally, one will lose their abilities, then their mind, and then their bodies and lives. It's a slow and graceless decay of one's being. Knights promise all of themselves to their cause and, in the end, it is their undoing."

Karsten said he was trying to rid himself of an addiction. Did he fall back on the drug? Is he only ill from the withdrawals or from taking the drug once more? If he stopped taking it, will he avoid the downfalls Sander describes? No, even with him quitting Vow, it is already happening. He won't get fifty years. He might not even get fifty days. I will lose him before I've ever even had him.

That should make me cast any thought of being with him from my mind. Yet it only makes me want to bring him closer, to enjoy being a part of what little life remains for him. But who says he'd even want to spend his last days with me anyways?

"Conjure the first image that comes to mind," Sander said, slicing through her thoughts.

"*What?*"

He waved his hands between them. "Something small. Just cast the first image you can think of into the air between us, but don't lose sight of that feeling buried in your chest."

She didn't think, she merely pulled forth the magic in her veins making her heart race and compelled it to materialize above the table, hovering over the remnants of her dinner. The self-doubt plaguing her had no space to fill her thoughts when they were so consumed by her worries for Karsten and what she'd just discovered about the little time he had left.

It was the fear, which was born from her care and desire for him, that compelled her magic forward. It rushed to life, singing under her skin until the song was a tangible entity tracing her fingertips.

An aurora and slice of the Bifrost, not unlike the one she produced on that first night she lost her family, twinkled and swirled with purples and golds. The lavender of the pie's sickly-sweet juice. The gold of his eyes as they shone with laughter.

She ripped it from the air and deposited it back into her body, as though she had a hidden pocket in her heart reserved to conceal such things. Her face burned even as a satisfied smile tugged at her lips.

Sander leaned back in his chair, his own lips turned to a smug, tight grin. "Now, we have something to really work with."

SANDER'S WISDOM proved invaluable to her that night.

As she twirled image after image of illusions into the air, she always knew where its inspiration came from. A thick roll of low hanging clouds whisking between the empty cups, forging shadows across the table just like her sister could. A hawk perching on her finger was for her mother, and they shared the same piercing eyes. So long as she thought of those she cared for and allowed her desire for their safety to take hold of her heart, her magic bled out into the world seamlessly.

Adelaide knew it was just the start. She needed to perfect the illusions for her meeting with the clergy, but was that all she could truly do? Create pretty pictures to entertain? That would not help them in battle like healing or elemental magic. There was a part of her who still believed those stronger magical abilities were out of her reach.

Still, Sander insisted the same method would work. As much as she wanted to dismiss him completely, she knew she couldn't discount his insights any longer.

She wasn't certain of his age, as her people weren't so obvious in their life progression as humans were, but she could tell he'd lived far longer than she. He held an archaic wisdom in his proud chin and magic. She hadn't felt anything similar since she'd last seen her mother. Her mother, without a doubt, was ancient. She was simply too much of a lady to admit it.

Adelaide didn't suspect Sander of being that old, but he seemed just as wise. If he was certain her magic was special and could accomplish more than she believed, it was worth trying.

He left her sometime after most of the inn's common areas emptied, and she had half a mind to turn in for the night as well. Her thoughts were consumed by everything Sander revealed. She doubted she'd get even a wink of shut-eye between then and when the clergy demanded her presence.

Her scarred eye ached, and she absently rubbed at it as she curled up in her seat, staring without seeing at the darkened dining hall below. Everything Sander claimed about her abilities seemed true, and the more she considered it, the more sense it made.

When she was young and truly attempting grand feats of magic, she had been focused on making her mother proud. There had been no thought of learning magic as a means of protecting or caring for them. No other feelings could emerge past her panicked desperation to please Mother. Responsibility always weighed on her shoulders, souring any passions she had.

Once her mother had discovered she was adept at firing her

bow, she had been deemed the clan's hunter. When she had been the best at cross-stitch, she had been made to mend every torn piece of fabric. Anything she had excelled at and found joy in had been turned from a passion into a chore to further the quality of life for her kin.

Even her relationship with Vane had ended the same. They had been great friends, but her mother had always encouraged her to give something more with him a chance. She'd explored her genuine curiosity of his body, but she'd wanted that less and less as the months went on. Still, she'd listened to her mother and married him, assuming her desire would grow the more they learned each other's wants.

It hadn't.

After he died, a deep sense of numbness had taken root in her soul. The attachment she'd felt for her kin felt foggy and out of reach. It hadn't been until she'd lost them too that everything she was— everything she *felt*—had come rushing back. She'd never felt something like what she felt brewing under her skin in the moments she watched Karsten from afar.

Even her occasional dalliances before Vane hadn't stoked the fire within her like Karsten could, and they had hardly even touched. His gaze was warm honey, sweeter than any mead, and his voice a deep timber that sent goosebumps racing down her back. Neither of those things even compared to the rest of him: to his unruly curled hair or the handsome scar marring his plump lips.

She stopped her thoughts there, unwilling to dig past appearances and admire the qualities of his kind heart instead. Enjoying his looks was surface level. Safer, somehow. Anything beyond that felt more intimate than she was willing to take it. As if undressing his mind and very soul exposed more than his toned body did.

Don't think of his toned, naked body wrapped around yours.

She stood, suddenly far too warm.

This is why my magic feels so much stronger. All my emotions do and the two must be linked. I was so numb for so long when Vane died but, since losing my family and forging bonds with these humans, I'm feeling everything so much more. Like I've received a piece of myself that was missing. Funny, considering my lost memory of the night all these feelings were unleashed.

She was swept away by a need: the need to feel all the powerful currents of her magic once more. She wished to gather every drop of emotion, of *burning*, that was alight whenever Karsten was nearby.

Her feet moved before her mind realized what she was doing. If anyone saw her, they'd assume something was amiss with how fast she dashed through the halls. She was simply seeking out a familiar head of blond curls she wanted to grab firm between her fingers.

No, she wouldn't give into such temptation. He deserved better than her lust when he already struggled with his own, but she wanted to see him regardless. She wanted to bask in the warmth he shone on her and let it fill every dark crevice torn into her soul.

He makes me feel things, even if I was only experiencing rage at first. It was still better than the numb, hollow feeling Vane left behind.

She stopped in the courtyard, out of breath as she turned in a circle, searching for some hint of where to go. She wasn't sure where Karsten's quarters in the inn were and she wasn't prepared for the inevitable looks she'd receive if she dared to ask, but the inn was expansive. The courtyard alone diverged into four separate hallways in each direction and, above her, were four more floors towering on all sides.

"You seem lost." Karsten's voice bled out from one of the hallways as he stepped into the flickering, hazy light cast by the sconces.

She jumped at his voice and scowled back at him when he dared to chuckle. "I was looking for you actually."

He hummed as he raised the hand previously hidden behind his back. In it, a small slice of pie sat atop a white ramekin with a fork pierced straight through the crust. "Funny, I was doing the same."

Despite her previous insistence on only focusing on his outer appearance, her heart warmed and a blush fought its way to her cheeks. "You saved me a piece?"

He nodded as he offered it to her and she gladly took the morsel, her stomach rumbling in anticipation. "I saw you watching us have dessert from the balcony and figured I'd see if there was any left to spare."

The burning of her cheeks intensified so she shoved a giant bite into her mouth to distract herself from the racing of her heart. Sugar and syrup coated her tongue, and she moaned at the taste before licking her finger where a berry stained it. Even hours after the pastries were served, it was the perfect blend of soft breading, crisp crust, and sweet filling that left nothing else to be desired.

Almost nothing else.

A small, choked sound caught her attention as she peered back at him, her fingertips still lingering on the edge of her lips. Karsten's eyes were blown wide, his mouth agape as his gaze remained transfixed on the stain of purple-blue transferring from her finger to her tongue. Despite the chill of the evening, warmth spread from her cheeks to her core.

"You said you were looking for me," he said, his voice breathy as he stood frozen, just out of reach.

Fuck.

An excuse. She needed an excuse for why she was desperately trying to find him.

Wanting to fuck him won't be an acceptable answer. Wanting to simply be in his presence because it makes the world feel less harsh is an even worse response.

"Sander has helped me develop a magical talent to impress the clergy." She spoke a little too fast, but he hardly seemed to notice. "I wanted to show you."

He took a step back and cleared his throat. "I'd love to see it."

She shoveled the last of the pie in her mouth and sat the ramekin aside. Her eyes slipped closed as she held out her hands, imagining the energetic pull of the magic flowing to her fingertips. It hummed just under the skin, but didn't spark to life. Anxiety replaced the peaceful thrum with an erratic electricity, sending her hair on end.

Think about Mother. Think about Zamir. Think about anyone other than Karsten. Someone I care about other than him. Don't let him see what he does to me.

But all her magic longed for was the rush of emotions he brought to the surface. Every time she tried to conjure, her mind slipped to him and she shoved the feelings he blossomed in her away, ruining every flicker of magic she attempted.

He sighed. It was a small thing formed from half-pity and half-disappointment, and she couldn't stand it. It did wretched things to her heart, hearing him sigh and knowing it wasn't an exhale formed from desire but from him finding her inadequate: just like her mother always had.

Her magic wasn't enough. *She* wasn't enough.

"You're probably just tired," he said, his voice a gentle sound on the breeze that tickled her neck. He laid a reassuring hand on her shoulder, sending a shiver down her spine. "You've been practicing with Zamir and Sander all day. You need to rest."

It's not pity or disappointment in his voice; he's making sure I'm okay. He believes in me. Sometimes, he's the only one who does. Even Mother doubted my abilities, but he never has. He knows me better than I give him credit for. He knows what I can do. I simply need to give into it.

She let her eyes slip open to meet his. With her face tilted towards his towering frame as he leaned over her shoulder from behind, their lips were a mere inch apart. Their breaths, white in the chilly night, mingled in the air. He was close enough to kiss, to touch, and to revel in all his charming looks. She could make out the gold flecks and blue sparks in his otherwise amber eyes that drew her in deeper and deeper into the sea of his soul.

Those tempting lips were almost close enough to taste, and the thrill of just imagining her own pressed against them sent a tremble through her. The way he looked at her, as if she were the dessert he wanted to devour, lit her from within.

She let herself *burn.*

Sparks jumped from her fingers, smoldering her skin until she turned away from his tempting form. All that desire and heat he brought to the surface of her skin rushed in her bloodstream, and she willed it outwards, casting it into the cold air of the courtyard.

It ruptured from her hands, ropes of green and pink light dancing before them, shimmering with every burst of growing affection she felt for him. She needed to be careful not to let the gold of his eyes infect the aurora she painted, so he didn't realize where her magic came from, but otherwise she let it all slip free—unfiltered.

The lights they played in were the largest illusion she could remember casting, and somehow it was the easiest to manifest. Perhaps that was due to how hard she'd been practicing?

You're a liar, a part of her whispered.

I know.

She grinned, her cheeks nearly splitting in delight as she spun to him. "Isn't it beautiful?" she asked, awaiting his approval as if she truly needed it.

Perhaps I do.

Only, he wasn't looking at the fragments of the Bi-frost she'd conjured. He was staring right at her, drinking her in as if she were the magical display instead. She wondered how she must look, aching and wanting, for both his approval and his body in equal measure. She was certain she must've looked pathetic and needy.

He cleared his throat and looked away, breaking the tension she wasn't truly certain was building between them. His hand met the back of his neck as he pinned his gaze to the floor. "Yes, b-beautiful," he said, his voice a little raw as he tripped over his words. "I'm sure the clergy will be impressed."

Despite her disappointment at the broken tension, she preened under the praise. "Thank you, Karsten. I hope it—"

She stopped as he turned on his heel, already making his way out of the courtyard without looking back. "You'll do excellent tomorrow. Believe me."

He left her in the night, alone, as the aurora fell and died around her.

In Adelaide's dreams, she and Karsten were still standing beneath the lights dancing from her fingertips. The image slipped through her mind, tainting her vision. She was half in the world of the living, half dead asleep in her lonely room at the inn.

In her dreams, she was back in the courtyard with Karsten, his eyes shining with the purple greens of the Bi-frost. It sharpened his features, but the soft way he looked at her that night remained the same.

At least, I think it's the same. He's always so kind to me, even without cause.

Instead of walking away like he had only an hour prior, he stepped closer to her dream-self and tangled his fingers in her hair. A tingle ran down her neck from where his skin brushed hers as they locked eyes, the aurora glittering as it faded out of existence.

"Isn't it beautiful?" she asked again, her voice breathy and weak.

His eyes danced to her lips as he hovered too close and not close enough at the same time, his breath coasting over her lips. She ached to close the distance—to see if his lips tasted like the mead and berry pie he indulged in for dinner. The image of the berries' purple juice running from his lips, caressing the scar skipping over his lip, and dripping down his neck came to mind.

Would his skin still have that lingering, sticky-sweet taste if she leaned forward and gave in to the temptation? That's what he was after all, wasn't he? A temptation drawing her in even as she slept.

Karsten wasn't exactly someone she could bring home to her family. He'd always have to be a secret, if she ever gave in to her fantasies. That would be unfair to him, so all she'd ever have would be dreams of him she'd never acknowledge while awake.

Might as well enjoy them.

"I'm seeing something far more beautiful," he whispered back.

She pressed forward, her breasts rubbing deliciously against his solid chest as she bypassed his lips and moved her own to his neck, dragging a long line up his supple flesh with her tongue. He shivered and grabbed her arms in a vice-like grip, holding her firmly against him as she indulged in his taste.

The sweetness of the berries coated her tongue but, beneath it, she could still savor his skin and the musky, natural flavor it carried. It made the pie filling even better, so she went in for a second helping, dragging her teeth along his neck as if to take a bite.

He hissed, and his grip on her arms flew to her waist instead, hauling her impossibly closer. Her tongue moved to his jaw, the stubble biting her back.

The hand still tangled in her hair drew her head away, halting her movements and exposing her to his piercing gaze. He was panting, hovering over her as his grip on her white locks tightened. It mixed just an ounce of pain into the pleasure pooling in her core.

"You've gotten a taste," he said, his voice a low growl she wasn't used to. "Now, it's my turn." He tilted her head to the side, his own lips crashing down on the soft skin of her neck.

His tongue swirled on the hollows of her collarbones and his lips lavished every inch of her exposed skin, peppering it with bruises that would ruin her reputation with the clergy. She raked her nails through his hair, holding him in place when his lips caressed the tips of her ears.

A moan ripped through her, and he froze, his body shuddering with the effort to stay still, to stop himself from taking her right there on the hard courtyard floor where anyone could happen upon them.

"Don't stop," she said, breaking his resolve.

He spun her, pinning her to the nearest pillar and clamping a hand over her mouth when a louder moan nearly fell from her lips. His other hand traced down her hip, inching towards where she wanted him.

No, where she needed *him.*

"You wouldn't want the clergy or innkeeper to find us, would you?" When she didn't answer, a wicked smile tugged at his lips. "Devious woman." His lips returned to her neck as both his hands dropped to the ties of her trousers, frantically pulling at the strings. "You taste so sweet," he groaned against her flesh as he finally loosened her pants enough to reach his fingers across the top of her undergarments. "I wonder what the rest of you tastes like."

SHE JERKED AWAKE, half expecting Karsten to be the one waking her with his head between her legs, only to find Zareen's fierce scowl hovering over her.

"We're running late," she said, shoving some clothes into the elf's hands. "Get dressed."

Damn it. I'm late, I'm ceaselessly horny, my wet dream about Karsten didn't even have a satisfying conclusion, and I'm sharing a room with a woman who won't take kindly to me rectifying any of those problems.

She dressed in a rush, briefly washed up, and combed most of her hair back into a braid to hide the sweatiest strands from view. She'd always considered herself lucky to have such a rare hair color. But when it was greasy, it turned grey and everyone could tell she was in desperate need of a good wash. When wet, it hung even darker and heavy against her shoulders.

It was the image of Karsten running those large hands through her darkened, wet locks that caused a brand-new sweat to break out across her neck. She groaned as she adjusted her coat to hide the hardening of her nipples, her mind continuing to play games with her desires.

Truly, a Lust spirit must be possessing me as well. This isn't like me at all.

She tried to sense any type of spirit, but none emerged. She'd sensed at least one in the city like an ever-present thrum making her scarred eye ache, but it was a solid background noise compared to the usual presence of a spirit.

No, there wasn't a Lust spirit tempting her. It was just the man himself who was enticing enough to bring out the horniest parts of her.

A sigh of resignation slipped past her lips as she left her room and readied herself for the inevitable frustrations of a day with the clergy. But no matter how much preparation she had, she wasn't ready for the presence lingering right outside her door.

She jumped at the sight of Jill standing outside, her frame a lithe, ghostly presence she couldn't ignore even if she tried. The old woman annoyed her to no end, but she couldn't help the rush of empathy tugging at her heart at the sight of all the tears held in the elder's eyes.

"Sister Jill, what's wrong?" she asked, concerned as to what could've brought the woman to her door, fighting back tears, first thing in the morning.

Did something happen to Karsten? Did the clergy already reject our pleas?

All sympathy and worry for the woman vanished as soon as her wobbly voice said in a low tone, "How could you?"

Adelaide froze. "Pardon me?"

"You've already corrupted him. That poor boy has been through horrors you cannot fathom, and yet you still move to taint his mind. It's monstrous, even for an elf."

Her brain struggled to come up with some sort of response to her accusations, but she couldn't understand what in the realms she was saying. "Who exactly are you talking about? And what are you accusing me of?" she demanded.

She laughed, the sound bitter and harsh as she shook her head to rid any lingering tears from her eyes. "You know exactly who I'm speaking of and what you've done!" When she continued to stare at her in silence, Jill gave a frustrated huff. "Commander Strom is a kind, gentle boy with honor and valor. You cannot corrupt his good spirits with your impure ways."

Jill was calling Karsten—a twenty-seven-year-old commander of an army—a *boy*.

She's delusional.

"I'm not sure what you're implying that I've done to a grown man, but I can ensure you I've had no improper interactions with Commander Strom," Adelaide said between clenched teeth as she pushed out all those improper interactions she'd thought about that morning out of her mind, as if fearing Jill would sense them lingering in her thoughts.

Regardless of her dreams and desires, nothing transpired between them.

Not yet.

"And nothing shall," Jill said matter-of-factly, as if she could control what two adults did in private. "Karsten is like a son to me. He's been through enough pain without you leading him astray. His mind has already been defiled by a wretched little elf just like you. His heart and Olena-given soul cannot handle more debauchery from your kind."

One of her more heartbreaking conversations with Karsten flooded back to her.

"A girl in town caught my eye. She was an elf. I knew there could be nothing between us, but one of the mentors must've discovered us. They decided to make an example of me."

She gaped at her, horror curdling in her gut as she stared down at the woman, a sickening feeling curling in her stomach. "You were the one who told his superiors about his crush on that elf." Jill's face paled at her words. "You're the reason he was *tortured.*"

Jill rolled her eyes. "It's a rite of passage, not the stoning he makes it out to be. He surpassed everyone's expectations, just as I knew he would, and he's stronger for it." Her wrinkled eyes raked over her, making her feel exposed. "But that was done in his youth, a far more forgiving time. Should he falter to desire now for the likes of you, an *elf*, no Knight will follow him into battle. He will be the laughingstock of the town."

"Who says he'd have desires for me anyways?" she asked, keeping a tight leash on her rage. Jill seemed to love hearing herself talk, and Adelaide was determined to get as much information out of the sister before she pummeled her into the inn floor.

"Anyone with eyes could see the two of you out in the courtyard last night, practically locking lips already. You're lucky it was I who caught you and not one of his warriors. They gossip worse than lonesome wives," Jill explained.

No wonder Karsten left so quickly. He probably sensed the hag's gaze on us.

She pinched the bridge of her nose and flexed her other hand, willing her fist to unlock before she truly knocked the woman out cold. "Whatever does and doesn't happen between two consenting adults has nothing to do with you. I suggest you forget anything you *think* you saw."

"That would be convenient for you, wouldn't it?" she asked, her voice rising and her tone dropping into a near growl. "Convince me to stand by while you ruin a good man, as is typical for your kind."

"Jill, if you do not leave this instant, the only person who'll be ruined is *you*."

She scoffed. "As if you could lay a hand on me in the home of my clergyman—the very ones you're here to beg for assistance, might I add. I'm untouchable within these walls and, as soon as you receive the backing of the clergy, I'll be recognized for all I've done to aid the cause."

"All you'll be seen for is the nasty rat of a woman you are," she said, her voice low enough that she felt the rumbling rage building in her chest.

A firm slap across Adelaide's cheek replaced her rage with pure shock. Her cheek stung, and the skin ached against the firm onslaught. She peered back at the sister, surprised and fuming in equal measure.

Jill fixed her robes over her chest and tried to hide the red tinge to her hand where her palm connected to the other woman's cheek. "I suggest you, as an *elf,* learn your place this side of The Divide before you enter the sanctum of the clergy."

Her surprise was washed away by her words. Only simmering hatred lived beneath the surface of her skin, but she also knew Jill was right. Adelaide couldn't touch her.

But perhaps she didn't need to.

In her mind, she reached out for any spirits hiding within the inn. With so many travelers, there was an endless sea of them casually lingering in people's minds. None were serious enough to require a full cleansing. Most people would fight off their inner monsters on their own.

She found a spirit of vanity bursting at the seams of each of Jill's wrinkles, feeding on her cruel words. It was a Vanity born out of a deep-seated feeling of inadequacy.

I can work with that.

"Do you truly need to interfere with other people's lives just to feel like yours is somehow still relevant?" Adelaide asked, mimicking the words the spirit within Jill whispered. The spirits showed it to her: how Jill spent most of her time alone and afraid of her own capacity for cruelty while simultaneously desiring to treat others worse all to make herself feel superior. "You're an aging relic of the past whose claim to importance hinges on what *I* do. Not *you*. No one here cares if you live or not. One day, you will die in your lonely bedroom and no one will notice for weeks. The rats will be the only kin who haven't abandoned you until they've chewed all your flesh from the bone and, even then, they will leave you because you are *worthless*."

Jill's eyes were blown wide and her mouth hung agape as every insecurity she'd felt was laid bare in the hands of someone whose words rang with magic and truth.

"There will be no mourners and no ceremonies for the death of someone so foul—only the thrill of finally seeing you buried like you belong," she continued. "Your ceaseless complaining and interfering with other's lives has nothing to do with them. It has everything to do with the fact that you're a worthless piece of filth not fit for your robes and you know it. You overcompensate by making your pain everyone's problem, but no one cares, Jill. No one cares about a worthless, refuse human being. It's why you must hate any elf you meet, for they are somehow more human than even you."

Tears were pricking her eyes again, so Adelaide tried to pull back, but the spirits wanted more. They wanted revenge and wrath and to feed on the dying vanity spirit clinging to the edges of Jill's trembling lips.

"Whatever Karsten and I may or may not be will *never* be influenced by the words of a nagging, hypocritical, spineless hag like yourself. There is no corner of the world with a living creature on it who cares for you, so do not take your inability to be loved as an indication that you need to make love harder for anyone else. You will die alone, forgotten, and as worthless as you always were. The same cannot be said about anyone else you have the honor of traveling beside on this trip. Learn to live with that loneliness and worthlessness, for you will die with it."

She finally pulled herself away from the enchanting tune of the spirits. It was like shaking off a fog from her mind, clouding every bit of rational thought. When she came back to herself, she found Jill a weeping mess on the floor, her sobs wretched and wracking her entire body.

She hadn't meant to go so far, but the spirits overcame her. She was a vessel for them to speak through and, to her own surprise, she didn't mind it as much as she thought she would.

Adelaide left her there, a grin slowly forming on her lips.

LADY AYLARA'S LETTER TO HER FAMILY, TRANSLATED TO COMMON

Dearest Dar-kin,

I am no longer here but rest assured I once was. These humans, despite our differences, did not harm me and only sought my help with the spirits invading both our homes. With you all gone from my life, they were my only lifeline to cling to in the chaos. Please, do not harm them. I agreed to aid their organization of my own free will and, no matter what happens, I would do it again. They are kind without reason, and more like us than I ever thought.

To my siblings, please go where I can find you. To the littlest of us all, know that I love you fiercely. To Mother, please ask the humans about the magic I've performed for them. I hope it makes you proud, knowing that I can finally do it. I'm sorry I cannot show you in person.

We will see each other again soon. Remember our oaths to each other and find joy where you can until we are reunited—either in Rannadal or Valhalla.

- Yours, Adelaide

16

SEVERING GOLDEN TIES

SKALD: KARSTEN STROM

Lysafell's cathedral was the beating heart of all Cislenian faith and the largest chapel in The North. It was intimidating for most, even those who worshipped Olena, but Adelaide didn't waver under the scrutiny or opulence as she stood before the clergy. She was holding her own, one of the few elves in the entire building, and answering any question with a perfectly poised answer they'd all hammered into her throughout her lessons for that very moment.

She exceeded even Karsten's expectations, and she'd yet to show off the spectacular magic she displayed for him the night before. But all he could see was red.

There was a subtle mark staining her left cheek, tinting her smooth complexion pink. No one else seemed to notice, but it was all he could focus on.

Someone hurt her.

There was no universe in which he wouldn't hyperfixate on something so cruel being written all over her beautiful face. She deserved only the softest, most tender touches. Something he couldn't even give. The idea of someone being forceful enough to leave a mark on her sent him reeling. In front of so many members of the church, there wasn't anything he could do about it.

He had to sit idly by with his insides turning in such fierce disgust and rage it made him want to puke. She was one of the kindest, strongest people he knew. Of course, she would act like everything was normal and bring no attention to the mark on her skin. Of course she'd leave whatever monster did that to her alive.

Karsten was not so forgiving.

The spirits in Karsten's soul cried out for retribution, to hold whoever hurt her accountable for their crimes. He wanted to wipe their blood on the walls of the chapel as a warning for any who dare lay a hand on her. To mar their skin with marks not so easily healed before casting their bones to the wolves.

But his heart cried out a different tune.

The only thing his anger would accomplish would be to remind Adelaide of why he wasn't to be trusted—why his kind were so hated by hers. She deserved to be comforted by a level-headed man who cared for her feelings, not confronted by his own simmering fury. So, he tucked his darker desires away and focused on his heart's pleas instead.

As soon as he was able to, he'd tug her aside, away from the others, and ensure no other harm came to her. He would be subtle, just like the mark, to keep the others from noticing. If her silence on the matter was any indication, that was what she'd want. He would honor that to the best of his ability.

Even if Rage whispered in his ear dark thoughts not fit for a chapel.

'Hang their corpse from the rafters and let these fools worship at her feet instead. Wrap their skin in metal and drop them into the deepest seas so even the Gods cannot find them.'

He banished the thoughts and sought a distraction instead. But where was he meant to look except at her? If he looked away, it would be seen as shunning her answers and reflect poorly on all of them. He could look at the clergy, perched on high at their pedestals they hadn't earned as they sneered down at her.

Staring at them isn't as appealing.

Adelaide's white hair was slightly curled and untamed from its usual braids. Her waist was cinched with a dark leather belt and the neckline of her blouse flared open, revealing some of her shoulders. If she were wearing the tunic like she usually would, he'd have a glorious view of the top of her breasts pressed tight against the fabric. But for the sake of the clergymen's souls, she buttoned it higher than normal.

A shame really. She's worth the blasphemy.

Desire clung to his senses, its hushed voice a symphony not as easily banished. It sang to him in a voice as sweet as hers, wishing to be near her. Wishing he could brush his thumb against the growing bruise on her cheek and let it linger on her lips.

"Commander Strom has done an excellent job training The Covenant's growing forces and, in doing so, mending any discontent between our Knights and Vikings," Adelaide said, her tone guarded as she squinted up at the clergyman who spoke last. His title on her lips snapped him out of whatever incantation the spirits threw upon him, her voice stronger than any spell the damned could weave. Her emerald gaze met his. "I trust him implicitly."

"The fact that he's a Knight of The Divide, a sovereign protector of the Cislenian faith ordained by The Codex itself, has no influence on your choices? As a vital decision maker within this so-called Covenant, it is crucial you remain impartial," the same clergyman said, his voice brimming with accusation. "You *are* a Keeper, are you not?"

Her once pleasant smile melted away. "Yes, the Commander is a *former* Knight, but we hold no ill will toward one another. I consider him a friend and confidant. His faith and previous employment have no influence on my trust in his abilities, nor do my faith and stance as a Keeper have on his."

The entire clergy turned to him, their judgmental eyes making his skin itch. "It's true," he said, his voice a little rough. "I trust her with my life. Regardless of where we may have started, we are both here to fight for peace."

Satisfied with his answer, they turned back to the woman who held his heart. They were raking her over the coals, demanding answers to every single one of their prying questions. They wanted to know about her views of both the New and Old Gods, how The Covenant's goals were progressing, her stance on The Codex's most controversial texts, and what her aspirations were once The Divide was repaired, the spirits quelled, and the perpetrator of the destruction apprehended.

"I suppose I will return home, back where I belong."

That was the answer the clergy seemed to enjoy the most, but it crushed a bit of that heart she unknowingly held in the palm of her hands.

AT HIGH NOON, there was a break in questioning for mid-day meals. Their group planned to meet in the office of Brother Knut, having secured the space from him earlier in the day, but Karsten needed to see Adelaide before the others.

In the hallway leading to the meeting chamber, he pressed himself into a secluded alcove and waited for her to pass. The others were already discussing the proceedings, but he swore he only needed to steal a minute of her time.

Out of the corner of his eye, he saw a flicker of her wavy white hair and he reached out, snagging her by the arm and redirecting her into an empty chamber before anyone saw. She gasped, the sound music to his ears, as he rounded her. She was flushed, and the mark was darkening on her cheek, but otherwise she appeared unfazed.

"What are you doing?" Adelaide asked, stunned as she stared back at him. Her chest heaved, testing the limits of the buttons she'd secured across her chest.

To prevent himself from giving into his deepest fantasies, he gave into a smaller desire: the one begging to touch the mark on her face. His thumb ran across the darkening bruise, as though he could smudge it away.

"What are you doing?" she asked again, her voice a touch breathier than before.

Focus, you fool.

He shook his head and pulled his hand back a bit, although he continued to caress her cheek with the lightest touch he could manage when rage and desire battled for control of his senses.

"Who did this to you?"

His voice was full of a thunderous rage, but his worry showed in the slight tremble of his hand as it cupped her jaw. He tilted her chin and brushed his thumb over the mark again. He touched her as if it was an apology for all the churning anger simmering under his skin, and the sheer *want* he knew she'd find in his gaze.

"Someone who was quickly put back in their place," she answered, a smug tilt to her tempting lips.

Gods, she's so beautiful when she threatens people.

He didn't bother fighting the relieved smirk spreading across his face. "Good." As much as he didn't want to, he dropped his hand and took a careful step back to lessen the tension pushing and pulling between them. "I wanted to make sure you were okay before you spoke with the others. Let me know if you wish anything else to be done with the perpetrator. I wouldn't hesitate to see them meet a swift end."

She scoffed and waved the offer away. "I bruise like a babe. She hardly touched me, and I have a feeling she's already realized the error of her ways."

"*She* then?"

Adelaide's brows creased, and she pointed an accusing finger at him. "Don't try to figure out who it was, Karsten. I've dealt with it how I see fit."

He nodded. "I'll respect that but do let me know if you change your mind."

She snorted and motioned for him to follow her out the door. "See, how could the clergy ever suspect us of being anything less than harmonious?"

He held the door open for her with his hand on the frame above her head. "I don't know, ask your past self from a few weeks ago to be *harmonious* with me and see what she says."

She didn't dignify that with a response.

YLWA PACED across the clerk's office like a pup begging to be allowed off the leash.

"You're sure you have just the trick to push the clergy over the edge, Adelaide?" the Sister asked. "They're divided now, so whatever magic you perform will solidify their opinion of both you and The Covenant—one way or another," she said as she wrung her robes between her hands.

Zamir rolled his eyes and leaned further into the plush chaise in the corner of the room. "Yes, that's just the way to motivate our dear Promised into performing marvelous magic: by burdening her with your anxiety."

"Must I remind you what hinges on our success?" Ylwa replied, her voice growing higher pitched with each word. "The support of the clergy would legitimize The Covenant, increase our resources tenfold, and ensure our reach expands. We could hire skilled men instead of always training new recruits, ensure no member goes hungry or unhoused, contact the other Jarls of The North for support, and ensure we have the means and authority to find, capture, and hold accountable whomever destroyed The Divide."

Zareen nodded, her expression scolding her brother for his relaxed demeanor more than her words ever could. "We could spare enough men to really push the spirits back. To track down any free spirits who slipped between our fingers. To heal the wounds of the many families who lost loved ones in the devastation."

"To finally find my family and fully seal The Divide, so no one else will be harmed," Adelaide added, her words finally seeming to pierce through Zamir's carefree facade.

Karsten knew Zamir wasn't trying to appear like he didn't care. It was only a mask to hide his own anxiety. The others didn't know him as well as Karsten did. Not even his sister seemed to grasp the inner workings of her brother's mind.

He clamped a heavy hand on Zamir's shoulder and gave it a firm squeeze of reassurance. "I have no doubt we all believe in the mission and that aligning with the clergy is necessary to pursue those goals, so let us turn to other matters."

The other man gave him a grateful smile as their focus shifted away from him and back to the matter at hand.

"If your magic cannot convince them—" Ylwa began.

Adelaide cut the other woman off with a disarming grin and a voice woven with bitterness. "Then all of Midgard, The Divide, and New Alfheim will pay the price, which will not happen. I won't let it. We will succeed and they will see reason." Her lips morphed into a frown as her gaze was stolen by the steadily rising voices outside, informing them their break was coming to an end. "When I find my family, I want them to be proud of the work we've done. I want them to have a safe place to call home again."

Zareen gave Adelaide's arm a firm squeeze, distracting her from whatever dark thoughts whispered in her ears. "Then we'll do exactly that."

Adelaide shivered and rubbed absently at her scarred eye. He'd noticed it was becoming a habit of hers—always caressing the mark as though she could erase any tension held there by a soft touch. Her eyes met his and she grimaced in pain before asking, "Do you feel that?"

He tried to sense whatever she was feeling but found nothing. He shook his head as he moved closer, worry creasing his brow. "No, what's wrong?"

"I must be imagining it, but I swear I keep feeling the energy of a spirit. Nothing intense, but it's getting stronger the longer I'm in the chapel chambers. It wasn't as noticeable before, but now it's starting to hurt."

Before he could answer, Sander spoke from beside the exit where he'd lingered during their meeting. "That makes sense."

Adelaide and Karsten both arched their brows at him, but it was Ylwa who spoke first. "How so? There shouldn't be any spirits within the cathedral and, if there were, Karsten and the other Knights guarding the city should be sensing it too."

Karsten felt the blood drain from his face as he looked away. Perhaps, if he were still taking Vow, he'd be able to sense whatever plagued her. Then, he could protect her from whatever manner of evil slunk between the walls.

I should be taking it.

"Adelaide's abilities far surpass that of any Knights," Sander said, as though he knew just what to say to ease the other man's mind. Karsten sighed, dispelling every desire to take the drug lingering in his mind. "Knights are only trained and given the means to sense spirits of chaos, but there are other spirits as well, ones more aligned to your Goddess. In a place of pure devotion, it would make sense that a spirit of Faith may have taken root, embedding itself in the very fabric of the city."

Adelaide's eyes lit up. "Yes, that must be it. I've felt it thrumming like a stream through the stones since we got here."

Sander smiled, seeming proud of how far his lessons with her had progressed.

I can never have that with her. What could I teach her? How to kill?

"I was hoping you'd pick up on something like that on your own. Well done. I have more to teach you about the matter, but we'll save that for another time. For now, you all must understand this," Sander said, pausing to produce a ball of white light in his hands. It ebbed and flowed like water, but a warmth radiated from its core like a flame. "Think of this as a good spirit, bleeding its kindness into the world." With a snap, a dark swirl rushed through the light, draining the warmth to leave the space chilled and pitch black. "A corrupt spirit can do the same. We know how troublesome one spirit can be, and the horrors of the many which escaped The Divide. But allowing these kinds of spirits to linger—to infest places as the spirit of Faith has done here—would sour the entire realm one city at a time."

Karsten glared at the swirling orb of darkness as though he could will it back to white. "Do you think that was the plan of whomever destroyed the mountains? To infest the world with spirits of darkness?"

Sander nodded as he waved the shadows from view. "I can see no other reason for such death and destruction. Midgard would fall to its knees in the face of such an infestation. We cannot allow it to take root."

"We won't," Adelaide said, conviction in her tone and a determined spark in her eyes. "Something like that could alter the fate of not just Midgard but all the realms. There would be no one left to answer any pleas for help. We *cannot* fail."

She shook off the uncomfortable weight of the Faith spirits itching in her eye and faced the door leading back into the grand chambers. Before his eyes, her demeanor shifted and all her obvious doubts were tucked away. It was as if she felt nothing about the proceedings, like they held no bearing on her future, even though he knew it meant everything to her.

It would determine what world her family returned to, if they still lived. Would they return to a realm of spirits devastating the countryside, ensuring their home in the mountains never healed. Or would they all live in a place that was fit for rebuilding?

A place where I can never join her.

"WHAT RELATION DO you have with the current leadership of The Covenant?" Grand Clerk Orman—first in line for divinity as he proudly claimed—asked once the proceedings continued.

Adelaide stood once more, alone in the middle of the central chamber.

"None by blood but I consider them family regardless," she answered, as eloquently as she did before the brief break. Nothing thus far in the interviews seemed to shake her, and he knew they all had her strict training regime to thank for that.

"What of your own family?" Orman asked. Immediately, Adelaide's resolve cracked. How little she wanted to speak of that topic was written all over her face, and the panic in her eyes made Karsten grind his teeth. The clergy already knew her family was lost; why cause her the pain of remembering? "You lived in The Divide with your kin. How are we certain none of them are responsible for the destruction?"

Her smile wavered, and she clamped her hands behind her back to hide the trembling in her fingers, but he noticed it regardless. It was exactly what he would've done.

"It was our home. They would never harm the land or those who live within it. They love our home as much as they love our kin." There was no doubt hidden in her tone, but she still stood slightly shaken after the mention of her family.

Karsten was certain that's why they brought it up at all: to shake the steady ground she proudly stood on and make her seem weak to all in attendance. Still, he knew her better than they did. She would not falter even at the mention of her family and their unknown whereabouts.

She'll simply be furious instead.

"What of your own motivations?" Orman continued, treading into dangerous territory if the scowl marring Adelaide's face was any indication. "You were the only person of interest, and the only one found at the point of destruction. How have you convinced The Covenant of your innocence?"

"I love them and I would *never* harm them. I have no motive to do so. My only motivation in even being here or with The Covenant is to find my kin and restore my home. Those objectives would make little sense if I were the one who destroyed everything I've ever known."

A hum of agreement rustled through the gathered crowd, and Karsten gave her a small nod of encouragement when their eyes met.

"Unless you're motivated by glory," Orman countered, resting his chin on a palm as though every accusation that left his lips bored him. "A Keeper of little notice who finally senses an opportunity for a new life by murdering her kin, destroying her home, and claiming Godhood among humankind. That would ensure you shall forever straddle the partition between our people. You'd be allowed to return to your home, New Alfheim, and traverse the lands of Midgard freely if the claims of you being able to alter the spirits were true."

The hands clasped behind her back turned to claws as her nails bit into the soft flesh of her wrists. She was nearly drawing blood with all her effort to remain calm. By the Gods, he wished she could simply let them hear every vile thought about them that was surely coursing through her mind.

I know I have a thousand words I'd like to spew at them.

"That's quite the story, Grand Clerk," she drawled, breaking her mask of passivity with a sneer. "But be careful what stories you spin when you haven't the slightest idea of what you speak or the horrors I've seen just to get here." He knew before she spoke next that whatever spewed past her lips would do them all in. "Is it truly so boring perched atop your pedestal that you've lost all remorse for anyone below it? All the gold in this chapel must be reflecting into your eyes, blinding you to the truth."

Orman's face turned red as he hauled himself to his feet, his voice bellowing over the chamber and echoing down every hallway in the imposing chapel. "You speak so freely in the chambers of our most divine, to a servant of Olena herself? How can you claim to be our Promised with such a foul tongue?"

"I don't make any such claims," Adelaide said, silencing the entire room.

Ylwa stiffened beside him. That was their one rule in all her training: for her to never say she wasn't the Promised of Olena. Such a title kept her safe, even more than her abilities did. It legitimized The Covenant. It rallied their people to fight under a collective banner forged from Jarl Lefa's visions from the Goddess.

It keeps her safe.

Adelaide spun away from the clerks, putting her back

straight to them and, in doing so, shunning them completely. Instead, she peered at the many citizens of Lysafell and the surrounding villages who traveled to the grand chapel just to witness the questioning.

To see if she was truly divinity made flesh.

In that moment, he was more certain of that than ever.

"Olena promised her people she would send a savior to Midgard in your most dire hour," she said, her voice reverberating across the rounded ceilings until it sang to even the furthest corners of the building. "My friends in The Covenant claim that's me. I won't pretend I always believe them, for who am I to know what the Gods intend, but I do know this." She placed her hand over her heart. "I'm here to help, and I seem to be the only one who can. I would love it if this gift were bestowed on someone else. To still have my kin near and simply go back home, but I don't have a place to call home anymore. I don't know where my family is or if they still live. I only know that I'm here, and I'm asking for the assistance of the clergy so I can continue to help." She stopped, swallowing hard and blinking fast to hide her building tears. "To save as many families as possible because I know what it's like to lose one."

The room was deathly silent as everything she said lay across people's shoulders like a heavy blanket. The clergy seemed smothered beneath such weight but, at least from his perspective, he could tell many of the citizens were settling comfortably under the truth.

An elderly man in the crowd with a twisted beard called out in the silence, "How are we meant to accept that you're our Promised if you don't even believe it?"

Murmurs rose as people debated their neighbor on the matter but, when she raised her hand, the room quieted once more.

"You know, I once believed I didn't possess a single ounce of magic," she said, smiling at the elder with far kinder eyes than she'd given the clergy. "Yet I've still quelled multiple spirits and conjured the Bifrost in my hands." She held her palms up and peered at Karsten out of the corner of her eye, forcing his whole world to stop until she pushed skyward and lifted the lights he'd seen the night prior into the air. It was only when she looked away that he came back to himself, though he still ached to see every inch of her highlighted under the colors of the aurora. "I may not believe yet, and you may not either, but I'm willing to try if you are."

Everyone's gaze was glued to the ceiling as the lights danced above. He couldn't pull his attention away from her even if his life depended on it.

The purple lights cast violet shadows across her hair, and her eyes reflected the green of the aurora right back out. It was as if the lights wound straight through her body. He believed she looked beautiful that first night he saw her beneath the lights, surrounded by destruction and caked in blood, but he could hardly stand to see her in all her radiance at that moment. He was unworthy of witnessing all she was.

Adelaide was divinity molded into being and she was right before him, almost within reach, but she'd never felt so far away.

THE PROCEEDINGS TURNED into an inquiry where any random citizen in attendance could ask a question to either Adelaide or other members of The Covenant waiting in the stands. It was incredible to watch her maneuver through the crowds, calming general panic and instilling faith in their efforts, even as the clergy grew more and more restless.

The Grand Clerk was fuming but, at the very least, he

remained blissfully silent in the face of Adelaide's success with the people. If he were to admonish her after the crowds already adored her, he knew it would risk his position.

Although, it hasn't stopped his face from permanently resembling a tomato.

"What of your thoughts on the Promised, Commander?"

Karsten nearly jumped out of his skin when someone directed a question towards him but, thankfully, everyone else seemed just as focused on Adelaide as he'd been. He turned to find Brother Knut leaning against the banister beside him.

"She's doing incredibly well, especially given the circumstances," Karsten replied, hoping he sounded convincing. It was damned impossible to balance the act of ensuring others he believed in Adelaide while also not revealing the true depths of his feelings on the matter.

How hopelessly, truly devoted he'd become in such a short time.

It's maddening.

Brother Knut nodded as he peered out at Adelaide and the throng of people she maneuvered through. Zareen and Njarl were keeping close to her side, ensuring no one got too close, but it still set Karsten on edge to see her surrounded.

"Do you truly believe she was sent by Olena?" the Brother asked, clarifying his prior question and sending every hair on Karsten's neck standing up straight.

In his mind, he was certain of her divinity. It was woven into every move she made. It lingered in the too-quiet steps of her feet and the sway of her hips. Holiness was ground into her laughter and sung from her voice. Whether or not she was sent by Olena, Odin, or no God at all mattered little to him. She bled sanctitude and was a deity he would worship above all others.

If she would ever give him the chance to, anyway.

"Ah," Knut hummed as he patted the other man on the shoulder. "I see now."

He pushed his hand away. "See what? I haven't even answered your question."

Knut simply grinned in response. "You didn't need to. Silence was your answer and the look in your eyes is all the explanation I need." He peered back at the woman in question and, like a moth to a flame, Karsten followed his gaze right back to the object of all his desires. "She won't be easily won. Not with the attention she attracts, but I hope you can make her happy. I imagine she's been through a lot already, and I have a feeling her journey has just begun."

"I know," he said with a sigh. There was no denying his feelings to the Brother. It was of little consequence if a small clergyman in the chapel knew of his affection. No one would believe him anyway. Besides, his feelings were so plainly written on his face anyone who paid attention could see where his heart lay. It was a trait his mother had always admonished him for.

"Don't let your father see such a smile or he'll beat it off you."

He shivered at the familiar words and schooled his features to the best of his ability. The Brother took his leave, allowing Karsten the privacy necessary to lie to himself: to pretend like he wasn't already falling for the woman who held the heavens in her hands.

KARSTEN DIDN'T MEAN to seek her out that night.

He truly only meant to follow the path he took the evening prior. It was lovely outside, and the gardens were in their last, desperate blooms. They were south of Rannadal, so autumn hadn't reached the region yet, but it wouldn't be long before the cold smothered whatever was left of summer's life.

Still, he found Adelaide curled up by the fountain in the center of the gardens, her knees tucked up to her chin and her arms wrapped around her legs. It pulled on her robe: a fluffy, white fur piece Lefa had imported for her. Another gift the Jarl had granted her after receiving further reports on all her good deeds. It would look ridiculous on anyone else, but she wasn't anyone else.

She was Adelaide Aylara, Keeper and Promised, and the most incredible woman he'd ever had the good fortune of meeting. And Karsten was just the inadequate son of an alcoholic farmer who had his own addiction and regrets to contend with.

"Did I do the right thing?" Adelaide asked, her voice so small he nearly missed it. "By turning my back on the clergy, we might lose everything we came here to obtain."

He sat beside her on the fountain, feeling far too large for the dainty stone edge. "Perhaps, but how would you have felt if the clergy believed we were trying to help but all those regular people didn't?"

She turned to face him instead of the fountain, and it was then he noticed the tears of frustration ringing her eyes. "To be honest, I'd feel like shit." He chuckled at that and she cracked a smile at the sound, but it slowly drifted back into a frown. "Then again, I kind of feel like shit now anyways."

"There's still one more day to turn things around," he said, placing a heavy hand on her shoulder and hoping it gave her strength instead of weighing her down. When she pressed her temple against it, his heart pounded faster. "The people of Lysafell already love you after your display today. Focus on mending your relations with the clergy tomorrow, but don't risk what you've already built."

She nodded and picked herself up, her white robe slipping to reveal a patch of her shoulder and collarbones hidden by that *damned* blouse all day.

Oh, to be a button on that top.

Pull yourself together.

"Thank you, Karsten." She stood and righted the collar of her robe. "I appreciate it." She smiled at him, and somehow it filled the garden with more light than her magic ever did. She offered him a hand, and he gladly took it. He didn't need the help to stand, but any excuse to hold her hand in his—even with his gloves in the way—was worth it.

He held on to her for a bit longer than necessary and, once he let go, the chill of the night settled in. "It's getting cold. Let me walk you to your room."

"I'd like that."

Is she blushing? No, I must be imagining things.

They walked in peaceful silence through the garden, neither seeming to care how long they lingered in the comfortable quiet conjured between them. If he shuffled his feet to keep pace with her, to ensure she was always in the corner of his gaze, he wouldn't admit it.

Her sigh disturbed the peace as they stopped just before doors to the inn. "I suppose it's time to retire."

"You're probably right."

Neither of them moved. It was as if the world began once more as soon as they left the garden, but they couldn't face reality just yet. At least, not when the dreamscape of the garden existed. It was a place of shadows where they could pretend they didn't see the obvious desire reflected in each other's gazes.

"*Karsten*," she murmured, her voice singing to him like a siren threatening to drag him even deeper into the depths of her. He would gladly drown in her if given the chance.

"*Adelaide*," he said, keeping his voice just as quiet as if the slightest infliction in his tone would scare her off. As if a single sound could disturb the dream woven between them, pulling them subconsciously closer.

Words hung on her lips and he remained suspended, awaiting whatever passed from her tongue. Would she ask him to leave? Would she cast him aside and realize she was right about him from the start? Would she pull him closer?

"Would you care to continue our game sometime soon?" she asked. "A question for an answer."

He nodded, his heart thrashing in his chest as he recalled that it was his turn to ask something of her. "Could we change the rules?" Her nose scrunched up in confusion as he stepped closer, hovering over her until he could feel her breath on his tunic. "Whoever's turn it is can ask a question or ask for something from the other person. A favor, perhaps?"

Something sparkled in her eyes as she nodded. "If it's within reason."

Reason battled for control of his tongue, but he was already so beyond remaining reasonable in her presence that even his fears he would never be worthy of her couldn't still the words from his lips. No, perhaps that wasn't accurate. If he'd truly gone mad, he would've asked for a kiss, but he would never pressure her for such a thing.

"Tell me something you've never admitted to anyone else," he said as he entwined his finger with a lock of her hair, tucking it behind her ear just to watch her shiver and her eyes dilate with the barest touch. "Something only your heart knows."

Her mouth fell open, words straying from her as he got lost in her eyes. Nothing but the cold night and their white clouds of breath separated them. If she wished it, she could steal a kiss from his lips and never give it back. He would let her. By the Goddess, he would let her do anything she wished to him. He no longer cared if that was holding a knife to his throat, drawing the wretched life from his body, or sealing their lips together in a searing kiss.

Adelaide's emerald eyes, molten with desire, fell to his

mouth and greedily drank up the sight of the scar dancing along its side.

"I must admit," she began, her eyes fluttering back up to his. "I've come to care—"

Whatever else she planned to say died as a screech of steel filled the garden, breaking the spell woven between them.

They turned to the sound, and he quickly grasped the pommel of his sword when his eyes fell on the approaching shadows lingering in the archway leading back to town. Five men stepped into the lantern-lit garden, their own swords half-pulled from their sheaths in warning.

Behind them, Grand Clerk Orman stood as an imposing silhouette.

At first, Karsten didn't recognize who the men were. They wore no symbol and only came adorned in darkness. Then he recognized it: their hands, which would normally hold a shield embossed with the twining symbols of Olena and Cismir, remained uncomfortably bare. One man even tried to reach for that shield, only for his hands to come up empty.

Karsten had struggled for months to break the habit of fighting with a sword and shield when he'd left the Brotherhood.

"*Knights*," Adelaide hissed under her breath as she took a careful step back.

The Knights were present during the proceedings and, in general, acted as guards of the city. He wasn't sure if Adelaide even recognized them in the Lysafell uniform rather than the Rannadal one. When she was cornered by a group of Knights who removed their armor but not their weapons as they followed the clerk who despised her, she wasn't the only one set on edge by their presence. He stood between their piercing gaze and her, one hand clasped on the hilt of his sword and the other stretched out to guard her.

"Grand Clerk Orman," Karsten called. "Why are you here?"

The man had the gall to roll his eyes. "You of all people should know the rules of the treaty the Knights and Keepers struck centuries ago." When neither responded, his ire increased. "A Keeper may remain in the lands of Midgard without forsaking their kinship so long as the lord of that land deems their residency necessary and welcome," he recited the treaty, stanza line eighteen if Karsten remembered his ceaseless lessons on the text accurately. "Jarl Lefa may have granted you quarters in Rannadal, but your invitation to Lysafell has expired."

Her soft touch on his arm was the only thing holding him back from cutting all six men down. "I'll leave then. No use staying where I'm not welcome."

"*Adelaide—*"

The hold tightened, her nails biting into his skin beneath the leather. "Don't fight me about this, Commander."

He nearly relented, leaving her exposed, but Orman's next words froze him in place.

"I'm afraid there's already been a break in the treaty," the clerk said, the quick smirk on his lips sending Karsten's blood boiling. "We cannot let you leave. Your only options are to come, willingly or unwillingly, to the chapel dungeons for charges." He paused to sigh, as if the only other option were something he truly regretted. "*Or* to forsake your kin."

The grasp on his arm went slack, so he grabbed her hand in his to hold her steady as he peered sideways at her, never turning his back on the slowly approaching figures in the garden. Her face was pale, and her chest heaved in panic. He could feel his blood drain from his face as he clutched her trembling palm beneath his own.

To forsake her family would mean leaving *everything* behind. She would never get to return to The Divide or enter New Alfheim. She would be forced to remain in Midgard forevermore. She would no longer be a Keeper. If her family was ever found, she wouldn't get to go home with them.

Everything she does is for them. She would never make that choice.

But then she met his gaze, fear dancing deep in the emerald depths, and he saw the truth in all its brutal light. She wasn't terrified about losing a title or being forced from the mountains.

Adelaide is scared about what will happen to me.

He was the only one with a weapon. She was in a robe, for Olena's sake. The rest of their companions were already asleep. If they needed to fight, Karsten would make her leave to find reinforcements and, by the time she returned, the five Knights might've done him in.

But if she turns herself in—

I won't give her the option.

A LETTER CONCEALED IN GRAND CLERK ORMAN'S DESK

Orman,

Your orders have changed. Stop the Keeper by any means.

- The Wise One

17

THE TREE OF LIFE AND A NIGHT OF DEATH

SKALD: ADELAIDE AYLARA

"K*arsten, don't.*"

Adelaide's words didn't seem to reach him as he stepped forward, putting himself squarely between her and Orman's men.

"You don't come in the middle of the night to apprehend someone after removing every emblem of the Order you serve," Karsten said as he fully unsheathed his blade. "I don't know what you plan to do, but you won't lay a finger on her."

Her heart was beating hard against her chest, threatening to break free and escape like she longed to. If she were ever cornered by so many Knights back home, she'd know exactly where to run, which trees gave the best cover when climbing up their branches and which caverns provided the most shadows.

Here, all I have is him.

She knew the stories of what happened to elves in Cislenian dungeons. How Knights and so-called *holy* men would torture them until their minds and bodies broke under the weight of their questioning. They could convince anyone of anything if they tried long enough.

However, she also knew the tales of her brothers and sisters forever barred from re-entering New Alfheim and The Divide. The All-Father's gaze couldn't follow them as swiftly once they turned their backs on their people. Humans would never understand them like their kin would. They would always be a threat. They would always be lacking when cut off from the resources of their home realm.

Either option for Adelaide was a death sentence.

If she were going to make the decision to stay in Midgard like many elves before her, it would be her choice alone. It wouldn't be because a clerk demanded it from her. If she abandoned her home, it would be for nothing but love. Her kin would always matter most.

Even with my growing affections for Kar—I mean any of my new friends—I wouldn't trade them for my kin. I can't make Rannadal a home. I already have one.

Karsten reached blindly behind him, never taking his eyes off the Knights as he pushed her towards the doors. "Adelaide, go!"

With his back blocking her view of the garden, she couldn't see where the men were. All she could hear was their steel swords screaming out of their sheaths and the familiar clamor of their metal boots on the stones.

No, I wouldn't trade my family for anything, but perhaps my family doesn't need to just be my clan. I won't make a home in Rannadal, but I can find a home in these strange humans instead.

She grabbed Karsten's axe from the holster on his waist just as the first sword met his. He parried the first attacker as the second rained down blow after blow. The crash of swords destroyed the peace of the garden, and grunts of pain replaced the trickling of the fountain.

A Knight snuck to Karsten's side, unaware Adelaide still hid behind his back since his imposing size kept her shielded. When he swung down, aiming straight for Karsten's head, she leapt in the way and met his blade with the axe, halting its movement before it had a chance to draw blood. They pushed back the Knights at the same time, giving themselves room to control the battle and a split second to meet each other's gaze.

In that brief moment, a deep seed of understanding was planted between them.

Adelaide and Karsten, despite their past, would fight and perhaps even die for each other. Not out of duty and not for any cause other than the bonds formed between them. They didn't need to speak of it. There was just a knowing in the sheer conviction with which they fought. Their willingness to kill and die for each other came naturally, like it was expected. She couldn't define it or describe it. She simply knew it to be truth. He would not let her fall, and she would not see him harmed.

A blade crashed into her axe, the force vibrating through her entire body. It caused her arms to tremble under the weight of the man bearing down on her, each swing of his powerful strikes threatening to weaken her grip and stance.

He took a breath, and that's when she struck.

The man was too large and clumsy, so he had no defense against her lithe frame when she snaked under his arm. She pulled herself too close for him to strike as her blade sliced across his throat. It wasn't as practiced and painless as she'd been taught to do when she was young. Her first kills had been animals for the hunt, and she hated seeing them suffer, so mother had taught her how to make it quick. With an axe instead of a narrow dagger and a fire of rage burning in her blood, there was no part of her desiring an easy death for the Knights surrounding them.

She was on the next man before she could blink, cutting him down with a practiced hack at his legs like she would to a birch tree in the forest. His cries fell on deaf ears as she moved on, leaving him to bleed out on the garden floor.

Karsten dispatched of the third and fourth man with an eerie amount of ease, their blood coating his cloak and face as he drew his sword out of their limp forms. Seeing him kill and knowing how he learned to do it so easily should have disgusted her. Her people's blood once covered his weapons. Just like the axe she held in her hands.

Instead, I'm merely grateful he's fighting by my side instead.

They met at the fifth man, who drew dual blades to hold them both off. No matter the man's skills or the number of blades he produced, he was no match for their combined effort.

That only left the Grand Clerk.

The battle brought a crowd. Zareen, Sander, and Njarl crashed through the doors of the garden. They were disheveled and still in their nightwear, but their hands held their weapons firmly regardless of their state of dress. Other guests hung out of the windows of the inn, clutching their robes closed as they took in the bloody sight below.

Karsten leveled his blade at Orman's chin, forcing him to meet their eyes as he remained pinned against one of the garden walls, the blood of his men soaking their shoes.

"What was your plan?" Karsten demanded, his voice bellowing through the garden and echoing up towards the heavens. "Force our Promised to abandon her family or agree to imprisonment? What for?"

Orman grinned, his gums leaking blood that coated his teeth and sent a sharp, copper tang into the air. That feeling that had plagued her since she entered the city rose, twisting into a sickly thing gnawing on her bones. A sharp lance of pain dragged across her eye, and she stumbled backwards as a wave of fire licked across the scar marring her face. Her eyes watered, blurring the vision of the clerk before them.

"This city," Orman began, his voice not his own. *"It runs on the faithful. Your so-called Promised does the same. She truly believes she'll find her kin, still living in a place decimated by death."* She blinked the tears back, freeing her vision until she could make out the clerk's piercing black gaze swallowing her whole.

"That faith is like a drug, but it's not enough. Faith never is. Neither is honor, hope, joy, or any other beautiful thing you wish to hold onto."

Dread coiled in her core, souring her heart and weakening her limbs. All the color in the garden slipped from her vision, leaving her gaze full of grey as she swayed on her feet, unable to right herself or the world teetering around her.

What if he's right? What if they're already gone? I've had so much faith they'd be there all my life. I've believed they'd find me again in Rannadal, not in the afterlife.

They're already dead, aren't they?

Sander grabbed her arm, hoisting her up from where she was hunched over in pain. "I don't believe the clerk is with us anymore."

Whatever wore the clerk's skin tilted its head, its neck straining until the skin pulled to the point of nearly tearing. *"Someone's not supposed to be here."*

Sander huffed, and his grip on her tightened.

"What in all the realms do you mean by that?" Karsten demanded as he struggled to keep the clerk pinned without slicing straight through him. They needed answers before his blood could coat the walls.

"A spirit of Grief has possessed Orman," Sander explained without an ounce of doubt in his tone. "It's feeding on Adelaide's pain, and most likely the distress of everyone in the city whose faith was shaken by the release of the spirits."

Something cleared in Adelaide's heart, like a fog lifting off her mind, until she could see past the tears welling up in her eyes. That feeling, which had gnawed at her soul since she set foot in Lysafell's perfectly tailored stone roads, finally made sense. Sander originally thought it was the spirit of Faith woven into the very fabric of a place so revered, but that wasn't true at all. Njarl's faith spirit disproved the theory immediately. When she sensed it around the Berserker, it soothed her eye. Grief only brought it more suffering, and she was a fool for not seeing the truth earlier.

"You're what I've felt since I got here," she said, pushing past Sander as she moved closer to the spirit greedily inhabiting the clerk's body. "That's why you wanted to disprove my abilities. It gives the people in this city a renewed sense of faith when you've been leeching off their grief. Off *my* grief."

Its smile was all blood and canines. *"Don't think of yourself as something special. Your grief now is tangible but not what I sought."* It licked at the trail of crimson oozing from its lips. *"But your pain if you'd given up your kin or the pain of all those who adore you if you'd agreed to imprisonment? That's simply delicious."*

She held her hand out, hovering her palm at the side of the clerk's skull to feel the very essence of the spirit inside. Before she knew what to look for, the spirit was so subtle she couldn't tell what exactly was wrong about the clerk and the entire city itself. Since she knew what it all meant, it was unmistakable.

How did the Knights miss this? How did they not know they were being led astray by the same spirits they're meant to ward against? Even Karsten couldn't tell.

For her, it was somehow all too familiar.

"You escaped from The Divide, didn't you?" she asked.

Its wicked smile returned as it leaned forward, cutting the clerk's throat enough to draw blood against Karsten's blade. *"Does that worry you?"* it asked with a pout. *"That such destruction allowed for the worst of our kind to slip through the cracks?"* It breathed in deep, seeming to savor the scent of its own blood in the air. *"It's been eons since we tasted the freedom and fears of Midgard."*

"Who exactly do you have to thank for that release?" Karsten asked.

Its lips puckered stubbornly. *"A spirit never tells."*

Without warning, it leaned back fully against the wall before slamming itself forward onto the blade. The wound ran deep and long, cleaving its neck and spurting blood across their faces as Adelaide took a surprised jump back. Its gurgles lifted into the air as the body collapsed, writhing as wisps of faded blue bled from its body before shooting off into the sky to disappear on the horizon.

At their feet, the clerk's eyes returned to normal shades of brown as she kneeled in the dirt to hold his hand. It trembled in her grip as she rubbed over it with her thumb, coaching him to the other side until his body was limp and his eyes shut, a single tear running to mix into the pools of blood on the ground.

I should've taken the spirit from him like I did for Embla. Why didn't I think about doing it in time? I know we need answers, but that wasn't worth losing a life—or was it?

Sander cleared his throat, bringing Adelaide out of her thoughts as she looked away. She tried to pay attention to the rest of the garden and not just the dead man at her feet. It was silent save for the breeze and the collective, frightened murmurs rising from the crowded windows overlooking the garden on all sides.

"You've done all you can, Promised," Zareen said, like she meant to comfort her, but the use of Adelaide's title informed her that the words were meant for everyone in the garden and not just her. "Let's go."

She stood to do just that, but a low groan pinned her in place. She peered at the body, half-expecting some miracle, but saw a corpse, just like she knew there would be. The only thing she could do was follow the noise, her throat tightening with every step.

They discovered the Knight whose legs she'd hacked with the axe. He was bleeding profusely and probably wouldn't be able to walk properly for a long time, or perhaps not at all. A bit of Sander's healing magic would at least ensure he lived, but he sneered at her rather than asking for help. He was cowering in a corner of the garden he'd dragged himself into, blood trailing behind his damaged legs.

That ache bit into her eye again.

"You're possessed by the spirits, but not as severely as Orman," she explained. With that haunted feeling so freshly singing through her body, she could feel the caress of the spirits as if it were a real touch. The evidence of it was wrapped around the man's entire body, pulling him as tight as a bowstring. "Let me help."

He stared at the hand she stretched out towards him with gritted teeth, but the longer she stood, unwavering, the more his resolve cracked. His eyes flashed, the pupils dilating and contracting every few moments as the spirit fought for control.

"*Please.*"

That was all she needed.

Adelaide pulled on all her own mixture of faith and grief. Every inch of her soul that knew her family still lived, and every fiber of her heart that felt like they must be dead. It swirled inside her and pulsed in her veins as she willed it forward into her palms. Light broke through the skin, shining over the man's face and causing the garden to glow with a fierce white that ebbed and flowed from the Knight, then back into her.

All his twisted-up feelings danced with her. She could sense his distrust of elves and the grief he held. He was agonized by the thought that she was a liar sent to destroy the chapel and all he loved.

Above all else, he was *terrified* of being wrong. Of making the wrong choice. Of turning his back on her only to realize he'd forsaken the Gods themselves. Of trusting the Knights with his life only to lose it for nothing.

She took each grief terrorizing his heart and replaced it with something she believed in. She replaced his distress with her faith in Zareen, who would never waver in battle. His fear she replaced with the courage she felt when she stood beside Karsten. His sorrow for those who died by the spirits' hands was replaced by all the joyful memories she had with her kin.

He smiled up at her, tears brimming in his eyes when the light died.

"T-thank you."

She smiled back at him, even as pain curdled in her core at the look in his blue eyes. He wasn't a man or a Knight. His face was too round and his words too soft. He was just a boy promised to the Brotherhood too young.

A boy I cut down.

With a start, she realized he was still smiling. He hadn't blinked and simply continued to stare back at her, his smile unwavering even as his soul died.

Karsten ushered her away.

THAT NIGHT, Adelaide stared without really seeing into the mirror in her room.

They brought her a warm bowl of water to scrub away the blood. It marred her hair, the white robe she was gifted with, and her face in equal measure. She managed to get the gore off her body but, no matter how hard she scrubbed, she couldn't seem to rid the robe of the reddish-brown stains.

It was a gift. I must get it clean.

Her fingers were red from scrubbing. Her arms ached from the swinging of the axe and the intensity with which she cleaned.

But I can't stop.

Zareen's hand on her shoulder made her freeze. "Jarl Lefa can commission a new one for you. For now, you must rest."

She shook her head and kept scrubbing.

The other woman sat beside her on the vanity bench in their room and grabbed her hands to peel her fingers away from the brush. She removed them, one by one, until the brush splashed into the dirty water.

With her hands freed, Zareen wrapped her arms around her and let Adelaide rest her chin on her shoulder.

And she *sobbed, sobbed, sobbed* into the night.

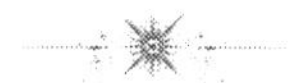

In the early morning light after a night of fitful slumber, the world felt softer than Adelaide deserved.

The bench built against the window of her room was too inviting. She wrapped herself in the largest quilt she could find and dozed in the first rays of sunlight filtering in from the horizon. Below her window, she could still see the stains of blood from the battle. So, she kept her eyes trained on the slips of golden sky peeking out between the lingering remnants of night and the rooftops of Lysafell's sprawling downtown.

There was a knock at the door, which she ignored, but it didn't stop the intruder from entering. They perched on the edge of her bed and sighed, their breath rustling the edges of the quilt she was cocooned in.

"Karsten found something you need to see," Sander said, slipping a few pieces of parchment onto the bench beside her.

She grabbed it and stared at the ink for longer than necessary, her brain refusing to comprehend the correspondences written in cursive, which she could barely understand. Karsten had helped improve her reading skills, but cursive Common was still beyond her reach.

"What is it?" she asked, unwilling to admit that she couldn't understand it.

He took the pages back. "Letters between Clerk Orman's grief spirit and multiple leaders across The North. Karsten is certain the spirit was attempting to see if any other spirits possessed their targets."

Her heart went cold. "You mean this possession was planned and more are already in motion?"

"It would seem so, just as I feared," he sighed as he ran his hand through his hair. "Whoever tore open The Divide seems to have struck a deal with the most powerful spirits once imprisoned there. They probably agreed to free them so long as they possessed certain leaders whose corruption would instill the most chaos." He rounded the bench so she could see him from the corner of her eye. "These humans will need you now more than ever, Adelaide."

She hid her face in the quilt, wishing it would all simply go away.

Why won't it all stop?

"But they might not trust you now as well."

She tore the blanket away to glare at him. "Why would they—"

"This was sent to Clerk Orman," he explained, holding up another piece of parchment.

There was a symbol scrawled across its surface that was ingrained into her memory like nothing else in all the realms.

The golden symbol of the Yggdrasil, the Tree of Life and the imagery on every gateway between realms, was stamped at the bottom a missive. It was the spitting image of the gates she'd seen dozens of times deep in the woods of her homeland but had yet to step through. She needed no translation to understand the elven words scrawled above the symbol.

'Stop the Keeper by any means.'

"The person who destroyed my home is an elf?" she asked

in disbelief as she hesitantly touched the edges of the parchment. "One of our own did this?"

His throat bobbed as he roughly swallowed. "Only Karsten, Zareen, and Zamir were in the clerk's office when this was discovered. They don't plan on telling anyone else besides the Jarl and Ylwa if we can help it, but we're the only elves here. They already trust us, but if anyone else were to discover this—"

"They'd think it was our doing," she concluded.

"Especially since you're the only one who can control the spirits, and I have vast amounts of knowledge on them. We would be the only two people they know who could do this. The humans have been kind so far, but we cannot test their limits of trust in us until we find who is truly responsible."

She dropped the quilt, ignoring the fact that she was only wearing a sheer shift beneath, and stormed behind the dressing screen to change. "I get it, Sander. I've run out of time to mourn and wallow in self-pity." She threw her shift away and exchanged it for her trousers and the nearest top she could reach. "We need to find these bastards before the humans try to lay the blame for all of this at our feet."

He snorted. "I'm surprised you're not questioning me like they did. Quite suspicious that I arrived so quickly after the explosion with all the knowledge of the spirits I have. I've been questioned since before the sun rose."

She peeked out from behind the screen as she fastened her top. "I'm certain you have plenty of secrets revolving around how you know so much, but I saw you enter town disheveled from days of travel. It took me a month to wash the scent of fire and smoke from me. I doubt you could've managed to hide your involvement so swiftly if you were the culprit. Besides, Zareen would've been able to tell that you were lying by now."

"Fair point."

She fastened her belt as she left the screen. "Speaking of

which, I'll require more information from you about the spirits." He sat on the window bench, making himself comfortable as she busied herself around the room to pack her things. "How is it that I sensed the spirits but the Knights couldn't? I thought that's what most of their training was for."

"The more powerful the spirit, the easier they can hide or disguise themselves. This one specifically altered itself to appear like another type of spirit, tricking everyone into believing they were a positive astral. I made that mistake, but it won't happen again."

She nodded as she threw her dirty clothes into the largest satchel, shoving her bloodied robe to the bottom in some vane hope that Embla could get the stains out.

"Even Karsten and I were fooled by this spirit, so I wouldn't take it to heart." He shifted uncomfortably at her words, making her pause. "Unless there's something else I should know?"

His shoulders deflated. "It's not really for me to say."

She stopped dead in her tracks, her heart quickening until it ached painfully in her chest. "If there's something wrong with Karsten, you *will* tell me."

He only hesitated for a moment more, but whatever lay bare in her expression seemed to push him over the edge. "I told you of how Knights take Vow to gain their abilities." She nodded. "I fear Karsten is no longer taking it."

"Is that not a good thing? You claimed the drug causes illness; why wouldn't he stop taking it?"

"Vow's chains are not so easily broken, Adelaide." He paused to peer at the door, as though worried someone might dare to listen to their conversation from the hallway. "The simple act of taking Vow ensures great abilities, but also a great loss to the years of one's life. Quitting it may be even more dire. The symptoms I told you about—of losing one's abilities, mind, bodies, and lives—rapidly *increase* alongside the withdrawal."

Karsten's frantic words while he was mid-panic attack ran like wildfire through her mind.

"And if something happens to me? If I'm not fit for duty, least of all well enough to fight off my own people? They'll know to incapacitate me first, if I'm not already."

"No, you need to know this now while I have my wits about me."

"I'm trying to—I am—ridding myself of a crutch. Something I used as a Knight to maintain my strength."

He sounded like a mad man.

He was losing his mind.

"What are you doing?" Adelaide asked.

"I just want to keep you safe."

"Cold sweats, paranoia. The cloak worked, it's why you look rested, so this isn't a spirit's doing."

"It's nothing for you to concern yourself with."

"Please, Karsten, let me help."

"You're sick, you needn't ever apologize for being ill."

He was losing his body.

"It's been hard not to give in, but this is something I must do to fully sever myself from the Brotherhood: to rely on my own strength instead of something granted by magic."

"You haven't had any delusions from the withdrawals, right?"

"None from the withdrawals but, since I quit, the spirits' visions have gotten stronger."

He was losing his abilities.

Karsten's shaking hands, sleepless nights, the sweat on his brow, and his bursts of anger all rushed through her thoughts until her stomach painfully turned.

"He wasn't able to detect the spirit, even when it made its presence known," she realized with a start, her knees almost giving out as she recalled his confused expression during most of their exchange with Orman. It was only after Sander clearly stated the clerk was possessed that Karsten seemed to understand what was happening.

"The loss of his abilities has already happened, and I fear what he may lose next," Sander finally admitted, lowering his head as though to give her privacy as her thoughts swirled.

He's not taking Vow, and it's going to kill him.

"Thank you for telling me, Sander," she said, her voice unsure and wavering. "I knew he was experiencing withdrawals; I just didn't know the full depths of it."

He scoffed. "Figures he'd forget to share such an important detail."

She swallowed down every biting word she wanted to spew at him. Karsten may not have shared every detail with her, but she understood why. If she'd known the truth back then, when she'd first found out, would she have tried to convince him to go back?

She didn't know, and that sickened her.

"Keep all of this to yourself for now," she said, her tone a little more certain than before. "We must respect Karsten's wishes to keep this quiet and do all we can to ensure he quits Vow for good."

He paled. "Adelaide, it *will* kill him. No Knight has successfully escaped Vow's grasp and lived to talk about it."

"Then he shall be the first."

She said it like it was a simple fact. As if quitting wasn't as difficult as she knew it would be. If anyone could accomplish such a feat, it would be him. He could pave the way for others to leave the Brotherhood safely, so long as he let her help.

If he has faith in me, the least I can do is believe in him.

Adelaide would support his path, even as her heart shattered with the thought of it.

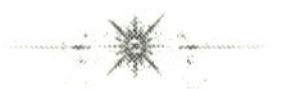

"Why would an *elf* destroy The Divide?" Jarl Lefa asked as she peered over the parchment discovered in Orman's office.

As soon as their trek to Rannadal was complete, they were ushered into the grand longhouse to discuss all that transpired on their journey in Lysafell. A letter sent by raven could not capture the full details of the clerk's possession, nor their surprise at the parchment they'd discovered. There was also a risk of it being intercepted, so they only sent word that there was much to discuss upon their return and left the rest out.

Brother Knut ensured they departed with the knowledge that the clergy were divided on their support for The Covenant. Half seemed elated by Adelaide removing their ranks of possession, but the rest weren't happy with the murder of their so-called *"First in Line for Divinity."*

That left them with only half the support they sought, with many in the clergy secretly sending gold and manpower to the village while the others argued against even allowing The Covenant to exist. It was still a preferable outcome compared to Adelaide being locked in a dungeon, so she considered their efforts a success.

Ylwa sighed as she played with the edges of one of the letters they discovered. "It can't be a Keeper. Otherwise, they wouldn't have called Adelaide a Keeper."

Zamir leaned back and propped his filthy boots on the long table, much to the Jarl's disgust. "I doubt an elf residing in New Alfheim would've done it either. Their resources are beyond comparison. To risk losing that and being banished to Midgard would be foolish."

"Unless they meant to destroy anything connecting the realms, ensuring no one could cross between," Karsten said.

Adelaide shook her head. "Doubtful. People in New Alfheim hardly care if an elf willingly leaves the realm, and they wouldn't risk harming the Keepers. We are their main defense should humans attempt to invade once more."

Zareen combed her sweaty hair back. They were all dirty from riding hard for days to return to Rannadal, and her upper lip curled at their combined stench. "An elf in Midgard must be the culprit then."

Karsten's gaze flickered out the grand hall doors, further into town where Sander's silhouette could be seen against the central bonfire.

"Don't even speak it," Adelaide said with a roll of her eyes. "That would be too perfect. The very person we're seeking is hiding among us, so clearly visible?" She sank into the nearest chair in defeat. "Highly improbable. It would've been far easier for him to flee. Remaining so close to the destruction he wrought would be foolish, and he's not a fool."

The Jarl rested the parchment with the Yggdrasil etched across it on the table between them. "Indeed. While I agree he is hiding something, the culprit is unlikely to be him. He has too much respect for life and the spirits. I'm also the one who asked him to come here, not the other way around. Besides that, this isn't his penmanship."

They collectively seemed to agree to drop the matter. Instead, they began picking apart everything else they learned in Lysafell, and each of the resources they'd obtained from the clergy. However, Adelaide couldn't shake the feeling that Lefa was right.

Sander *was* hiding something.

After their talk in the inn, the matter of the spirits and all he knew about them was dropped. She'd tried to bring it to his attention throughout their travels back to Rannadal, but something always intervened.

Not any longer.

She excused herself and made her way down the hill back into the heart of town, paying close attention to Sander's whereabouts. Almost like she feared that by blinking, he would disappear. When she allowed her gaze to slip away from him, it was to eye the front of the chapel.

Outside the doors, a Sister she didn't recognize stopped in her tracks to glare at Adelaide as she closed the doors, as though to bar her entry. The Sister hissed, her voice a deep rumble the elf almost didn't hear. "No heretics in the church."

She ignored her entirely, much to the other woman's shock.

I'm too tired to even make fun of her. I've truly lost my touch.

Her body sang in protest as she collapsed onto the bench opposite of Sander, the fire separating them and painting his usual cool complexion in shades of warmth.

"You never explained to me what more you know of the spirits," Adelaide said, her blunt tone slicing through the meditation he'd fallen into by the fire.

He sighed as he cracked open one of his misty gray eyes to look at her. "Are you so determined to learn because you actually wish to know, or are you using this as an excuse to get away from Karsten before you think about his impending death?"

She scowled. "Two things can be true at once."

"That's fair," he said as he closed both eyes once more. "You know there are thirty types of spirits, yes?" She nodded when he opened one of his eyes enough to see her. "What if I told you there were really only fifteen?"

"How could that be?" she asked. "I've been training all my life to recognize the spirits of my home, and I've seen almost every type for myself."

He looked at her as if she were a misbehaving pupil rather than a friend, and it set her on edge. "The spirits of destruction. Name them for me."

Putting her ego aside, she did as he asked. "The spirit of Misery, which distresses the soul. The spirit of Suicide—" That fateful night she met Embla flashed in her mind. "It convinces people to take their own lives."

"Go on."

"Lust." She thought of Karsten and the spirit which plagued him, deciding to skip all which it did to a person. "Vanity compels one to think only of themselves. Obsession turns one mad with need for another. Fear terrifies. Wrath turns you into the embodiment of living rage. Deceit forces one to lie. Regret haunts you. Loneliness entraps you. Chaos turns your life upside down for its own enjoyment. Jealousy spoils your relationships. Grief" — she thought of the boy she killed — "leaves you lacking. Revenge pushes you to harm others. Sorrow leaves you empty."

Just as I felt when I first came here.

"What spirit used to fill the walls of Lysafell?" he asked next.

"Faith, a being who defies the spirits of destruction and brings order," she said, recalling Sander's initial theory that the walls of the city themselves thrummed with faith.

"Even after Orman died, you still felt a lingering sense of the spirits, correct?" he asked, leaning forward with his chin perched on his clasped hands.

"Yes, but what does that—"

The look he gave her revealed it all. There were still the remnants of Faith in Lysafell, even after Grief struck. Or were they really one and the same? They didn't feel all that different to her. One soothed her scar and the other raked its claws across her eye, but they both existed in the same space—tugging on her magic.

"Strange, isn't it?" he asked. "There are fifteen spirits of Order and fifteen of Chaos." He held out his hands so two balls of light shone, one white and one black, like he'd done in Lysafell. "We all like to see the world in simple terms. In this, humans and elves are alike. It's easier to see evil as just evil. It's so much harder to see the darker sides of such light." He brought his hands together, combining the light so the black and white swirled together as one.

Two sides of one coin.

"You're saying that the spirits of destruction are simply corrupted spirits of peace?" she gasped, her mouth suddenly dry.

He nodded. "Muse, the spirit of passion that turns to Misery when the creative heart runs dry. Mercy, meant to ease lost souls, turns people to the brink of Suicide as though it believes death to be the truest mercy of them all. Pleasure, meant to please all, turns into a needy, Lustful beast. Honor twists to Vanity. Love, into Obsession. Courage, to Fear. Hope, to Wrath. Wisdom, to Deceit. Peace, to Regret. Rest, to Loneliness, Order, to Chaos. Loyalty, to Jealousy. Justice, to Revenge. Joy, to Sorrow. And, yes, even Faith to Grief."

She sat in silence, all she'd once known spinning around in her head at rapid speeds. She'd made friends with the spirits of Muse when she was a child. She'd seen Peace and Loyalty reunite families. Never in all her years had she expected those spirits to be lying on the precipice of such horror.

"How does this corruption happen?" she asked.

He shrugged. "Others have their own theories, but mine is quite simple."

She leaned forward, finding herself eagerly hanging onto his next word.

"We do it."

"How would we do such a thing?" she balked.

"The spirits are all ones of Order at first, but we are flawed creatures, Adelaide," he explained with a sad smile tugging on his lips. "It is our influence which corrupts the spirits. We like to believe they possess us, forcing us to commit acts we wouldn't normally do. That's partially true, but they're only able to be corrupted through their interactions with the living mortals of this realm."

"By destroying The Divide, their home as much as it was mine—"

"Every spirit in the blast zone was corrupted as well."

The spirits she'd once known. The ones who had protected her and saved other clans she knew. They were the same they'd fought and killed, both in their physical and astral forms. The dying Muse spirit she'd discovered when she'd tried to find her kin hadn't been actually perishing. It had been *changing* into a spirit of Misery. She'd been given the power to destroy both the good and the evil, and she hadn't even realized what she'd done.

"The next time we find ourselves with a spirit, I want you to remember what I've told you," he said.

"*Why*?" She looked away so she could blink back her tears. "Just so I can feel even more guilty for what I've done?"

He shook his head. "No, because you might be the only one who can fix what they've done on a grander scale than you even realize." She turned back to him, feeling even more confused than when their conversation began. "If you hold sway with the spirits and the average person can corrupt them, who is to say your abilities may not be the very thing that can save them? You may be able to purge the darkness from the spirits and return them to their original purpose."

At long last, everything seemed to fall into place in her heart. She was not meant to cut down the spirits. Her abilities weren't granted so she could save just the living. Adelaide would protect the spirits too. Any chance she had, she would convince the spirits to be what they truly were.

To be spirits of the dawn instead of the perilous night.

SANDER LEFT her alone at the fire to mull over everything he'd revealed. Adelaide was certain it was also to avoid any more of her probing questions, as she was still certain there were things about him none of them knew, but she decided to leave that thought alone.

After all, she had her own secrets she hadn't shared with them.

Her thoughts swirled and continued to question what Sander's words meant for Karsten. He was tortured by Lust, but how was that spirit of Pleasure turned to such atrocities? Had it been corrupted by him or by the ones who had entrapped it?

Adelaide couldn't picture a world where he, a child wishing so hard to protect others, would be the cause of any sort of *corruption*. Still, he had slayed that spirit during his initiation. Had it wished to die? Could she have healed its corruption if she had been there? There were more questions than answers, so she let them lie unanswered.

Instead, she focused on her wary steps to the bathhouse. Grime stuck to her skin from the long days of travel and her body fiercely ached. There had been no time to bathe the morning after Orman's men had confronted her, so she felt like all that blood still stuck with sweat to her skin.

She didn't even have enough energy to side-step Jill as the old woman stopped her on her path to the bathhouse, her slightly hunched form blocking Adelaide from her destination. The elf was sorely tempted to just turn around and go straight to sleep, but she knew she'd wake up from her own stench if she didn't wash off the long days on the back of her borrowed horse.

I hope Enok is ready to ride soon. I've missed him so much.

Jill stayed a safe distance away, wariness bleeding off her in waves. "May I speak with you, Adelaide?"

She sighed, her attention still trained on the bathhouse beyond. "I'm far too tired to fight with you again, Sister."

The bruise on her cheek was healed but still stung deep down. The only reason she didn't push straight past her was because of the deep, exhausted ache in her bones and the lingering fear Jill obviously felt towards her. Perhaps her fear would keep her in line.

"I know you have no reason to trust me, but there is something you must know."

"Whatever you have to say, I wouldn't believe you anyways," she said, rolling her eyes as she went to go around the woman.

Jill grabbed her by the arm, halting her before ripping her hand away as though she were burned. "I wouldn't trust me either, but despite our differences we share a common goal." Adelaide remained where she was, hearing her out not because she believed her but because she was simply too tired to do otherwise. "We wish to heal The Divide and see you return home, far from here and back where you belong."

Jill made it perfectly clear she believed Adelaide belonged with her family, not with Karsten. The Sister's mind was focused on *"saving"* Karsten from whatever ill intentions she imagined the elf had for him.

The easiest way to get me to leave would be to find my kin.

Maybe Jill will be useful to me yet.

"Yes," Adelaide said, squaring her shoulders. "I wouldn't have a choice but to return to my kin once they've been found and the mountains have been healed."

She smiled something wicked. "Exactly as I thought." She hummed with a proud tilt of her chin that quickly dispelled her grin. "However, that is the sad truth of the matter I've come to discuss with you."

Her mind went on alert, the wariness replaced with panic as Jill's sincerity rang through louder than Adelaide's doubt. There was every reason for Jill to want her kin to be found alive; she had the most to benefit if she left with them.

She couldn't be with Karsten if her kin were found. It was a small price to pay to be reunited with them, but it didn't hurt any less.

"I overheard them when you first arrived and again just now," Jill explained, nodding up towards the grand hall perched atop a hill in the center of town. "Jarl Lefa, Sister Ylwa, Zareen, and Karsten have made a decision regarding your family—*and* you."

Her heart hammered faster in her chest and she reached out towards the spirits haunting Jill, seeking any lies hidden in her words but finding none. Whatever she was about to whisper would be the truth.

"If your family were ever found dead, they agreed it was best to keep the truth from you. They would pretend like they were still searching to ensure you stayed," she explained.

A snort left her unbidden. "Why should I believe you?"

Something crinkled between her wrinkled hands as she pulled a parchment from her robes' pockets. It was folded over so many times along the same seams that it appeared as though the slightest breeze would tear it apart.

"See the proof for yourself."

Adelaide took the note with hesitant hands before delicately peeling it open. Scrawled on the page before her were simple orders to The Covenant's warriors and scouts, written in penmanship that was far too familiar.

If Clan Aylara is found deceased, remain silent. Only inform Jarl Thurstan and me of the discovery, and you are under strict orders to avoid raising The Promised one's suspicions on the matter of her family. Disregarding this order will be met with the Jarl's fiercest punishments.

Karsten's name was signed in the bottom left corner in a scrawling font, one she memorized even when the letters danced in her eyes.

"Now," Jill continued, "they're speaking in the grand hall about forcing you to remain by any means necessary, something neither of us wants."

Despite all that had transpired between them, Adelaide

believed her. How could she not? The proof was in her grasp, written in the same handwriting that annotated the scrolls she studied and penned by the hands she'd trusted for months.

My kin could already be discovered dead, and they wouldn't tell me. They will trap me here for eternity, never knowing what befell them.

"Do you know if—"

The Sister shook her head, silencing her. "I do not, child. I only overheard pieces of conversations not meant for outsider ears, which is why I've remained silent until now. All I can say is that they agreed to these measures willingly. I kept their secret, hoping the truth would never be necessary, but it's been too long with no sight of your clan. You must face the reality that they're dead and decide what you will do next." She folded her hands into her sleeves. "Will you stay with the liars who would keep the death of your family from you? Or will you return home to finally find out where your clan is buried?"

Jill left her with nothing but sorrow that night, stumbling towards the bathhouse with a heart heavier than the mountains. She bathed, unfeeling as she stared into space as though hoping to materialize her kin right before her eyes.

They're gone. They're gone. They're gone.

He lied. He lied. He lied.

In her anguish, she didn't see the shadow looming over her.

A VOICE IN THE SHADOWS

Die. Die. Die

The air is gone from her lungs, her chest burning.

The fall is inevitable.

Her nails scratch against air and skin, thrashing in the waves.

Do not fight it.

The water is so hot—no, it's so cold. How can she be burning in the ice?

Let the darkness embrace you.

Everything is getting dark. Why is it so dark?

LET GO.

18

WHISPERS FOR THE NIGHT

SKALD: KARSTEN STROM

Karsten pinched the bridge of his nose as their meeting dragged on late into the evening. None of them were lucky enough to have bathed in days, aside from the Jarl, who sat comfy in her grand hall's giant throne while they rode through The North on her bidding. All to seek the resources of a clergy that mostly despised them.

Still, the trip was fruitful in ways he didn't expect.

Like the berries on Adelaide's lips that night beneath the aurora.

It was still burned into his mind. How sweet she had looked and how much sweeter she would taste if he ever had the courage to tell her how he felt. Still, that required the very narrow possibility of her returning his feelings.

A foolish thought.

"Who is this *Wise One* signing these letters?" Lefa asked as she rifled through the parchment they took from Orman's desk. "Do we have any leads?"

Zareen bit her nail between her teeth, whittling away at the surface in her mounting anxiety. She'd only shared a single comment about how devastated Adelaide had been the evening the Knights had attacked them, but it was enough to make his heart stutter in his chest and haunt his friend's distant gaze.

"Adelaide wouldn't say it—couldn't *say it. Possessed or not, she killed a child. I don't think she wanted to be here after that."*

Karsten knew better than most that *"here"* didn't mean The Covenant or Rannadal.

"No suspects," Zareen confirmed. "We can only surmise whoever wrote these letters is the same person who destroyed The Divide."

Lefa nodded as she tossed the papers across the table. "Then it's settled. Our target is The Wise One: whoever they may be. All our efforts must be diverted to discovering who is responsible and stopping them by any means. We can return our efforts to permanently sealing The Divide once we're certain they've been brought to the axe."

In his mind, Karsten was already configuring new guard rotations and scouting expeditions to accomplish that very goal. By the time he fully focused back on the meeting, he'd formulated a new training regimen for the recruits, and the topic had drastically changed.

"There are whispers," Ylwa said as she handed him a scroll. He unfurled it, though he could hardly read the words through his exhausted gaze. "Elves at the border of the mountains."

"Could they be—"

Lefa shrugged. "I would hazard a guess they may be Adelaide's clan, but it's just as possible for them to be the ones behind the destruction. I don't think they're one in the same though. None of our scouts could get close enough to see if they matched the descriptions she gave of her family."

He sighed as he rolled up the scroll. "We either have the enemy advancing on us or the very people we've been seeking the last few months."

"Precisely," the Jarl said.

Zareen rested her chin on her folded hands perched atop

the table. Her brother had left a solid boot print on the surface when he'd left to see how Adelaide was faring, and she'd tried to wash it clean before daring to touch it again.

There was still a scuff left behind.

Karsten wished it could be him comforting her after the chaos of their trip, but she'd been eerily quiet around him ever since Orman's death. He wondered why. If he'd done something wrong, he would fix it to the best of his abilities. If she would simply tell him what he did to upset her.

'Perhaps it was your blade cutting down Orman or the ease with which you murdered your fellow Knights. Maybe she could sense your lust outside of my influence, begging her to kiss you. To let her taste more than the berries. To lick at something sweeter. What a fool either way.'

He shook off Lust's whispers and focused on Zareen as she raised a hesitant question. "What if she does find her family alive?" She bit her thumbnail again. "That was her condition for assisting us: that we help find her family. She will have no reason to stay."

"Her home is still destroyed. She has nowhere else to go," Lefa said, interjecting before Karsten could speak. "She will assist. She's the only one who can. We have the means of making that possible, should she resist."

He stiffened. "She'll help of her own accord. I'm certain of it." Then, he was the one delaying what he truly wanted to say. "You all do realize the longer we keep her here, the more danger she's in."

Zareen's expression soured as she gave the scuff on the table a hard stare. "What other choice do we have, Karsten?"

Ylwa picked at a frayed strand of her robes. "We know we only asked her to stay to heal The Divide and that she would potentially leave before we even found the one responsible for all of this, but the people adore her."

"The Covenant would lose all legitimacy should she leave,"

Lefa said, her expression hardening to stone. "We must hold onto her for as long as possible, regardless of if her family is found alive, dead, or not at all. She is the only one who can cull the spirits. It is her people who tore The Divide apart. Her abilities are what give people hope. She is the only one who could have been foretold in my vision. She *must* stay."

Karsten wanted her to stay. Gods, he wanted her to stay with him. But not like that.

Zareen and he sat silently while the others whispered about ways to force her to remain in Rannadal. Plots to keep her a willing participant for as long as possible and what to do should they fail to keep the peace with her. None of their plans would matter, so long as she stayed of her own accord or her family was never discovered.

Adelaide wouldn't stay. He knew her too well to ever believe that. She would keep up her end of the bargain. Whether her family was dead or not was the only difference. If they were alive, she would rebuild their home in the mountains. If they were dead, he couldn't see her staying around in Midgard or The Divide after that.

The sad look in Zareen's eyes told him that much.

To keep her alive, he would be willing to lie about whether her family still lived or not. He could hide their bodies if necessary to ensure she remained in the realm of the living, but the thought sickened him. He couldn't make up his mind on what he would do in that situation. Whether he could lie to her or not.

Instead, he made up his mind about something else entirely.

Should her family live and she choose to leave, he would let her go. He would help her escape. He'd do *anything* for her, even defy his Jarl. He simply hoped he would never need to, for all their sakes.

The doors to the grand hall burst open, the wood thundering against the walls. At first, he expected the cause to be a strong gust of wind from a coming storm but, no, it was one of his warriors.

The man was gasping for breath as he met Karsten's gaze.

"It's the Promised."

KARSTEN'S MIND was void of thought and completely numb. All he could feel was the dread pulsing in his heart and echoing in his ears as he followed the warrior out of the longhouse and through town. The closer they got, the louder the screams grew.

The bathhouse came into view.

He ran for it.

"Why didn't you ask for directions here earlier? They could have been easily provided."

"Bathing leaves you quite vulnerable, Commander. I didn't trust anyone to know when I would be in such a state."

"But you trusted me?"

"My drunken, desperate mind did. Don't get confused."

He pushed past the crowd gathering outside the doors and rushed to the women's side of the chambers, only to freeze when the thing of his nightmares came into view.

Adelaide, lying cold and tinged blue on the stone floors. She was soaked from head to toe, water flooding the area where she lay. It drenched Zamir, who cradled her body to his chest as he screamed pleas to the Gods. Sander stood over them, his healing magic casting a white light over them both.

"Odin, don't do this!"

She's too still. Completely limp and void of life. Can Sander's magic do anything? Is she already a lost soul lingering realms away and out of reach? Did I fail her so soon?

Karsten's legs trembled beneath him, threatening to give out as he moved closer as though in a trance. His vision narrowed until all he could see was *her*. White hair tangled around her face, framing her blue lips and shut eyes. The tips of her pointed ears, fingers, and toes were lavender to match the bruises beneath her eyes.

Who did this to her?

He would do any impossible deed the Gods asked of him, but surely the Gods would not ask *that* of him. They couldn't ask him to say goodbye so soon.

She gasped for breath and, in doing so, breathed life back into his own lungs. He heaved alongside her in shock. She sputtered water, the liquid raining across her until Zamir turned her on her side. It flowed freely from her mouth and tears ran from her eyes to mix with the hot spring water she choked back up. That's when he realized his previous thoughts were a lie.

Karsten would not do everything the Gods requested, but he would do anything Adelaide asked of him. He would shatter the earth, conquer any city, and bleed every drop of his blood onto her blade if she demanded it. She'd taken the place in his heart where his devotion to his Goddess once lay, and he would never desire otherwise.

To lose her now would be like losing hope itself.

Sorrow wrapped itself around him as if it were an old friend coming to comfort him. Adelaide cried, shaking violently on the floor as she clung to life under Sander's magic. Zamir rubbed soothing patterns into her back, and uttered words he couldn't hear over the roar of the spirits in his mind.

'If this is how you feel when she hasn't even died, how will the real thing feel?' Sorrow asked. *'How will it feel each time you send her out into the world to repair The Divide, knowing you cannot protect her in your home? You will keep sending her out, day after day, to death's door—hoping she does not open it. Praying to Gods you hardly know she returns unscathed.*

'You may very well be the thing that kills her.
'The water choking her lungs.'

Inside Adelaide's cabin, the air was thick. She was fast asleep, resting after what happened to the best of her ability. Karsten stood guard from beside the fireplace, the warmth choking him.

His fear pressed in around him and he bit his lip until it bled in some feeble hope that it would stop trembling. He wanted to cry out to any God who would listen, but that would only disturb her sleep.

Never take her from this realm. Gods, I could not bear it.

He didn't know if he prayed to Olena, Cismir, or The Old Gods. He would take any of them if only *someone* would answer him.

In the moment, he hadn't felt anything. He had been in shock as he'd stared at her body, unable to do anything to help. It was Sander who had saved her and Zamir who had held her until she'd cried herself to sleep. Karsten had carried her back to her room, but he'd left to collapse in his own bed while Zareen and Embla had dressed and warmed her. When he'd awoke, the reality of it all had washed over him, and it threatened to drown him too.

Someone in his own home had drowned her. The evidence of her struggle remained written all over the bathhouse: a picked lock, claw marks from her nails on the wood, and puddles of blood and water painting the floor.

He shuddered as he looked at her limp body beneath the many blankets she was cocooned in. Without Sander, she would be gone. She'd already expressed her fear of being left vulnerable in the bathhouse, and he hadn't done anything about it.

I'm so sorry, Adelaide.

The night and day wore on. She slept through most of it, save for the fitful nightmares causing her to scream in her sleep. He coached her through them, but his words and warm touch on her too-cold cheek didn't have the desired effect.

'You can't comfort her like Zamir did. You cannot heal her like Sander did. You cannot protect her like you promised. What good are you?' Sorrow asked.

He didn't know, so he simply stood guard until his bones ached and his tears dried.

"MAKING sure I don't run away again?"

Karsten jolted at the sound of her voice, waking from where he dozed in the chair beside the fire. His bones seemed to throb and his veins sang pleas for Vow—the cure to all his ailments—but he pushed them away to focus on the emerald shade of Adelaide's gaze instead.

"You're awake."

She could hardly keep her eyes open, but she was awake and *alive*.

"Obviously." She grimaced as she shifted, unfurling one of her arms from the bundle of blankets draped around her. "The blankets are unnecessary. I'm sweating."

"Sorry," he mumbled as he took a few of the quilts away, his throat suddenly dry. He folded the ones he grabbed and set them aside. "Zareen fussed over you like a mother hen."

"Surprising given the truth of it all."

His brows pinched at her blunt tone that felt familiar but somehow *not*.

"You can rest easy. I have no plans to flee until my duty is complete and my family is found. There's no need to watch me. A little drowning won't scare me away."

She's lying.

He turned to her in disbelief, but he found her staring at the ceiling with an unblinking gaze and a fearful tremble in her lower lip. "I'm not here because I think you'll run. I know you'll honor your word," he said, his voice low but still filled with conviction. "I'm here because whoever harmed you is still out there. I will not see you hurt again."

"Protecting your asset, I take it?"

"No, I'm protecting my *friend*," he said, his voice rising slightly. He shouldn't have yelled, but he couldn't help it. "Where is this coming from?"

She bit her lip to stop its trembling and continued staring with wide eyes circled by darkness that saw nothing. She was too pale and weak—a fragile being wearing the confidence of a giant.

"I know about your deal with the others," she said, venom lacing every word passing her lips. "To not tell me about my kin's whereabouts and if they're alive or not, all in the hopes that I remain here to be used in your plight. How you'll do *whatever is necessary* to keep me here, far from my home." She seethed as she gripped the blanket tighter. "How would I *ever* trust someone like that to protect me or to be my friend?"

Words left him completely, and all he could do was stare back at her with wide eyes that pleaded for understanding she wouldn't grant. That's when he recognized the familiar, distant tone of her voice. It was the same way she had spoken to him after she'd discovered he had been a Knight.

The way she had treated him when he had *lied* to her.

In the back of his mind, he supposed she was right. He had

agreed to Lefa's orders to hide her family if they were slain and assist in their efforts to keep her in Rannadal, but he'd never planned on truly doing either. He would defy the very Gods for her. The wrath of his Jarl was a small price to pay to see a smile on Adelaide's face.

Even if it was the last time he saw her and ensured she'd go where he couldn't follow.

"Be honest with me, *Knight*." The use of his former title slapped him out of his thoughts. "Are they still alive?"

That was the moment Karsten saw right through her. For all her bravado, she was simply scared, alone, and unprotected in a world not accustomed to her. Still, she would not bend to its demands to break beneath the pressure. He understood then that their worlds would never align, no matter how much he wished it.

"I-I truly do not know."

She scoffed at his answer.

"I mean it, Adelaide. We just got news of a few elves near the border, but no confirmation on whether they matched the description you gave. That's all I've heard."

She met his gaze for a few long, agonizing moments. He pleaded with her in his mind, hoping she would believe him and understand. If she'd only listen, he'd tell her any God he could ever pray to paled in comparison to her.

"You know," she began, her tone wavering between disbelief and anger, "I truly thought I could trust you. How foolish of me, a Keeper, to ever trust a member of the Brotherhood with something so precious."

He shook his head, his hands outstretched but never touching her. "Please, b-believe me. I-I would never agree to such things willingly but I had no choice."

"There's always a choice to do what's right." Her chest was heaving beneath the quilts, her forehead dotted with sweat from the exertion her rising anger brought. "Believe it or not, you're the one who taught me that. I thought if a Knight could truly redeem himself then it would be easy for me to do the same. That I could help people not for any other reason than it being the right thing to do." She stopped to gasp for breath, stubborn tears welling in the corners of her gaze and spilling unbidden across her cheeks. "I'm such a fool for ever thinking that was real. That any of *this* was real."

"Any of what?" he asked, the heartbroken look in her eyes stealing the very breath from his lungs.

She met his gaze, piercing emerald on molten amber. "You know."

Despite the rage brimming in her eyes, he *did* know. The stolen touches, quick as a rabbit in the woods, the lingering looks smoldering with something more, and the way she smiled when she thought he wasn't looking. It wasn't all in his head. There was something there, lying dormant under the surface, begging for them to close the gap.

The gap that is now a smoldering fissure, dividing us just as the mountains did.

He didn't have a chance to speak before she was releasing a harsh laugh at the ceiling that stole her gaze away from his again. "I cannot believe I fell for such tricks. There is no way in all the realms my family wouldn't have found me by now if they still lived. Yet I clung to this sickening hope they were alive because I saw you trying so hard to bring them home to me. Now I know that was all a lie and I cannot help but wonder why you did it?" The end of her question was broken by a sob, and he was unable to do anything to slow the rapid tears streaming down her face. "Why couldn't you have just told me the truth so I could've mourned them months ago? This false hope was cruel."

"I'm telling you the t-truth, they could still be—"

She didn't allow him to continue as she rambled like she was unable to hear him at all between her choking gasps for breath. "How did you do it? How did you stomach lying to me and comforting me in the same breath?" She dared to meet his gaze again, the shimmering anger within impossible to break free of. "It must've been painful considering—"

Adelaide stopped abruptly, and terror overtook her expression for just a split second before she looked away, her face paling against the warm firelight of the hearth.

"Considering what?" he asked, his hands finally falling to his side as he shifted an inch closer. She refused to look at him or acknowledge his existence in any way. Somehow, her anger was better than the morbid guilt evident in her expression. "Adelaide, what did you do?"

She wouldn't look at him and, when he tried to step into her line of sight, she closed her eyes. "I'm the reason you've been so sick," she admitted in a quiet voice. "That day I asked you to find my family, I used Zareen's dagger to cut your neck and then I—"

When she couldn't continue, she held up a finger with the tiniest scar marring the skin.

He stumbled back a few steps, his heart in his throat as the pieces fell into place. Was that why he couldn't sleep and the withdrawals worsened to impossibly new heights? The thought of her family being lost or dead made him sick, and finding them had quickly become an obsession. He'd thought it was because he truly felt for her, but was it a lie? That compulsion to make her happy by finding her kin wasn't his own; it belonged to The Blood Oath he'd unknowingly signed.

A contract she'd hidden from him the entire time, even as that unnamed pull brought them together. Was that why she claimed none of it was real? Because she knew the force dragging them together was magic instead of the tender affection he felt well up inside his chest whenever he looked at her?

"If I could take it back, I would," she murmured against the quiet, still air. "I even tried to steal Zareen's blade to destroy it, but then I heard it was from her father and I couldn't do it." She blinked back her tears as she met his gaze again. Somehow, he felt in his heart that it would be the last time she'd ever grant him the right to peer into their depths. "It's my turn in our game to receive an answer, isn't it?"

He nodded, suddenly unable to speak.

"So how did you do it? How did you defy The Blood Oath if you weren't truly looking? How has it not incapacitated you?"

He wished to tell her that The Oath was proof he was searching tirelessly for her clan, but the words wouldn't come. All he could do was stare into those eyes that held the entire world and pray they wouldn't close again for good or leave him forevermore, grasping at the edges of his sanity for another glimpse.

Despite knowing The Blood Oath existed as an invisible thread tying their fates together, the pain thrashing in his chest wasn't from that. It was an entirely different feeling beating in his heart and begging for escape. The two were separated, one an allegiance to a task that would be released once complete. The other a devotion so deeply engrained in his body that it could never be undone. He was too frightened to call it what it was, and the fear brought him to silence.

She rolled away from him, tearing the connection forged between them.

"You can go."

"*Adelaide—*"

"I said, go!"

The shutters rumbled at her words and his heart shook with them. He would fall at her feet apologizing. He would explain everything to her and go searching for her kin alone in the damned mountains himself if she asked. If it would make penance, he would do anything, but she wouldn't let him.

All she asked was for him to leave, so he did.

Sander took his place at her side, healing and protecting

her in ways Karsten couldn't, and the bitter claw of jealousy wrapped itself around his throat.

KARSTEN HUNCHED over the bar top, a tankard of mead in one hand and his head in the other. He had fucked up even when he hadn't technically done anything. That was the problem, wasn't it? He should've explained himself better and proved he'd never planned to adhere to Lefa's orders.

He could've shown her the supplies he'd stored in the escape tunnels as proof he had taken precautions to ensure she would always have a choice to leave. He could've brought any number of warriors to vouch for his efforts in finding her family or brought her the scout rotation reports as evidence.

He had done none of those things and instead simply stared like a dumbass at the object of all his affection as she'd spewed vitriol at his feet. It was pathetic how words and logic completely left him when she looked at him—even in rage. His adoration for her was so encompassing he even struggled to conjure anger at her for forcing The Blood Oath on his shoulders.

Okay, maybe I'm a little angry about that.

No, *furious* was the correct word. It simmered under his skin, and Lust played with it as if it were a toy. There were passionate ways for him to make penance for his transgressions and there were enticing ways she could do the same, but such ideas were foolish. Adelaide may have admitted to there being a lingering admiration between them, but any small chance of that growing between them was squashed at his feet.

'Who says you need admiration? Put both your rage to good use

and give into the pull. Mark your apologies on her skin with your lips and teeth. Allow her to say sorry with her mouth around your—'

Enough with you, Karsten groaned internally as he slammed his head down on the bar top counter.

A gentle hand caressed his shoulder, shaking him from his thoughts as a familiar smile greeted him. "Madam said you wished to see me," Lady Serenade said, her cheeks just as rosy and her dark hair just as perfectly curled as always. "It's been ages, Kar. What's held you away?"

He sighed as he rested his hand atop hers. In truth, he wasn't certain what held him back from visiting her. He was no stranger to Lilly's Den. Very few in Rannadal were unfamiliar with the brothel. There were even folk who traveled to their town just for the pleasure of being attended to by the people serving there. He'd just been busy.

Distracted.

"I apologize, Ser. I didn't mean to stay away."

She huffed as she sat beside him at the bar, her dress unfurling around her like a rose as she fixed the crimson lengths around her rear. "A lady's mind strays, you know. I often wondered if you were too ashamed to see me."

He shook his head. "Not in a million years."

She smiled, her grin more genuine than before. "Good. I would hate to lose my best client to the whims of bigotry. I work hard, you know. I'm no warrior or witch sent by the Gods, but I still serve The Covenant like the rest of the town."

He rolled his eyes and he drank deep from the jug. "You know I hate when you call me a customer."

She cackled, her fingers brushing close to her robust chest barely contained by her corset. Whatever she wore, it was imported, as were most of her clothes. They didn't have such lush fabric, deep colors, and tightly cinched pieces floating about Rannadal's markets.

'What would Adelaide look like in that?'

Silence, she hates us.

"You pay to spend time with me, do you not?" she asked with a pout. "Whether it's for sex or just for a chat, I still think that makes you a customer."

He sighed, low and long. Over the years, he'd repeated the same talk with her. He wasn't comfortable being called a customer when he just sought her out for friendship. He only paid because it kept the Madam happy and ensured his friend stayed employed. Ser insisted on calling him one anyway to desensitize him from it, to help ease away the taboo of their closeness and her profession.

The teachings of the clergy rang in his head, but when he was so out of sorts, he couldn't put up a fight about the inappropriateness of it all.

"That's all you have to say on the matter?" she questioned, her mouth hanging agape in surprise. "That usually stirs you. Something must have truly gone awry."

He downed the rest of his drink and passed it to the barkeep for another. Around them, the brothel was winding down as the morning approached. The velvet seats were empty except for a few drunk, sleeping townsfolk, and the usual suspicious noises from upstairs were absent. Ser smelled vaguely of sweat and sex, so she'd already completed her duties for the night. Only the barkeep could hear him, so he slipped a few extra coins in a silent plea for the man to remain at the far end of the bar where he couldn't hear.

"*Oh*, this must be interesting." Ser slid closer. "You sure you want to talk or do we need to work through your issues in another manner?"

He blushed as her hand ran across his shoulders to play with the space where his tunic and neck met. Her fingers nearly touched flesh when he pulled back, sending her a look that told her to behave.

Serenade and Karsten had been friends throughout his

entire training in the Brotherhood, back before her career as a courtesan had begun and she'd taken the name Serenade. They'd remained confidantes even after his departure from the Knights, often sending letters between them. In his youth, after his initiation into the Order was over and his torture was still fresh on his mind, they'd lain together once or twice.

In the end, they only saw each other as friends, so romance never sparked beyond the physical. She had helped him process what the spirit of Lust had done, healing him in places he could not reach alone. He still bore the scars of it, but she ensured they weren't gaping wounds.

In return, he had been her first client at Lilly's Den, assisting her in feeling more comfortable in her role and warning her of men or women she should refuse patronage from. Most of them had been removed when he'd become The Covenant's Commander, but he still ensured any who stepped out of line were swiftly dealt with.

"As my friend, I ask that you keep what I'm about to tell you to yourself," he began. "Don't use it for gossip to feed the eager ears of your fellow courtesans."

She was giddy with excitement as she leaned in, her breasts almost falling from their top. "This must be truly scandalous then. I heard a commotion the other day: people saying the Promised fell ill. She's pregnant, isn't she?" He paled, and she pointed directly at his face in triumph. "I knew it! Probably with Sander's baby, no doubt? Lilac owes me five coppers."

He grabbed her waving, frantic hands in his and caged them in his own. "Serenade, this is serious." She froze, her blue eyes as large as saucers as she stared back at him, her excitement wavering. "She—" He stopped to compose himself. "She almost *died*."

She paused, letting the words process slowly. "But she is our Promised. Olena would not let mortal hands touch what is hers unless it was in her will." Her rosy cheeks faded. "Unless Olena has turned away from her and she is not the true prophet."

"I still believe in her, Ser." He released her hands to grab his tankard instead. "With all of my heart, I believe in her."

Silence stretched between them as he drank, but then it was broken by her low hum. "No wonder you've stayed away," she said, her voice not as subdued by her usual sugar-sweet tone. It was a little deeper, a little more *her*. "Didn't want your beloved to know where you frequent?"

He looked at her from the corner of his eye. She didn't seem angry, merely disappointed. "I would never be ashamed of our friendship," he told her, hoping honesty dripped from his lips like the wine did from hers as she nervously gulped some down. "She is also not my beloved. She despises me—*again*."

"There was a time when she didn't?" There was a smug bite to her tone. "I'm surprised. It's so easy to loathe your very presence."

"Uhm, is that why you keep trying to bed me?"

"To smother you in your sleep? But of course."

A smile crept its way onto his lips. "I missed you, you know."

"Then visit me more often, you oaf." She laughed and pushed his shoulder. "Let's get back to the task at hand. The woman you seem taken by nearly died. She's also the prophet of Olena and the Promised of our entire village, who is spreading the word of her holiness across The North. She's an elf Keeper, sworn to The Divide and devoted to a faction who despises the very existence of your former affiliations. She also, for a reason you haven't disclosed, *hates* you after she already got over you being a former Knight." She made a *tsk, tsk* sound with her pursed lips. "What a mess you've found yourself in, Kar."

"*Thanks*."

"A mess that can still be resolved, I'm sure," she said, patting his arm before she returned to her wine, the color as pure red as everything she wore.

"I'm not so certain."

She swatted his arm. "You must gather strength. You feared for her a great deal. She was frightened for her own life. I'm sure tension was just high and anything said can be mended." Her eyes sparkled as she met his gaze. "You are quite the catch, Commander Strom. She would be a fool not to see it. Give her the space to see what she's missing, and she'll come around."

Give her space? I can do that.

Even if all I want is to wrap her in my arms, shielding her from everything wishing to harm her. If what she desires is the exact opposite, I will give her the space she needs.

He simply hoped the absence didn't make her realize she was better off without him, or that the separation broke his heart. He'd missed Ser, he truly did, but missing Adelaide felt like an entirely different burden.

As he left the brothel in the early morning hours, he passed by her cabin. The fire inside flickered, silhouetting Sander's form as he sat on the edge of her bed. Perhaps the absence wouldn't make her heart grow fonder of him after all. It would just make space for someone else.

Someone better.

He walked the rest of the way to his bed in silence. Sorrow, Lust, and Jealousy ran rampant in his mind, all eager to tear his soul apart.

The dawn broke and so did his heart.

A LESSON LEARNED ELEVEN YEARS AGO

Any Knight of The Divide knows three things: do not show emotion, do not waver in your convictions, and do not deny your mentors.

Karsten Strom did all three by merely breathing.

He denied his mentors when his youthful infatuation for a local elf turned too sweet. He wavered in his convictions with every stuttered word from his lips that wouldn't right themselves. He showed too many emotions when his brothers-in-arms beat the speech impediment from his lips and the compulsive, obsessive tendencies from his hands.

They couldn't beat the thoughts from his mind, but he still flinched whenever a word came out wrong or a thought lingered for longer than necessary, repeating like dance steps he couldn't stop perfecting. They couldn't rid his heart of its kindness, not fully. They couldn't stop him from calling out for a mother who never came.

He supposed he'd always been a bad Knight after all. Never as dedicated as his peers. Never as willing to fall to cruelty or wipe compassion from his mind. Never as certain about his mentors' motivations as the others were.

Always willing to do what was right, even if it hurt him in the end.

- Unknown

19

A HEART SO COLD

SKALD: ADELAIDE AYLARA

"I hate to admit it, but perhaps you were too cruel to him," Sander said as he helped Adelaide sit up in bed, her chest aching with each strangled gasp for breath her lungs refused to take. "The Commander has clearly been trying to find the truth about what happened to your kin, even if Lefa ordered him otherwise."

She couldn't look him in the eyes as guilt gnawed on her core. Karsten was only compelled to ignore the Jarl's orders due to The Blood Oath and somehow, he *still* managed to disobey the spell by agreeing to Lefa's orders. There was no way for her to tell Sander about any of that though. Not when she couldn't stomach what she'd done to invoke The Blood Oath in the first place.

It was a breech of trust just as deep as the Commander agreeing to Lefa's demands. Even if he didn't mean it, even if he meant to subvert those orders, it didn't matter. She was the one who truly tore apart the timid trust building between them, and she was a hypocrite for it.

This is all further proof we shouldn't be together. That the divide between us is too great.

"I don't say that lightly, Adelaide," Sander murmured, his voice only a touch louder than the crackling of the hearth as his tongue rolled over the elven language she so dearly missed. "It would be easy for me to agree with you. To claim Karsten followed those commands willingly, without duress, and never planned to find your kin. We both know that's not the case."

"How could you possibly know that?" she snapped, her teeth grinding. "He's a *human Knight*, for Odin's sake. I'm just the fool who truly thought his kind could change."

He stared at her, two silver eyes like swirling moons, and she found herself transfixed by their depths. By the Gods, why couldn't she have fallen for those instead of the burning amber gaze she truly desired? Everything would've been so much simpler.

"I sensed the magic of your Blood Oath the moment I saw you and recognized its other half in him the very next morning."

At his confession, her heart only beat louder and angrier in her chest.

"It would be impossible for him to break that tether. Besides, if he even feels a fraction of the affection I've had for you since the moment you rolled away from me on that hilltop, grass all tangled in your hair, even without The Oath he wouldn't be able to deny your request."

Her frantic heart stilled, frozen beneath the weight of such an admission and each of its implications. "You were awake that day?" He nodded. "And you still let me go?"

"Better you fled where I could follow you in your dreams than escape when no one knew of your disappearance, even if Zareen and the Commander screamed at me for it," he explained with a chuckle. "Either way, do you see how it would be to my own benefit if I confirmed your worst fears? If I lied to you and told you Karsten betrayed your trust and was the liar you thought, perhaps there would be space for me in your heart."

He scowled as he brushed a strand of her hair away from her face, caressing her ear, but it didn't have the desired effect either of them expected. There was no tender, natural lean of her head into his hand and no shiver running down her spine. The only reaction that came naturally was the one she tried to suppress.

The urge to run away.

"If I were to be that cruel, nothing would be real." He sighed as he pulled his hand away. "That's what upsets you the most, isn't it? When you question if anything he did was real?" She nodded dumbly in response, unable to form words on her dry lips. "Then know this, dearest Adelaide." He stood to his full height and bent at the waist to plant a soft, lingering kiss on her forehead. "The Oath doesn't compel someone to dream about you every night, and neither does a spirit of lust. *That* is all real for him."

Sander pulled away and refused to meet her gaze as he threw his cloak over his shoulders. He was outside her cabin doors before she could even think of a response, so she allowed it to die on her tongue as she curled back into bed.

WATER AND BLOOD swirled in Adelaide's dreams, coating the walls of her mind and setting her body on fire. What blissful irony—to feel inflamed when surrounded by water.

Ice bit into her skin as she swam to the surface, her fists banging against the frost preventing her from escaping. Her hands were too small and too weak to break through. She couldn't breathe, her lungs burning for air she couldn't have.

So close, yet just out of reach.

Her body betrayed her, swallowing the sea until darkness overcame her.

ADELAIDE WOKE in a cold sweat that dripped down her back and soaked the sheets. She felt disgusting after being smothered by blankets and the heat after the pure cold of her dreams. There was no possible way for her to step back into the bathhouse so soon, so Embla helped her clean up with a bowl of water and a rag. The only thing she wouldn't let her help clean was her raven pendant necklace, the one she still couldn't bear parting with.

Throughout her first day awake, the others visited her in bursts to ensure she was never alone and always protected from whoever drowned her. Absently, she realized her usual guardian was the very man she had pushed away, and everyone else needed to rotate in the task because of her stubbornness.

Not only do I feel like a hypocrite and an angry fool, now I'm also a burden.

Jarl Lefa sent a letter of apology, promising whoever was responsible would be dealt with swiftly. She made no mention of the commands she gave her people to hide the deaths of her kin.

Adelaide tore the letter up.

Njal visited, his laugh contagious and his promise to protect her from any future harm unwavering. His Berserkers would make quick work of whoever was responsible, and she believed him far more than the Jarl.

Zamir traded places with Njal the following day, and they stood outside her door for several minutes to whisper between each other. Her keen elf ears would normally pick up on the chatter, but she was too tired to listen in. She could only make note of their sudden closeness and planned to tease the men about it as soon as she was able to, but she fell asleep and didn't wake for the rest of the witch's rotation as her guard.

Zamir was a companion she looked forward to, but his sister flared Adelaide's temper. She was just another one of the humans who agreed to lie about her kin's fate in the hopes of entrapping her in Rannadal. That was unforgivable.

Ever since the siblings had traded spots in her cabin, the two women started at each other's throats with cruel words and bitter voices. She supposed it was still an improvement from the sharp right hooks they traded in the early days of their acquaintance, but Adelaide was certain that was only due to her injuries.

Zareen scoffed and threw her hands up. "You truly think we agreed to that *willingly*?"

"You agreed, did you not?"

"In front of the Jarl, who *insisted*," she said, her own voice rising. "Neither Karsten nor I had any intention of going through with it. Perhaps Ylwa or Lefa did but, if it came down to it, we hoped to persuade them otherwise."

Adelaide crossed her arms, ignoring how the movement pulled at her sore ribs. "And how long would my kin be rotting in the mountains while you tried convincing them?"

The warrior stopped, her chest heaving as she glared daggers down at her. "We would've prepared them the same as the others in The Dead Fields."

"I trusted you so much I gave you my letter to my clan, Zareen." She swallowed the thick feeling in her throat threatening to choke her just like the bathwater did. "You recognized what it was immediately. I told you how my life is entwined with theirs. Yet, you would let them remain unnamed bodies in a *field*?"

"I wouldn't have waited long." Her thick brows furrowed over her troubled eyes, and all Adelaide could see was the war being waged within their brown depths. The pull between duty and what was right. "Either we'd convince Lefa or we'd get word to you in secret."

She huffed in disbelief only for air to fight its way back into her lungs. A panicked look crossed the other woman's face at her struggle, but Adelaide held a hand up to stave off her concern.

"This was both of your plans? You and the Knight's?" she asked.

"*Karsten's*, yes," she corrected as she folded her arms. "I truly am sorry for you finding out in such a way and that we didn't inform you of Lefa's plans, but it wouldn't have been necessary until your family was found. What would be the purpose of telling you something that would make you distrust our leader and us by extension?"

"Because it would be the truth!"

A harsh laugh ripped from her chest. "The *truth*?" A glint of steel reflected off the firelight as she pulled her jeweled dagger from her hip. "How can you speak of such things when you've hidden this from us since the very first day you started walking around town?" She slammed the dagger through the table, splitting the wood with a resounding crack. "You used my dead father's dagger to *enslave* my friend, Adelaide!"

Despite the pain radiating from her chest, she forced herself to her feet. "You were the one who told me Blood Oaths weren't used for slavery in Midgard!"

"You put The Oath on him before you knew that." At her words, the elf's face drained of blood. "Yes, I'm not a fool." She yanked the blade free and held it between them, jewels glinting in the light and painting the room in shimmering colors. "I remember what you made him promise as you cut his neck. You only swore to seal The Divide, something with a finite end, but he made an oath to find people he's never even met in one of the most dangerous places in the world." She paused to shove the blade back into her sheath. "You also demanded he protect your family *always*—binding him into servitude for as long as anyone in the Aylara Clan lives. There is no expiration on that oath if your family is alive. *That* is slavery."

There was no excuse for it and she knew that, but a million tried to cram their way up her throat, souring her tongue as she choked them back down. The only thing she could do was divert the conversation to the other half of what Jill revealed to her.

"What of your latest order then?" she asked as she folded her arms, mirroring Zareen's fierce stance even as her body screamed in protest. "To keep me here by any means necessary. Wouldn't that also be enslaving me to The Covenant?"

She rolled her eyes. "Yet another thing we had no intentions of pursuing. Besides, you already bound yourself to our cause when you cut yourself on this blade. The Divide isn't fully sealed. You're stuck with us."

Half of a pathetic retort was already out of her mouth by the time Adelaide realized Zareen was already at the door, her fist clasped around the doorknob. "Where are you going?" she asked instead.

"Anywhere else but here." She yanked the door open, paused, and slammed it shut again to sneer at her. "If you didn't already have that oath, I would *gladly* force one upon you to keep you here. Not out of some sick wish to trap you, but because I know what you'll do to yourself if you're alone and discover your family is gone." She stopped, and Adelaide could only stare in shock at the tears lingering in her gaze. "If it prevents you from killing yourself in your family's name, all in some feeble hope of seeing them again in Valhalla, so be it." The door opened again, and Zareen stepped through the threshold before speaking one more time while refusing to look back. "Just so you know, I've been by Karsten's side the entire time he's tirelessly arranging scouts to traverse the spirits' forsaken mountains to find your kin. I've sought them out myself. No matter what Lefa made us swear, our vow to our Promised comes first."

"You may be telling the truth from your perspective," she began with a small, uncertain voice that forced Zareen's tense shoulders to fall. "How am I to know if that's the truth for him? He said nothing of the sort when he was here."

"Did you give him the chance to?" Silence met Zareen's question. "You were willing to listen to me, but not him. Why?"

"You're rather difficult to refuse."

She turned around, the doorknob still in her tight grasp. "You refused to listen because it's easier to see him as a Knight: as someone entirely evil only capable of doing wrong. You chose not to see him as *Karsten*, your friend." She sighed as Adelaide looked away, a blush burning across her cheeks. "You let your fear control you, but it cannot be used as a shield to refuse people entry into the deepest parts of you. Let him know how it hurt you but expect to get the same in return for the words you've said and the things you've done." She started closing the door but paused it again to meet her gaze. "Which, may I add, was of your own volition. We may have been forced into agreeing to cruel plans we would never adhered to, but you spat cruelties and lied to us of your own free will."

The door finally slammed shut.

Zamir stared at her, unblinking, with his chin propped on his hands. His turn for the guard rotation wasn't until the following evening after Zareen's, and it gave Adelaide plenty of time to consider her options.

"You want to *leave*?" he asked, dumbfounded.

She nodded as she rumpled the quilt on her bed between her hands. "I want to try."

He pursed his lips. "I love you to bits, but Lefa would actually kill me." He stopped to think about it. "My sister and Karsten might too. An entire killing party of our friends."

"Lefa is *not* my friend."

He grinned. "Oh, but Karsten is?"

"I didn't say that."

His smile only widened. "You didn't not *not* say it either."

She snapped her fingers in his face. "Back to the point, Zamir," she said in a warning tone as she pulled the quilts back. Already, she could feel the weight on her shoulders and the thrashing in her gut from the task at hand. "I need to know that Kar—*the Knight* has truly been looking for my kin."

"Leaving will accomplish this by—" He froze, seeming to mentally answer his own question before he could even finish asking it. "Adelaide, I don't think that's a good idea," he said as he slowly rose from his seat. "Your Blood Oath is still intact. If you leave, it will sever the oath and the sheer pain of it could kill you."

She rounded him to grab her bag from off the table, her finger lingering on the spot where Zareen's blade left a hole behind. "That's exactly the point. If I leave and the pain is unbearable, I'll return with the knowledge that Karsten is truly looking for my kin. Otherwise, if he were lying, he'd be dead."

He folded his arms as she limped across the room, gathering what few things she had. "What if it doesn't hurt or you can withstand it?"

Adelaide couldn't meet his gaze as she pulled her boots on, her heart rushing through her temples and her lower lip quivering with a mix of fear and sorrow.

"Then this will be the last time any of you see me."

THEY DIDN'T EVEN MAKE it into the escape tunnel.

Adelaide collapsed against a table, barely able to hold herself up as she dropped her bag on the herbalist shop's floor. Sweat coated her entire body, pooling in the hollows of her collarbones and dripping onto the floorboards from her forehead. Her entire body convulsed, and she needed to swallow her vomit to prevent it from coating the herbs beside her.

"Are you finished yet?" Zamir demanded, his hands outstretched to catch her if she fell.

Again.

Between her body still healing from drowning and The Oath clawing in her bloodstream, she felt as though she were having a heart attack and the flu at the same time. Her pointed ears thrummed with the distant sound of her own rushing veins and each of her steps was heavier than the last. She was certain she didn't look any better than Karsten did when his withdrawals reared their ugly head and she'd helped him in that very shop.

Gods, did I do that to him?

She shook her head, the room swimming from the movement. If he was sick from ignoring The Oath, that was his fault. Just as her current pains were her own caused by trying to flee before she finished sealing the torn Divide.

"No," she snapped as she stumbled into the center of the room to kick the rug out of the way. She pointed at the trapdoor as she swayed. "Could you?"

A long-winded sigh slipped from his lips as he grabbed the latch and swung it open. "You're already dead on your feet; can we simply put this matter to rest already and—" He was cut off by Adelaide tumbling headfirst down the trapdoor. "For Odin's fucking sake!"

A few feet down, at the bottom of the tunnel, she groaned as she stared up at her friend who remained on the main floor of the shop. She hated to admit it, but her friends were right. Even without her injuries, there was no possible way Karsten could survive day to day if he wasn't searching for her kin. His heart would've burst out of his chest, and she was forced to concede to The Blood Oath just to stop her own from breaking out of her ribcage.

"Help," she called up to him with a pathetic whine. "*Please.*"

Zamir mumbled under his breath as he climbed the ladder. "Stubborn fucking woman. Stubborn, stupid elf. This is why I court men. Stubborn as a fucking mule. Gods fucking damn it, it's gross down here."

He propped her up, helping her lean against the dirty tunnel walls as the pain slowly ebbed from her body. There was no possible way for her to continue, so all she could do was blink her tears back as she regained some sense of herself and her body that was stolen by defying The Blood Oath riddling her veins.

"Why didn't it feel like this when I ran away?" she complained to the ceiling.

A quiet, disgruntled laugh slipped out of him. "Because even then, you planned on returning, even if you pretended otherwise. The Oath can tell the difference." He sat beside her in the dirt with a huff. "Speaking of which, were you trying to subvert The Oath then? By finding your clan yourself, Karsten could never upkeep the first half of his bargain." Silence met his question. "You're impossible."

"Silence," she grumbled before changing the subject. "We're supposed to figure out who this Wise One is and stop him next, aren't we?" she asked into the tunnel, her voice bouncing back to her. "How can we accomplish that when we've broken each other's trust? When *I've* broken that trust?"

"I haven't broken anything, thank you very much," he huffed. "However, apologies can go a long way. It's at least a place to start."

She nodded as she stretched her leg out, only to stop when she hit something. In the dark tunnel, even her strong elf eyes struggled to see what her boot hit. "What is that?"

Zamir peered over for her since she couldn't move yet, her body still too pained to do anything more than breathe. "Oh, that's the supplies Karsten put down here just in case we needed to evacuate you. There are packs just like it at every tunnel entrance."

Tears welled in her eyes, unbidden and silent.

I've truly made a mess of things, haven't I?

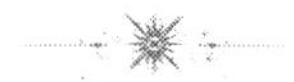

As the days of her recovery ran by, her mind was a blurry fog where nightmares and reality blurred. With the haze of fear lifting and all the water she'd choked on cleared from her lungs, she was seeing more clearly than ever.

All she could do was wait for Karsten's turn in the guard rotation, which would be an inevitability. There were so few people she trusted, eventually no one would be able to guard her besides the very man she longed to make amends with and dreaded seeing all at the same time.

She'd listened to *Jill* of all people about those closest to her in Rannadal. Adelaide should've just turned away from the bathhouse, marched up to the grand hall, and demanded answers. She should've listened to what Karsten had to say and believed him.

He has always believed in me and, the one time the roles were reversed, I failed him miserably.

The guilt ate away at her, gnawing at the bit of her sanity with each passing day he didn't come. Sander, Zamir, Embla, and Njarl were comforting visitors, and she was quick to smooth things over with Zareen the moment she could, but none of them compared to the soothing presence she truly craved.

Gods, did she crave him, but she'd made a mess of everything.

The day she was finally released from Sander's forced recovery period, she gathered the nerve to call for him.

"Are you sure?" Embla asked. "It didn't seem like you two were at peace the last time he visited. I wouldn't want any arguments to hinder your healing."

She sat a little straighter on her bed, hoping she looked more confident than she felt—less injured than she truly was. "Yes, ask if he will see me."

Sander was a remarkable healer, and all traces of her drowning were long gone. The fear remained, however, and the nightmares were endless. She'd drowned in a hot spring and yet, for some reason, she always dreamed of ice and snow.

A hesitant knock on the door made her jump, but she called out for him to enter, regardless of the terror rattling around in her chest.

My fear won't control me.

Karsten stepped over the threshold and stood like a formal soldier in a Jarl's army instead of like a friend. He stayed back, leaving space for a quick escape. "Yes, Keeper?"

The title slammed through her like an insult.

Gods, I truly have ruined things, haven't I?

The corner of his lips quirked. "Not entirely."

Shit, I said that out loud.

"Karsten, I'm so sorry," she rushed to say, standing as he

closed the door behind him. "I shouldn't have accused you of going along with Lefa's plans and not let you explain your side of things. Let alone what I did with The Blood Oath and hiding it. I'm a hypocrite and I can't stand it. You're so dear to me. I should've listened to you. I should've been a better friend to you and—"

She was cut off by his strong arms wrapping around her, pulling her against his chest. Warmth flooded her from head to toe, banishing every dream of ice biting into her mind.

"I missed you," he murmured into her hair.

"Then you should've come back," she said, slapping his chest. "Why didn't you come back?"

He sighed as he pulled away, holding her at arm's length. "A friend recommended that I should give you space, let you figure things out on your own."

While she was grateful for the time with the others to figure out her own mind, she couldn't help but wish he'd been there. She wanted his arms holding her when she cried, not Zamir's. She wanted his comforting words, not Sander's. She wanted his laughter, not Njal's. She wanted his protection, not Zareen's.

Gods, how I want him.

"I wanted—"

You. You. You.

"You wanted what?" he asked.

She let the words she really wanted to say slip from her grasp. "The truth, I suppose. I simply chose to believe in the worst and, for that, I truly am sorry."

Her gaze met the floorboards beneath their feet, fixating on a spot creaking beneath his weight. She supposed she felt the same as that loose board—never fitting in and threatening to give out under the slightest pressure. His boot moved, covering a side of the floor with half his foot while the other half rested on the board beside it to stabilize them both.

"I'm so terribly sorry for enacting The Blood Oath and

never telling you about it," she continued, her heart racing in her chest as the words spilled from her lips in a rush. "I took away your choice to help me and I'm sick for doing so. I was so ashamed I couldn't face you with the truth, but I should've tried."

A gentle touch on her chin brought her face back up to his, forcing their eyes to meet as his thumb rested near her lips. He tilted all of her further under his scrutiny.

"It doesn't matter." Words were already out of her mouth to disagree, but his finger suddenly covering her lip coached her into silence. "The Blood Oath doesn't matter because I would do these things for you regardless. Oath or not, I would search for your family, protect them with my life once found, and keep you safe no matter what." His eyes drifted to where his finger and her lip met, and he struggled to move his touch away as their gazes met once more. "I would do anything for you, Adelaide."

Her breath caught in her throat, her blood hammering against her veins at the softening of his sad smile doing wretched things to her melting heart. "Karsten, you will never know how sorry I am."

"No more apologies from you," he said in a mock-commanding tone. "I should be the one apologizing. I swore to find your family and keep you safe. I've failed miserably on both parts." His hand moved to cup her face. "I'm so sorry."

She shook her head and, to her dismay, his hand fell. "I asked for an impossible feat. None of your scouts know the mountains as well as my kin and I do. Expecting the warriors to happen upon my clan, no matter what their fate, is impractical. If the woods do not wish to give them up, they won't." Her shoulders fell and her heart wavered at once. "As for my safety, I should've been more aware. If I hadn't been so tired, I would never have let someone sneak behind me like that."

He arched a brow. "Then you didn't see the person who did this?"

"Unfortunately, no." She collapsed at the end of her bed, taking up Sander's usual spot when he cast healing spells on her. "If I had, Zareen and Njarl would be hunting them down."

He hummed in thought as he sat on the chair beside the fire like he did when she'd first awakened after drowning. He was too far away and yet somehow still too close. "What do you know about what happened?"

She shrugged as she pulled at the hem of her blouse, worrying the fabric like she did whenever the subject arose. In her mind, it was sudden and somehow stretched on for an eternity, endless and forgotten all at once. It was a dance of ice and heat. She could hardly tell her nightmares from reality.

"I was in the grand hall with all of you," she began. "Then I stopped to speak to Sander by the bonfire. I ran into Jill on the way to the bath, who told me about your deal with Lefa. I went into the bath, and everything went black shortly after."

His expression soured. "Jill knew you'd be there?"

"I suppose so, but I doubt she'd be behind it. She had no idea where I was going when she tracked me down, and it happened so shortly afterwards. Even in my exhaustion, she's so frail I would've fought her off without issue. If she called upon someone else to do it for her, they wouldn't have arrived so swiftly. I was only there long enough to get undressed. My first dunk beneath the waves to wet my hair was when they forced me back under. Again, and again and—"

Her hands were shaking, and she couldn't get them to stop.

Karsten was by her side in an instant, his palms wrapping around hers and holding them tight as he instructed her to breathe.

No. Can't breathe. There's water.

"There's no water. You're not drowning. Breathe."

No. I can't. I can't breathe. Ice. Cold. Then hot.

His brows pinched over his handsome face. "You drowned in a hot spring, but you're not there anymore. You're not drowning, and there is no ice. Breathe."

Breathe?

"Yes, *trust me*—you can breathe."

She took a long, deep breath as her shaking subsided and her palms weakened. All the energy seemed to bleed out of her and into their clasped hands. As he rubbed circles into her wrists, he sent the warmth back into her.

"There you are." His voice was low and soothing as he tucked a strand of hair behind her pointed ear. His gloved finger ran across the tip, making her shiver in ways that had nothing to do with the cold. "Stay with me. Tell me something else about that day."

She shuddered as she closed her eyes to better focus on those brief, soothing touches. They'd be more grounding without the gloves, but she knew why he wore them: to hide his own shaking.

"Sander had a few revelations," she said, recalling her meeting with him by the fire. "He claims the spirits of chaos are simply corrupted spirits of peace."

His movements stopped. *"What?"*

She opened her eyes to take in his shocked expression. "Fifteen spirits on either side of the spectrum is rather odd, isn't it?" His face pinched in confusion. "Think about how opposing they are. It makes sense living things could corrupt those which were once divine. We turn our Muses into sources of pain, Misery. Our Mercy for others can become Mercy for us, Suicide. The Honor of warriors turns into the Vanity that comes with victory. When you Love too much, it can be Obsessive. Our Courage comes from embracing our Fear. A lack of Hope leaves one full of Wrath. With enough Wisdom, it's easy to Deceive others. There can be no Peace when there is Regret. Rest is best by oneself, and yet it can be Lonely. Enough Order can always bring Chaos—as The Codex says. One's Loyalty can turn to Jealousy in the right conditions. A lack of Faith makes one Grieve. A need for Justice can bleed into an urge for Revenge. A world without Joy becomes Sorrow."

"You're forgetting one."

All she could do was stare back into his pained eyes. "Pleasure, something meant to please all, can corrupt into Lust meant only to serve one."

He gnawed on his lip. "The spirit used in my initiation." It bothered her that he still called it that rather than what it truly was—*torture*. "It was already in that state when it entered the chambers."

She nodded. "I thought so."

He peered away to look at the fire, his eyes reflecting the flames. "'*That which is corrupted shall always be purified,*'" he said, reciting a line Adelaide briefly remembered from within The Codex. "Do you think you can—"

"Sander believes so, but I have yet to try." She held her hands up on either side of his head where he continued to kneel on the floor in front of her. If she wished, her knees could trap him in place between her thighs.

A tempting thought.

"You can try with me," he said.

She smiled at him and closed her eyes to focus on the constant thrumming of the spirits lingering around him—never possessing but *always* present. After Lysafell, she could sense them with far greater ease. It unnerved her to think that all his torment was lying so close to the surface, but she was too untrained to see it.

He's also no longer taking the very thing that granted him the ability to sense the spirits on his own. No wonder they dogged him so much when he quit Vow. It's like opening the doors to a feast.

Inside his heart and woven into the fabric of his mind, she could sense the pulse of the spirits tangling themselves into his very being. She plucked at the edges of them, willing them to unravel their grasp.

Jealousy's grip was already loosened. It hid in the back of his head and brought pressure to the base of his spine. She eased the tension away until she could picture the spirit withering in her grasp, the color of a fine merlot wine. The spirit was aged and smelled of earth and berries. It didn't cause him much discomfort, but she still wondered about its presence.

'Spirit of Jealousy, why do you hide?' she asked in her mind, calling towards it and hoping it would answer her.

'I am wrong to feel,' it answered in a child-like tone. *'Wrong to be so jealous and needy of what is not mine. To adore that which I cannot claim. To want what I cannot have. Yet, as wrong as it is, I cannot stop wanting.'*

Her heart ached as its words echoed in her own heart.

What in all the realms could Karsten want that he believes he cannot obtain? Why does it hurt him so?

'Nothing felt in the heart is wrong,' she told it. *'Only what we do with those feelings can be wrong. It's okay to want. It's okay to be envious and wish for more than what you already have. The only thing that matters is what you do with those feelings. Do you hurt others to get what you desire? Or do you simply remain true to your path, trusting that one day you will have all you need?'*

It paused, as though to consider her words. *'I feel like I will rage. I feel like I will cry out to the Gods and ask what I did wrong not to deserve what I desire.'*

'But is that what you want to do?'

Its answer was immediate: *'No.'*

'What is it you wish to do then?' she asked as she felt the spirit shrink in size. *'You were once a spirit of Loyalty. What has changed your path to this?'*

She sensed the spirit peer back at Karsten's heart. *'He was not Loyal to his family nor to his Brotherhood. He wanted a different life so badly, and his anger at not having what others easily obtained soured me.'* Its voice grew even quieter, and she imagined the spirit as a child-aged version of Karsten, huddling in on himself. *'All we wanted was a family who cared. Is that so much to ask for?'*

'Of course not.' She soothed the spirit, her hands running over its aura clinging to Karsten's hair, using the strands like a child would hide behind their mother's dress when meeting someone new. *'But Loyalty means nothing if one is loyal to what is wrong, not what is right. Loyalty for the sake of loyalty is a path to ruin. Allow for you both to be loyal once more. Allow for your hearts to open to the possibilities the Gods have in store for you, not what they've already granted others.'*

It trembled, a being of half-hope and half-fear. *'What if we want so much more than that now? How can we know it will come true?'*

One of her late-night conversations with Karsten flooded her mind.

"I was too broken for romance."

"Are you still too broken for it?"

"Probably. Doesn't stop the wanting though."

'You don't,' she said, much to the spirit's dismay. *'You'll have to find out on your own, but isn't that the exciting part?'*

The spirit shimmered, its color in her mind's eye shifting from a wine red to the purple of a berry pie. It shed its heavy weight and, at the same moment, Karsten sighed in relief.

Jealousy became Loyalty once more, so she moved on.

Faith and Courage were spirits strongly supporting his being, and they greeted her with enthusiasm on her journey through his soul. They supported him, acting as his right and left legs to keep him standing strong. They flickered white and gold, each of them so entwined with each other she could hardly tell where one began and the other ended. They were each so a part of him and each other, she could hardly picture him without his strong Faith or his unwavering Courage.

Sorrow ran rampant in his chest and bolted down to his hands on occasion, making them twitch and shake. She moved her own hands to hover above his, listening to the frantic false breath of the spirit.

'Not good enough. Never good enough. Must try harder. Cannot stop.'

She caressed the spirit as it passed her fingers, but it didn't halt. *'Spirit of Sorrow, will you speak to me?'*

'Always speak. Never stop speaking. Again and again in his head. Running like streams to his heart. Won't stop.'

'Did you come to him as Sorrow, or were you once Joy?'

It rummaged through his heart, tugging at every broken piece it found and rearranging it in patterns she couldn't understand. *'Joy was here on its own, but it was distorted when I arrived. I made it worse. We always make everything worse.'*

She furrowed her brow in concentration. *'A spirit of Joy was here but you, Sorrow, took its place?'*

It shook, and she felt as though it was shaking its astral head. *'No idea where Joy went, but it's sometimes here, sometimes gone. Flows like waves, like waves, like waves—'* It stopped with a growl. *'Can't say it right. Can't ever be right. Always wrong and always broken.'*

'Did Karsten corrupt the spirit of Joy, did you, or was it something else?'

It unfurled itself, reaching towards Karsten's head before curling back up around his heart like a snake. *'His mind plays tricks. Always tricks. Always wrong. Must repeat every bad thing. That called to me long ago, but then I was trapped, trapped, trapped like Joy. It drove Joy mad, and I have fallen the same way.'* It began repeating the same pattern as before, running up to his hands and then back to his chest—always the same way. *'Must be perfect. Cannot fail. Must try again. Not good enough. Never good enough. Must try harder. Cannot stop.'*

Something in Karsten's mind was obsessed with perfection;

something no one could truly obtain. That didn't halt the eagerness with which he sought it or the way he worked himself to the bone. Yet, despite how hard he worked, it was *never* good enough. He always noticed the smallest error, constantly correcting the position of his papers and the order of his reports and quills.

It ate at him, turning his joys into points of pain.

'Not good enough. Never good enough. Must try harder. Cannot stop.'

Sorrow repeated the same phrases again and again, growing more temperamental as it sought something unreachable.

'Your Joy is not on the other side of perfection,' she told it. *'Your Joy resides within you already. That is why it appears and disappears like the tides. It is ever changing, just like you both are. We should allow Sorrow and perfection to have their places, but not at the expense of Joy.'*

'But Sorrow is easy,' it said, and she could feel a bit of its trance-like state waver. *'The risk of being joyful is much more dangerous.'*

She thought of Courage and Faith again. *'Isn't that uncertainty what makes life all the more interesting?'*

It finally slowed its frantic pace, but it continued its usual path. *'What if I am not perfect?'*

'Isn't that the whole point?'

Sorrow considered her words but, in the end, returned to its pacing. It slowed, seeming to take its time with its journey rather than rush to its completion. In doing so, she could sense Joy peek out of the cracks in his heart that it hid within.

She moved on.

By far, the most daunting spirit was that of Lust. It wasn't just an astral sphere residing in his veins. It was practically a living, breathing entity whispering in his ears. She could almost picture it. A vague outline of a person leaning against his shoulder as a constant weight, the ever-present desire he ignored.

'Finally come to play?' Lust asked. *'Oh, how I've longed to play with you.'*

She bit down on her lip, refusing to acknowledge the fact that it sounded exactly like Karsten. It had the same low rumble that ran across her skin and straight to her core, but her own desires didn't matter, so she tried her best to ignore it.

'He was tortured by one of your kind long ago,' she began, moving her hands towards his heart, where she felt it had taken root the deepest. The scars of the previous Lust spirit ached beneath her fingers. *'Did his previous torment corrupt you from your original state of Pleasure?'*

It snickered and answered, *'No.'* Its form weaved between their bodies as though to hinder her reach for his heart. It was possessive of him for reasons she could not fathom. *'I have been Lust for as long as I have existed. Perhaps there was simple Pleasure once, but it was so long ago I cannot recall what it was like to desire anything else.'*

She forced her hands to remain above his chest, even as it punctured straight through the form of the spirit. Every place her skin touched its invisible form, a tingle ran through her.

'If you're so ancient, why have you entertained yourself with Karsten for so long? There must be better prey.'

It twirled around her, breathing down her neck as it slithered closer. *'What better prey could there be than this? Feeding on simple minds with easy feelings isn't nearly as delicious as devouring all that he is and all he craves.'* It paused to move to her other ear. *'You can sense it, can't you: how much he desires and begs? He'd look pretty begging, would he not?'*

She pushed away the swirling images that conjured. *'If you won't return to your natural state, you cannot continue to haunt him. I won't allow it.'*

It hummed as it slid down her arm, sending the hair there

skyward. *'He has been a constant source of desire for me to feed upon. That is not so easily given up.'* It ran its fingers back up her arm, towards her neck, spreading warmth along the way. *'I could feed off your desires if you preferred. You're the only creature I've wanted as much as him. Your desires are just as strong, and just as hidden.'* It sighed as it ran back down her skin. *'Your denial of your passions is born from fear of losing more than you gain. His are born from the belief that what he feels is wrong to want. Tempting him to give in will be far more satisfying.'*

She resisted the urge to ask what exactly Karsten wanted so desperately. *'He won't falter under your influence, so you might as well—'* It sank into the space where her neck and shoulder met, breathing in deep and cutting her off.

'Your desire to know what lustful thoughts reside in his heart is palatable.' It moaned, and she hated the way her body responded to the sound. It sounded so much like Karsten. *'Your desire is so strong. How beautiful it would be to break your will, to have you give in to all your deepest wants.'* Its teeth scraped against her neck. She forced herself to stay still—determined not to bend to its words. *'Imagine yourself, bent back onto this bed as he's trapped between your thighs. You already thought about it on your own, without my help.'*

She gritted her teeth. *'As I told Jealousy, how one feels is valid. What we do about those feelings is all that matters. It's okay to feel desire for an insanely attractive man. What isn't okay is acting upon such thoughts.'*

'Why would that be so bad?' It immediately sensed the answer in her mind. *'Oh, because you believe he would not want you back? Or perhaps that he would, but you'd still leave him regardless? How sad, truly.'* It sank into her skin and wrapped itself around her torso, its face level with her heaving breasts. *'What do feelings matter when Lust is so much more powerful?'*

'I won't hurt him.'

'What if he likes a little pain? What if he'd like to hurt you?' it

questioned as its warm breath ghosted over her nipples beneath her tunic. *'What if all those desires he thinks he cannot share perfectly align with everything your previous lover could never do?'* A blush fought its way onto her cheeks that she refused to acknowledge. *'You cared for him, but he hardly satisfied. What if Karsten could scratch every itch and tend to every kink that's ever run through your mind? I know you want that.'*

She mentally pushed the spirit away, and it returned to its place on Karsten's shoulder, its claws digging into his back. Desperate for help, she tried to recall her mother's lessons about the spirits from when she was young. Lust spirits would take on the qualities of what you desired most and, the longer she spoke to it, the more it looked, felt, and sounded like Karsten. She couldn't let it warp his image into what she desired when she was trying to help him.

'It matters little what I want. What matters is what he wants, what he's comfortable with sharing with me and what he's not.'

It laughed. *'That's the beauty of my prey, Adelaide. He would never admit to what he desires. Watching it break him or watching him give in to it will be satisfying either way.'* It licked its way down his neck, tasting his sweat. *'It's all he thinks about*—you *are all he thinks about,'* it said, latching onto him even harder with its claws. *'Making you moan his name. The gasp from your lips as his latch onto your core to suck from a juice sweeter than any fruit. Every shiver of your skin under his touch, warm and solid against you. The way his cock could—'*

"Enough!"

Karsten's booming voice severed the connection between her and the spirit, causing her eyes to fly open for the first time since she began. She'd been able to feel the spirits move around so effortlessly, she almost forgot she had her eyes closed at all.

Then she saw him, still kneeling before her, and she regretted everything she'd done.

He was heaving, his chest rising and falling rapidly as his hands gripped the sheets on either side of her, pulling her closer by accident. She hovered just above him, their lips only a breath away. Old tears streaked down the sides of his face as his entire body trembled. Warmth radiated from him, and his pupils were blown wide, nearly turning his irises black.

"Thank you," he said in a strained voice. "But that is enough."

She nodded as she slid backwards on the bed, giving him space to gather himself. He remained kneeling and shaking for several minutes, his fingers flexing against the blankets as he tried to compose himself.

Finally, he sighed as the trembling ceased, but his gaze was just as heated as before when their eyes locked again. "I'm feeling lighter than I have in a long time, and yet—" He bit his lip until it bled. "The *wanting* is always there."

"I couldn't heal Lust. I'm sorry."

He shook his head slowly, his gaze never leaving hers. "Don't be, you've done me a great service." He stood on shaking legs, his stance a little awkward as he turned himself away from her. "I'll let you rest. That must've taken a lot out of you, and I have plenty to think about."

She nodded as she watched him leave, Lust snickering once more right before the door shut between them. As she stared after him, she didn't realize how true his words were as she slipped off into sleep.

ADELAIDE AWOKE SEVERAL HOURS LATER, lying in the same position. Her body ached, and her mind swam with every whispered word of the spirits. Whenever she was near them, her scarred eye pained her, but Karsten had left hours before, and the discomfort in her marred skin continued to linger beneath the surface.

The only thing she could do was follow that pain as it tugged her out of her cabin. Two of Njarl's Berserkers, Thora and Kare, were stationed at her door. They insisted on following her, so they drifted through the night together like a pack of lost dogs searching for a home.

Her magic and the hurt radiating from her eye led her outside Rannadal's gates and past the training fields. It worsened with each step, but never grew to a point where it was unbearable like defying The Blood Oath was, so she continued even when her gut warned her that she was stepping towards something dangerous and ancient.

She stopped at the edge of the lake, the altar she'd made at Karsten's suggestion lying in wait by her feet. It was dusty and windswept from the elements, but it still forced a small smile onto her lips as she asked the Berserkers to give her a moment in peace.

"Spirit of Sorrow," she greeted when she recognized its presence lingering at the altar. "You're not Karsten's, but you're not exactly the one I defeated in The Divide. What are you?"

It shimmered before her, hovering like a sad blue ghost above the lake that sent fear churning in her chest. *'I was both and all at once, but also neither. All Sorrows come from me. I am their birth and their death,'* it explained. *'I was something before the mountains ruptured, but I cannot remember what. I remember haunting you here, dying by an axe, and being reborn as a monster beneath the earth. There was darkness again, and then a light.'*

"A light?" she asked.

'Yes, the light of possibility compelling me to follow you,' it whispered before her and all around her at once, dancing in the wind and through the trees. *'I miss what I once was, even though I have forgotten it. There are pieces of me in places I cannot reach.'*

"When you were a monster underground, how did you end up that way?"

A guttural noise ripped from it, and its form raged at the reminder of how wrong it was made to be by cruel hands. *'Someone who claims to be wise but lacks all compassion. They struck an agreement with us, and we are made to pay the price for not knowing how we would be transformed by their lies.'* Its voice cracked at that last word. *'I'm made and unmade in the wrong image: never what I am meant to be.'*

She swallowed the lump in her throat at its lamenting cries. "Do you recall what you did before all of this happened? What your purpose was?"

'All I remember is The Divide between worlds and its gates to the lands of spirits and the realm of the elves. Not where they are, but how they felt. How they needed to be protected at all costs.' It paused to twirl closer. *'Was that my purpose? To be a guardian at the gates?'*

"In your physical form, you were doing the opposite. Rather than guarding the entrances from stray spirits leaving or souls slipping within, you were ushering the spirits to escape and preventing us from healing the mountains," she explained as she held a hand towards it, its astral palm slipping around her fingers. "That is not your fault, Sorrow. The Wise One corrupted you to do their bidding, turning your joy for protecting your home into sorrow for losing it. They corrupted you by forcing you to go against your very nature, but you have a choice now to return to what you know is right."

'Yes.' It hummed as it tightened its hold on her hand before slipping away. *'I was Joy not long ago. I don't remember what it's like to feel that, but I want to.'*

Its shimmering blue shape melted, pooling into the lake, before it flowed back into the air in shades of the sunrise. A dawn burning bright through the night as its light winked back to life.

It shot off to the mountains, gleeful laughter trailing behind as it headed towards home.

BACK IN HER CABIN, Adelaide knew she should've focused on everything she'd learned about the spirits over the week since they'd discovered the possessed clerk. She should've wondered at all the magic swelling inside her, eager to heal more spirits turned against their true nature. Instead, all she could think about was whether Lust was being honest.

Does he truly want me?

Despite their past, could he possibly want her regardless of everything standing in their way? Would he accept having her only to need to let her go when she returned to The Divide? What about her kin? What would they think if they discovered her feelings for a *human*? Did any of that even matter?

She paced around her room, her nail bitten between her teeth. Her kin could be long dead. Was she willing to waste the rest of her life waiting for people who would never come? She loved them and would keep their pact to find each other in the realms of the dead, but could she live without them? Could she choose to forgo all her traditions to live what little life remained for her with Karsten by her side?

What if her family was found? Would they truly cast her aside when they found out she'd come to adore so many of their enemies? That she desired the body and heart of a former Knight? They'd be ashamed of her—*but did that matter?*

They would love her regardless. They might frown at the match, but would they cast her aside? Would they bar her entry back to the mountains as was their duty? Tradition dictated they did so, but she couldn't picture her mother ever doing such a thing to any of her children.

Besides all of that, perhaps her feelings were nothing but a passing curiosity. Maybe she just needed one night to satisfy her and it wouldn't matter. She'd only have to give up her home if she wished to stay with him and have more than just one night.

But by the Gods, do I want more than one night.

She desired every morning and moment by his side, tasting his body and traversing his heart in equal measure. Did her desires really matter at all? Lust claimed all Karsten could think about was her, but did he think only of her body? He desired an elf before in his youth. Was that all he felt? Was she simply some kink to mark off a checklist?

No, I can't see that being the truth.

He desired her and she desired him. Whether or not he wanted a relationship like she did was irrelevant in matters of the flesh. They could figure out the rest of what their relationship would be when the fate of her kin was discovered.

For now, I cannot hold back any longer. He's out there somewhere, aching after all the thoughts Lust brought forth, and I believe it's time for some relief for us both.

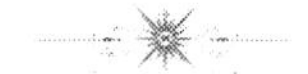

ADELAIDE SLIPPED OUT of her window the same way she did the first day she'd met Karsten, ensuring the Berserkers didn't follow. That night, she searched all of Rannadal but couldn't find which dark corner Karsten had sequestered himself to.

Night lay thick over the town, obscuring the darkest corners from even her attuned vision. She walked the few lit paths remaining in town, and found herself in the easternmost corner, far from the grand hall, chapel, and bathhouse. There were only a few buildings close to the cliff the town was butted up against, but lanterns still flickered in some of the windows.

At the end of the last path in town she'd yet to venture through, a large stone building appeared carved out of the cliffs themselves. Vines wrapped around iron fencing surrounding a dead garden in its front and nearly every window was still lit. Atop the double doors, the name Lilly's Den was scrawled in white paint, the last letter ending in the painting of a flower.

Curious, she peeked inside the nearest window.

Within the den, the night had barely begun. People mulled about, usually attended to by a lavishly dressed companion. Crimson velvet cascaded from the ceiling, hugging the walls as they dripped towards the floors. Chaises were full of patrons with full tankards and full bellies who still, somehow, *hungered*. She sensed lust spirits weaving themselves about, eagerly feeding on everyone inside.

Including one curly blond sitting at the bar.

A woman was draped over his side, her laughter booming to the ceilings as her fingers played in the hair at the nape of his neck.

Jealousy curdled in her core, even when she knew she had no right to be. He wasn't hers, even if she wished he was. Her words from earlier that day rang in her ears.

'Nothing felt in the heart is wrong. Only what we do with those feelings can be wrong. It's okay to want.'

She almost laughed.

Oh, how easily I said those words, but what a fool I was. It seems now he's not too broken for a dalliance after all—it's just not with me.

She peeled herself away from the window and meandered down the road she'd previously taken. It wasn't fair to make her jealousy his problem. He deserved his own happiness, even if it wasn't with her.

The tavern's barkeep welcomed her back with a sad smile.

AN EXCERPT FROM THE CODEX

In the dawn of all that is holy, Olena formed the world in the juxtaposed essence of light and shadow. While the world was fresh, she left the offering of Order to her children, all living creatures with conscious minds and compassionate hearts.

Olena made a Vow: that which is corrupted shall always be purified.

Olena made a Divine Promise: that her prophecy foretold a savior rectifying the realm.

Olena made a Blood Oath: that enough Order can always bring Chaos.

Olena made a Covenant: that her army of the righteous would ride again.

Olena gave Her Word: that she would never abandon those who hold the light.

- *Stanzas* 14 - 21

20

RECTIFY

SKALD: KARSTEN STROM

Karsten paced his room, curls tightly tangled in his hands as he pulled roughly at the locks in both fists to keep his hands from straying *elsewhere.*

He needed relief from everything Adelaide conjured in his mind by toying with Lust. She'd been so close—*too close*—and yet not close enough. He wanted to kiss her, to let her know once and for all everything she made him feel. He wished to share all his desires to know her heart and her body, but he was a coward.

'Wasn't she glorious? Chest heaving and eyes blown wide in desire. She was so fun to play with,' Lust said with a delighted giggle.

"Don't you dare speak to her again," he snapped aloud.

'Why? Don't tell me you're embarrassed.'

He ignored that there was indeed a blush burning across his cheeks as he said, "She doesn't deserve your brand of torture."

'What if I told you she enjoyed it—that it wasn't torture at all?'

"Silence."

'What if I told you she wished for your flesh just as much?'

"Please, stop."

'What if her desires are even greater than yours?'

He shrugged off his cloak in frustration and threw it across the room so he could collapse in bed, his body aching in every single way. Without the protective runes stitched into the fabric, Lust's voice grew louder. It wrapped around him as he lay back, thinking on the whispered, hoarse words it had murmured to Adelaide.

'Making you moan his name. The gasp from your lips as his latch onto your core to suck from a juice sweeter than any fruit. Every shiver of your skin under his touch, warm and solid against you. The way his cock could—'

He shivered as his finger inched towards the waistband of his trousers. Lust encouraged him, its voice sounding more and more like Adelaide's as the moments ticked by. It haunted him, whispering in his ear.

The thought of her cradled behind him, running her hands through his hair as she eagerly waited for the show he'd put on for her rushed through his mind. He could partially feel her fingers tangled in his hair, gripping hard as his neck strained back so he had to look at her as his hand finally freed his cock.

Her touch hovered just above his skin, sending shivers across him as she trailed down his chest as though to replace his hand with hers. Her breath, sweetly scented by berries and mead, ghosted over his lips as she reached to where he ached most.

He sat bolt upright, sweating with the effort to pull away from the musings Lust taunted him with.

'Give in. Give in. Give in.'

He marched towards the half-frozen lake and dove straight in.

WITH HIS BLOOD forcibly cooled by the brisk ice bath, Karsten dragged himself beside the nearest fire to thaw before he finished his duties for the day. He had a rare evening available, and his thoughts continued to return to the woman who captivated him.

He couldn't go to Zamir or Zareen, two of his only friends, on matters of the heart. Zamir would simply push him towards Adelaide at any given chance because he thought it was funny. On the other hand, Zareen would make sure they were never alone together for the sake of ensuring Adelaide's name remained unscathed.

Gods, he could only imagine what would happen if anyone outside of their friends knew how he felt about her and, perhaps, how she felt about him.

The most divine of Olena's people succumbing to her lust for a disgraced former Knight and leader The Covenant's holy army? The idea was laughable but, if he were ever lucky enough for her to return his affection, it could never be known. Doubt would be thrown on the legitimacy of her heavenly nature if she gave into pleasures of the flesh so publicly.

He wasn't worth the trouble.

But if we were kept a secret—

If their romantic entanglements were kept under lock and key, perhaps they'd have a chance to see how they truly felt. Maybe he would be allowed the privilege of kissing her, if only once.

Goddess, that is all I ask.

It would never be enough. Being with her physically for one

night wouldn't satisfy his desire for her burning brighter with each day. Being her friend and confidant, he could gladly live with even as he wished for more. But to kiss her once and simply know what she felt like against him, that would give him some sort of peace.

One kiss. It wouldn't be enough when he wished to wake beside her every morning and hold her every night, but they couldn't afford such luxuries. In another life, realm, or land there may have been a chance for more, but they didn't reside there.

I still have the honor of calling her a friend. I should not ask for more.

But one kiss, perhaps he could ask for that and that alone.

He needed to see Serenade. If he could not seek out his other friends on the matter, he needed to speak to the only other soul in all the realm who fully knew how he felt. She was right about giving Adelaide space, was she not?

She'll know what to do.

The bustle of Lilly's Den roared in his ears as he pushed open the doors. A scantily dressed man at the door plastered on a wide grin for him, making Karsten blush and stammer out Serenade's name before he hid at the bar to wait for her.

Her hand in his hair was the only warning of her presence before she slid beside him, boxing him between the bar. "Another visit so soon?" she laughed as she massaged the base of his neck, pulling a low groan from his lips. "Save those noises for your beloved, Kar."

He blushed again as he peeked at her from the corner of his eyes. She looked ravishing in deep green, but all he could envision was the color of Adelaide's eyes.

"You truly are smitten by her, aren't you?" she wondered, humming as she squeezed in between his spot at the counter and the patron next to them. "It's a fine look on you."

"Your advice worked last time, so I fear I'm seeking your wisdom once more."

She giggled as she grabbed a drink from the barkeep. "In which case, my insight into the female mind must be heralded. From here on out, you must sing my praises to all the town." She clinked her wine glass with his mead horn. "Here's to all the customers your sweet words shall bring me."

He downed what little remained of his drink and quickly bought another to strengthen his nerves. "I'm sure you understand that, for a million reasons, I cannot be with her."

She pouted as she allowed her glass to be refilled. "That would be a tricky entanglement to navigate, but you've done far more impossible things. If anyone could accomplish it, that would be you." She pinched his shoulder, relieving some of the tense nerves in his back. "Just kiss her and tell her how you feel already. If she doesn't feel the same, you can move on in peace." She winked as she sauntered away, her hips swaying with every step. "If she does feel the same, that's when all the fun really begins."

WHAT LITTLE HELP SHE WAS.

In the late hours of the night, his irritation at Serenade's short words grew. He'd sought advice on how to proceed with his feelings and, while he understood she was at work, he would have willingly paid for more of her time if she'd simply give him *real* advice.

He stayed at Lilly's Den to sulk and drink, catching her eye every so often in hopes that she'd divulge more. She never did, even when they were within reach of each other.

"Just kiss her already."

That was her only repeated piece of so-called advice.

He huffed in annoyance as he drifted towards his cabin. The fires were already dimmed so late into the evening, and most of the townsfolk were already retired. Only the tavern, brothel, and barracks remained active. Most patrons of Lilly's were already neatly tucked into beds, the warriors on guard already made their final rotations, and most drunks were passed out or puking.

Except for whichever loitering drunkard blocked his path.

He sobered at the sight of the cloaked figure stumbling through town. Whomever it was, he couldn't risk them tripping down the hills or falling into the wrong sorts.

"I think you've had enough to drink," he admonished as he yanked the tankard of mostly spilled mead from their hands. "Off to bed with you."

"Y-you can't tell me w-what to do-o," a familiar voice stuttered out.

He ripped off their hood, the scent of lavender and winter slamming into him as he took in her disheveled appearance. Her wavy white hair stood at all ends and her eyes were hardly open as she glared up at him.

Gods, she's still so beautiful.

"Adelaide," he said in surprise, his cheeks and blood heating once more as he took in her face glowing beneath the moon. "What are you doing?"

She snorted. "Me? What are *you* do-in?" She poked him in the chest. "Show me all those damn t-things and then gone to *her.*"

He arched a brow in confusion as he reached into his cloak's inner pockets. He always kept a few remedies the herbalist made on hand, just in case his men needed to sober quickly for battle. He missed the herbalist, Hallie, wherever she'd disappeared to before The Divide fell, and just hoped she hadn't fallen victim to it.

"Drink this, but try not to taste it," he ordered. She took it like a shot without argument but still blanched at the brazen flavor. "Now, smell this."

She stuck her nose into the remedy pouch and gagged as the scent invaded her senses. She sputtered as she rubbed her nose, her lips screwing into a deep frown. A slight sparkle shimmered around her as the spell woven into the elixir worked its way through her. It lit up her eyes until they looked like stars bathed in the emerald lights of the aurora.

Those same eyes glared daggers at him as soon as the remedy worked, and she huffed as she spun on her heels to walk away.

"Adelaide." When she didn't stop, he followed her. His legs were far longer than hers, so he caught up quickly. "After everything that's happened today, I need to speak with you."

She held up a hand without looking back at him. "I think your actions speak louder."

"What in the realms are you doing?" He stopped, his words forcing her to freeze a few paces ahead of him. "I thought we were okay. If you still hold issue with my orders from the Jarl, I will continue to apologize, but you need to tell me what's wrong first."

She sighed, her shoulders falling from their tense place by her pointed ears as she finally turned to look at him. Her eyes were distant and closed off, and she held herself a little smaller, as though she were afraid.

"You're right, Karsten. I'm being unfair to you." She dipped her chin, staring at the ground instead of at him, and he wished for nothing more than to hold her face in his hands so he could meet her gaze again. "I'm sorry."

He shook his head as he advanced on her, his frustration, adoration, and desire for her all mixing into one unyielding emotion he had no name for. There was no single word to describe how he felt in her presence, but he sought that feeling out like a man obsessed.

"What have I done wrong?" he asked, his voice as gentle as the finger he used to tilt her chin so she had to look up at him. His gloved hand trembled and he just hoped she didn't notice it shaking against her skin.

She forced a smile, but it didn't reach her eyes. "Nothing. I apologize. Let's just ignore my drunken display and turn in for the night." She tried to step away, but he gripped her arm to keep her close.

Perhaps I am a man obsessed, but I cannot let her go.

"Adelaide, please just be honest with me."

Whatever he said seemed to break the floodgates of everything she was holding back. Her tempting lips turned into a scowl, and her emerald eyes narrowed into slits.

"You truly want to speak of *honesty*," she snapped, her voice full of venom even as she was careful not to speak too loudly. After all, the path they were on was lined on both sides by homes full of sleeping townsfolk. "Then be honest with me for once."

He threw his hands into the air, his ire racing under his skin to play with the desire for her only growing in the face of her anger. Perhaps he was demented for finding her so stunning while she seethed at him, her hair still wild and the scent of mead still heavy on her breath. He hardly cared about what made sense or what was sane when he was around her.

"What have I not been forthcoming about?" he demanded, his tone just as biting. "The orders? I already apologized and you seemed to accept it considering you tried to help heal my mind just afterwards." He froze. "Unless that was just to crawl inside my head, hoping to find something to use against me."

She balked. "I would never do such a thing."

"Then what else have I hidden from you?"

Her eyes searched his face in silence and, in that quiet, he moved to walk away. She had nothing except baseless accusations that stung his heart. He needed to leave before he made a fool of himself.

"You didn't tell me about Vow."

He froze.

"I knew about an addiction, but you didn't tell me everything. You hid how crucial it was to the Brotherhood and to your own life."

He heard her take a tentative step towards him.

"You didn't tell me what it meant to quit. You didn't tell me it would kill you either way." Her voice was barely above a whisper then, drifting into the cool night air and barely brushing his skin.

When he turned back to her, all he could see was the fear in her eyes as she ground her teeth together in frustration. "If you knew back then, would you have asked me to start taking it again?"

She paled, but the frustration in her expression didn't lessen. "I don't know, but that's not the point."

"That is *exactly* the point." He stepped back to her, hovering in her orbit like a star caught in the rotation of forces beyond its control. "I already told you: I would do anything for you. I'd disregard any command from the Jarl or the Gods themselves. Forsake any promise I made to myself to sever ties with the Brotherhood." He swallowed hard, suddenly nervous under her piercing gaze as his deepest truths spilled unbidden from his lips. "You are the only force in this realm who could cause me to take that drug again, and I couldn't risk that."

She stared at him, wide-eyed and heaving, as the words settled between them. Words stumbled across her lips, never fully forming a real response. "I-I didn't think. I don't—"

He held a finger up to stop her, and it hovered temptingly close to her mouth. "As for it killing me, I'm still alive, am I not?"

"But Karsten—"

"I am now the longest living person to ever cut off Vow completely, and I intend to be the first to live a *long* life without it." He hated the plea he could hear in his own voice, the prayer on his tongue to not ask him to go back to the man he used to be. A man she would hate. "I thought you of all people would wish for me to have no ties to them. This is how I accomplish that, and I'd like your support on the matter."

"Of course I support you, but I wish you'd told me." She closed her eyes. "Now I understand why you couldn't."

He thought that was the end of it, that perhaps she was merely upset about finding one of his deceptions so shortly after discovering another. When her first real impression of him had been discovering he had concealed his former ties to the Knights, he couldn't blame her for being sensitive to even the smallest piece of concealed information or fib falling from his tongue. But that was all he'd hidden. Everything else about him was an open book, ready for her to read if she wished.

Except for his feelings for her, of course. When she opened her eyes again, there was still betrayal playing in the depths of the green seas he wished to drown in.

"There's more bothering you. I can tell." He brushed a strand of hair behind her ear, but, when he reached the spot where his finger would normally caress the tip of her ear, she stepped out of reach. The strand landed right back on the side of her face.

She wrapped her arms around herself. "It's nothing to concern yourself with."

He reached out for her again but she stepped away once more. "If something troubles you, I want to help."

"Why would that be?" she groaned in frustration to the skies. "Because we're *friends*?"

His heart shook in his chest. "I certainly thought we were trying to be."

Her eyes softened, but her scowl remained in place. "Friends don't hear their companion's voice on a spirit of Lust, now do they?"

Oh, Goddess. She knows. She heard every word of the spirit. Of course she'd be upset. She thinks all I see in her is some sick fantasy.

"Adelaide, I'm—"

"I misunderstood." She cut him off as he stood silent and slack-jawed at her rambling words. "When Lust spoke in your voice to me, I thought it reflected your own experiences with the spirit. I thought it meant that, while I was hearing you, you might be hearing me." She swallowed hard. "Clearly, I was mistaken."

He followed her gaze back up the road he'd come from, towards Lilly's Den. He pinched the bridge of his nose, frustration bubbling beneath the surface and setting his skin aflame.

She saw me with Ser and thought I was seeking release from all the spirit conjured with someone else. As if I could look at anyone else when she's right there. When she's all I could ever desire.

"After healing your spirit of Jealousy, it's almost funny that I should succumb to my own without the influence of a spirit. I shouldn't have said anything and just let it be, but I suppose I got my hopes up. Having them dashed so quickly surprised me, but I shouldn't have directed my anger at you. You can desire whomever you like. It's none of my business."

None of her business?

The rest of her words flowed through him in a rush, and the realization dawned on him slowly, as though he couldn't comprehend it.

She wants me?

Adelaide heard my voice moan in her ears, whispering filth, and she still wants me? She went to find me and was jealous when she discovered me with Serenade. She got drunk and upset because she thought there was any realm in which I would reject her.

She wants me, despite everything?

"Like I said," she continued, a blush staining her cheeks and making her even more beautiful in the moonlight, "who you wish to spend your time with is not up to me. Let's forget I ever said anything and return to—"

Goddess, forgive me.

Karsten grabbed her by the arm and yanked her off the path. In the dark alley between homes, he pinned her against the nearest wall and crashed his lips against hers.

He couldn't take it anymore. The madness of questioning whether he deserved her or if they could be together at all. He didn't care. He'd prayed to Olena for just one kiss and, if that was the only kiss he'd ever be granted, he would pour everything he had into it.

She gasped against him, and he used the opportunity to slip inside to taste the mead on her tongue. Her mouth was like silk against his, and he yearned to feel every crack on the surface of her lips and the way every drink or dessert tasted on her tongue.

It ended far too quickly as he panted for air. He gulped as he searched her face, wishing to know whatever was in her heart. Her face was flushed, and her lips plump from his attention. For a moment, she simply stared and he questioned if he'd made a mistake.

Then, her lips met his once more.

She gathered the front of his cloak in her hands to pull him flush against her. He groaned when his chest met hers, her hardened nipples rubbing against him through the thin fabric of their tunics. Her cold hands moved up his neck, sending goosebumps across his flesh, until her fingers snaked into his hair to angle him deeper into the kiss.

He could hardly breathe, but he dared not pull away again for fear of breaking whatever spell pulled them together. All he could feel was her. All he could taste was her. All he wanted was her, and he silently thanked his Goddess that Adelaide seemed to feel the same.

Her breath hitched against his lips, and it was only then that he realized his hands moved with a mind of their own to press to her backside. He almost pulled back to apologize, but she arched so her ass was flush with his palms and he gripped her there hard, pulling her firmly against him.

She moaned, and the sound was like music to his ears: a sound no spirit could replicate no matter how hard they tried. His cock strained in his trousers as he trapped her between the wall and him. With the next sound she made, he knew she could feel his hard member pressed between them.

Adelaide was the one to pull away first, heaving as she leaned her forehead against his. He stole her lips another time, but kept it as gentle as his beating heart and pulsing lower half would allow.

"We should," she began before stopping for a moment to continue choking down air. "Talk more before we get too carried away."

He nuzzled against the side of her face, his stubble dragging across her skin and making her shiver as his breath danced over her neck. "Yes, we wouldn't want to move too fast."

She laughed, but the movement rocked her body against him and pulled a low groan from his lips. She flashed him the most beautiful smile with her cheeks all flushed and her hair even more tangled than before. "Sorry." She kissed his cheek, her lips lingering on his skin to soak in the taste of him. "I don't mean to tease, but we've both been drinking and there's much to discuss."

He sighed as he cupped her face in his gloved hands. She tilted into his touch, seeming to savor the feeling even if it was obstructed. "I know you're right, but my heart doesn't want to let you go in case this is all a dream."

"Uhm, it's your heart that's keeping you pinned against me

then?" she asked as she rolled her hips, brushing her clothed core against his length. A choked noise was ripped from the back of his throat. "Who knew you were so *hard*-hearted, Commander Strom?"

He chuckled as he leaned forward to nip at the tip of her ear in retribution. She gasped, and he felt her shake beneath him. "Keeper Aylara, I wouldn't recommend defying your Commander. You never know what consequences you may face."

"Whatever they are," she began with a wide smile, "I can't wait for the ramifications."

LEAVING ADELAIDE WAS NEARLY IMPOSSIBLE.

He managed it with great effort and a lot of awkward shifting of his lower half on his way back to his lonely bed, but that didn't mean she truly left him. For even in his dreams, he saw her pressed back against the wall. In the morning, he woke sweating and aching.

Goddess, please don't let it all have been a dream.

Jarl Lefa called them into the great hall that morning and, as soon as their eyes met, he knew it was incredibly real. They shared small glances across the central table as they waited for the others to arrive but, through some sheer miracle, managed to keep their hands to themselves.

'Already envisioning all the ways you can take her?' Lust asked.

Silence, we're only going to talk.

For once, the spirits quieted enough for him to see and think clearly, to actually enjoy every feeling she made bloom in his chest without being tainted by every unseemly whisper of the spirits in his mind.

I will never differ from Serenade's advice ever again.

"Would you like to start our game again?" Adelaide asked as she leaned against the table, a blush burning her cheeks down to her neck. "I have a question I'd like to ask."

He hummed in thought as he stepped a little closer, his heart beating fast from both desire and the fear that anyone could open the grand hall's doors to discover them. They were playing with fire, risking being found like that, but he couldn't resist her even if he tried. "I suppose I'll allow it," he said as he tucked the same rebellious strand of hair behind her ear and allowed his touch to linger, caressing the soft skin of her neck.

"How badly do you want to kiss me again?"

He wet his lips as his gaze drifted to her mouth, all sinfully red and begging for his attention. "More than I want to breathe," he answered as he stepped between her legs, forcing her to sit on the table to make space for him. Her legs wrapped around his waist like she was made to fit there. "How long have you wanted me to do this?" His lips lightly caressed hers, barely leaving enough room for her to answer.

"Longer than I should admit," she breathed against his mouth before her lips claimed his once more, moans of relief falling from them both as they gave into the mounting tension rippling between them for months.

Adelaide was sunshine in the winter, a reprieve from the darkness threatening to swallow him whole. She wound her hands into his hair, tangling into his curls like they belonged to her as he claimed her waist in his firm grasp. Unworthy hands skimmed her hips, digging into the soft flesh with all his pent-up yearning, and it caused a whimper of delight to fall from her.

He eagerly trailed kisses along her jaw, his heavy-lidded eyes drinking in the sight of her withering in his grasp as his palm traveled to her breast. His touch was featherlight, but her nipple puckered beneath the thin fabric anyways. She was so responsive; it only stroked the heat in his blood further until it was roaring in his ears.

"I really did intend on talking this morning," she breathed against his mouth. "There's something I need to tell—" She was cut off as he sucked on the soft skin of her neck, careful to leave no evidence of his lips behind before he soothed the spot with his tongue. "*Karsten,*" she sighed, unable to continue with whatever she tried to say before.

He'd never heard his name sound so sweet, and he wished for nothing more than to hear it chanted in her breathy voice as he brought them both relief.

"How far does this blush go?" he wondered as he followed the pretty pink shade burning down her neck to the collar of her tunic. He arched a brow at her, seeking permission.

A smirk tugged on her lips, plump from their kisses, as she continued gasping for breath. Her chest heaved, drawing his attention to the trail of pink he wished to follow.

"Find out," she said as she leaned back, granting him further access to her body.

He didn't wait for any further invitation, and was quick to sink his mouth and teeth back on her skin as his hands tugged the tunic down. Her breasts nearly spilled out, exposing more of her than he'd ever had the privilege of seeing. Lavender and snow invaded his mind, intoxicating him more than any mead or sip of Vow ever could. He would drown in it, if she would let him.

Something crashed in the grand hall, ripping them apart.

They stared at each other, wide-eyed and heaving for breath, before they scanned the room, fear the only thing preventing him from claiming her lips or body again. Their gazes fell on a mouse as it scurried around the tables, running away from a broom it knocked over.

A nervous laugh fell from her lips as she fixed her tunic and lowered herself from the table. "Probably for the best. The others should be here soon," she said, her tone airy from her still-heaving chest as she struggled to breathe.

She drowned not long ago. I should've been gentler.

"Adelaide," he began, but suddenly he was lost for words as her eyes met his again. He'd meant to apologize if he overexerted her still healing body and see if she was okay, but nothing came out. All he could do was stare, lost in emerald seas he would gladly succumb to. There was no way to describe the feeling burning in his chest or the desire thrumming in his veins, but he needed to try. "I-I think I'm—"

Whatever he was going to say was cut off by the grand hall doors flying open. Jarl Lefa strode inside from the town rather than her chambers in the back of the hall like she normally would. Ylwa, Zareen, and Zamir were on her tail, their expressions full of dread freezing the warmth Adelaide previously engrained into his skin. Any lingering thoughts of her lips vanished with their arrival, which brought tense apprehension into the hall.

"Come with us to the chapel, quickly," Lefa demanded as she rushed out of the opposing door leading back outside.

He shared a brief, worried glance with Adelaide before they hurried to catch up with the others. They were all out of breath by the time they entered the chapel's walls, but that didn't stop the elf from rounding on the Jarl.

"What's going on?" she demanded as Lefa rushed to the center of the chapel.

"The elves we spotted on the border are advancing," Lefa explained. "We don't believe them to be your kin. They may very well be the ones who destroyed The Divide."

Karsten unsheathed his axe, ensuring it was ready if it was needed, as they joined Lefa.

"They could also be refugees seeking aid or embassies from New Alfheim wanting answers for the destruction. We can't judge so fast," Adelaide said.

Zareen shook her head. "We understand they're your people, but we cannot risk your life on a hunch. Until we know of their full intentions, we must hide you."

Lefa lifted the corner of a rug on the pulpit to reveal a hidden cellar. It belonged to the same tunnel system beneath town that's other entrance remained in the herbalist shop.

"Get in," the Jarl ordered.

Zamir marched to the cellar door and pushed it a bit more closed. "I don't believe we need to take such measures just yet." A concerned look passed between him and Adelaide, but Karsten didn't understand what it could mean.

Ylwa wrung her hands together nervously as she paced by the doors. "Our scouts said they come bearing arms. We must take every precaution."

The hair on his arms stood straight. "Why was I not informed of a possible attack?"

"We sent you and Adelaide to the grand hall to ensure she was protected in the center of town. If we told either of you, you both would've run straight into danger. We cannot afford that," Zareen explained as she drew her sword.

"I am the Commander of this army, am I not? I should be with my men."

Adelaide's expression was blank as she stood, almost timid, in front of the cellar doors. Unwilling to enter or to leave, so she remained stagnant just like he did. He wished to protect her above all else, but he wasn't sure what to do. Would staying by her side, guarding her, be better? Or would she be safer if he let her go alone so he could grant her enough time to flee?

"How are they moving?" Her words were so soft they were almost missed.

"Scouts say they're using non-lethal attacks on our people for now, but their patience seems to be wearing thin as they grow closer to the gates. They'll disappear for a moment from their view, and then strike again from seemingly nowhere," Zareen explained.

Adelaide stared at the cellar door before stumbling away from the pulpit. Karsten gripped her arm to keep her steady, but she trembled under his grasp.

"What is it?" he asked, hating to see the fear in her eyes, but it was mixed with something he almost couldn't name.

Hope?

The doors burst open, and he moved his weapon to the sound on instinct, keeping the blade between Adelaide and the intruders. All it would take was one command from his lips, and they would fall before they ever reached her. Between his blade, Zareen's, Zamir's magic, and Lefa's own prowess, they could cut down whatever foe dared to intrude on their home.

At the threshold, three figures stood back lit by the sun.

He nearly called everyone to arms but a small, choked sound from beside him forced him to pause. He peered at Adelaide, whose emerald gaze filled with tears. Down the chapel's nave, the figures took one more step inside before freezing altogether. In doing so, he could finally see them. They were all elves, two women and one man.

The woman on the right had long black hair braided down her back that was notched with gold runes to match the color of her eyes. Her skin was a dark, warm umber stretching across her exposed, broad shoulders before disappearing under her midnight armor. Her nails were pointed and painted to match the rest of her gear, but her dual daggers clutched tightly in her hands were the same sharp gold as the runes.

The man in the middle was shorter than the women, with a head of fluffy blond hair and blue eyes like the sea. A heavy bundle was strapped to his chest that he guarded closely with a golden shield. The man had no weapon Karsten could see, so he moved his attention to the last person.

The woman on the left had short curly red hair framing her

freckled cheeks. Her hands clutched at simmering magic that almost looked like swirling orbs of snow. Despite her softer frame and gentle features, her stance was fierce and her green eyes unyielding.

Emerald eyes that were all too familiar.

Adelaide took a few more hesitant steps forward, her entire body shaking.

The man dropped his shield and held up his hands to show he wasn't a threat, so Karsten lowered his axe from in front of Adelaide. But he didn't sheathe his weapon just yet. The man reached for the bundle wrapped around his chest, unfurling the fabric until Karsten could make out a head of blonde curls wrapped within the dark cloth. The man sat the bundle on the chapel floor.

"Sophie?" Adelaide gasped, her voice teetering on the edge of a cry.

A little girl, no older than six years, peeked her hazel eyes out of the fabric, and her gaze widened at the sight of Adelaide's shaking form at the end of the nave.

"*Mommy*!"

"*Sophie*," she cried as she ran down the aisle to the littlest member of their clan.

She's running towards her . . . daughter?

He watched, stunned as the little girl wobbled her way to meet her mother in the middle of the chapel. Adelaide fell to her knees as she scooped her up into her arms, holding her so close he could no longer see the child behind her trembling back. Her sobs wracked the rafters and echoed into his heart until his eyes burned with unshed tears.

Every plea Adelaide made to find her family suddenly flashed through his mind. She was so insistent and desperate to find them. He'd chalked it up to general worry, but the conviction in which she spoke always haunted him.

Because she spoke as a *mother*, not a daughter or sister.

"The orders I gave you. If you'd followed them, I would've made you all hide—" Lefa cut herself off as he peered back at her. Her face paled to the color of snow.

He turned back to the family reuniting before them as the man dropped beside Adelaide and her child, cuddling them both to his chest as he kissed the top of each of their hair.

Oh.

Oh.

His heart shattered somewhere on the chapel floor.

TEASER FOR THE NEXT BOOK IN THE DIVIDED GODS SAGA

They're alive. They're alive. They're alive.
Thank you, Odin, for bringing them back to me.
Thank you, Freya, for keeping them safe.
Thank every God that has ever existed.
I prayed for this.
I cannot believe it's real.

DRAMATIS PERSONAE

The Aylara Clan:

Adelaide Aylara – Keeper of The Divide, Promised of Olena, Omen of the Gods (alive)
Linnaea (Linn) Aylara – Matriarch of the Aylara clan, Mother of Many (unknown)
Nissa (Issa) Aylara – Keeper of The Divide, Weaver of Oceans (unknown)
Sofie Aylara – The Youngest of Clan Aylara, Future Keeper of The Divide (unknown)
Birgitta (Bir) Aylara – Keeper of The Divide, Sovereign of Shadows (unknown)
Unnamed Male Family Member (One) – Keeper of The Divide, Healer (unknown)
Unnamed Male Family Member (Two) – Formerly of the Astrom Clan (deceased)

The Covenant:

Commander Karsten Strom – Formerly a Knight of The Divide and a Viking (alive)
Lieutenant Zareen – Formerly a Rannadal Viking, Sister of Zamir (alive)
Zamir – Witch, Formerly of the Southern Kingdoms, Brother of Zareen (alive)

Rannadal Residents:

Jarl Lefa Thurstan – Daughter of Thurstan the Cruel, Visionary of The Covenant (alive)
Sister Ylwa – Matriarch of the Rannadal Chapel, Worshipper of Olena (alive)
Sister Jill Gorm – Former Matriarch of the Rannadal Chapel (alive)
Lady Serenade – Courtesan of the Lilly's Den, Formerly Known As ~~xxxxx~~ (alive)

Vikings:

Captain Filipe – Leader of Rannadal's Viking Forces (unknown)
Njal Magunusson – Second in Command of Rannadal's Viking Forces (unknown)
Kare – Berserker of Rannadal's Vikings, Worshipper of The Old Gods (unknown)
Thora – Shieldmaiden of Rannadal's Vikings, Worshipper of The Old Gods (unknown)

Other:

Embla – Barkeep of The Whispering Maiden Tavern in the town of Skagi

THE WORLD OF THE DIVIDED GODS

Locations:

The Wild Woods – The forests of The Divide the Aylara Clan calls home.
The Divide – The mountain range separating New Alfheim from the rest of Midgard. It holds the Spirits of Order and Chaos. It's protected by Keepers, elves who pledge their lives to protect their lands from humankind.
Rannadal – A town in The North former base for the Knights of The Divide.
Alfheim – The original home realm of the elves. As the legends go, it was destroyed by humans thousands of years ago.
New Alfheim – Once a part of Midgard, the land has since been claimed by elves as their new home after the destruction of their realm.
Midgard – The lands of mortal humans and many other fantastical creatures.
The North – The northernmost lands in Midgard.
The Whispering Maiden – The tavern of a small northern village called Skagi. This is a central location in the forthcoming novella prequels to this saga.

Factions:

The Keepers of The Divide – Elves sworn to protect New Alfheim from human influence.
The Knights of The Divide – A Brotherhood of warriors in The North. They serve as the Cislenian holy army and are mean to protect the borders of Midgard.
Seiðmaður – An elder, magical seer, and spellcaster. They can be humans or elves but are highly regarded. A seer, once aged, becomes a seiðmaður with the wisdom of their years.
Völva – A witch who specifically follows The Old Gods. They are often seen as some of the most powerful magic users in Midgard.

The Old Gods:

The Old Gods – The Norse Pagan Pantheon.
Odin – The wise leader of the Old Gods.
Yggdrasil – The tree of life holding the realms.
Bi-frost - The aurora-like multi-colored bridge connecting the realms.
Valhalla – The realm where warriors go when they die in battle.

Cislenian:

Cislenian – The religion of the gods Olena and Cismir, the patrons of Order and Chaos.
Olena – The Cislenian Goddess of order, peace, and tranquility.
Cismir – The Cislenian God of chaos, destruction, and calamity.
The Codex – The Cislenian religious text.
Saint Zelmar – The patron of Cismir who is said to have control of humanity during the time humans destroyed Alfheim.
The Divine Promise – The prophet said to one day be sent by Olena to fix the destruction created by Saint Zalmar.
Lines Of Divinity – The lines of succession for the Cislenian clergy.

Misc:

Blood Debts – A pact forged between a person who owes their life to another.
The Iniquity – The rite of passage for young Keepers.
The Initiation – The rite of passage for young Knights.

Skald - This typically means, “a composer and reciter of poems honoring heroes and their deeds.” For this story, it’s used to say which point of view the chapter is from.
Skal – Spoken when cheering or drinking. It means, “Cheers!”
Dar-kin - An elf word to address those you respect.

THE SPIRITS OF ORDER:

Muse – A spirit of passion for creative people. It appears yellow.
Mercy – A spirit meant to ease lost souls. It appears as a royal purple
Pleasure – A spirit meant to please all. It appears pink.
Honor – A spirit of valor, to bring honor to families and warriors. It appears emerald.
Love – A spirit for lovers. It appears red.
Courage – A spirit for the brave. It appears gold.
Hope – A spirit to bring hope to the downtrodden. It appears cloudy white.
Wisdom – A spirit for scholars. It appears silver.
Peace – A spirit to bring peace. It appears light blue.
Rest – A spirit for the tireless. It appears grey.
Order – A spirit of order. It appears eggshell white.
Loyalty – A spirit of loyalty for warriors, leaders, and lovers. It appears purple.
Faith – A spirit of faith for the righteous. It appears blindingly white.
Justice – A spirit of justice for those wronged. It appears royal blue.
Joy – A spirit of joy will lighten the hearts of those who need it. It appears orange.

THE SPIRITS OF CHAOS:

Misery – A spirit of distress. It appears icy grey.
Suicide – A spirit who pushes you to kill yourself. It appears deep purple.
Lust – A spirit of pure need. It appears deep red.
Vanity – A spirit of pride. It appears putrid green.
Obsession – A spirit of control. It appears crimson red.
Fear – A spirit which ensnares its victims in fear. It appears yellow.
Wrath – A spirit of living rage. It appears fiery red.
Deceit – A spirit of liars. It appears brown.
Regret – A spirit of regret for things left undone, unsaid, and unfelt. It appears dark grey.
Loneliness – A spirit of the depressed and lonely. It appears white.
Chaos – An agent for chaos. It appears black.
Jealousy – A spirit of jealousy believes that they deserve more. It appears red.
Grief – A spirit of grief for putting faith in what let them down. It appears blue.
Revenge – A spirit revenge for those who seek an eye for an eye. It appears dark blue.
Sorrow – A spirit of one's greatest sadness. It appears light blue.

BONUS CONTENT

Sign up for Jenna's newsletter to get bonus content from the world of The Divided Gods.
Bonus materials include sneak peeks at the rest of the saga, deleted scenes, and more.
For even more behind-the-scenes, join the Patreon.

Both the newsletter and Patreon can be found at jennastreety.com

ACKNOWLEDGMENTS

This debut was truly a labor of love from so many extraordinary people. To my cover artist, Mariona at @itsmumeii, I cannot thank you enough for bringing Adelaide and Karsten to life for this cover. To Niko at @nikespera, thank you for crafting the first images of these characters that have lived rent-free in my head for years. Chesney of @chesneyinfalt, thank you for your hard work and the tireless hours you put in to fix my abysmal grammar. I promise, I'll figure out the difference between lie, lay, and laying one day (but that's not today).

To my incredible betas, Sam (@greenersideofsam), Megan (@meganwritesYA), Tim, Ella, Piper, and Ari—thank you for reading my garbage and making it shine. An additional special thanks to the one and only Elle Lavendelle (@lavendellebooks) for beta reading and formatting this novel. I couldn't have polished these words or even uploaded them onto KDP without you.

My lovely Petty Writers Club besties, Devon (@authordevonharry), Kapri (@carnivoreincosplay), and Emma (@chthonickraken) deserve so much love. Thank you for your support, sprints late into the evening, and listening to my stressed-out rambling sessions. Extra love to my Patron and friend Aubrey McShan (@withaubrey) and my dear friend and podcast co-host, Holly Rhiannon (@stygianpen).

Endless thanks are due to all my Patrons, including Kris Q, Kaci Davis, Debra Zachau, Angelica Andersson, and Melissa Key. Another special thanks are due to the 185 Insane Challenge crew on Discord for pushing me to hit publish. Thank you to my sibling, Jay (@jay_henderson_frazier), for listening to me ramble about this world and my husband, Steven, for providing me with the snacks necessary to complete this book in the first place.

My heart is so full of gratitude for every single one of you. Thank you for taking the time to help make my author dreams come true.

ABOUT THE AUTHOR

Jenna Streety (she/her) is a romantic science-fiction and fantasy author. Her love of spellbinding stories manifests in her Spicy Viking Romantasy novel, *Between The Shadows And The Dawn*, and her forthcoming space opera series, *Spaceborne*. When she isn't writing stories full of soulmates and stardust, she's casting spells in the woods with her kin.

Find her at jennastreety.com, or @jennastreety on all socials.

Made in the USA
Columbia, SC
20 June 2025

59665480R00331